12.12

KINGDOMS OF THE NIGHT

KINGDOMS
of the
NIGHT

BY ALLAN COLE
AND CHRIS BUNCH

A Del Rey® Book
Ballantine Books • New York

A Del Rey® Book
Published by Ballantine Books

Copyright © 1995 by Allan Cole and Christopher Bunch
Map copyright 1995 by Christine Levis

All rights reserved under International and Pan-American
Copyright Conventions. Published in the United States
by Ballantine Books, a division of Random House,
Inc., New York, and simultaneously in Canada by
Random House of Canada Limited, Toronto.

Library of Congress Cataloging-in-Publication Data
Cole, Allan.
Kingdoms of the night/Allan Cole, Chris Bunch—1st ed.
p.   cm.
"A Del Rey book."
ISBN 0-345-38731-7 (alk. paper)
I. Bunch, Chris. II. Title.
PS3553.04485K56 1995
813'.54—dc20   95-1036
                                                        CIP

Manufactured in the United States of America
First Edition: June 1995
10 9 8 7 6 5 4 3 2 1

for
Charles
and, as always,
Li'l Karen

Kingdoms

of the Night

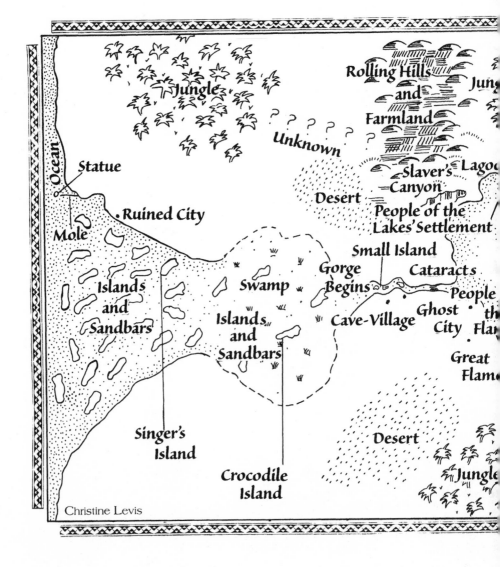

Rolling Hills
and
Farmland

Jun

Unknown

Jungle

Ocean

Statue

Desert

Slaver's
Canyon

Lago

Ruined City

People of the
Lakes' Settlement

Mole

Small Island

Islands
and
Sandbars

Swamp

Gorge
Begins

Cataracts

People

Islands
and
Sandbars

Cave-Village

Ghost
City

th
Fla

Great
Flam

Singer's
Island

Desert

Crocodile
Island

Jungle

Christine Levis

BOOK ONE

GREYCLOAK

CHAPTER ONE

THE MAD
CHARIOTEER

W ho shall ever read this, heed me: I am Lord Amalric Emilie
Antero of Orissa. Know that this journal and its bearer
are under the protection of my family and myself. If you
deliver them speedily and safely to my agents you will be paid two
thousand gold coins.

But beware—my generosity is double-edged. Do not harm or
delay my servants in their mission, or the consequences to you, your
family and descendants will be most severe.

All this I swear on this sixth day of the Month of Frosts in the
fifteenth year of the Time of the Lizard.

MY DEAREST NEPHEW, Hermias. I write to you from the Far Kingdoms—
the *real* Far Kingdoms, not the false rune of Irayas which Janos
Greycloak and I found nearly fifty years ago. I should have realized
we were wrong: The wonders of those distant kingdoms that so enthralled us then pale in this realm of miracles and magic.

Poor Janos. He betrayed all he loved and sold his very soul for the truths he believed resided there. And it all turned out to be a monumental lie.

The old Janos—the Janos who was once my friend—would have laughed at his self-delusion.

"The best jests of the gods," he would have said, "are those that reveal you as an ass. The man who believes himself wise walks in darkness. Only someone who knows he's *truly* a fool can see the light."

He would also have been glad, I realize now, because our very victory in finding the Far Kingdoms held the seeds of his destruction. For after that, what else was left of value for Janos to discover? If only he could be here now to glory in how much we missed the mark.

That said, I should tell you that in all likelihood as you read these words I will be dead.

Do not grieve. My life has been long, for the most part fortunate and spiced with much incident and achievement. It amazes me that after all that has happened since we last embraced, there is spark enough to guide this pen.

At an age when most men survey all empty ground for a suitable grave, I set out for my last great adventure. I crossed the Forbidden Sea of the East to the unknown far shore, dared uncharted rivers, desolate wastelands, and frozen mountain peaks. I've seen dreams shattered, mended, then imperiled anew. Few men or women have been gifted with a life such as mine. And now that I've been granted experiences and adventures that would easily overflow another full span, I can say if the gods don't love me, at least they haven't ignored me.

But I must not ramble. This is not a journal of reflection, like the first.

I write to warn, not to edify.

We are in great danger from forces I am just beginning to understand. Soon my enemies will come for me. And if I should fail in my last task, another *must* follow to pick up the fallen banner.

That is the purpose of this journal.

Although I must write in haste, I will spare no detail, so wiser eyes may see what I did not. Study these ink spatterings closely, my dear nephew. And seek the counsel of our bravest and most perceptive friends.

Tell them the end of history is rushing upon us. And if I die, it is *they* who must stop that Mad Charioteer.

IT BEGAN in the Month of Flowers. All around my villa blossoms were bursting through the earth, filling the air with their essence. Gentle winds played sweet music on the garden chimes, and from my study window I could see a pair of lovers strolling the grassy fields, birds bursting from cover in front of their wandering feet. Just beyond them was the meadow where there were colts at play. But all that beauty was lost to me. I sat before an unseasonable fire, toasting my bones, a rug pulled over my skinny old man's legs, nursing a cup of brandy and damning what little life I had left for a prison. I pined for Omerye—my life's mate. She'd been dead a year, and in one corner of the garden I could see the small tomb with her flute-playing likeness carved into its face.

I'd never expected to outlive her. This doubled the shock of the quickness of her death. One moment she was my lively Omerye— full of laughter and music and wisdom—the next, a corpse. We made love the night before she died. I'm grateful of that. Despite our age, our passion for one another was as deep as ever. She fell asleep in my arms. That night I dreamed we were young again, wandering the wilderness together in search of new horizons.

The next morning I awoke early thinking I heard her pipes. The music had the dawn's cheer to it, the refreshing chill of morning air.

But I found the Dark Seeker had come and gone. Omerye lay pale and cold beside me, her pipes nowhere in sight.

I'd known such tragedy before—I lost my first wife and daughter to the plague. But I'd been young then. There were days enough for hope to still live. As I sat in the study I thought of the treasures Greycloak and I found in the Far Kingdoms and all the marvels I brought back from those once-mythical shores. The greatest treasure of all was Omerye—court piper for King Domas himself. It was she who healed me—she who made my days worthwhile.

There is a land I know of, where it is not only acceptable but considered admirable to take one's own life. There are priests who make an honorable profit assisting. They ply their customers with an elixir that brings on the happiest of memories. A basin of warm, perfumed liquid is provided and a spell cast so all pain is pleasure. The sorrowing one—who sees clearly that his best course is to lay down the burden and close the final door—takes up a sacred knife, summons the Seeker, then slits his veins.

I was considering this recourse when Quatervals came to collect me. Imagine what a morose, self-pitying sight I made. He groaned as if to say, "Not *again*, my lord!"

Quatervals was head of my household guard—tall, ruddy-cheeked, and bursting with muscular good health. A former Frontier Scout recruited from one of the hill tribes outside Orissa, he was an able soldier who'd risen through the ranks to lieutenant. But troubles at home had forced him to desert, since his tribe believed blood feud the highest duty and justice. Unfortunately, when matters had been settled to his satisfaction and his enemies interred, he'd had the moral rectitude to return to his unit.

He had been headed for the executioner's block when his plight came to my attention. I rescued him from that fate for motives I've occasionally regretted, and he joined my service as chief of my guard. He was good at his job, and the only complaint I had was that he sometimes didn't treat me with the respect a man of my position is occasionally fool enough and weak enough to believe he deserves.

When Quatervals saw me, his face darkened, his brows arched, and his bearded smile of greeting turned to a grimace.

"You're not dressed, my lord," he admonished. "We have to hurry or we'll be late for the ceremony."

"I'm not going," I said. "Send my apologies and tell them I'm ill." I did my best to look wan—touching my forehead as if testing for fever, then sighing as if I'd confirmed my worst fears.

"You don't look sick to me," he said. He glanced at the brandy, then at the half-empty crystal carafe. "Feelin' sorry for yourself again, are you, my lord? Te-Date knows what you've got to complain about. You're richer than any man has a right to be. Prince of the greatest merchant empire in Orissa's history. Beloved and honored by all. Well, almost all. There's some that's got sense enough to see you're as common a mortal as the rest of us."

"Meaning you?" I said.

"Meaning me, my lord," he replied. "Who else would care enough about such a cranky old man to keep an assassin from doing us all a good turn?"

"Don't be impertinent," I snapped. "I know whether I'm sick or not."

He said: "My lord—if you wanted a polite liar for chief of your guards, you shouldn't have hired the likes of me."

Despite my foul mood, I had to bury a smile. Quatervals' fellow tribesmen were a fierce, independent lot noted for always speaking the unvarnished truth. They wouldn't lie for any reason—even when polite society demanded.

"The only thing that ails you, my lord," he went on, "is a bad case of the mopes. You need fresh air, sunlight, and the company of others. So, stir your stumps, Lord Antero, because that's exactly what awaits you."

"So now you're a skilled physician, as well as a swordsman," I said. "I want to be left alone, dammit! I'm *old*. I have the *right*."

"Sorry, my lord," Quatervals replied, "but I've got a grandmother twenty years your senior and she's been up four hours by now chasin' the goats in for their milking. You're not feeble. But you will be soon if you don't quit acting like it."

I was getting angry, still clutching my specialness—my sorrow—to my bosom. But Quatervals beat my bad temper to the finish.

"Besides, this is a ship launching, my lord," he prodded. "Your family and employees have been planning the ceremony for weeks. You not only agreed to attend but promised you'd do the honors of blessing the ship."

"I changed my mind," I said.

Quatervals grimaced. "That'd not only be rude, my lord, but bad luck as well. What if something happened to that ship later on? Jumped by pirates or sunk by storm? It'd practically be your fault for givin' it a bad start."

"You don't actually believe that superstitious nonsense," I growled.

Quatervals shrugged his hefty shoulders. "I'm a landsman, not a sailor," he said. "But whenever I've been to sea, I got down on my knees fast as any old salt when the winds blew fierce. That's when the gods *really* make themselves known." He laughed. "But you'd know more about that than the likes of me, sir," he said. "You're the famous Lord Amalric Antero. Slayer of demons. Rescuer of maidens. The greatest adventurer the world has known."

Then his look turned mournful. "What a pity," he said, "that such a man should dry up like dust and blow away."

"Oh, very well," I said. "I'll go . . . if only to shut you up. But it'll be on your head if I catch a chill and die."

"I'll chance it, my lord." He laughed. "Now stir your bones so your man can get you dressed."

With that he exited.

I drained my brandy and slammed the cup down. That son of a poxed whore! I'd teach him! But as my blood boiled I realized that once again I'd fallen prey to his game. The famous Lord Antero, indeed! Quatervals ought to apply to the Evocators' Guild for a license. Look how he'd turned self-pity into anger and anger into a renewed interest in life—if only to contemplate how pleasant it would be to toast his bones.

I laughed and called for my manservant. I had to hurry or I'd miss the launching.

I looked out my window and saw that the lovers had disappeared. My eyes were still keen enough, however, to make out the place where the tall grass shadowed into a fragrant bed. I saw the grass moving in a steady rhythm.

Perhaps it would be a lucky day after all.

IN MY YOUTH it had been a pleasant if lengthy trip from my villa to Orissa. I was always invigorated by the ride through the countryside, past sleepy farms, through cool woods and across musical brooks. But the city has burst its old limits and tumbled to within a mile or so of my door. Only a few of the farms remain, and the woods have been gouged for timber to construct the homes and buildings that line the crowded streets. As much as I love our city, I am not so blind as to call her a thing of beauty. She's grown in a haphazard fashion, from the age when the first Orissan judged that the best place to build his fishing hovel was upwind from where he gutted his catch, to the present, where any bare spot that you can cram a stick and brick into is considered a prime building location. Land was so scarce that in some places towering tenements had been hurled up to such heights that they leaned crazily over the street, casting everything into shadow. These buildings reminded me of the crowded squalor of old Lycanth—the city that had been our archenemy for generations until my sister, Rali, slew the evil Archons who ruled it and reduced it to rubble and ashes.

My bleak mood crept dangerously close again when I thought of Rali. Now there was a hero we'd never see the likes of again. I'd admired my older sister since I was a toddler. If truth be told, my exploits were puny things beside hers. She'd been a warrior's warrior. Commander of the all-woman Maranon Guard. Rali had pursued the last Archon of Lycanth to the very ends of the earth in what had to be the greatest voyage in history. She'd caught and killed him and rescued Orissa from destruction. Rali had also been blessed—or cursed, by some lights—with magical talents that rivaled those of our best Evocators.

She'd gone missing on an expedition to the frigid regions of the South many years before. Every day since, I'd awakened half expecting news of her return. Then the ugly truth would dawn and I'd realize once again that she must be dead.

It seemed all my contemporaries were gone. I'd outlived friends and enemies alike. Perhaps that's why I felt so useless. It seemed long past the hour for me to shuffle off and leave the world for the next generation to do with as it pleased.

The carriage jolted as it hit a rut, shaking me out of my joust with villainous Regret. I'd long complained to the Council of Magistrates that the roads were falling into disrepair. Their condition was not only uncomfortable and dangerous, but an eater of profits as well. Goods and wagons were damaged daily while the Magistrates fought their private wars for more prestigious offices and who would get the best seats at public ceremonies.

"It's not us but the Evocators," the Chief Magistrate said. "We paid good city coin for spells to protect our streets from wear. The last they cast they vowed was good for ten years or more. But that was less than a year ago and just look at the state of our roads!"

The Chief Evocator replied it was the Magistrates' fault for building with materials so poor that not a spell in history could preserve them. This earned a bitter retort from the Chief Magistrate, who retaliated in kind, and back and forth it went with nothing being done while the roads and bridges crumbled around us.

So far the Magistrates held the upper hand in the blaming game. For although few trust a Magistrate, *everyone* is wary of a wizard.

Adding to the poor public view of the Evocators was a rash of apparent failures in the past year. The gift of magical knowledge I'd brought back from Irayas had blossomed mightily. We commanded the weather that nurtured our crops; the purity of the streams; the woods and fields that gave us fish, flesh, and fowl; and we even controlled the plagues that once ravaged us at will, plagues that had killed my own Deoce and little Emilie.

But in recent months cracks had appeared in the protective walls. There'd been sick cattle in the countryside. The last grain harvest had been afflicted with a voracious beetle. And in the marketplace the witches had been treating a mysterious outbreak of skin infections. In my own household an entire storeroom of meat had to be destroyed because somehow it had spoiled. Even in the old days the most common spell cast by the Evocator assigned to the Butchers' Guild would have prevented such a thing.

Naturally, the Evocators were given the greater share of the blame. There had been much public discussion of how lazy, greedy, and thieving our wizards had become. Although I didn't think on it much—the incidents, after all, were fairly minor—when I heard such talk, I quickly put the rumormonger straight. In my youth the Evocators had been the sworn enemies of the Anteros. Their graft was enormous, their secrecy impenetrable, and some of them had even plotted with Prince Raveline of Irayas against our city. My own brother, Halab, had been a victim of their evil. In my lifetime I had seen all that change. The doors of knowledge at the Evocators' Palace were open to all with talent, and the wizards now take an oath to work only for the public good. Obviously—human nature being as it is—all hearts were not pure. But the ideals had been hoisted higher.

My thoughts were on matters such as these as my carriage passed the hill where the Evocators' Palace sits. It had once been contained behind forbidding walls at the summit. Since then it had grown as much as the city around it. Buildings and gardens sprawled down terraced hillsides. Even in the daylight the magicians' workshops gave off a magical glow and the air—heavy with the scent of sulfur—buzzed and tingled with energy. I could see a group of fresh-faced acolytes being marched up the hill to their classrooms by a stern Master Evocator. Although I have no talent for magic, I knew the books they study well. They contained the wisdom of Janos Greycloak, or at least what wisdom *I* had been able to remember and repeat.

His theories—his search for the keys to all natural law—had turned wizardry on its head. For the first time in history magic was tested and examined for cause and effect. There were even a few young wizards, I was told, who wondered if Greycloak's ultimate guess was correct, that magical energy and common energy were the same. In sorcery a thing can be changed from one form to another, can be transported, duplicated, protected, or destroyed. Greycloak speculated that identical forces ruled the falling weight, the rushing stream, the twitching compass needle, and the fiery hearth, as well as the very light that allowed one to see such commonplace marvels. He wondered if all things—both of this world and the spiritual world—might be built of identical grains of something, whatever that substance might be, and the behavior of that stuff might have a single motivator. Find that motivator, he said, and all things will be possible. The search for such a thing was Greycloak's greatest goal. He thought he was close on its heels when we reached the Far Kingdoms. I think he would have caught it if it hadn't turned in its tracks and killed him first.

My carriage turned toward the river docks and I was swept through the neighborhood where I'd once pursued the fair Melina— she who was a witch of the flesh and my young, lustful soul. It had been a dank and dangerous place then, with rotting tenements whose walls concealed pleasure palaces Orissa is unlikely to see again. There was no erotic fantasy ever dreamed of that wasn't once satisfied by Melina and her courtesan sisters.

The tenements had been torn down and replaced by fashionable apartments. The street had been broadened, beautified with plantings and fountains, and it was lined with expensive taverns, clothiers' saloons, and shops a-glitter with trinkets for children of the rich. If the likes of Melina and her procurer, Leego, had appeared there, they'd soon have been rousted from the street by a burly watch officer.

I suppose it's an improvement over the wretchedness of the neighborhood's past. But whenever I pass over those daily scoured cobbles, along the gardened avenue, I regret the loss of that tawdry jewel.

We continued on around the bend and I could see the docks and waterfront warehouses ahead. People in workers' clothes with toil-etched faces, calloused hands, and hard musculature made way for my carriage. Some of them called my name in greeting. Others turned to their children to explain who I was.

It is my vanity to believe I am a fair man, known for honest wages for honest work. I am wealthy, but not ostentatious. I'm generous, charitable, and sympathetic to the troubles of working men and women. But there are others who can claim the same, and to be honest, all merchants are at heart thieves. We steal a man's time for his labor, a woman's purse for our goods, and a voyager's dreams for our commerce.

So I'm not as good as I like to think. But I did one fine thing in my life, and I don't mean the great expeditions I shared with Janos. Or even the blessings I brought back for my people. It is the reason I was looked upon with fondness by those I passed that day. It was I who forced the others of my class to free the slaves of Orissa. Some of my kind hate me for it to this day. I cherish that hatred.

Just before the docks, we turned down the river, making for the yard where my new ship was waiting to be launched.

Between the docks and the yard the broad grassy banks of the river sprang free, running nearly a mile along the course of a park marked only by paths where families, couples, and solitary dreamers strolled. The park made a sharp point where retaining walls kept the river back when it was fat with showers and rising snow.

The Month of Flowers that year was rich with both, and I could see the sleek, overfed river moving swiftly past the point. A spray misted up from where the water punished the rock for being stubborn. The mist from that battle which the rock must someday lose sprayed over my carriage as I went by. The rich smell roused the river rat in me, and I felt my senses perk up, my nose twitching with curiosity. I saw a ship with storm-tattered sails limping for the docks and wondered the same wonders that had so captivated me when I was a boy playing on those same banks.

The ship was old, ill-painted; its hull and sails were rimed with salt. But old as it was, it rode the river with authority. It was a ship that had seen every sea, every sunset, every storm. I could almost smell its tarry breath and feel the worn, firm planks under my feet. I imagined horizons fleeing before me, the pitching deck, the cracking sails, the barefooted seamen swarming up the masts.

By the gods, I love to wander! It was what separated Janos and me. He was a seeker, I a rover. He was obsessed with reaching his goal. I am at my happiest between one gate and the next. Odd, when I think of it. Greycloak was a rough spirit who'd trod hard paths and knew the ways of the wild shore. I was raised in luxury and had known not a care until I set out with him for the Far Kingdoms. It was then that I was afflicted with this malady.

Its symptoms are a racing pulse, a chilly spine, and a sudden, uncontrollable distaste for your surroundings. It comes without warning. The sight of a deep-sea merchantman can fire it, or a long-distance caravan bringing its goods to market. Small things can be equally as dangerous: A sound, a smell, the feel of old leather can summon memories of a place and time when nothing existed but the beckoning road.

From across the water I heard the pilot's mate call the mark, and I had to heave back a sob from the need to be going. I thought: Your travels are done, Amalric Antero. There'll be no more adventuring. You're too old, my friend. Too damned old.

Quatervals shouted for the crowd to make way, and my matched blacks drew my creaking carcass into the yard where the Anteros had gathered with our friends and employees for the blessing and the feast.

Strolling musicians serenaded the celebrants. Enormous roasts turned on spits over fires made of alder. There were tables of food everywhere, and scores of servants ducked in and out of the crowd bearing trays of liquid refreshment. Everyone was costumed in their best, which in that month meant the most glorious colors to complement the flowers springing up all over Orissa. The smells and sounds and colors infused me until I was almost looking forward to the remainder of the day.

So many milled around to greet me that I exited with difficulty. My son, Cligus, broad-shouldered his way through to help. He was dressed in his finest uniform, with three heavy chains of gold slung from his neck to call him general, lest someone miss the gleaming badges of rank on his shoulders and breastplate.

"Father Antero!" he cried in his booming, crowd-pleasing voice as he bounded forward to take my arm. "We feared you might not be well and be unable to honor us with your presence."

I glanced at Quatervals, who gave me a sardonic grin, shrugged and turned away. I shook off my son's hand, suddenly irritable.

"Sick?" I said. "What makes you think I'm sick? Why, I've never felt better in my life."

My son beamed, patting me affectionately, and announced to the crowd: "Did you hear that? Father Antero says he's never felt better in his life.

"We should all take inspiration from his words. By the gods, a man is only as old as he acts! And there's the proof standing before us, my friends. The great Lord Antero, knocking on the doors of seventy, and still feeling alert and vigorous."

He embraced me. It was all I could do not to draw away from his rich man's musk and humiliate him in front of the others.

I loved my son. I truly did. But in adulthood he had formed

habits that grated on my sense of rightness. Cligus was in his forties and had made his mark in the military. I didn't know if he was a good soldier, although he'd had his victories. He had crafted a public face he believed would make all love him: a magnificent speaking voice, an arsenal of pleasing phrases, and a willingness to boast of his abilities and deeds. Also, it seemed to me he overused the Antero name, calling me Father Antero when others were present, as if he believed the name itself trumpeted honor. The result was that some feared him, some respected him, but from what I could gather, few liked him. His own father, I'm ashamed to admit, hovered near the edges of that final crowd.

Feeling like a traitor to my only child—fruit of my happy marriage to Omerye—I turned my sourness to a smile and took his arm again. Cligus beamed with pleasure.

"It's good to see you, my son," I said. Then I raised my voice so the others could hear. "Now, shall we get these festivities started? There's a ship that needs blessing, food that needs eating, and a whole river of drink to be drunk."

My remarks were greeted with much cheering and loud praises for the merry Lord Antero. Now where do you suppose Cligus had learned his manner?

As we made our way to the blessing platform, Cligus leaned close to me. "You promised we'd talk soon, Father," he whispered. "About my future and the future of our family."

Cligus was alluding to the status of my estate. He and others in my family had been after me for many months to name my successor as head of the Anteros' commercial empire. As my only child, Cligus naturally saw himself filling that role—dismissing the rights of any rival among my many nephews, nieces, and cousins. I was not so certain he was the wisest choice, and had been delaying the decision. The delay had become a sore point. In a way, I suppose, he was caught in a cycle of my making. The more I delayed, the more he feared, and the more he feared, the more his nervousness led him to do or say the wrong thing.

Although I knew I wasn't ready to face the issue yet, I forced certainty into my response. "I've not forgotten my promise of a meeting," I said. "It's near the very top of my list."

"When would it be convenient?" he pressed. "Seeing you look so well gives me hope that appointment might be soon."

Suspicion tangled its roots with guilt and I snapped back, "When I'm ready, by the gods, and not a moment before."

Cligus flushed. "I'm sorry, Father," he said. "I didn't mean to overstep my bounds." I saw Omerye in his eyes and the stubborn tilt of chin and regretted my outburst.

I squeezed his arm. "Pay no attention to my temper, son. I've much on my mind."

He took heart from this. "Then we will talk soon?"

"You have my word on it," I said.

The platform loomed up near the riverbank, decked with bunting, streamers, and huge, extravagantly decorated maps of our far-flung trading routes. Framing the platform was an enormous pavilion blazing with color, which hid the new ship and its cradle from view until it was time for the unveiling.

As I climbed the steps of the platform, a handsome young man beamed down.

"Uncle Amalric!" he said with honest pleasure. He grabbed a cup of cold, spiced wine from a passing server and offered it to me. "If you drink it quickly," he said, "I can get you another." He laughed. "I happen to be well-connected to the fellow who's paying for all this."

"There's a good nephew," I said as I took the cup from Hermias. I hoisted it up. "Just to let the gods know we're serious!" I drank and the wine stoked my cheer at seeing him.

"Now, this is the proper way to greet a fellow," I joked to Cligus. "A cup of wine to light the panoply."

I was instantly sorry for my silly little jest. Cligus glowered, taking offense where, if implied at all, it had been by accident.

"Do you really think it's good for you, Father?" he said. "Wine, so early?"

I pretended I didn't hear—one of the few benefits of age—and merely smiled and took another deep drink.

Cligus gave Hermias a look that needed no words to sum up his feelings. He thought the young man was an opportunist of the worst sort, who pandered to the more foolish desires of his elderly father.

Hermias pointedly glared back. I was surprised to see loathing in his look and wondered what Cligus had done to earn it.

My son had cause to see him as his rival. Hermias was in his middle twenties, grandson of my late brother, Porcemus. Since he'd first come to my attention, Hermias better matched my own view of the child Omerye and I should have produced. He was intelligent, honest, and aware that high birth made him no better a man than any other. He didn't have the same flair for the traders' art I had at his age, but he labored hard to make up for it, working every position, no matter how low, as he climbed in my esteem as well as my organization. Adding coin to the growing heap in his bowl was the fact that he'd recently returned from his Finding—a long and difficult maiden trading voyage whose jump-off point had been Jeypur, that distant and most barbaric of ports. From all accounts, it had been a great success.

If any should doubt that the ways of the gods are twisted, consider this: Porcemus was the laziest, most cowardly and unpleasant of all my father's many children. As the oldest, it was he who expected to take over the business from Paphos Karima Antero. But my father, that canny old devil, had seen a spark in me—a wastrel if there ever was one—that he nurtured with more care and understanding than I can ever claim to have done in my dealings with Cligus. My father had not only backed my expeditions to the Far Kingdoms, but had skipped over all my kin—to Porcemus' special displeasure—to name me head of the family. I had only been a year or so younger than Hermias. Now I was in my father's position. Actually, it was a little worse. He was forced to choose one son over another. I was contemplating picking a nephew—and a great-nephew at that—over my own son. Mind you, I'd never hinted at my thinking, and at the time of this launching, despite speculation by others, it was only a vague possibility.

I finished my cup and looked for the promised other. Hermias caught my glance at a passing tray of brimming wine cups and plucked one off.

"There's thirsty winds ahead, Uncle," he said. "And it's my professional observation that you've only got one sail raised."

"Then by all means," I said, "let's hoist the other." I reached out to trade my empty cup for its more bounteous sister.

But just as I did, Cligus blurted, "*Please*, Hermias. Don't encourage him!"

Without thinking, he thrust out a hand to block Hermias. Instead he knocked the cup from Hermias' grasp and wine spilled down the front of my tunic.

"Look what you've done, Cligus!" Hermias said, wiping at the stain with his own sleeve. "Since when did you become your father's conscience? A man doesn't need a son to judge his limits."

Again I marked Hermias' distaste for my son. There was more boiling under the surface of his remarks than competition for my favor.

"It wouldn't have happened," Cligus blustered, "if you hadn't tried to interfere. It's my place to serve my father. Not yours."

Then he looked quickly around, and seemed relieved when he saw no one had been close enough to witness the incident.

"Gentlemen," I chided, not wanting a stupid argument to spoil the day after I'd gone to so much effort to rouse myself. "There's no harm in a little wine, be it inside—" I scrubbed at my tunic "—or out."

Hermias chortled, his good temper restored. But now Cligus was stricken with remorse. Whether from his actions or for being so revealing about his dislike for Hermias, I couldn't say.

"Please forgive me, Father," he said. "Shall I send Quatervals back for a fresh tunic?"

"Don't worry yourself," I said, although I noted it was Quatervals he volunteered, not himself. "It's not the first time I've had wine spilled on me. Although when it happened last I was in a rather low tavern and the fellow didn't spill it but hurled it into my eyes. Then he came at me with a knife."

"What happened?" Hermias asked, although he knew the answer, since the tale was a variation I'd told in many forms over the years.

"He killed me," I said.

Hermias chuckled at his favorite uncle's tired jest, and Cligus recovered poise enough to make perfunctory noises of appreciation.

Another voice broke in. "Hells an' green hells! Could that be me master, lads? Drunk ag'in with wine stains on 'is tunic?"

The day brightened considerably as I turned to embrace Kele, my most trusted ship's captain and a woman I was honored to call friend. Kele was short and sturdy, like her father, L'ur, who'd captained for me since the days of my expeditions to the Far Kingdoms. He'd died some years before, but although I missed him, his daughter did her able best to fill the void.

Kele clapped me on the back. "Heard you was dead, or worse, m'lord," she said.

"What could be worse than dead?" I asked.

"Eatin' cold porridge 'n' wet bread," she said. "Pleased to see for meself 'twas all tavern lies."

I saw Quatervals watching from a distance. I flushed, even though he was too far away to hear. But it didn't keep me from repeating the tale I'd tossed into Cligus' lap.

"Lies is right," I said. "Why, I've never felt better in my life."

Kele was friend enough to know it was a falsehood—and, more importantly, to ignore it. As she chatted on, giving me a quick update on the fortunes of mutual friends and enemies, I thought what a godsend she'd been. She was a bit over forty summers—near Cligus' age—and had wide experience from her voyages. Many a pirate had felt the keenness of her blade, and many a cheating trader had knuckled under the hammer of her business sense. When Hermias had made his Finding, it was Kele I chose to captain his ship. If his greenness had gotten him into danger, I knew Kele would pull him out.

As she talked, however, I sensed tension. I saw her glancing between Hermias and Cligus. Worry bit her brow. I'd woven my way through too many fog-shrouded passages with her not to suspect that something unpleasant lurked ahead. Were those waves I heard beating on rocky shoals?

The crowd stirred and the black, symbol-studded carriage of the Chief Evocator entered the yard. All was a-hush as his footmen ran to set up the golden steps and open the ornate door. The man who exited was tall and skeletal. His face was long, fierce—made longer and fiercer still by his jutting dark beard. His robes were blue-black, edged with gold, and as he stepped down, everyone inched away in dread.

Palmeras' head rose and his glowing eyes flew over the crowd like a hawk. When they struck me they stopped, glowing brighter still.

"Antero, you old dog!" he thundered. "Who does a wizard have to curse around here to get a drink?"

It was time for the blessing to begin.

PALMERAS was one of the new breed of Orissan Evocators, as much politician as sorcerer. He was middle-aged—young for a man in his position—and his influence stretched beyond the wizards' palace on the hill. If it weren't for the instinctive uneasiness Evocators create in most of us, he would have been one of the most popular men in the city.

As his assistants made ready for the ceremony, and with me at his side to bolster his image as a man of the people, Palmeras strolled through the crowd spreading his charm. Worker or high-born, he treated everyone as if they were important. He had an affinity for remembering personal detail—congratulating a grizzled carpenter for just becoming a grandfather or praising a noble lady for the good taste she displayed in the new garden she'd created at her country home.

Moments before all was ready, he grabbed us both another drink and drew me aside. He glanced over at Cligus and Hermias, who were jammed together at the edge of the crowd, each ostentatiously ignoring the other.

"Such a remarkable display of kinsmanship," he said dryly. "Warms the heart to its very core."

I sighed. "I expect you have more on your mind than a ship launching," I said. "Other than his deep regard for an old and dear friend, why else would the Chief Evocator attend such an ordinary occasion?"

Palmeras laughed. "Such cynical suspicion is unworthy of you, Amalric."

"But accurate," I said.

"Yes," he said. "But unworthy just the same."

"The subject, I presume," I said, "is when am I going to let loose the reins of the family business and name my son to replace me."

"You overshot your presumption, my friend," Palmeras said. "Most of us think you're wavering between your son and your nephew. And that is the reason for delay."

"Not so," I said. "If I had to make an announcement tomorrow, I'd be proclaiming Cligus as my sole heir."

Palmeras gave me a mocking grin. "We'll really hear this tomorrow? Good! May I alert my aides of the news? Or is this just between old friends?"

I laughed. "Speaking of overshooting a presumption. I distinctly said *if* I were going to make an announcement tomorrow."

Palmeras turned serious. "Then it really is true," he said. "Hermias *is* a candidate."

"I didn't say that."

"You don't need to," Palmeras said. "The whole city is abuzz with it, my friend. Whether you like it or not, your very delay has people believing Cligus has lost your favor and Hermias will be your successor."

I remained stubborn. My hair may have turned from deep red to white, but I hadn't lost my contrary nature. "They can believe what they like," I said. "It won't affect my thinking."

"As a favor to your fellow Orissans," Palmeras said, "do something soon. Our friends on the Council of Magistrates are worried. It is unsettling to commerce and politics to have such uncertainty from the city's leading family."

"Oh?" I said. "If that's how they feel, why didn't they come to me themselves? You *are* their emissary, are you not?"

"If the Chief of Magistrates approached you," he said, "it would only heighten the rumors." He studied my face a moment to see if I was in pace with him. I was. He continued. "No one has the temerity to tell Amalric Antero what he should decide, much less the timing of it. However, I'm sure you can appreciate how unsettling the delay has become. Much power sways before the winds of your house, my dear friend. There is a scrambling going on as we speak. Even here! Look at the faces around us—studying your son and nephew, wondering which will wear the crown."

I glanced about. There was no mistaking the looks Cligus and Hermias were getting. In a few places I saw enough naked ambition to turn my stomach.

Seeing my reaction, Palmeras said, "I'll tell the Magistrates you won't delay much longer," he said. I nodded and Palmeras went on. "They'll be relieved. These are anxious times. No one trusts their leaders the way they once did. I can't say I blame them. Spells gone wrong or too weak. Public facilities deteriorating. Why, you should see the state of the Grand Amphitheater. Shocking! Simply shocking. And of late, it seems even our trade abroad is suffering."

Palmeras was touching on a recent concern of mine. There hadn't been a successful expedition opening new trading opportunities for two or three years. Not only had most been turned back by hostile conditions in the unexplored lands, but a few had failed to return at all. And it seemed to me when I looked at a map of the known world that in places things had even been pinched back slightly and once-known territories had been lost.

This only heightened my concern about Cligus. If new discoveries *were* to be made and lost territory regained, was he the Antero to do it? He only had his diplomatic success not long ago at Jeypur to show he might.

Despite his youth, or perhaps because of it, Hermias impressed me as someone who would set a firm course and not turn back if adversity threatened.

"Out of curiosity," I said, "and with the understanding that nothing I say indicates my thinking . . ."

"Understood," Palmeras said.

"Who is most favored by the public? Cligus? Or Hermias?"

Palmeras mused, then said: "Of the two, Hermias has the largest and warmest following. His house and the neighborhood around it fairly swarm with his supporters. Each morning people seeking his favor line the street to his door. But don't think your son doesn't have his constituency. Although it's mostly among the military—

and even then his most fervent backing comes from his own officers and men."

"Interesting," I said. "Although this is hardly a popularity contest . . . if it's a contest at all."

Palmeras laughed. "The businessman as complete autocrat," he said. "I like that description of your profession, although I imagine your fellow merchants would cringe."

"It's easier to rid yourself of a merchant than a king," I said. "If the quality of my goods is poor, my prices unfair, you have only to turn to my competitors."

"How true," he said. "But what that also means is . . . if Cligus fails . . . that is the end of the Anteros."

He looked at me, attempting an unassuming face. But there is no blunting a wizard's sharp gaze, and I felt suitably chastened. He'd steered a course identical to my own thinking and fears.

A young Evocator sounded the gong that all was in readiness, saving me from a response. We hastened to our positions for the ceremony.

The speech I gave was not one of my better efforts, so I won't repeat it, except to say it ran along the usual road of such addresses. I thanked everyone for coming and talked at length about the symbolism heavy in such an occasion . . . new ship, new ventures, rebirth, and other such inspirational blatherings. Experienced as I am at public functions, and despite my reputation as a phrasemaker, I fear I was mired by an awareness that each word was being examined in a glaring light. Those who supported Cligus and those who favored Hermias and those who were merely curious looked for deeper meaning in my every word. So I obfuscated wherever I could, and the result made not much sense at all.

Then horns sounded, gongs rang, and Evocators passed through the crowd swinging smoking pots of thrice-blessed incense. Over in the cattle pen two white oxen bellowed as they were led out for the sacrifice. Before their misery could sour our luck, an Evocator blew magical herbs in their faces, calming them. They were bled and killed, and the best cuts were taken from their carcasses.

Eight strong young acolytes mounted the platform bearing an

idol of Te-Date—the king of gods and protector of ships and travelers. One hand was stretched out, iron palm up for the offering, while the other held a large chalice. With drums pounding and chanters singing, the furnace in the idol's belly was fired and smoke and flame boiled from his lips.

Palmeras and I stepped to the idol, flanked by four other wizards who carried big trenchers of sacrificial meat and a cask of blood from the slain oxen.

The Chief Evocator was an excellent showman, and he put his best dramatic efforts into the business at hand. He threw back his robes so they billowed in the breeze off the river, and his arms shot up above his head as he addressed the heavens.

"O Great Te-Date," he intoned, his magically amplified voice thundering over all of us, "once again we gather before you to seek thy blessing. Your kindness to travelers and seekers everywhere is legend. For long centuries you have especially blessed the people of Orissa, who live by the river and trade peacefully and honorably with the world. Our caravans and ships have carried your exalted name into the wilderness, where it lights the savage darkness and shows us the way. Today a new daughter of Orissa is born. She bears our dreams and our fortunes.

"We beseech thee, O Lord Te-Date, to raise thy splendid shield to protect her from any misfortune."

Palmeras whipped his wand from his sleeve and flourished it high. The other Evocators bowed their heads low to help concentrate and guide his power.

Lightning cracked from the wand's tip.

The wizards stepped forward with their offers.

The crowd gasped as the idol stirred into life. The god's iron hands reached out and the wizards quickly tumbled flesh into one palm, then filled the chalice from the cask of blood. Te-Date's mouth opened, fire bursting out, and the hand bearing the meat tilted it through metal lips. The smell of scorched flesh filled the air. The other hand jerked upward, spilling the blood into Te-Date's fiery maw. The godform became still and the crowd groaned in satisfaction. Te-Date had accepted our offerings.

More flourishes from Palmeras, and black smoke spewed from

the idol, billowing thicker and thicker until it became a dense cloud hanging over the godform's head. Sparkling lights danced in the smoke, which swirled and columned upward into a funnel.

"Behold, O Great Te-Date," Palmeras roared. "Gaze upon thy daughter. We pray you find her fair."

The smoke shot toward the huge cloth pavilion that hid the ship. It hovered over it for an instant, then a hole opened and the smoke hissed through. Palmeras thrust upward with his hands and the tent quivered from the magical force of the smoke inside. Then stakes burst, lines ripped free, and the giant tent lifted up and up until we could glimpse the bright painted timbers of the new ship.

Palmeras shouted, "Away!" And the pavilion filled like a sail and was swept off to the side, completely baring the vessel.

I've seen many such a thing before—although I must admit Palmeras' unveiling was easily the most spectacular—and I knew what to expect. Still, I caught my breath. There are few things as moving as a newly born ship.

Palmeras whispered to me. "Quick, what's to be her name? I forgot to ask."

The naming of a new ship is always important, and those of us who can claim parentage—and even those who can't—spend long hours considering and discussing the options. Like a human child, the ship's birth name seems to affect its future. Ask at any dockside tavern and you'll hear many a tale of ships with awkward names or unlucky names that came to misfortune. Some are even true. A large list had been presented to me, all, as I'd requested, of water-dwelling birds. I'd reduced the list to my favorites: shearwater, petrel, tern, and . . . ibis. I'd seen whole flocks of that graceful, heronlike creature fishing a marvelous lake in a distant land I'd once visited. The ibis, with the subtle beauty of its black and white plumage, is worshiped in that land, and once you've seen one with its spearlike beak stalking the shallows on its long, slender legs, or soaring on the midday breeze, you understand why. So that is the name I chose, and that name is the name I whispered:

"Ibis."

"Quite fitting," he said, and turned back—his position as Chief Evocator forgotten for the moment—to gawk like the rest of us.

The *Ibis* was a lovely thing to look upon. She didn't have the efficient carnivore lines of a ship of war, nor was she as fast. She was a shallow-drafted merchantman—ninety feet long and twenty abeam—built to take any seas and carry people as well as cargo in comfort. When she was completely rigged for sea, she'd carry a single mast, but just now there were flagpoles mounted for the ceremony, flying colorful banners. There was a quarterdeck at her stern with the wheel, a main deck forward, then the small-decked forecastle where the sailors would sleep. There were big cabins in the stern whose interiors would be lit by large, square, many-paned windows.

This was a ship ideally suited for exploring new seas to win new friends for Orissa and customers for the Anteros. Besides her sails, she could be powered by six large sweeps. She'd roll some at sea, but with her shallow draft and maneuverability, she could sail up rivers or hug any coastline and still have grace enough to impress a savage king. Although she could carry twenty-five men and women with ease, she'd need no more than six or seven to crew her. I like my ships to have a bit of flair, so I had her painted in bright, eye-pleasing colors, which at the same time did not detract from the bright skies and sparkling seas she'd soon sail. The only decoration still missing was the figurehead, which required not only much artistry, but magic as well. It wouldn't be finished for some days yet. The family who had created such masterpieces for several generations was notoriously precise—some said picky—and besides, it was bad luck to mount a figurehead until the ship sailed.

Someone shifted at my side, and I noticed Kele inching forward to sneak a better look. As an excuse for joining us, she had the green and gold ceramic flask that held the blessing potion. At the right moment I was supposed to break it against the side and officially launch the ship and name it.

"I'd trade my left tit to command her," she whispered.

I smiled, as taken by the craft as she, and slipped the flask from her grasp. Palmeras nodded, signaling me to get ready.

The ship sat in a cradle, a frame made of wood that would collapse when she was launched. She was held in place by thick-beamed shores angled up to steady her. And the whole elaborate contraption rested on freshly tallowed ways she'd ride down into the river.

Palmeras raised his wand and a hush fell over the crowd. But the sudden stillness let another voice carry loudly through.

"Damn you!" I heard my son roar. "How dare you take the word of a stranger over your own blood?"

We all jolted to see Cligus nose-to-nose with Hermias. Both of them were so absorbed in their confrontation they didn't notice that all eyes were on them.

"This is not the time to continue such a discussion," my nephew said.

"I'll not have you spread your filthy slander," Cligus said.

My son's hand went to his dirk. But Hermias beat him to it, his own hand shooting out to grasp Cligus' wrist.

I recovered and found my voice. "Stop it, you two! Remember *who* you are!"

My words jolted them to awareness and they turned, flushing in embarrassment. I let my glare sweep over the crowd, putting all my authority into it, and I saw the looks fall away and return guiltily to the business at hand. So much anger was in that glare that even Palmeras quickly dissolved his "I told you so" look into one of complete disinterest.

I raised my hand and the musicians caterwauled into what quickly smoothed out into stirring music of the sea.

Still angry, I braced to hurl the flask. But then I hesitated as the ship seemed to speak out to me, beg me not to let such emotion soil her luck.

"I'll make it up to you," I promised under my breath.

I flung the flask and it crashed against the ship's timbers. The heady scent of the blessing potion cleansed the air.

"Before all who witness," I declared, "I name thee *Ibis*. And may all your tradewinds be fair!"

Palmeras gestured with his wand, and the air crackled with the force of the spell he cast. The ship tilted forward, the cradle collapsed, and the *Ibis* slid smoothly along the ways to enter the water as royally as any princess slipping into her bath.

There was much cheering and music. Men and women pressed around me to congratulate the Anteros for the newest addition to their fleet. The merrymaking began in earnest then. Roasts sputtered on their spits, wine flowed, and couples, young and old, danced.

Cligus melted into the crowd and disappeared to sulk at home, I supposed. Hermias found a moment to come to me and apologize.

I waved him down. "I don't have to tell you that you acted the fool," I said. "Just as you don't need me to admonish you and say that I shall be angry at your behavior for some time. If you are the man I hope you are, you'll know you deserve it and suffer in silence."

Hermias blushed and bowed his head. He was wise enough not to speak.

"But I would like to know what you and my son were quarreling over that was so important."

Hermias shook his head. "I'll not say. Please don't press me on it, Uncle Amalric. I'd hate to earn your further wrath by refusing. Refuse, however, I must."

I could see there was no point in demanding an answer. He was an Antero, after all, and no one can match our stubbornness.

So I called for Quatervals and my carriage and headed home.

The day had left me in an even deeper quandary than before. I couldn't delay much longer. But the incident at the launching did nothing to grease the ways for *me*.

I REPAIRED to my villa garden to listen to the fountain play beneath my mother's shrine. She'd died when I was a boy, and I had little but my child's imaginings to remind me what she was like. And that was mixed up with the gentle myths my sister Rali had told.

Isn't it odd to think an old man might still want his mother's comfort and advice? Odd or not, this is what I wished for. And then a different light pierced the facets of that wish and I found myself mourning for Rali, my strong warrior sister whose common sense had been invaluable to me for many years. A final turn dredged up Omerye's face and the memory of her flute, which used to charm reason out of any mess I'd made of things.

I was Lord Amalric Antero, a man whose wealth and good fortune was the envy of many. But I had no one to lean on when weakness threatened.

No one I could trust to help.

Outside the villa walls I heard a horse trot up. Then a stranger's voice hallooed the house. I rose from the stone bench and went to the grated window in the garden wall.

It was a woman. Despite my age, my eyes are sharp and I could see her clearly.

She was young, fair of skin and form, but with a commanding presence. She sat tall and easy in the saddle of a fine gray. She wore a hunter's tunic of forest-green over a tight-fitting black body stocking that showed off shapely but muscular limbs. Her hair was dark, cut short, and on her head was perched a jaunty hat with a long feather of green to match her tunic. A simple chain of silver or white gold gleamed about her neck. Small studs of a similar metal winked at her ears, and as she waited for a response to her hailing, I saw her draw off elbow-length riding gloves, revealing a pair of wide silver bracelets on each wrist.

Impatient, she slapped the gloves against the saddle, then dismounted. On foot she was not so tall as her high-split limbs had made her first appear. She moved with a wiry grace, full of energy and purpose. And I noted that her high boots were expensive if well-worn from travel. About her narrow waist was a sturdy, large-buckled belt that bore a slim dirk in a scabbard on one side and what looked to be a leather wand case on the other.

She hallooed the house again. A servant came out, and although I couldn't hear the conversation, I gathered the young woman was asking for me. The servant shook his head, no, the master was not available. He was resting and had given orders not to be disturbed.

This was true. But curiosity overcame weariness and I hastened to send someone to tell the servant I'd changed my mind and please show her ladyship in.

When she strode into the garden, a large purse of well-worn leather slung over one shoulder, I was not disappointed. She was a dark-eyed beauty, and close up there was no mistaking her royal bearing. Only a slight bump at the bridge of her nose—hinting of an unset break suffered in some adventure—marred her chiseled perfection.

But I was too old to be dazzled by such things, so it was not her look that impressed me. Her eyes glittered with an intelligence that was so familiar I could almost say its name. I'd never met her, but somehow felt I'd known her long ago. And she was far too young for the number of years my mind was leaping over. She smiled, white teeth glittering against her dark features, and once again I was reminded of someone I once knew.

A double jolt struck me when she spoke and I heard the rich timbre of her voice. It was feminine, but deep and firm, and I felt an old ghost trying to roust itself from the tangles of my memory.

"Good evening, Lord Antero," she said, bowing.

"Good evening, my lady," I said. "Thank you for gracing an old man's day. Please bless me further by revealing your name and what I might do to assist you."

She drew a breath and firmed her nerves, as if this were a task she'd long awaited but was now hesitant to perform.

But when she answered, her voice was steady and strong.

"I am Janela Kether Greycloak," she said. "Great-granddaughter of Janos Greycloak—the man you were once proud to call friend."

I was rocked by her announcement—left gasping with amazement. For there was no doubt from the look of her and the sound of her that what she said was true.

But what came next struck harder still.

"As for the second question, my lord," she said. "I've come to ask you to accompany me to the *real* Far Kingdoms."

I sputtered. "What do you mean?"

"You and my great-grandfather were wrong, my lord," she said. "The Far Kingdoms have yet to be found.

"And only I know how to find them."

JANELA

I've been ambushed by that jester, Surprise, many a time. I like to think I've handled most such encounters with the harlequin well. I've bargained with cannibals, amused touchy giants, and dodged demons who ate a hundred souls for dinner and coveted mine for dessert. But I never expected I'd be confronted with the ghost of Janos Greycloak, telling me it wasn't over yet.

The young woman standing before me wasn't a ghost and she wasn't Janos, but she might as well have been. There was no denying her likeness. She had Greycloak's far-seeing eyes, his sardonic smile, high, stubborn cheekbones, and a voice that bade you listen. Even lacking demonstration, I could tell she was a wizard. She had an aura about her of tightly coiled magical energy waiting to be released.

I needed time to recover. Time to think. So I said, as calmly as I could, "I believe we could both use a brandy, my dear."

I called for a servant to fetch a bottle of my best, and yes, thank you, we'd prefer to have it served in the comfort of my study. As I led her there, pointing out a few interesting treasures from my travels on the way, I could see the mask of calm I'd donned had been effective. She seemed pale, tense, and there was barely disguised wonder that I seem unaffected by her announcement. I thought, What a cold, stony heart she must think beats in this old breast of mine. If only she knew how shaken I *really* was.

But by the time she'd had a sip or two of spirits she was ready to recommence the hunt for the old lion in his thorny lair.

"I have proof, sir, of my claims of kinship to Greycloak," she said. She didn't hesitate to see if I would instantly demand it—which I would have. I've been tangled in too many lies not to be wary, especially from someone who used that name.

Janela drew back the flap of her purse. It yawned open— showing it was even more voluminous than it first appeared—and she reached inside. Although it seemed full of all manner of things, both mysterious and common, her fingers quickly found a sheaf of papers which she spread out on my desk. There were gilt-lettered documents of introduction from half a dozen kings and princes, all of whom I knew well and whose word I was accustomed to accept. She had other proof, including testimonials from wizards noted for being scholars of sorcery. They praised one Janela Kether Greycloak—great-granddaughter of Janos Greycloak—as an able student who'd surpassed teacher after teacher, and who now, despite her youth, had the powers of a master wizard.

So I'd guessed correctly on that, I thought, leafing through the documents with fingers as numb as my brain. As final proof she unrolled a scroll from Irayas itself, proclaiming her as a daughter of a noble family who had the favor of the king.

I looked at the family name on the scroll. I saw a discrepancy and seized it.

"It doesn't say Greycloak here," I said.

Janela nodded, eyes intent, determined to convince me. "My great-grandmother, who was called Sendora," she said, "was a Lycus. So that is the name you see inscribed. It's a family renowned for the beauty of its women. Until Sendora, they were known for their purity, as well."

"Ah," I said. "So you're claiming you are the result of scandal? A child born on the wrong side of the bed?"

"Not just any bed," she said with a wry smile. "It was Janos Greycloak's bed my great-grandmother crept into."

"I knew him well," I said. "Better than any man. And I never heard him speak of a child, much less a child conceived in the Far Kingdoms."

"Irayas," she corrected. "I've already told you, sir, that you and Janos were wrong. The Far Kingdoms lie elsewhere."

"We'll get back to that later, my dear," I said. "I hope you don't mind me calling you that. I know it's out of fashion and some young women take offense these days, but I'm too old to unstick that once-gentle phrase from my tongue."

"You may call me anything you like, sir," she said, "as long as it's understood you are referring to a Greycloak."

I sipped my brandy to cover the laugh bubbling up. Greycloak or not, this was a very impressive young woman. She'd come better prepared for this meeting than many a sharp businessman, and refused to let me wander off the path she'd blazed with such care. From her short-cropped, easy-care locks to the simple elegance of her traveling costume, this was a woman who breathed confidence and efficiency.

"Go on," I said. "If you please."

"Do you really doubt," she asked, "that my great-grandfather left children behind?" She laughed. I liked the sound of it. Although it lacked Janos' boom, it resonated with the same free and easy humor that had charmed me when first I'd met him.

"His victories with women," she said, "were the stuff of legend. Why, he bounced more eager damsels—virginal, or otherwise—on more mattresses than any man I've certainly ever encountered."

From the flash in her eyes I could tell she was not a woman totally inexperienced in such matters. A passionate nature was another thing she seemed to have inherited from Janos, I thought. I grinned, remembering that Greycloak, who was also a master of many tongues, once said the best language book could be found in the arms of a charming native.

"How many languages do you speak?" I asked idly.

She seemed surprised. "Oh, twenty or more, I suppose. That's without accent. I can get on well enough in twenty others. Why do you ask, my lord?"

"No reason," I said, feeling a little ashamed for wondering if she favored the same learning devices as Janos.

I went on. "There's no denying Janos' reputation. But when we were in Irayas together, as foreigners we were kept away from the daughters of the highborn. Janos dived into the fleshpots, to be sure. But to be frank, they were orgies of the most decadent sort and with the most decadent of people. I wouldn't be so quick, if I were you, to shame your great-grandmother by including her in such activities."

Janela shrugged. "She was young," she said. "No more than sixteen. When she saw Janos at court, she fell hopelessly in love—which is not uncommon at that age. However, as you said, there was no normal way such a thing could ever be consummated. But she was a determined young woman. She bribed a courtesan to let her take her place at an orgy Janos was attending. And she showed him so much ardor that their affair lasted some time. He didn't live long enough to learn her true identity."

"And Sendora became pregnant," I said. "That *would* have been a great scandal."

"As soon as the family learned of her condition," Janela said, "and who was responsible—a filthy foreigner, and a dead one, to boot—they took quick action. In a false act of piety they had my great-grandmother make sacrifice at the Temple of Virgins."

I knew of the temple. Several times a year maidens of some very religious families offer their virginity to the gods. They must accept the embrace of any man who presents himself during the night they spend there. It is presumed that a god enters the body of that man so he can accept the gift the maiden offers.

"In other words," I said, "the child was said to have been conceived by a god."

Janela chortled. "Considering my great-grandfather's vanity," she said, "perhaps they weren't lying as much as they believed." She sipped the brandy, amusement crinkling the corners of her eyes. "I've heard a particularly ugly beggar became a very lucky man the night Sendora made her sacrifice. He was so amazed to hold such fresh, clean beauty in his arms that he took his own life the following day, knowing nothing so grand would ever occur in his life again."

"But even if your family went to such extremes to avert scandal," I said, "there would still be doubters. There'd still be ugly talk."

"Exactly why they married her off to a country lord," Janela said. "Which was where my grandmother was born, only to wed another rural squire and produce my mother. None of the women bred in those marriages has ever been permitted to leave the countryside. All to protect an old family secret."

"*You* left," I said.

Janela's face darkened with anger. "I am not a woman to bear shackles of any kind, sir," she said. "My family disowned me for it, as I have disowned them. I've taken my great-grandfather's name—my birthright—and for ten years I have made it my purpose to see that his dream was fulfilled."

"If your family has disowned you," I said, "how do you live?"

"I have my own money," she said. "My great-grandmother learned more things than passion from her experience. She learned what it was to be helpless, to be forced to bow to family rule. She set aside funds her entire life in case her daughter should ever find herself in dire need of independence. My grandmother added to that, and *my* mother, as well. So, although I am not as rich as you, my lord, I am quite well-to-do."

"Was your mother among those who disowned you?" I asked.

"My mother is dead," she said, so flat-edged I knew better than to ask the particulars. As one who suffered the same loss, I was sensitive to her feelings.

"The reason," she said, "I believe I was the first to break from that prison—and soft as it was, it was a prison just the same—is I am the only one who was born with Greycloak's powers. I cast my first spell as a child—to repair a favorite doll that had broken. I was no more than three. It had a ceramic head which shattered when I dropped it, and I was desolate. But suddenly it came to me that I could make it whole again. So I did."

"Did you actually will the doll's head to be healed?" I prodded. "Or did something else happen?"

She frowned. "To be completely accurate," she said, "I thought of that doll as it had existed before I dropped it. Then I . . . reached into that place . . . and traded one for the other."

I nodded. This was exactly how Janos once described a similar experience. Except it was a scorpion, not a doll. And we were more than desolate because we were dining with the Lord Mortacious at the time and he was a *most* difficult host. I shuddered at the memory.

"Do you accept who I am?" she asked briskly, anxious to move on to the next part—the part I dreaded the most.

Still, I had no choice but to answer: "Yes."

She put the papers away and drew out something else. I craned to look, but she kept it hidden in her palm.

"You can't imagine how long I've dreamed of this meeting," she said. "A Greycloak and an Antero together again. Over the years I almost made the journey several times. But I knew I was not only too young and inexperienced, but that I would need absolute proof to convince you. To gather that evidence I've traveled from land to land and court to court. I've studied with the greatest masters of magic and learned enough so that I someday hope to approach the abilities of my great-grandfather. Wherever I went, I sought and studied all the tales I could find of the Far Kingdoms. I've read your book as well. And your sister's, too, because although you may not know it, Rali added greatly to the solution of the mystery. To be truthful, I'm not yet sure where the pieces fit, but I am certain that they *are* pieces."

"I don't care how much you studied, or how far you traveled," I said. "You were wasting your substance. If you will only draw back you'll see your fascination with Janos Greycloak has made you twist the facts to meet your dream of emulating him. Forget it, my dear. Take your talents, your energy, and your intelligence and devote them to making your own life, not someone else's. I was there, my good lady. Janos and I walked that road shoulder to shoulder. We buried comrades. We overcame much. But in the end we succeeded. We found the Far Kingdoms. How can I deny what I saw with my own eyes?"

"Deny this, then," she said. And revealed the object hidden in her palm.

It was a small silver figurine. I recognized it immediately— Janos once had its twin strung on a chain. Janela's fingers twisted and the figurine dropped, until it, too, hung from silver links. It was the likeness of a beautiful dancing girl, hands stretched above her perfect head, one holding a feather, the other a veil frozen in mid-twirl. The maiden's face was alight with happiness, as if she knew her next leap would set her free and she'd fly away like a bird.

As if drawn by a magical force, my hand stretched out to take it. Janela let it fall into my open palm.

"Behold," she said, "I give you . . . the Kingdoms of the Night!"

As soon as the dancer touched my flesh she came to life. She pirouetted, her gossamer costume swirling about the naked form beneath, giving tantalizing glimpses of her slender limbs and small, shapely dancer's breasts. But this was no courtesan's dance of seduction. She seemed innocent, unaware that she might be an object of passion as well as art.

At first the dancer was similar to the magical talisman Janos once used to convince me the Far Kingdoms really existed. Except his figurine had been tarnished and broken—deformities that eventually vanished the closer we came to Irayas. But as I watched, the scene began to change. I goggled as glorious music swelled and the maid's surroundings and audience misted into view—this was a sorcery far beyond the one Janos had so prized.

She was dancing in a courtroom of tremendous wealth. The tapestries were rich beyond measure. The walls they hung from were smooth, milk-white, and as lustrous as a rare gem. As royal musicians played in a pit beneath her dancing platform, noble men and women—in exotic costumes whose like I had never seen—craned for a better view of the dancer's artistry. Overseeing it all was a handsome monarch and his beauteous queen. They sat on twin thrones made from the same milky gem as the walls. The king was young, with long muscular limbs. His features were fair, sharply defined, his beard gold as the band he wore for a crown. The queen was also young, her skin the color of ivory, and she had long black hair that tumbled from beneath a simple emerald crown. I saw the king lean over to whisper to the queen. She smiled, and her beauty became so dazzling that if I had been a young man that smile would have broken my heart.

Even in miniature the power and sophistication of that court humbled me. I felt as small, ignorant, and barbaric as when Janos and I had first stood before King Domas in far Irayas. But with that feeling came a flush of anger that here was knowledge my own people had been denied. I yearned to visit that court and set matters right.

Janela whispered, "Look closer, my lord."

I scanned the scene, searching for what I'd been too bedazzled to note before. And then I saw him—lolling in a favored viewing box near the throne.

He was a demon dressed as a man. He had the snout of a wolf and the brow of a great ape, which beetled over a single yellow eye. As I watched, he extended a taloned paw. Dangling from it was a single rose, and I felt my flesh crawl, for somehow this seemed an obscenity. He laughed, exposing long fangs, and hurled the flower at the dancer. It fell at her feet, petals shattering from the blossom head. The dancer missed a step; she glanced down at the broken flower, then at the demon. A look of immense loathing and fear marred her perfect features. Then she smiled and took up the dance again.

I drew back, my eyes sweeping the audience, where I saw other demons scattered about the room. It was apparent that the people in the crowd—while studiously acting as if the demons' presence was normal—shrank from full contact, leaving a space about each beast.

Janela touched the dancer. The dancer froze, becoming a mere figurine again, and the scene vanished. Only force of will kept my hand from shaking as I handed the talisman back to her.

"Do you believe me now, my lord?" she asked, voice low—confident.

I could still have denied it. Pointed out that by using the description of the figurine from my book, an elaborate magical forgery could have been commissioned. Or that because the scene was remarkable, it didn't mean it necessarily came from a mythical second Far Kingdoms—which she had dubbed the "Kingdoms of the Night." All sorts of other quarrels and attacks could have been raised. An unbreachable wall of logic, mortared with pure reason.

But that isn't what she'd asked. She'd hoisted another banner entirely—the flag of Belief.

I looked at her and saw Janos in her eyes, and I could never deny Janos the truth.

So I answered: "Yes."

Janela swept the figurine into her purse, closed the flap, and rose.

"Think of it, my lord," she said. "We can talk again at your convenience."

Janela turned to go.

"Where will I find you?" I asked, somewhat befuddled by her brisk exit.

"At the Inn of the Harvest Moon," she said. "I'm using Kether—my Orissan name."

Then she grinned Janos' grin, saying, "I didn't think it wise to let everyone know there was another Greycloak about."

And she was gone.

Memories welled up, then spilled over to rush by in a torrent. My adventures with Janos were uprooted and swept under the long bridge that rose from our chance encounter in a villains' tavern and ended in the swamp of confusion that was the present day. One particular memory tumbled over to smite the pillars of the bridge: the Fist of the Gods. To aid my recollection, I hastily pulled the journal detailing our expeditions from the shelf of my desk. I leafed through the pages that had enthralled so many at the bookstalls.

I found the description of the vision that had greeted us in the Evocators' Palace when Janos and I had won their blessing for the first voyage: . . . *hunched upon the horizon was a mountain range. It sat upon the land like a big-knuckled fist. There were four squat peaks in the range, with a curved fifth that made the clenched thumb. The peaks were of black volcanic rock, dusted with snow. Snowdrifts picked out each digit of the fist. The valley between thumb and forefinger rose smoothly upward—passage through that black range. A passage to . . . my thought was completed by Janos' whisper of awe . . . "the Far Kingdoms."*

I gulped brandy to still my nerves as I riffled forward to the place where Janos and I had stood before that same gateway to our hard-sought goal.

. . . Beyond was the mountain range. There were four peaks in the range and a fifth that twisted like a huge thumb. We had reached the plain that stretched to the Fist of the Gods. It was yet too early for snow, and we appeared closer than in my vision, so I could tell there were striations in the peaks beyond just black volcanic rock . . . I turned to Janos . . . Both of us went a little mad for the next few moments—mazed shock, imbecile gape, then both babbling, neither hearing the other . . . "We found it," I said . . .

But we hadn't—and I saw our error plain. Just to make certain, to grind the sands of failure deeper, I turned to the last page. I re-lived the terrible moments when I tended the flames of Greycloak's funeral pyre. Then:

. . . I wipe wetness from my eyes . . . Suddenly I see a vision of great clarity. Far to the east across dazzling seas, where they say no man lives, a trick of light lifts a mountain range above Horizon's curve. The range looks like a great clenched fist, and between thumb and finger I see the glitter of a pure white blanket of snow. The mountain fist exactly fits the vision I saw when the Evocators cast the bones that began our quest . . .

I groaned when I read the last sentence. The mountain range I'd seen in both visions *was not the same* as the one we had stood be-fore in person, much less climbed. *Where was the snow?* Janos and I had laid its absence to the warm weather. But damn the eyes of the gods who lied to us, weather had nothing to do with it. The moun-tains of the visions rose much higher—so high snow would never melt. Now I thought of it, there were other differences we should have noted if we hadn't been blinded by our obsession.

I slammed the journal closed. I refilled my goblet, drank it off, and filled it again. I continued this course until—for the first time in many a day—I was quite drunk.

When Quatervals came to fetch me to bed, I thought he was Greycloak and I cursed him for being such a fool. I cursed myself even more bitterly, for as a fool I was his royal superior, and what was worse, Janos was dead and I was old and there was nothing that could be done about it.

Nothing.

THAT NIGHT I dreamt I was young again, burning with the need to make my mark as a man my father could be proud of. I was in the camp of the Ifora, watching Janos' savage dance. His scimitar flashed in the firelight, routing the imaginary enemies that peopled the tale he told. Beside me the beautiful nomad whore, Tepon, smiled. I smelled rose and musk and her robe fell open, revealing gleaming dark skin and high breasts heaving with desire. I was young and strong and I mounted her like a wild desert stallion, my hands gripping her firm hips as I thrust. She looked over her shoulder at me, laughing and urging me on. She shook her head and black tresses whipped about like the mane of a high-spirited filly demanding the stallion be worthy of her gift. In that moment everything was possible. There was no sea I could not cross, no wasteland I could not dare.

And the Far Kingdoms were mine for taking.

I WAITED two days before I saw Janela again. I was using the old merchant's ploy of delay to rattle her confidence. But when she greeted me in her sparse but tasteful rooms in the Inn of the Harvest Moon, I saw the light of victory in her eyes. She was dressed as before, except this time she wore a blue silk tunic over the black body stocking. Her hat bore a matching blue feather.

I was determined to make her sell, and sell hard. I needed to test her mettle, much as Janos had tested mine.

I let her fuss over me, making sure I had a comfortable seat by the fire and a goodly amount of brandy in my goblet. Her bracelets rattled softly as she leaned across the table. Anticipating an easy first parry, I struck hard.

"Why me?" I asked.

She frowned, caught unaware. "I don't understand," she said, playing for time.

"Why do you want *me*, of all people, to accompany you?" I said. "After all, I was responsible for your great-grandfather's death."

She nodded. "I know that, my lord," she said. "Just as I know you had no choice if you were to save your own life, much less to save your people from ruin. I'm well aware of Janos Greycloak's many faults. I'll admit that when I first read your book I was furious. I believed you lied when you wrote of the evil bargain he made with Prince Raveline. Just as I believed you lied when you said Janos betrayed you."

"What changed your view?" I asked.

Her brow deepened in thought. Then she said, "First off, the rest of your book rang so true. You made no effort to show yourself in a favorable light. You swore to tell the truth in the very beginning, and I could find no other place that rang false. You stripped yourself naked in your writing, plainly struggling to come to grips with your feelings for a man who was once your friend, but who betrayed you. In the end I think you proved that despite his betrayal, your friendship extended beyond his death."

"Thank you," I said. I toyed with my goblet, waiting.

When I didn't take up the banner of conversation and carry it forward, she had to struggle to complete the answer.

"I didn't leave it there, however," she said. "I've never thought feelings or beliefs proved a thing. Even my own. So I checked your claims quite thoroughly. And I found nothing that would contradict them. Actually, you were probably kinder to my great-grandfather than many others."

I shrugged. "False friend or true," I said, "no one could deny that Janos Greycloak was a great man. You must examine one at the same time that you consider the other."

"I have great admiration for you, my lord," Janela said. "I've been living incognito in Orissa for many months. I've observed you and your family quite closely. I've read everything I could about you and your remarkable sister. I've spoken to others as well, and I found that even your enemies respect you. You are a great man yourself, Amalric Antero. As great as Janos, in many ways. And that is why I have come to you."

I studied her closely as she spoke, and was certain she'd answered as honestly as she could. But I gave no hint of my thinking.

"That's all very kind," I said. "But it is only a partial answer. You said you were not without substantial funds, so you don't need my money to mount such an expedition."

Janela laughed. "Don't be so quick about the money, my lord," she said. "I said I was well off. But I'm not as rich as you. I doubt many are. Still, your point is well-taken. It isn't money that draws me to you. The facts are these, sir. All the spells I've cast indicate that alone I have only a small chance of success. But with an Antero at my side the chances rise considerably. I think my great-grandfather sensed this after you'd met."

I snorted. "Then you should have approached one of my younger relatives," I said.

Janela's eyes narrowed and I could feel the strength of her will. "I told you I have observed you and your family closely. I won't tell you what I think of your son, Cligus, for I hope that we can at least be friends. Besides, only you and your late sister have the spiritual—read that 'magical'—wherewithal. You plainly inherited abilities from your mother. If other Anteros possess it, they are still at suck with their wet nurse."

"If they are too young," I said, "I'm plainly too old for the journey. I might die on the way, and then where would you be?"

Janela's eyes narrowed. "That much closer to the Kingdoms of the Night," she said flatly.

The answer was as cold as pure honesty could make it.

Then she said, "As for your age, my lord, I think you're just feeling sorry for yourself because you feel useless. Why, the whole city is talking about your reluctance to pass the torch of your empire. I wonder if that reluctance is because when you finally do so, you truly *will* be useless."

She leaned close, eyes glittering. "I'm offering you a chance to redeem yourself, sir," she said. Her tone was low, harsh. "You were wrong, and as it is, when history is corrected, you'll be nothing but an ironic footnote—the man who came so close but missed by so much."

The harsh tone shifted to a soft plea. "Come with me, Amalric Antero. The place we seek lies far to the east across seas it is forbidden to sail. Those seas beat on mysterious shores no man or woman from these parts has ever trod before."

Her hand fell on mine. It was small but strong, and so full of the life of a seeker that it burned. "Come with me," she said again. "And we will do great deeds together."

My pulse hammered, deep emotion stirred by her speech. Janela must have noticed. She smiled and withdrew her hand. "You are not so old as you think," she said. Then: "There's time enough for dreams if you'll give yourself the chance."

She was right. At least that is what I sorely wanted to believe.

A long silence fell, unbroken except for the crackling of the fire.

"Will you give me your answer now?" she asked.

I shook my head. "No," I said. "But I promise you shall have it soon."

With that I tore a page from her book of tricks and departed wordlessly.

She would not sleep well until I returned. But then, neither would I.

SO, AS I NEARED my seventh decade I found myself at a crossroads. But whichever path I chose, a single mountain stood in my way. I had to pick a successor. If I did not, I would leave all that the Anteros had built over the generations at the edge of a precipice.

Who should it be? Cligus or Hermias? Once more I made the lists, naming each man's virtues and vices, trying to keep my feelings out of the judgment. But I could not. Cligus might be my blood, but I found no wellspring within me. On the other hand, was I being too much the romantic, since Hermias seemed to have a bit of the flash, flair, and gods-blessed foolishness I remember myself as showing in years gone by?

I finished the lists and shrugged. Nothing was new, nothing had changed. With one exception: What had happened out there beyond the Narrow Seas that caused the near fight between the two at the christening of the *Ibis?*

I couldn't ask either of them about it, which left only one person who would likely know and who could be trusted: Kele. I called for Quatervals and my carriage and set out to track her down.

I found her dockside, in the fitter's shed next to the *Ibis.* On the table in front of her was a stand with a horizontal brass rod resting on two mounts. Impaled on the rod was an intricately carved wooden model of the ship. Kele was delicately placing small blocks of wood on the model's deck. It teetered, teetered, and then, as she chanced one more, spun on the rod—"capsizing," sending the wooden blocks cascading to the floor.

"Pack eighteen tons'a deck cargo, more an' she'll roll like a whaleshark . . ." she muttered, and made notes in a logbook. Then she noticed me, stood and touched her brow.

"Lord Antero," she began. "Di'n't expect you or we could've had some wine sent—" She stopped abruptly. "Dyin' sea gods," she said. "Sorry to be jestin', since you've got death an' despair writ large 'crost your forehead."

I managed a smile. "Maybe it's good I'm not going afield any more, Captain, if I'm *that* easy to read." In truth, after all the years as my employee and friend, she ought to have been able to read me as easily as she could decipher the fathom marks on a chart.

She didn't answer, but led me out of the shed. "It's a nice day for a walk," she said.

"It'll be raining in an hour," Quatervals said.

"A *very* nice day," she went on, "for a stroll 'side the quay where there's no hidden spaces where someone c'n cock an ear f'r what'd well be none'a their business."

Quatervals looked worried and glanced about as if the imaginary spy Kele had named was lurking within earshot. Kele was *always* this cautious. If she had a lover—and even after all these years I had little idea of her private life—he or she would've gotten more pillow talk from a mute.

That was one of the many reasons Kele was my most trusted seafarer—far beyond a mere ship captain, actually, since she'd frequently served as my eyes and ears on foreign shores, and even, on occasion, as my very quiet ambassador without portfolio. Another of her talents was the ability to report a conversation *exactly* as it happened, so even if she herself spoke like the salty mariner that she was, she could mimic the speech of an Evocator or lord as if she were born in their ranks.

We strolled down the embankment. There weren't many people about on that day since, indeed, rain clouds did boil and threaten overhead.

Kele, as usual, waited for me to speak. I had barely begun my request when she began shaking her head violently. "Not that, sir. That's somethin' I can't . . . won't talk on."

"Why not? I desperately need to know what happened, and also your advice."

"First, Hermias swore me t' secrecy that night in Jeypur, a'ter the man—after what happened. Second, I'm nowt a fool, sir."

"I never thought you one."

"Isn't any soul who steps in the middle of a family fight a fool or worse? Wouldn't I be best advised keepin' my blessed mouth clamped?"

So the incident or whatever it was *had* happened in Jeypur. That barbaric port was a crossroads both for ships and merchant caravans striking off into the west. It was from there that Hermias' Finding had begun and where he'd stocked his pack animals before setting out into the interior to cement his new trading territory. Jeypur was a city that had no allies beyond the moment, no friends beyond those who could profit her. It was said crime was very low in the city because nothing was illegal and all of the best thieves were in the government. It was, in short, a place I'd always found intriguing.

I took a minute before I answered, weighing my approach cautiously. "I could say, Captain, that I could put my own agents out and possibly find out what happened. But I need to know right now. There is more at stake than pacifying two Anteros who nearly came to daggers-point in a shipyard."

I told Kele a bit of what was happening, although I did not tell her who Janela was, or of her search for the Kingdoms of the Night. However, if I did decide to accompany her, I'd already decided the *Ibis* would be my flagship and Kele, if she chose, its captain. But at the moment she didn't need to know any more than that I proposed to undertake a voyage of great risk and length.

Kele looked out at a passing pair of trawlers, setting out to net the river's mouth. "Bastard, bastard, bastard," she muttered. "And now I'm like you, 'tween a lee shore an' a reef. If I *don't* tell you . . . but then if I do . . ." She fell silent. Then: "And you *are* my bound lord and that's my first duty. So . . ." Again, there was a long silence. "How many souls work for the Anteros?" she asked.

I puzzled, but remembered Kele always had her own way of toothing a problem. "Over five thousand. Quite a few more, I suspect, if we count our contractors' people, all of our trading houses overseas, and the caravansaries we've opened in the last year. But let that number stand as the least," I said.

"So if you choose wrong," she said, "that'll be five thousand wights who'll have me an' my curs't vows to thank. Hells and green hells!"

"Would a brandy make your decision easier?" I asked, trying to lighten the path. "Or some time to think?"

"What happened isn't a tale for a taproom, sir. Nobody should overhear. An' if I'm to break my vow, I'd as soon start bein' a fool now as takin' time to think about doin' it. One thing—if I violate my promise to Hermias, you have t' swear he'll never learn of't. 'Least, not till after it doesn't matter any."

"I so swear," I said.

"D' you remember," Kele began, with no preamble, "five or six years gone, when General Cligus went to Jeypur?"

I did indeed. It was one of my son's honest triumphs, a task I'd felt him completely unsuited for, yet one that he'd accomplished perfectly, covering himself in glory and making me wonder if perhaps I wasn't being too harsh and perhaps he *did* have the necessary skills of diplomacy, subtlety, and common sense the Antero empire must have to survive and continue its growth.

Jeypur was ruled by a council whose members and even size

varied depending on which factions had the greatest power. This
particular time a new group had gained the palace and announced
that no longer should Jeypur exist as the cat's-paw of other golden-
ribbed cities, that it deserved its place in the sun. They were referring to Orissa. They meant to acquire this glory and wealth by
placing a fifteen percent surtax on *all* caravans, cargoes, and ships
entering, being purchased, *and* leaving the city, which meant a trade
item could have its price nearly doubled—fifteen percent when it entered the city, fifteen percent when it was bought by an outside merchant and stored for sale or transshipment, and a third fifteen
percent when it left Jeypur for its final market. At the time, about
twenty percent or more of all western traffic, including many items
brought from the faraway islands of Konya, passed through Jeypur.

That was intolerable to the merchants of Orissa, particularly
since we thought, with some justification, that the rulers of Jeypur
differed from the pirates of the Narrow Seas only because they
robbed by decree, not dagger. There were angry meetings with our
Magistrates and a determination that something must be done and
done immediately. Some of my hotter-headed colleagues wanted to
fit out an expedition. I advised a diplomatic mission, but one that
should have a few soldiers attached just to make sure Jeypur understood that Orissa had more than words in her arsenal.

My idea was seized on and blown up like a pig's bladder at
slaughtering season. Not only should there be soldiers, but a soldier
should be in charge. I argued, but unsuccessfully, so I retreated
gracefully and began thinking of various members of our army
known for their tact and charm. While I thought, Cligus and his
supporters acted. He was named to head the mission, and elected by
acclaim. There was nothing I could've said to change it. How could
I object to an Antero, least of all my son?

So off they sailed, and I grimly wrote letters to my various fac-
tors in lands around Jeypur, advising them that a small, silly, but
trade-ruining war was likely in the offing. I *knew* Cligus would confront the council, insult them liberally, dare them to stand against
the might of Orissa, and then, most likely, kick over one or two statues of their favorite gods as an afterthought on the way out.

To my astonishment, none of that happened. Admittedly, luck

helped him, but luck is often an excuse for failure by those unblessed. Before the delegation had been in the city more than a
week, three of the ruling council's members fell ill and died. Their
replacements listened to reason, which of course included some private enrichment, and the proposed tariff vanished like smoke
wisping from a temple incenser.

Cligus, when he returned, was granted a special day of feasting,
and his name was read aloud in the Great Temple at the end of the
year when the priests told the gods which Orissans were especially
suitable for blessing.

Yes, I remembered well.

"When we arrived in Jeypur," Kele went on, "the presence of
an Antero was cause for the criers to bellow their lungs out. It mattered not to either Hermias or myself, other than the higher prices
we'd have t' pay for the caravan animals, since where Hermias'd be
tradin' was already known, and I'd pass the time waitin' for him to
return rechartin' those demon-blasted sand islands to the west of the
city, where I blessed near wrecked a few years gone.

"We took quarters, unloaded our trading cargo from my ship,
and started buyin' all of the gods-blest million-and-one things for
Hermias' journey.

"On the third day, quite late, as I was havin' a final tod with
Hermias in his quarters, the innkeeper tapped at his door and said
a man wished converse with us.

" 'This late,' I told Hermias, 'this man's trade'll either be dis-
honest, like most matters here in Jeypur, or bloody.'

"Hermias laughed. 'So far, my good captain, this trip has been
lacking in adventure. We could do with a footpad or two to enliven
the tale we'll come home with.' He ordered the keeper to show our
late visitor in and bring him whatever he wished to drink.

"I slid my chair around so my back was to the bulkhead and
made sure my blade was in reach. Hermias hadn't learned yet adventure's best in the tellin' 'n' seldom in the experiencin'.

"The man that came in looked fair ordinary. He was dressed
quietly, if expensively, and appeared quite sober. In a crowd most
people wouldn't notice him, or if they did, would imagine him a factor or perhaps a magistrate's clerk. He introduced himself as Pelvat.

"Hermias asked him his trade, and he looked sly an' said, 'Perhaps milord might care to think of me as a harvester. Others might call me a gardener.'

" 'Since we're to be in Jeypur no longer than a week,' Hermias said, 'what gardening would we need? Although I imagine you're being inexact in your words.'

" 'Not at all,' Pelvat said. 'A gardener goes across his land and decides which plants are flowers and are to be watered and tended and which are weeds to be plucked and tossed away. So I've been described, although I work mostly in the city among men.' "

" 'An assassin!' I said, my stomach curling a little.

"Pelvat made no reply, nor did his face change. He paid me no mind, I suppose correctly, since Hermias was the lord whose keep he was seekin'.

"Hermias himself took a deep breath, and I saw his jaw firm. 'I am an Antero,' he said. 'We have no need to hire murderers. Not now, not ever. So what in blazes impelled you to approach me?' I could see his face flush as he realized who was sittin' opposite and anger spread. Pelvat rose. 'My apologies for having disturbed your lordship at such a late hour and for such a . . . misunderstanding. But it was quite natural, since I was able to perform certain services for a kinsman of yours some years ago and he, at least, found my scythe to be quite keen and exact.'

" 'Who?' Hermias demanded.

" 'General Antero himself. You don't think those councillors who fell ill most conveniently and passed on in spite of the best efforts of wizards and leeches alike just happened to have the gods frown on them, do you?

" 'A skilled gardener not only knows how to distinguish flowers from weeds, but also how to distill other plants to make his task of beautification easier and less, shall we say, obvious.'

"Hermias was white with rage. 'Get out!' he snarled, and his hand went to the table where his dagger lay in its sheath. I myself reached for my own weapon.

"But there was no need. Pelvat bowed once, slightly, and slipped into the night. We never saw or heard from him again.

"Hermias and I were awake until dawn, talkin'. Somehow, sir, we felt the murderer spoke the truth, at least as far as he knew it."

She ended her tale, looking away from me in embarrassment. It was many moments before I could speak. Finally I fought my way through the heavy surf of emotion to address her. I said, "Kele, you've served me well once again, not only as my servant, but as my friend."

"I hope so," she said, and her expression was troubled.

There was nothing else to be said. We parted and I returned to the villa. I had Quatervals cancel all of my appointments for the day and retreated to the solitude of my study, where I brooded for many hours.

Somehow the use of poison made the crime worse. A poisoner is someone who gloats over the dark power of death that only he or she is privy to, someone who watches his victim writhe and die with pleasure.

Cligus. My son.

THE NEXT DAY I arose remarkably refreshed—cheery, even. In the faint light of dawn I'd held a trial, totted up the evidence, and found myself guilty of being the worst parent in Orissan history. But what was done was done—and considering that I had reached the age where I had wasted more time than I had years left, I decided it was time to move on to the firm ground of action.

I sent for Janela, and when she joined me in the garden—and found a comfortable place beside me on the ancient carpet the servants had spread on the grass—I came right to the point. All who know my smooth merchant ways know how much out of character that is. But I was through with wit dueling. I wanted plain answers to plain questions.

"You've shown me that Janos and I erred," I said. "Now tell me what makes you certain you know how to correct that mistake. How did we misread the fables of the Far Kingdoms?"

Janela caught my brisk mood, and after a wondering look at my sorrow-hollowed eyes, struck directly for the heart of the matter.

"You didn't misread the myths at all, my lord," she said. "Unfortunately, as ancient as those tales were, they are striplings compared to the originals from which they sprang. As a researcher, you see, I had the advantage of following in my great-grandfather's footsteps. I learned that there are two sets of myths. The newest begin shortly after Irayas was founded and prospered. As you know, Irayas and the rest of Vacaan was built on the ruins of the Old Ones."

I nodded. Greycloak had sought the answers to the riddle of nature itself in the volumes of knowledge those mysterious people had left behind.

"The other myths began during the days when the Age of Darkness first descended. When—as all schoolchildren are taught—the Old Ones were destroyed."

I, too, as a boy had reveled in adventures that were not my own, and my favorite stories were the myths of the Golden People who were said to have once ruled the land. We were children, less than savages compared to those wise folk, the tale-tellers claimed. All knowledge was theirs to command; all art, all song; in short, all that was beauty and made life worth living. A thousand years or more ago a great calamity struck and the Old Ones disappeared, leaving only their magnificent ruins to haunt us, humble us.

"I found the first spoor of those old myths," Janela continued, "while studying the origins of my own people. We were first nomads, driven from our ancestral lands by a now-forgotten enemy. When we stumbled on the ruins of the Old Ones and their treasure stores of knowledge, our future greatness was assured. We'd heard tales ourselves of the Far Kingdoms, and a few even thought perhaps Vacaan was once that place. Then people in other lands started thinking that *we* were the fabled folk, and to suit our own purposes we encouraged those new myths. It made potential enemies fear us, allowed our rulers to seal us off from evil influences, and—to be frank—it gave us a sense of vaulted superiority over others."

I knew that trait. One of the first things I'd noticed about Irayas was the people had little interest in the doings of others and thought there was nothing we barbarians could do that they couldn't do better. One of my fellow voyagers—Sergeant Maeen, I believe—said the people of Irayas walked around with their noses tilted so high that they were in danger of drowning whenever it rained.

"The first difference I noted," Janela said, "was that in the old tales—before our coming—the fabled lands were said to lie on the other side of the Eastern Sea. And in those stories they were called the 'Kingdoms of the Night.' As soon as I realized that, I searched for all legends that made reference to such a place. Everywhere I traveled I sought those myths. In dusty tomes, wizards' vaults, and even in the camps of nomads where stories have been handed down intact over scores of generations. Those myths all agree the Old Ones fought a mighty war against an unimaginably powerful and evil enemy. The survivors retreated across the Eastern Sea, where they now wait for an eventual return."

She patted her purse. "It was in one of those camps that I found the dancing girl," she said. "According to the witch I bought it from, it came into her people's possession long ago when they raided the last caravan that traded with the people of the Kingdoms of the Night."

"It *must* have been long ago," I said. "There's little I don't know of trading tales, and I've never heard of anyone who has ventured those waters."

"I tried once," Janela said. "But I was turned back by our coast watchers. If it weren't for my family connections, they would have summarily tried and executed me when they boarded my ship."

I was most impressed—not just because of her courage and initiative, but because among her people such a voyage to the east is forbidden. Although Vacaan is named after the supreme god of the Old Ones, Janela's people become quite disturbed when the ancients are mentioned. Fear is part of the reason. But I think it's more because the Vacaanese can't bear the comparison to such mighty people.

Still, they honor the Old Ones in many ways. For example, behind the city of Irayas, there is a mountain peak where the east wind always blows that the ancients held holy, a mountain whose plateau holds haunted ruins of those Old Ones. When a great Vacaanese wizard dies, his body is turned to ashes on a funeral pyre so the winds can carry his smoke—his essence—across the Eastern Sea, where the gods are said to dwell. That was where I'd performed such a ceremony for Janos.

"Did you know," I murmured, "Janos thought light itself had physical properties? That it actually bent when it followed the curve of the horizon?"

On the surface, my question had nothing to do with our discussion. But Janela immediately took my reference.

"Yes," she said. "And it was that which captured my imagination when I read the last lines of your book. And you described the vision you saw of the Fist of the Gods. That was no vision. A trick of light—bending light—revealed those mountains to you."

Barely containing her excitement, she whipped up her voluminous purse. From it she took a much-battered chart and unrolled it between us. I leaned to look and saw the coast of Vacaan and, spreading out from there, the eastern seas. Beyond those seas was a coastline, and many marks showing mountains, rivers, and deserts. Far inland—farther than most would be comfortable imagining—I saw a rough sketch of a fistlike range. It was labeled "Antero's vision."

"I began this chart," Janela said, "when I first began my studies. On it I transferred every clue I found in the myths of the Kingdoms of the Night." She grinned ruefully. "As you can see from the mess I made, many of those clues turned out to be false starts."

I laughed with her. The chart's surface was marred in many places where she had rubbed out her mistakes.

Then I said, "Where do we begin?"

I heard Janela's sharp intake of breath. "You've decided!" she crowed.

"Yes," I said flatly—disguising my own excitement. "I'm going with you."

Janela's eyes glowed with victory. But following my lead, she forced calm. A slender finger stabbed at the map.

"There," she said. "The jumping-off point is Irayas itself!"

I sent for strong spirits to seal our bargain.

As the servant poured, Janela said, "I have to ask, even though I fear it may weaken your new resolve: Pray tell me, my lord, what particular bit of evidence made you decide in my favor?"

And I answered, "Oh, why don't we just lay it at the feet of the persuasive powers you inherited from your great-grandfather?"

"I'll accept that, my lord," she said. "Even if your answer has more honey than substance to it."

She was quite correct. My decision had been built on the ruins of my son. I had failed with Cligus. Just as I still believed I'd failed with Janos. But I swore I wouldn't make the same mistakes with *this* Greycloak.

I owed Janos that.

I raised my goblet in a toast. "This time," I said, "we'll get it right."

CHAPTER THREE

THE WOLF
IN THE
PALACE

A few days after my decision, a strange sense of uneasiness began to plague me. I was sleeping restlessly, although I'd never
really been able to sleep well since Omerye had died. But
now I would wake near dawn with a sense of dread. It was as if I
were a boy again awaiting punishment for a piece of mischief.

At first I thought it was base worry, since I still hadn't announced my plans to the family. Then I thought perhaps I'd become
like too many old men I knew, letting my body sit idle and boil up
strange juices that flowed like oil of wormwood through my mind,
fertilizing dark thoughts.

I began exercising, not only to clear my mind but also because
I certainly couldn't traipse out into the wilderness as the doddering
old wreck I was. I remembered the soldierly setting-up exercises
Janos Greycloak had favored and began doing them morning and
night. After the midday meal I swam for an hour in the garden pool.
I hired a dueling master and spent several hours a week stumbling
around the mat with him. But these were light tasks compared to

the most onerous of all. Every morning before dawn, rain or sun, I stripped, save for a tie about my loins, and ran with Quatervals as my companion. He'd been running, heat of summer, storms of winter, every day since he joined my household, and was forever going on about how much fresher it made him feel. I maintained that all his straining accomplished was making him familiar with the inevitable aches and agonies of old age when he was still comparatively young. To be truthful, I was Quatervals' companion for only a moment, since I faded rather quickly while he went on to Mount Aephens and back—running the full three leagues to the mountain, then up and down its league-high crags.

At first I wasn't even out of sight of the villa before I sank to my knees, wheezing like a greedy harbor seal with a fish blocking its gullet, but each day I managed a little more. It was a real victory the day I went far enough to see Mount Aephens rise out of the dawn mists.

As for my diet, that had never been a problem, since I never was one to put on weight, and after Omerye's death the pleasures of the table vanished for me.

What my household thought of all this I didn't know; I made the mistake of asking Quatervals.

"Why, they think you're trying to make yourself strong enough to give the wench a tumble she might remember longer than a moment or two."

I hadn't told anyone who Janela really was nor our intent—other than Quatervals and one or two others—but I'd forgotten that people make up their own stories when there's an absence of fact, and the most lascivious is generally the best believed and the quickest to spread.

"Thank you, my friend," I snarled. "Now I understand why you come from such a *very* small tribe."

Quatervals snickered but took no injury. It was remarkable that unlike most people who pride themselves on the truth, he was decidedly thick-skinned.

Hesitantly, I told Janela about the problem, fearing damage to her reputation. I was hoping she might produce an explanation for her presence that involved an area somewhere above the genitals.

She just laughed. "What do you think they said any time I put myself under the tutelage of a man?" She heard the echo of her words and laughed once more. "Yes, sometimes I did just that, but it was my desire, not theirs."

I said I was amazed she'd found so many sensible and understanding people to study and live with. I knew too many masters who thought their power over their servants included the bedroom as a matter of course.

"It wasn't that they were understanding," she said. "But words, sometimes magical, sometimes not, can change a man's mind, if indeed he's thinking at a time like that. It always surprised me how quickly a jest can turn a stiff tool into a limp cloth."

I told her she needn't go in search of the Kingdoms to gain riches—I could name a dozen households in Orissa where the maids would cheerfully pay a week's wages to learn those jests.

She smiled and said that in the current matter, what people said didn't bother her, so we could let the problem lie as far as she was concerned.

"If you say nay, you'll be the first man I've ever met with gray in his beard who *does* object to people saying a young woman thinks he has something under his tunic she finds worth passing time with."

That ended *that*, and I retired, a bit amazed I could still blush. Janela's somewhat bawdy honesty would have made Janos proud.

None of this changed the sense of dread that haunted me. I even wondered if my mind might be weakening and soon I'd be one of those old loons who sit in parks, nodding in the sun and trying to remember the path back to where bread drenched in milk awaits their toothless pleasure.

Then I remembered I'd had this feeling before. But the knowledge brought me scant comfort because I also remembered when and where. It was when Janos Greycloak and I sought the Far Kingdoms. There'd been wizards searching for us, trying to find and destroy us from several directions. First there'd been the Archons of Lycanth—and I spat reflexively at their memory, hoping their dead souls were even now screaming in some demons' embraces. Far worse was the watching by the one who controlled the two Archons, Prince Raveline, the sorcerer who'd seduced Janos and then helped him destroy himself, the evil one I'd slain with my dead brother's help in that haunted city above Irayas.

Once again I felt I was being *watched* or, more correctly, looked for, the way a hunter scans a thicket for the stag he's certain is hidden within. By whom, I had no idea. So I tried not to think of him— for so I thought this entity, although it might as well have been her or it—which was foolish, much like telling an honest man you'll fill his cloak pockets with gold if he can *not* think of a blue pig for the passage of an hourglass.

Fortunately, there were other things to take care of, the most important being the finishing of the *Ibis*. I also sent word by fast courier boat for two of the vessels I kept ported in Redond across the Narrow Seas to refit according to my instructions for an inshore trading expedition, in an area where great storms could be expected. This way their captains would have no clue as to my intent, yet would be ready for a deep-water crossing and whatever lay at the voyage's end. Once they were ready, I ordered them to anchor just off Orissa's river mouth, to await further orders.

I would rather have had three ships identical to the *Ibis*, but we hardly had the time. These two, sister ships named *Firefly* and *Glowworm*, were single-deck hoys, smaller than *Ibis*, less handy and luxurious, but as close as I could come to ships that might meet any problem I could imagine.

All this was most important, but in the course of all these details of ships being here and there, Amalric's gut shrinking from here to here, his ability to trot from there to there . . . something was ignored.

I discovered what it was one night not long after dusk. There'd been a chill wind blowing, a reminder of winter's storms with brief spatters of rain, the kind of night that makes a man grateful when he sees his home loom up out of the blackness, its windows alight from a fire someone has thoughtfully laid for him, and his mind turns toward a warm brandy and spiced roast fowl and perhaps a blanket across his knees. Such were my thoughts as I huddled in my cloak while Quatervals turned our carriage out of Orissa's heart, where I'd spent an exhaustive afternoon at one of my banking houses making sure they understood our new currency exchange policies.

I felt something touch my spine. Not fear, not dread, but . . . a warning, perhaps. It wasn't of danger, but more like what a man feels when he's ridden out and can't remember whether he left his door unbarred and so turns back.

"Quatervals," I said. "To the yards. I wish to see the *Ibis*."

I was not telling him exactly what I did feel, since nine times of ten the man comes back to his house and finds to his embarrassment that not only is the door securely barred, but bolts are slid and the latchstring pulled inside.

Janela should still have been at the ship, since two days earlier I'd told her which cabin would be hers, and against her not-very-sincere objections, told her she could decorate as she pleased since she'd be spending long hours in it during our journey. Further, she should keep in mind that she might well be entertaining important visitors there. Those guidelines had produced a flurry of yardage merchants, painters, and chandlers, as well as a quickly suppressed moan on my part as I realized what most of Orissa, and not just my household, must now be thinking about goatish old Amalric Antero, his "trading ship" being turned into a floating bedroom and his newfound obsession with the woman of short-bobbed dark hair and soul-staring eyes.

But I'm afraid I let my concern show as I asked him to put the horses to a trot. Quatervals looked at me sharply, tapped the reins on the horses' backs, and adjusted his sword belt so his blade was handy. I thought of telling him it wasn't *that* bad: I was just being a cantankerous old man.

The yard workers were gone and the docks deserted when we pulled up. I muttered, seeing that the yard lamplighter was amiss in his duties and hadn't bothered to fire the torches that sat on posts along the wharf the *Ibis* lay at. But there were two lanterns burning at the ship's gangway and I could see another light flaring from the windows of Janela's cabin. All was very peaceful. Feeling even more a fool, I got out of the carriage and started toward the ship. Quatervals gave me a skeptical glance but followed.

We'd just gone through the gates when I heard a shout from the *Ibis*, a woman's shout of anger and surprise.

"Janela!" I said, but Quatervals was already running, his blade whipping out of its sheath as he went. I went after him as fast as I could, cursing myself for being a fat, comfortable fool.

Quatervals ran down the slight incline toward the finger wharf, and two men sprang out at him from behind some bales of cargo. I saw steel flash as Quatervals lunged at one, who screamed in agony; but the second smashed at him with a club and sent him spinning off the quay into the water.

The man came at me, club high, as I panted toward him. At one time when I'd been a bravo, I would've lugged out and spitted him like a cockerel as he charged. But not now, not carrying all these years. All I had time for was to slip out of my cloak and swirl it out like a bait net, waist high. Gods be blessed the wool was heavy and wet, with enough weight to send him stumbling to the side, clawing for his balance, then going to one knee.

Before he could recover I saw a long pole, a tool of some sort, and seized it. It had a heavy ball at its end, and I swung as hard as I could. The weight struck my attacker in the head and dropped him. He lay motionless, but I had to be sure and stamped hard on his throat.

I could feel my heart thudding against my chest, trying to burst free. A few feet away lay the sprawled body of a man, the lamplighter, struck down before he could accomplish his task so the villains would have benefit of the dark. I held the pole he used to light dock lanterns, a long stick with a heavy ball of tarred twine at the end.

On the deck of the *Ibis* I saw figures and again heard Janela shout with rage. I ran, staggering actually, down the dock, a buffoon armed with a match. As I went past, I saw Quatervals reach a piling and laboriously begin pulling himself out of the water.

The *Ibis* was beside me, her deck and bulwarks not much higher than the dock. On the ship were four struggling figures. One of them was Janela, and I saw the glitter of her dagger as she cut at an attacker. The other three carried swords and wore dark clothes.

I stood helpless, trying to determine what I could do. Then amazement hit as I watched Janela defend herself.

I had never—*have* never—seen *anyone* fight in such a manner, and I've witnessed, in demonstration or for blood, a thousand ways of war. It's possibly easiest to understand if I describe what I saw rather than try to explain. One man lunged at Janela, but even as his wrist straightened for the thrust, she'd slipped inside his guard and slashed and I heard a shriek. A second man was bringing his sword—a great two-handed blade—up over his head, but as he did she shifted sideways and the blade smashed into the wooden deck, bedding itself. Before he could yank it free, she drove the dagger into his chest.

The third man struck at her back, but again she was not there for the blow to land. But she'd had to move in such a hurry that her weapon was still bedded in the second man's chest as he tumbled backward.

Now Janela was unarmed, and the first man struck. His attack cut nothing but air.

It was as if she could anticipate what her attackers were going to do and move accordingly. But no matter this strange skill, now she was doomed, facing two armed men empty-handed.

All of this I took in as I hurried up the gangway gasping, a roaring in my ears and looking at the scene as if I were staring from inside a cave.

I had the presence of mind to touch the lamplighter's pole to one of the gangway lanterns and it flared up. The flash made one of the men turn. He shouted something and dashed at me. I may have been old and feeling my years, but no one with a three-foot spear, for so the man was trying to use his sword, can successfully perforate another who's carrying a ten-foot lance.

As he came at me, I shoved the burning ball of tar full in his face. His long hair caught fire and he howled in agony and stumbled back.

The last man saw his mate dying and spotted Janela as she pulled her attacker's sword from the deck and, holding the great blade as easily as she had her dagger, came at him. It was his turn to shout in fear, and he ran for the ship's side, intending to leap over onto the dock.

Waiting, a long piece of wood in his hand, was Quatervals. The tough was trapped. He turned back and Janela was on him. I saw he was a trained swordsman because in spite of his fear he went on guard and lunged. Once more neither she nor her blade were there . . . but a foot and a half of steel stuck out from the fellow's shoulder blades and he gargled blood and was dead.

Quatervals jumped on deck and his face was a study of anger and shame at his failure to protect me. His mouth opened and I motioned savagely for silence.

"Janela! Are you hurt?"

"No. No," she managed. "The bastards startled me when they burst into the cabin. But I've taken no harm." She looked around the deck. "Three of them."

"There were two more standing guard at the head of the dock," I said. "Quatervals killed one and I stopped the other."

Janela nodded, chest heaving as she recovered her breath. I realized I was still holding the lamplighter's torch and tossed it over the side. It hissed as it struck the water and went out.

"A big gang for such slender pickings," she said. "None but the first would have had pleasure from me." She smiled, a tight grin without mirth. "And there's little gold in my purse."

"No," I said. "I don't think they were thieves."

Both Quatervals and Janela looked at me.

"Thieves, rapists, murderers . . . they're cowards," I explained. "I have yet to see one stand and fight, except when they're trapped, and then they can show the savagery of any cornered animal. These men stood their ground. By rights they should have run as soon as they saw Quatervals and me."

Quatervals nodded. "I've never heard of robbers willing to stand away, on guard, when the others have found . . . gold," he said uncomfortably, not wanting to say what he knew they'd intended for Janela.

Janela smiled. "Lord Antero," she said, speaking formally in Quatervals' presence, "I know you think yourself old and helpless.

Yet you came down that dock as proudly as any warrior I've ever seen."

I muttered something. Even as a youth I never knew how to accept praise, and still haven't learned the lesson, although I admit my bravado had surprised me.

To change the subject, I walked over to one of the corpses, the one Janela had stabbed. He lay facedown and wore cheap homespuns with a cap pulled over his head, like any other night bully out of Cheapside.

"I'll go for the watch, Lord Antero," Quatervals said.

"Wait a moment." I toed the body over and swore. I heard a start of surprise from Janela.

Hanging around the man's neck was a large torc, solid gold with gems set in it. It sparkled in the lantern light.

"That's not loot," Janela said. "Look at his shirt." Around the torc shone green filigreed silk, exposed now that the disguise of homespun had fallen away.

The necklace and the silk had not been the surprise for me. I had recognized this man.

And I knew this night's troubles had just begun.

"LORD PALIC, EH?" the sergeant of the watch said. "I'm not surprised to see him weltering in his own gore. Lord Antero, you and your servant Quatervals have done Orissa a service. Mayhap some of his friends who swagger the streets thinkin' they're above the law'll see where their nose-slittin' and brawlin's like to bring 'em. But it's only a hope, and a weak one at that. They're the sort who never learn."

He turned to his men. "Haul this one off with the others, lads," he said. "I'll send someone to his family to see which priest gets the gold for holdin' 'is nose an' pratin' at the death-ceremony."

The sergeant pulled a bit of the homespun over the late Palic's face and stood as the guardsmen slid the body onto a stretcher and carried it off the *Ibis* to the bank where the bodies of his four henchmen rested.

"Will you be seeking death damages, lord?"

"I shall not."

"Sir, I'll not record your words t'night. Perhaps you'll rethink in the calm of day. Lord Palic's family was warned and warned again about him, once even by m'self, but paid no mind, sayin' the boy's just full of himself an' no more'n a fun-lover. Boy they called him and he's touchin' thirty." The sergeant thought about spitting, remembered who I was, and swallowed hard. "He's got two brothers now, who're shapin' to be his mirror images, an' maybe, you pursuin' the matter an' touchin' what they find dear, their vault, might change things."

"I said what I meant, Sergeant."

"Very well, Lord Antero. But I think . . . ah, it doesn't matter what I think." The sergeant was silent for a minute. "And here I thought Lord Palic might've changed his ways since we'd heard no wind of what he must've called adventures for nigh on a year, year and a half. Damme for a milk-fed dreamer. 'Night, lord. Lady." And he trudged off down the gangplank after his men.

Janela was looking at me curiously. I waited until the sergeant and his detail were gone, then motioned Quatervals and her into the cabin, where there'd be no possibility of my words being overheard.

Palic had, indeed, been a terror. I knew more about the man than the sergeant did. He had not exactly changed his ways, but found a sponsor for his mischief. If he hadn't been of the nobility, he would've been described as "in the employ of," but naturally no one of his high rank ever held a real "job."

Instead Palic was the "boon companion" of one of our newest and fastest-rising Magistrates, Lord Senac. I'd had word he was so enthralled that he did *nothing* his mentor didn't order.

Now, tonight, I said, I proposed to visit Lord Senac and inquire as to just what errand, if indeed there was one, Palic had been running aboard the *Ibis*.

Quatervals' eyebrows climbed. "Aren't you puttin' yourself a bit too much in harm's way, lord?"

"I'm old," I snapped, "not dead. At least, not yet. And I'll not put someone to a task I'm afraid to touch myself." That ended that line of discussion abruptly—and I saw Quatervals grin approvingly.

Janela furrowed her brow. "I've never heard of this Senac, Amalric. Is there any reason he might be an enemy?"

"I know of none. Which is why I wish to speak to him."

Quatervals was looking at me. I nodded: He could speak freely in front of Janela.

"Are you sure you aren't looking at mist on the mountain and seein' a storm, lord? Maybe the sergeant was right and Palic was just rippin' and tearin'."

I shook my head, not sure of why I was so certain, but I was.

"There could be," Janela said, "a way to confirm your thoughts."

She drew her dagger and went out.

Quatervals made sure the door was closed behind her. "Lord," he said, "I failed this night. I think I should find another way to pay the debt I owe you than being your guard. Any fool that runs into a trap like I did has no more business carrying a sword than a priest does holdin' a blood-debt."

"Shut up," I advised. "I didn't think anything was awry, either."

"But—"

"The matter is not open for discussion. If you wish to expiate your many sins, next time I ask you for an opinion, make me feel good and lie."

Quatervals hissed through his teeth but obeyed orders. I didn't add that he wasn't the only one who'd been a cursed fool. I'd committed to this plan of Janela's knowing there was danger but forgetting that such a voyage brings hazard the moment it's thought of, and so went about with no weapon sharper than my tongue. Perhaps I shouldn't have strapped a sword on again—that would've made even more tongues wag—but I certainly should have been carrying one hidden in the carriage and had more than one guard with me at all times. I remembered something Janos had said to me, long ago in a weapons shop when we'd been arming ourselves for our quest.

I'd bought a sword and then he'd handed me a dagger, saying, "This will be your corpse-, carcass-, or thief-cutter, which you will keep always beside you. The sword you will find uncomfortable and tend to leave by a campfire or tied to your saddle, especially just before you need it. And this dagger can be your salvation."

That I could manage, and from now on Janela would have guards around her and I wouldn't venture out without at least two men besides Quatervals. I'd also make sure our villa was properly guarded day and night.

Janela came back, carrying her dagger level in front of her like a priestess returning from the sacrifice. On its bare blade was a dark, congealing liquid.

"Blood will talk," she said, and went to her bag and began fishing through it. Quatervals glanced at me.

"Lord Antero, I'll be outside." And before I could say anything he was gone.

"Another one that magic bothers," Janela said as she took out a small pouch containing vials.

She unfolded the legs of a small brazier and sprinkled herbs from the vials onto it. "Golden seal . . . myrrh . . . white willow . . ."

She scraped the drying blood from her dagger's blade onto the bare deck.

"This will not please your shipwrights," she said, "but steel gives the edge over chalk's bare image. Also, this blade has had certain words said over it to give it potency in matters like this."

She cut twin crescents into the decking and a circle around the gore, and I realized it represented an eye. Above, below, and to either side of it were carved four figures, letters or words, perhaps, in lettering I didn't know. She held her finger over the brazier and whispered words I couldn't make out. Smoke wisped and I could smell the herbs burning until their scents filled the room. Then she chanted:

"Blood can see
Blood can tell
The man is gone
The secrets are bare."

She said this thrice, and above the brazier a shimmer formed between the narrow wraiths of smoke, and it was if we were peering through a peephole into a luxurious chamber. There was a man standing in front of us, pacing back and forth talking, and I squinted, trying to make out who it was.

"I don't want to make it bigger, for fear . . ." But as Janela spoke I recognized the figure. It was Lord Senac. Then came a flash, but not of light, of darkness, like a cloud of night building over the brazier, and Janela seized another vial and sprinkled herbs. I smelt something foul, then the sweet smell of a forest in autumn, and the ball of darkness, of night, vanished.

Puzzled, I looked at Janela.

"That man—" she began.

"That was Lord Senac," I interrupted. "The man who employed Palic."

"I was attempting to cast back in time, using Palic's blood, to see if I could read his last few hours," she said. "And then came that . . . blast. I don't know what it means for certain. If I were using this spell to spy on a sorcerer, I would guess I'd been found out, which was why I cast oak bark powder on the brazier, to break the contact. But Lord Senac isn't an Evocator, is he?"

"I've never heard of him having any dealings with sorcery," I said. "This is another question we shall ask him."

Janela began putting her powders away. When she finished, she closed her bag and looked at me, her face showing concern.

"We must go carefully, Amalric. I feel this path turning as we begin to walk it."

LORD SENAC was the heir of one of the oldest noble families of Orissa. The family had fallen on hard times and had even been forced to move out of the city a few generations ago. About twenty years ago it was quietly announced—as all the great families announced everything from birth to death—that the Senacs had been fortunate enough to find gold on their property.

Once again the Senac fortunes were restored and the family mansion in Orissa rebuilt. Only the finest marbles and inlaid stones were used, and the most exotic plants and trees went into their gardens and mazes. The grounds were fenced with thorn trees from the wastelands, and there were tales told that Lord Senac had hired Evocators to put guardian spells around the estate. He had no human guards, nor even dogs, and in fact lived a very plain life with only a handful of servants.

When all was finished, Lord Senac took residence. He threw small affairs and four great parties a year at the beginning of each season, and invitations were widely sought, since only the top tier of Orissan society was invited. Within a few years Lord Senac was named a Magistrate. It did not hurt that he was slender, young, good-looking, and known for his quiet wit and intelligent conversation.

Now I wondered what his interference in this matter meant and was determined to find out at once.

We went to my mansion and I woke four good men—Yakar, Maha, Chons, and Otavi—and armed them well. Yakar and Chons were gardeners, Maha was a kitchen apprentice, and Otavi, like his grandfather J'an, was my head stableman.

J'an, incidentally, was one of the fellows who'd stood firm beside me when mobs, influenced by magic from Irayas, thought they could destroy the Anteros. Otavi was about twice the size of his father, who had comfortably wielded a butcher's axe as his favorite weapon, and was as monosyllabic. I noted that more than silence had been passed down, since Otavi was leaning on a huge axe that we normally used to split steers' carcasses after we'd poleaxed and gutted them for the kitchen.

As they got ready, Janela took me aside. "When my spell was broken," she said, "that ball of darkness could have been the beginnings of a counterspell. I wonder if perhaps the goose should take a moment and prepare a relish for a gander."

"You *are* expecting magic?"

Her eyes had a hard glitter to them that reminded me of Janos when he thought someone or something might be standing between him and the Far Kingdoms.

"I expect everything, I expect nothing," she said shortly. "But I prepare for everything." She asked for a servant to take her into the kitchen and to follow her bidding. By the time the men were outfitted, she'd returned, carrying her bag and a small oilskin pouch.

"Would you ask your men to line up?" she asked politely. "I'll need a bit of sputum from each."

All of them save Yakar complied reluctantly, since no one cheerfully gives any part of himself into a wizard's keeping. Yakar shook his head stubbornly, his lips pressed together, and said only, "I'll have no truck with that."

Otavi glowered and asked if I wanted another servant summoned.

Before I could reply, Janela said, "No man should be forced to do something like that against his will. And if he does, whatever benefits a spell might bring would be negated or lessened."

Yakar looked vastly relieved. Janela took a wand from her belt pouch and touched it to the rag the spittle was on, then drew out two round mirrors and tapped each of them with the wand.

"That's for the invisible. Now for the visible," Janela said, and went into the arms room.

She scanned the weapon racks with the easy familiarity of an expert, then chose a slim sword, almost a rapier but with the blade sharpened and a delicately worked hilt and guard. I found a favorite sword from years gone by, an ondanique broadsword with a simple guard, intended for battle, not for display, and slung it from a baldric.

Finally all of us donned thin chain-mail shirts under our clothes, arranging everything as discreetly as possible. The last thing we wanted to do was look like a war party.

Our social requirements met, we set out to call on Lord Senac.

WE RODE the back ways to Lord Senac's estate, wanting to attract as little attention as possible. And when we arrived, we tied our horses in a wood near the mansion. We crept to its gates and I motioned for my men to remain still as Janela pushed her senses out, sniffing the air like a big cat on the stalk. Then she frowned and beckoned me close.

"Very odd," she said. "I feel no magic from here, and surely I would've perceived the presence of any guardian spells." She looked worried.

The stone gates were large but, I knew, cunningly set on a counterbalance so it took but a finger's push to open them when they were unlocked, which they weren't at this hour. We'd brought a padded grapnel and rope, but a bit of knowledge I'd gained from a supposedly reformed thief in my employ turned out to be a better tool. He'd told me one of the best ways to enter a place is next to where the guards are the most alert. It's easier, for instance, to slip into a palace through the main entrance than smash glass, pry bars away, and clamber through a window.

So it proved here. The thorn trees were taller than the gate. But when I forced my weight between the gate and the first tree, shoving branches apart, there was a considerable space—a passageway unintended by the landscaper, who no doubt was proud he left room for the gate's stonemasons to work. All entry would cost us would be a few pinpricks. I motioned my men forward, but Janela held out a hand. She plucked a long blade of grass from the ground, bent it back and forth, touched it to one of the thorns on the tree, then bent it again, whispering:

"This is your cousin
Feel how she moves
The wind turns her
The rain turns her
Join with your cousin
Just for this hour
Join with your cousin."

She nodded for me to go ahead. The prick of the thorns I'd been expecting was gone and they turned aside like blades of grass. My passage was no harder than pushing through any thick shrub.

Once all of us were inside the grounds, I waited for Janela to check for magical warders. Once more there were none. Quatervals touched me on the shoulder and in the dimness I could see his hand make a circle. I nodded and he vanished into darkness, as silent as any questing beast. Moments later he returned and spread his hands. No physical guards to be seen, either.

We unbarred the gate's lock and swung it open, and I sent Maha and Chons for the horses. When they returned, we swung the gates closed and I left them to guard our rear, with whispered orders to come running if they heard trouble.

The five of us went swiftly up the long winding drive to the house. Quatervals had wanted us to creep through the gardens but I said no. We already resembled a murder party, and I wanted to confront Lord Senac as an equal, not a midnight skulker. I was glad Senac had paved his drive rather than graveling it like most.

What little noise we made was covered by the blustering wind and occasional rain squalls. This was indeed a night for somber deeds.

There were lights ahead. Someone in Lord Senac's household was still awake. Just before the house, we took cover behind some slender trees whose branches hung down limply, touching our faces with chill fingers and sending a shudder down my spine.

There were no horses or carriages drawn up in the courtyard, but two big torches flared into the night, hung on either side of the mansion's immense entryway. This stood open, and a long shaft of light stretched out across the yard. In the middle of that shaft was a body.

There was no movement except for the whip of the trees in the wind, and no sound except the branches and the spatter of rain on the paving. My sword came out and I crept forward to investigate. The old movements were coming back to me. How to creep, how to crawl, how to dart, although I'm sure I was still most laughable as I gaited across the open ground to crouch over the corpse. It lay faceup, and my stomach roiled at the sight. I may have seen worse, but it had been years, and the stomach does not retain memory of horror. Savaged though his face was, I was fairly certain I knew him as Lord Senac's castellan, and the ragged remains of his clothes were the lord's livery. I do not wish to be specific about what the corpse looked like, but if you envision a man tormented to his end by playful hyenas, you know enough.

I motioned the others up but moved away from the body.

Quatervals and perhaps Janela might see what remained of the man without sickening, but not so the other two. Quatervals glanced and his jaw tightened. He drew a question mark in the air: Did I have any idea what could have killed him? Or why? I shook my head. All of us had our weapons ready, except for Janela. I noted she had nothing but that small oilskin pouch ready and wondered what sort of spell or potion she'd prepared.

She leaned close and whispered, "*Now* I smell magic. The air reeks of it."

I sent Quatervals back for the other two. We had more need of swords here than at our back. In a few moments they trotted out of the darkness. My men were puzzled, well out of their depth. I'd told them we were going to Lord Senac's to discuss some treachery he might've done, but what was this? Had something attacked the lord's mansion? Were we now on some kind of rescue errand? They looked at me for reassurance and I tried to look firm, but I was as ignorant as they were.

We went up the mansion's broad single flight of steps and entered. The house was lit as if expecting guests, but the long foyer was empty. We moved as silently as we could, but I swore I could hear the sound of our breathing echoing against the shiny marble walls and floor. We went down the passageway that led to the dining room, and its doors also gaped wide.

We walked through the portals and I heard one of the men behind me inhale sharply.

There were three long tables in the room, reaching from end to end. They were set for a banquet. Fine porcelain dishes were placed on the whitest linen, where silver settings and crystal goblets glimmered richly and red velvet hangings gave the room a royal backdrop. But there were no diners, no servitors.

The plates were not empty, waiting for the diners to enter and the meal to begin, but piled high with food, and the goblets were filled with wine. It was as if the banquet had been begun and then abandoned six months ago. The food was black, and I could smell the reek of decay.

Yet I knew Lord Senac had hosted a feast in this room not two nights earlier.

I heard the buzz of flies as they savored their repast. The smell grew stronger. I backed out, my men moving with me. Quatervals was at the door, looking out, reflexively serving as a rear guard. Now the stench seemed to fill the entire house.

We went on down the passageway. At its end rose the staircase that led, I imagined, to the private rooms and bedchambers. I'd never been above the first floor, however, and knew of no one who had. There was a closed door to the right that led to Lord Senac's meeting room, half library, half gallery, half museum; the room was often remarked on for its collection of strange and wonderful objects, some known, but more from lands no Orissan had ever touched. We had been told that in their day the Senacs had been a far-traveled family.

There was blood, a great pool of it, just in the middle of the passageway. It stretched from wall to wall and appeared to be more than one man's body could hold. We stepped as carefully as we could, but when we went on, each of us left a sticky red trail on the white marble. There was no body, nor any signs of a struggle on either side of the gory pool.

At the stairs I started up, then decided to look into the meeting room. I opened the doors quietly. A fire guttered low at either end of the high-ceilinged, dark wood chamber.

In the center of the room crouched horror.

It was blood-drenched, and I could see bits of what it had feasted on lying about the room, fouling the carpets.

Imagine a direwolf, but a direwolf bigger than any the most drunken fur hunter could imagine, perhaps twenty feet tall. Now imagine such a beast without a pelt but with a parchment-yellowed skin, stretched impossibly tight, so the creature looked starved or mummified. Where a direwolf's eyes gleam yellow, this thing's shone red, like the embers of a fire. Its twisted fangs were brown and stained. Instead of a wolf's claws, there were curving talons like a lion's, which incessantly went in and out of the paws. I could smell it across the room, a stink of corpses and decay.

A sound came from it, part growl, part high whine, like a dog finding a scent.

The demon rose from its haunches and came toward us, unhurriedly. There was no need for haste—there was no way we could have reached the exit even if this were a mortal creature.

Fear grabbed me, fear like I hadn't known for years, but I refused its embrace. Instinctively we spread wide, as hunters try to circle a cornered wolf or boar.

Janela had her wand out, moving first in a small circle, then over her head, then in a small circle in front of her. She began speaking, and I was amazed because her voice was as calm and certain as if she were discussing her plans for the day.

"Let the mirror lie, let the vision blur
The few of us are many, the few of us are strong
The steel we bear is doubled
The hate gouts up
The fear is gone, the fear is gone
It pours like water
Out to our foe.
The laws are here, the laws are now
The rules are of this world not another
Let that from another be ruled
Let that from another take heed
The death is here
The death is real
There is no gate, there is no door
There is no return
His doom is now."

And yes, the fear was gone and courage bloomed afresh. I heard growls of rage from my men as her spell took effect on them as well.

Across the room the demon was still snarling, but the note was higher, almost as if it were taken aback at our mettle.

The first part of Janela's incantation had also taken, and looking at my tiny band of servants-turned-warriors was like looking at a reflection in a pool shaken by ripples. Now I saw one, now I saw several, now I saw many, shimmering, changing.

All of us but one, and that was Yakar, the man who'd refused the spell. The demon's snarl grew louder and he padded toward us. Yakar may've been afraid of magic before, but his heart was great now. He shouted, not a battle cry but a scream of blind rage, and charged, brandishing his sword. No soldier, no warrior, he waved it like a club as he went.

The demon sliced at him once with its foreclaws and ripped his body almost in half. Yakar began to topple. Before he could fall, the demon's jaws snapped, ripping a chunk of flesh from my poor gardener's corpse. The night-beast swallowed and bayed triumph, and the walls shook around us.

I forced myself forward and Quatervals ran at the monster from the side. The demon lashed out at Quatervals but he ducked away and slashed at the creature's foreleg. The demon howled and his blood—not honest red of this earth, but dark, decaying green with golden flecks in it—sprayed.

Its head turned toward me, fangs dripping, and I swear I saw knowledge flash in its eyes. It knew me and I was its only prey, just as a boar will choose one hunter to attack from those who have him mewed.

It lunged at me and I tried to duck, but old bones betrayed me and my feet went from under me on the slick room's floor and I fell heavily. But even as I thudded down I managed to roll to the side, my sword coming up, not thrusting so much as trying to ward off a blow, and it stuck firm in the demon's paw as it lashed down.

Again the horror bayed pain, if that was what it felt, and snapped its paw, flipping my sword out like a beast would rip away a thorn. Its jaws gaped wide. I saw Quatervals and the others running to my aid, but they were moving slowly and would be too late.

Once more I heard Janela's voice, although I couldn't see where she stood or what she was doing. It was still calm, still certain, but this time it filled the entire room.

"This foulness is not ours
This terror is of another
Earth take heed
Earth defend

Earth give of yourself
Give me desert sand
Give me desert wind
Earth reach out
Earth give
Help your sons
Help your daughter
Mother Earth listen
Hear the plea."

Between me and the demon a small tornado began, no more than a dust devil I might've ridden past in the Wasteland beyond ruined Gomalalee, and then I could feel the bits of sand drive at me and sting my face as the wind grew and firmed, and I could see it, gray, turning black.

The demon-wolf snarled and snapped at it, then yapped almost like some earthly creature as the bits of earth drove into him.

Still the wind grew, and I dragged myself back, feeling it suck at me. The demon howled and the wind howled louder still until I could hear nothing else.

The cyclone reached from floor to ceiling and began to move, swaying, seductive, like the hips of a dancer, and it closed on the demon and took him into its embrace.

The monster roared in agony and rose on its haunches, and I could barely see it as the hard-driven grains of sand lashed at him, cutting him like millions and millions of razors, and again I saw his green ichor spurt and I felt sticky spray across my face.

There came a final scream and the wind was gone, although it took me moments to realize that what I was hearing was no more than the roaring of my ears.

The demon fell back on its front legs, and its skin was gone, flayed away by the wind. Once more it bayed, a howl of rage and betrayal, as if this world and its puny peoples should have had no defense against it, then fell heavily and rolled to its side.

It still writhed and twitched in death spasms, but Quatervals paid no heed to its death agonies and raced in, his curved sword lifted high. He hewed once, twice, and then Otavi was beside him, striking with his butcher's axe, and the beast's head rolled free from its body.

My hearing came back and the room was silent. I could hear the small crackle of the dying fires at either end of the room.

I picked myself up. Death being gone, at least for the moment, my body allowed itself the luxury of feeling the pain of the fall.

Janela was beside me. "I . . . wasn't sure *that* one would work. I've only cast it once before and that was in a magus' study." No longer was her voice sure and certain, but shaken, and her face was as pale as the rest of ours were.

I was about to ask what boon I could grant for her saving my life when I heard a shouted oath from Quatervals.

Lying in the middle of the floor in a blot of blood where the demon's head had been was the severed head of Lord Senac.

THE VOYAGE BEGINS

We rode away from Lord Senac's estate at a gallop. Behind us the building roared into flames and fire gongs began sounding alarms across the city. We'd deliberately fired the mansion as a cover for what had happened, although I sensed the night's affair wouldn't be cleansed as easily. We lit fires in several rooms and found other bodies, all members of Senac's retinue, all butchered as gruesomely as the castellan. We did not venture upstairs—Janela said the place reeked of sorcery and was afraid watchguard spells still lingered. The orders were welcome—none of us had the slightest desire to explore a demon's home, even after he was dead.

I myself torched the library and noted as the flames grew that the body was slowly changing from the wolfish form back into the human shape of Senac. Janela said she supposed that meant a most powerful enchantment had been cast for the creature, even in death, to retain an unnatural form.

We cut across open land as soon as we could and rode a circuitous course back to my villa. We went unobserved and unchallenged.

At the villa I roused two hostelers and bade them to take care of the horses. I led the rest to my study. It was just dawn, and the kitchen staff was awake and the fires were burning. But after Yakar's death and the horror we'd seen, none of us had an appetite.

I took our party into my study and had wine and spices sent in with a pot, and Janela mulled it over the fire. I added a dram of brandy to each tankard as I served it. My three servants appeared uncomfortable being served by their master, but said nothing.

I said a prayer for Yakar and said we would sacrifice to his memory in a day or so. He came from a village outside Orissa, but no one knew if he had a family there. I told the others I would find out and, if so, would see they were provided for.

When the three finished their mugs, I told them to go to their quarters and get what sleep they could. I asked them to please try to refrain from telling of tonight's events, and they so vowed.

As the door closed behind them Quatervals said, "I remember my first battle and the first time I saw dark magic. I'll vow most of them'll spend the hours staring at nothing."

"They'll sleep," Janela said. "I said words over the wine as I added the spices."

Quatervals half smiled and rose. "Then I'm for my own chamber, before the spell hits me and leaves me sprawled in the hall. Wouldn't want anyone thinking I'm a simple drunkard." He went out.

Janela sipped from her mug and looked at me curiously. "A question—no, two, Amalric. You could've asked me to cast a spell of silence over them. Or you could have offered them gold to keep their lips sealed. Why did you choose neither course?"

"I could have," I agreed. "But gold's more likely to cause talk than not. I'll reward them in quieter ways in time. As for asking you to cast a spell of silence or forgetfulness, I don't think anyone who commands has the right to force obedience with magic. Not if he is anything other than a tyrant."

Janela nodded approval and changed the subject. "This is a very dark matter," she said.

I managed a wry smile. "Somewhere in your travels you've learned to bring understatement to perfection. One of Orissa's most respected Magistrates is a murderous demon . . . yes, I'd perhaps call that dark. Or at least twilit around the edges."

Janela laughed. "I meant that at no time did I sense Senac's presence, and demons most generally broadcast an aura even a nonmagician might feel. Was he ever a man? And what was his purpose? I come fresh to Orissa, so I've got no theories."

"I'll wager the one we called Senac was never a mortal. Think about the convenience of a poor family, living in a remote area, suddenly finding riches and being able to return in triumph to Orissa. That is the stuff of romance. I think this was an immense spell or series of spells cast over the years. When it began . . . I have no idea. *Why* is a better question, and that is what frightens me."

Janela sat waiting. I told her about the dread that had been haunting me for the past few weeks, and how long it had taken before I'd identified it as that same sense of being watched that I'd known so long ago in Janos' time.

Janela muttered a curse. "I, too, have felt such an odd sensation," she admitted. "But for several months now. I'd never felt it before, and so never had anything to compare it to and identify. I thought it might've been no more than the currents that accompany anyone who uses sorcery."

"So both of us are being watched."

"Are we? Do you still feel it?"

I fought off the sensations that filled me—the fatigue, the sorrow for Yakar's death, the terror of the demon and the battle, the worry for the future—and tried to "listen." I shuddered. I did sense it, but very faint, very distant.

Janela caught my expression. "I do, as well."

"So Senac was not the linchpin. He has—had a master."

"Perhaps," Janela wondered, "someone from the Kingdoms of the Night. Or someone—something—from the other worlds. It matters not, at least not yet. But we already have a great enemy, and our quest's not mounted."

"We have only one choice," I said, knowing she was right. "We must move more rapidly. Sooner or later there'll be another Lord Senac, or a host of them."

Janela smiled, oddly. "Now I see why my great-grandfather knew you were the companion for his search. You never think of turning back."

I made no response, but drained my mug.

"Three weeks," I decided. "We sail then with what we have."

IT HAD BEEN some time since I'd personally overseen the mounting of an expedition, and I thought I'd be rusty at the craft, especially since this journey would be as hazardous as any I'd set out on, from the day of its departure until wherever it ended, whether with our bones scattered on some desolate heath or at the Kingdoms of the Night. I also felt my problems would be compounded by the haste we must take and, more immediately, by the problem of my successor occupying most of my attention.

The preparations were, however, surprisingly easy and took less than a week and a half. I'd estimated I'd need about seventy-five men between the three ships. The two hoys already had crews on board of about fifteen men each, so that lessened the number I'd need to find.

We never posted broadsides or sent criers around announcing the expedition. But somehow the word spread to those who wanted to hear. There would be a knock at my door, and a man I hadn't seen for ten years would be there, hat in hand. He'd stammeringly say, well, he'd heard Lord Antero might be mounting some sort of a trading expedition again, and he'd heard this one would be sort of special and perhaps the lord would remember him, back when we made the first contact with the swamp dwellers on Bufde'ana, right terrible time it was, too, and well, he was more than willing to go, seems that Orissa just couldn't hold him like it used to and . . .

. . . And another one was signed on.

So it went. He would have a friend, or perhaps three of my former fellow adventurers would send a representative. Or sometimes it was a man from much time past, too broken by his years or the wounds he'd incurred in my service, who sent a son or cousin or nephew.

Other men I sought myself, not only men who'd been with me on other expeditions, but sometimes competitors, small traders who'd made notable voyages of their own to strange shores.

Some of these men came from my own household. Otavi came to me and said if I wished, he and the others who'd companied me to Lord Senac's wouldn't mind going along.

"Since we was in at the start, I'm supposin'," he said, "I'd like to see the outcome. Besides, it'd keep Da from sayin' on an' on there ain't no men like there was in his an' Grandda's days."

That pleased me no end, especially when I realized that Maha, the kitchen apprentice, was ready to be promoted to beginning cook. I've noted that more expeditions wreck themselves on the shoals of indigestion than enemy spears and had no intent of following their lead. As Quatervals put it, "Any fool can be miserable if he wants, without even tryin' at it."

I told Kele the details of our expedition and asked her if she wished to be the admiral of this tiny fleet. Kele grinned and said she'd been getting worried, not having been asked, and would've either killed herself or me if she hadn't. She was also able to put the word out through the waterfront dives and collect enough experienced seamen for the *Ibis* and to fill out the crews of the two hoys.

Quatervals himself brought twelve men, all ex-Frontier Scouts. It seemed that not all of the soldiers in the regiment chose to return home after their retirement or leaving the service. Others stayed in Orissa doing, as Quatervals said, "whatever comes up that seems right."

They were a hard-looking bunch of hellions, some young, some old, and I gladly welcomed them. From their ranks I'd most likely choose my subofficers.

As an aside, there might be those who think that men who go on journeys into the heart of danger such as the one I proposed are of a special breed. They are, but not as those who listen to the epics might imagine. They probably envision a young man, fair of hair, keen of expression, muscles like iron bands, silent, determined, trained in arcane skills from nomadic languages to killing with no other weapon but those the gods gave him. A man who wishes for nothing more than to throw himself into the lion's den, a smile on his lips and a song in his heart.

I've been looking for such a stalwart for years and intend, once I find him, to require Orissa to reinstate slavery just to keep this man perpetually in my service.

Let me contrast the epic hero with one of my *real* valiants, Pip. When Pip stands erect, which is seldom, he's a full inch short of five feet. He won't off-balance a hundredweight on the scales—so skinny that Quatervals once said he's got to lean thrice to make a shadow. Pip comes from Cheapside, and until I signed him for a journey nearly twenty years ago, had never been outside the city and thought anything green was probably dyed that way. Pip is my best scout. The cunning that kept him alive in the alleys of Orissa served equally well beyond Laosia and in the wastelands west of the Rift. Pip cannot finish a sentence without a curse and, when a journey is over, can spend a full day whining that he's not sure he hasn't been cheated out of his fair share of the gold. I would no more set out without him than I would without my sword or Quatervals.

So let me briefly give the qualities I seek in an adventurer, Hermias my heir, for the time you come in search of my remains.

First, the ideal man or woman must have a sense of humor, most pointedly at themselves. If they cannot laugh at their plight when toppling into a mud hole after staggering all day long under a pack that would fell a woolly elephant and then find there's no water for bathing, then they'll never travel with me. I'd say such a candidate must not be stupid, but I cannot define stupidity. Is someone who speaks ten languages but can't learn to read and write stupid? I don't think so.

They must be clean and always keep themselves and their equipment in perfect order, or as perfect as the road and weather permits. They must be hard workers, but also be ones who'll see a task waiting and set to it without orders. They should be in good health, although I've had men and women I swore were on their deathbed stagger on beside me a league, a league, and then another.

As for skills and talents—all of them can be learned enough to suffice. It doesn't hurt for one of my company to be able to cast a knife unerringly into a coin's center from a dozen paces ten times running, but I'd as lief have someone who can realize a fight is in the offing and then find soft words to turn the wrath away—or a side passage fit for the running. Skills can be taught, from languages to killing to even bargaining—although I like to fancy there's *one* area where talent is uppermost, and that Anteros are peculiarly gifted in that arena.

There is one final quality or pair of qualities, and I am not sure how to put it. The ideal fellow must find the peaceful life impossibly dull, so dull he'll do anything, including foolishly join an expedition more likely to produce painful death and a forgotten corpse than fame and riches. The paired portion of this is he should not have much of a home. A man who pines for Orissa the minute the river takes him beyond sight of the Palace of the Evocators should be shown mercy and set ashore at once. Homesickness can blind one as much as fatigue or stupidity.

I was most proud the day that I found my seventy-fifth such hero or fellow fool and then wondered how I could most politely turn away the other one hundred fifty who'd either come to mind, presented themselves, or been mentioned by Quatervals or Kele.

A day later Palmeras summoned me to the Palace of the Evocators.

I'D BEEN EXPECTING something of that nature—the mysterious fire that killed Lord Senac and his entire household was still the favorite chatter in the marketplace, and I was hardly unworldly enough to think that a few minutes work with flame could cover what'd happened from Orissa's Evocators, as skilled as bloodhounds in tracking magical scents.

Even if what'd happened went unexplained, I couldn't leave Orissa, my home and my pride, without somehow giving a warning that once more dark events were circling the city. But I wasn't entirely sure of how to present matters or to whom I should go—even an Antero cannot dance into the Palace of the Evocators or Citadel of the Magistrates and calmly announce that, well, yes, I butchered one of Orissa's leading Magistrates because it seems he tried to murder me, but don't worry, he wasn't really a man at all but a demon and you should be careful because there may be more demons in your midst or arriving soon by hellish charabanc.

When the summons came, I was pleased it was from an Evocator, since these matters were sorcerous, rather than a Magistrate, and certainly felt I could have no better judge than Palmeras in the matter.

I admit to being nervous when I arrived at the Palace. I was greeted civilly by one of Palmeras' aides, a senior wizard wearing a red sash over his robes, not accompanied by guards, which was a good sign. I was escorted to an anteroom, not to the huge dark cavern where the Evocators' most sacred and dangerous hearings were held, which was also good.

I was not offered refreshments, which was not good. And Palmeras entered in his robes of office, which also was not heartening.

Palmeras asked me to be seated and sat across from me at a rectangular table. He didn't speak for a long moment, probably to let the awe and grandeur of his office overwhelm me. But waiting is second nature to a merchant. Eventually he spoke.

"I'm sure, Lord Antero," and I liked it not that he used my title, "you're aware of the strange death of Lord Senac."

"I am, lord."

"There are some . . . peculiar aspects of the matter that interested me . . . and some other members of the Council."

"I'm not surprised."

What might've been a smile flitted across Palmeras' lips. "Amalric, I won't fence with you. Would you be so kind as to tell me what happened? I vow that whatever you say will not be heard officially, although I must warn you this is a most grave matter and unless satisfactorily explained may well result in charges of the highest degree."

If I'd been told that by a Magistrate, I would have clamped my mouth shut and refused to say *anything* out of a proper court. But this was different. I counted Palmeras a friend, or at least as much of a friend as an Antero could permit an Evocator to be.

I said I would tell him everything. But I insisted he swear an oath of secrecy: Unless he deemed the matters surrounding Lord Senac required a criminal charge, none of what I was to tell him was to be passed along to his fellow Council members—*until time and circumstances made it necessary.*

Again Palmeras' lips quirked, but this time the smile remained. "Only an Antero," he sighed, "would have the fortitude to set conditions to the chief of all Orissa's Evocators in a matter that could involve the Kissing of the Stones. The only reason I'm agreeing is that I probably know more than you suspect.

"Not hours after the fire was extinguished, I was called to Lord Senac's estate, or what remained of it, by one of the watch officers who's had an interest in magical matters over the years. He asked if I would sieve the area for emanations. I suspect the man has more than a bit of the Talent, although he denies it. I was a little piqued that he'd ask a man of my rank rather than a lesser Evocator. But I obeyed his request and discovered some most unusual matters. Now, tell me your tale."

I did, from the arrival of Janela until the time we rode away from Lord Senac's mansion. I had to pause for a time after I'd told him who Janela was and also her conviction that the real Far Kingdoms had never been reached. At that point he sent out for wine, and while it was being brought, went to his own chambers and returned with sorcerous materials and cast a Dome of Silence about us, so not even his fellow Evocators could eavesdrop on what was being discussed.

Then I finished my story.

"I said *unusual* matters," he mused. "But these are far darker, far deeper, than I'd dreamed. Let me say right now I believe you completely. Among the other things I found when I cast my magical net of senses through the ruins of Senac's house was signs of magic not of this earth, or at any rate not of any earthly arts I'd ever encountered or read of. At first I thought they could belong to that young woman all Orissa seems to think you're having a mad affair with, but these signs went back more than six years."

"That," I remembered, "was about when Lord Senac, or whatever was calling himself by that name, arrived from the hinterlands and had the mansion rebuilt."

"Just so. That made me *very* curious, and so I cast further spells. I could go into details about what I discovered: The slain retainers whose bodies I could find bits of to sample had been killed hours earlier, at a time when you were still being questioned by the sergeant of the watch at the docks. Or some things I found of Lord Palic's sudden infatuation with sorcery and servitude. But this is not a court, Amalric, although I'm still the knowledge-seeker, but in much greater areas.

"What lies ahead? You and Lady Greycloak *must* continue on your quest. I must admit to still being taken aback that a descendant of the great Janos Greycloak is in our city, and wish times were different so we could celebrate such an event properly. I am accepting without question that there is a *real*, or at any rate a greater, land called the real Far Kingdoms or the Kingdoms of the Night that is reachable from this world.

"But what of Orissa? What does this demon's presence mean? I remember in your account of seeking the Far Kingdoms you wrote of Watchers who were magical sentinels for the late King Domas, long may his memory shine. Was this Senac a Watcher of a different sort? For someone else, in another place?"

I answered truthfully: I did not know, and the few spells Janela had gingerly cast, not wanting to attract more attention than we already had, had found nothing.

"But I do know," I finished, "that Orissa must be on alert. Almost as if this were wartime, although I doubt if there will be armies marching against our gates, at least not for a while."

Palmeras sat thinking for a very long time.

"Yes," he finally said. "We—or at least such Evocators as I choose to admit to this secret, given your permission—must become sentinels. Sentinels and even warriors. I once heard that being around you Anteros almost invariably was interesting, and the person who told me that added hastily he could wish for nothing more than for his life now to return to dull, drab boredom.

"What do you need of us, Amalric? How does Orissa help?"

"By maintaining silence, Lord Palmeras, as long as possible." I wasn't sure why I knew this to be vital, but it was. "Other than that, we have almost everything we need. I might ask one favor—if

Janela Greycloak has need of any sorcerous materials that you might have, may I have them? I shall use Quatervals, whom I trust as much as myself, as courier, since I think Janela's visiting this Palace would cause even more of a stir."

"Granted."

Palmeras lifted the silence spell and led me to the door. "I wish," he said a bit wistfully, "there was time and place for me to talk to Lady Greycloak. If, as you say, the sorcerous talent has been handed down, there could be much for me to learn, in spite of what people believe about my vast knowledge. Oh well. Life, I've been thinking, is sometimes little more than a series of missed opportunities.

"One thing, Lord Antero," he went on, his mood changing as he reverted to formality. "There is one matter you *must* deal with before your departure."

His wizard's gaze pinned me. He said no more. It wasn't necessary. I knew what he was referring to.

I DID NOT HANDLE the matter well. I should have launched a quiet investigation into the Jeypur incident. I also should have gathered evidence on other sins I was certain Cligus had committed as well. Then I ought to have summoned my son into my stern presence and—supported by a stack of reports detailing his crimes—denounced him. Told him that as a son, much less a human being, he was a failure and a grave disappointment. Furthermore, I should have then banished him from Orissa—sending him into golden exile to some faraway place. And if he violated that exile, not only would all funds be cut off, but the list of crimes would be revealed to all.

I thought of all those things, but in the end I didn't have the heart. After informing Hermias of my decision, I drew up a will naming him as my heir, and as a sop to Cligus ordered a goodly percentage of income derived from the sprawling Antero empire to be paid to him annually for the rest of his life.

Cligus was not satisfied.

"How can you do this to me, Father?" he shouted after I had laid out my plans privately in a meeting in my study. "You are destroying me!"

"On the contrary," I said. "I've just made you a very wealthy man."

"But I'm your son," he said. "Everyone will believe that you've disowned me."

"If you review the wording of my will," I said, "you'll see that I've praised you for your military prowess and stated that I think it best for you continue to serve Orissa in your capacity as a general."

"They'll think it a lie," he said. "I'll be the laughingstock of the city and all my friends."

He pounded my desk. "It's Hermias, isn't it?" he thundered. "He's been speaking against me. Filling your ears with slander."

"Hermias hasn't said one word against you," I said.

"I'll fight it, Father," he said. "I won't rest until this is overturned. This I vow."

I sighed. It was time to show him my stick.

"If you do," I said, "then you really will be ruined. I've added a codicil stating that if my decisions are protested, you are to get nothing at all."

"All my life," he said, "I've lived in your shadow. No matter what I do, I'm known merely as the son of Amalric Antero. I've been denied a normal existence. Denied a chance to make a mark of my own. And now you are damning me to trod that same road even when you're gone. Except now it'll be worse. Now, people will say I never was good enough to be worthy. I'll be spurned. Mocked."

Tears welled in his eyes. "Why are you doing this to me, Father? What have I done to deserve this?"

"Do you really want me to answer that question?" I asked, unmoved by his pain. "Shall I detail your misdeeds? Beginning with a man named Pelvat?"

Cligus paled. Then his eyes narrowed and I saw hatred flare. "So," he said. "You *have* been talking to Hermias!"

"I have ample resources of my own," I said. "Did you really think I'd never find out?"

My son became quite calm. He rose to his feet. He stared long and hard at me. I found myself looking into the eyes of an enemy. I saw him reach some kind of decision.

Then he said, "Very well, Father. If that's how you want it." And he turned on his heel and stalked out.

As the door slammed behind him I wondered once again how such a man could be my son.

I made my decision public the following day. The seers of business immediately made their approval known as investors besieged my trading offices to plunk down their gold for shares in our enterprises.

Poor Cligus. The city had voted with its coin, sealing his disgrace.

WE SET SAIL not many days later. By that time the gossipmongers had tired of their tavern-stool speculation on why I'd chosen Hermias over Cligus to be the new head of family. There was no panoply to mark our going, no parades or elaborate ceremonies, no stirring music to hearten voyagers off on such a daring venture. Only a few well-wishers gathered at the docks to bid farewell to our small fleet and view the simple blessing Janela performed to entreat the gods to aid us. It was almost as if we were sailing in secret. In a way we were, for I'd told everyone I was embarking on a grand tour of all the Antero holdings—a tour that would take at least two years to complete.

In the whole city, only Palmeras knew our true purpose, and I'd asked him to stay away so his august presence wouldn't rouse suspicion. Before we boarded, I took Hermias aside and gave him a letter containing the real nature of our mission. I told him not to open it until well after we were gone.

We hugged, and Hermias swore he'd devote his life to covering the family name with glory. Which I'm sure you have, my dear nephew.

It had rained the morning of our departure, and Orissa was sparkling in all her beauty under the clear, sun-kissed skies. A fresh wind carrying the odors of hearth and home filled our sails, bearing us swiftly down the river.

As Janela and I stood at the rail watching the city grow smaller, my emotional barometer rose and fell with each heartbeat. Just before we rounded the bend I saw a rainbow arcing over the city, framing her in the colors of bright promise.

As we sailed out of sight it came to me that I'd never see my home again.

RETURN TO IRAYAS

N o matter how many times I'd entered the mouth of the immense river that coils like a snake from the Eastern Ocean through the Kingdom of Vacaan to its capital of Irayas, I would thrill. Not only in memory of that distant day when Janos Greycloak and I came within sight of what we'd then called the Far Kingdoms, but in the present as well.

It always seemed the day was fair, the sea calm, the breezes blowing perfumed and gentle off the land. So it appeared this time, almost ten years since I'd last seen Vacaan.

Our passage from Orissa had gone smoothly, the weather more like balmy summer than early spring, and we encountered no storms that lasted for more than a day or so, enough to give our sailors a chance to make certain everything was as shipshape as Kele and the captains of the hoys wanted. Those captains, Berar and Towra, were natives of Redond and longtime servitors of the House of Antero. One thing that pleased and surprised us all was the lack of fitting-out-brawls, which happens all too often when strong-willed people sort out their differences at the beginning of a hard and dangerous voyage. We'd chosen well.

Even though we sailed through seas that were hardly pacified, we'd expected no problems from pirates and in fact encountered none. Four sails had rushed down from the horizon toward us, but when their lookouts had seen the device blazoned on our sails, they'd sheered off at full speed. This was but one of my secret "weapons"—many years ago, Domas, then King of Vacaan, had granted the Antero family leave to fly his royal banner when traveling to or around his realm, and so our mainsails held the crest of the huge coiled serpent, set against a sunburst.

When his son Gayyath had assumed the throne after Domas' death, it'd taken several subtle approaches by my factor within the kingdom, a very solid man named Hebrus, before the privilege was renewed. He is another of those heroes who are never found on temple friezes. Hebrus was the only man still living of the party that accompanied us on our final expedition. He was a year or two younger than I, although he looked ten. Before he volunteered to journey into the unknown with me, he was a music teacher who, when bored, dearly loved to climb temple or palace walls, moving from cranny to crack without benefit of ropes or belays. Hebrus is a man I once heard described as "hardly having enough strength to blow more than one petal at a time from a flower without fainting." But I've seen him carry two men's packs in addition to his own without sweating after those stalwarts sagged and dropped them in a long hasty march.

Hebrus had decided to remain in Irayas rather than return to Orissa, since their customs were more tolerant of his tastes, and I'd made him my factor a few years later. He'd never returned to his home city, but stayed on, companioned by a long succession of younger and steadily more handsome men as the years went by. It was him I was counting on to help us with the necessary permissions and to expedite our passageway east, as well as for an honest picture of what had happened in Irayas since I'd last been there. Certainly he'd sent regular dispatches, but all communications from Irayas were still censored by the court, yet another remnant of the days when the great kingdom hunched like a hermit crab in its isolated shell.

As I said, the journey upriver appeared normal at first. It did seem that the mirror atop the emerald watchtower at the river's mouth sent its interrogatory flashes of light a little longer than I remembered. And the war birds that came swooping, bright colors masking their fighting spurs and murderous beaks, flew escort longer than usual. But at the time I didn't think it important.

What I did notice was the increased number of patrol boats on the river. Vacaan had always guarded its approaches well, but previously the steel had been somewhat hidden inside a glove of velvet. No longer. I counted ten riverine watch craft in our first hour's passage upriver. They weren't cleverly disguised as fishing or pleasure boats, either. These were small sweep-propelled boats, no more than thirty feet long, and looked to be shallow-draft. Each boat was open, with a canopy over the center compartment from the bow halfway to the stern. That was hammered metal, less a spray shield than a guard against arrows or spears.

I asked Quatervals his opinion. "They're the sort of scow you'd use if you'd taken a country but held no more'n the rivers and ports. Boats like them'll keep the waterways pacified, convoy your tax men around, or put ashore a landing force in minutes." An occupying force? In their own country?

Another oddity was the men crewing those boats. The oars were manned by ragged unkempt men who might've been slaves or condemned criminals. There looked to be two or three seamen aboard each craft, but the rest of the crew, about ten per craft, were soldiers, wearing a uniform I'd never seen before: tight-fitting black breeches and tunic, with a bloodred armored vest over it and a close-fitting helm of the same color.

I asked Janela, and she knew nothing about them—when she'd left Vacaan, no such force existed.

One of those patrol craft, a small flag at its jackstay probably indicating that it was the flotilla's leader, closed on the *Ibis* and its officer hailed us. He asked, in a tone more like a demand, permission to send a man aboard. Kele looked at me and I shrugged—all this was new but not necessarily a problem.

One man wearing the black-and-red of the soldiery, with a small pack on his back, leapt deftly from the bow of the patrol boat, found a foothold in one of the boarding cleats, and swung over the rail, ignoring the hands that had been stretched to help him. A sailor brought him to us.

The man was hard-faced, with a seamed scar running down his neck. His sword belt was old and well-worn, as were the hafts of the dagger and sword sheathed on it. He welcomed, or rather greeted us by name, which didn't surprise anyone—the sorcerers of Vacaan were more than competent to espy us several days out at sea. It seemed that a scowl touched his face when he addressed Janela, but if so, it was gone in an instant. He said his name was Rapili and he would be our escort to Irayas.

"Escort," Kele wondered. "Didn't know we'd be needin' a pilot. Never had one before."

"Not pilot," Rapili said. "Escort is what I said and meant." His manner was cold, formal.

"There's been a change since the last time we arrived in your kingdom," I said, sounding a bit apologetic. "New customs, it appears."

"Customs change with the times," he said. "And the times are more dangerous than they were."

I waited for an elaboration, but none came, and I somehow did not want to ask. We offered him food and drink, which he declined, saying the practice was for Wardens to provide their own. He said he would, however, wish a compartment, since he would company us all the way upriver to our destination.

I told Quatervals to find him a space, and waited until he'd gone belowdecks before drawing Janela aside, saying, "His own food and drink? Does he think we plan to poison him?"

Janela shook her head. "I don't know. But that was a pawky excuse for a welcome. If they treat *us* like this, I would certainly hate to be a newcomer wanting to trade with these people."

"*These* people," I said, half smiling. "You mean your people, don't you?" She didn't answer. I shrugged. "When first we came to the Far—" I caught myself, but so I still thought of Vacaan. "—to Vacaan, we weren't greeted like long-lost kinsmen, either. We changed their minds before too long, at least to a degree. And as the soldier said, customs change."

Janela started to answer, then stopped short, her gaze pulled away. I turned and I also stood amazed as the *Ibis* rounded a high-banked bend. In the distance was that great blue mountain, many leagues and days' sail farther than it appeared. Below it would be Irayas, Vacaan's capital, the grandest city in all the known world, place of marvel beyond marvel.

The mountain was the deepest blue, as blue as the river we rode on. But the sky above did not match. It was gray and a storm hung over Irayas.

That mountain always sent two thrills through me. The first was joy. But the second, stronger, was fear. In a cavern below that mountain's plateau I'd been brought close to death by Prince Raveline, and in the ruined eldritch city above it I'd slain him. And on a plateau just at the mountain's farthest reach toward the east, I'd burnt the body of Janos Greycloak after I'd killed him and sent his spirit soaring into the skies.

There would be another ceremony on that mountain after we reached Irayas.

I tore my eyes away and turned back to the river as our three ships slid upstream like swans on a summering pond. But always behind us were at least two, generally more, of the patrolling boats and their red-clad warriors.

Near dusk we sailed past the huge port city of Marinduque, the hub for trade of the seventy principalities that made up Vacaan. I'd always been astonished by its cleanliness and efficiency. No longer. Not that it had fallen into ruin, but now it looked no different from Redond, Jeypur, or Luangu, and appeared no more than a huge port where a merchant could sell or buy a cargo and a seaman could find as much or little trouble as he desired. It also no longer looked as prosperous, and as we sailed past, I saw a long line of ramshackle, half-sinking boats tied up at what was their last mooring, near a ruined warehouse district, the boats swarming with the people who lived aboard. Vacaan had its poor, of course, but I'd never seen people forced this low.

Times *had* changed here, and not for the better.

Rapili joined us at dinner, although eating his own rations from his own plate. I attempted to ask him about the changes and how the Vacaanese fared under King Gayyath. He made short noncommittal answers, ate quickly, and excused himself, leaving us with nothing.

I asked Kele and Janela to join me at the taffrail and made sure the watch officer and helmsman were out of earshot.

"I'd assumed," I began, "that stopping here in Vacaan would be little more than a formality, beyond winning King Gayyath's endorsement of our voyage. But something is wrong here and I'm not quite sure what it is."

"I think the same," said Janela. "I chanced casting a few prognosticative spells, but it was as if I were trying to see through a fog bank. Nor can I *feel* ahead to what Irayas might look like. I'd suggest we be prepared for almost anything."

Kele grunted understanding, and from that night on posted two additional lookouts fore and aft, weapons unobtrusively ready. If Rapili saw them, he said nothing.

Janela noticed the next upset. One of the greatest marvels of Irayas was how the river was carefully managed by the kingdom's wizards. There were no locks, carries, or portages as the river wound through and up into the country. Only a shimmer would mark where a spell had been cast to raise the water to its new level. The spells still held after a fashion, but now there was a noticeable surge and we had to man the sweeps to push our way onward, as if fighting rapids.

I also noticed the marks of flooding where the river had overflowed its banks. I remembered how well it had been managed, with high and low waters being ordered by magic to suit the needs of the farmers who worked along its banks. Neither of us thought it wise to ask Rapili about this, since the matter would be high court magic and not seemly for an outlander to show interest in, no matter how long I'd been an honored guest there.

Two days after entering the river we saw our first real shock: We passed the fire-blackened ruins of a small city. I chanced asking Rapili what had happened. In a tone of complete indifference he told me the town had risen against King Gayyath and it'd been necessary to make an example of it. I forced my luck and asked for more details.

Rapili said, "Just another one of those damned peasant risings. Sooner or later they'll learn to blame misfortune on the gods, not on our good king. If not . . ." He said no more.

Another rising? And what were these misfortunes? Although Hebrus' dispatches had always been guarded, he *had* said Vacaan had been having troubles as severe as Orissa's. But . . . Rapili was looking at me intently, so I just thanked him and, after a few moments, found an excuse to go below.

I noted that the people we passed, fishermen, laborers, merchants, weren't nearly as contented as they'd once seemed. Some of them, when they saw the royal emblem on our sails, turned their backs or just stared, their faces blank, as if a cruel master was parading by.

One sound I heard less than before: laughter. The most common sound on this river had been the shrill laughter of happy children. Now it came infrequently, and the expressions of the young ones we passed were stolid, like people who've known little joy and to whom misery is a constant companion.

We wound our way through the kingdom, day by day, past city after city. There was no consistency to what we saw: Some lands were fertile, green, some cities exploding with life; other lands were dry, barren, or barely fertile, and the cities around them on hard times.

I hardly knew what to think and, quite frankly, was beginning to dread seeing what Irayas itself might look like. If that dream-city was changed, cut by time's wounds . . . I could not let myself think that.

We came on it at dawn, and the river channel, already nearly half a mile across, flared into a lake with a thousand green islands aglow as the sun's fingers touched the city. It was still magic, and the day's fresh fires shot prisms of color through the towers of crystal and sent dazzling beams against my eyes from the golden domes. Now there was birdsong and I thought I could hear music from around us as the many fountains shot plumes into the crisp air.

No. Irayas had not changed. In fact, it was even more splendid than my ten-year-gone memory said.

I looked at Quatervals. His hard, leathery hillman's face showed the simple awe of a babe before he caught me looking at him and forced control. This was the first time he'd been to Vacaan.

"Well?"

Quatervals took a long time to think before saying, slowly, "There's not many times you know you're seein' something that appears to have come from the gods, is there?"

Rapili, standing behind him, overheard and smiled tightly, and I could also read *his* thoughts—it was well the foreigners knew what they were seeing when they saw it. Of *course* there could be nothing in this world or any others to match the glory of Irayas.

Janela's expression was unreadable. I moved close beside her and said, very softly, "And what is my lady thinking?"

She answered as quietly: "Just that no matter how you might believe you've shed your feelings for somewhere that was home, especially after it's treated you . . . the way I was . . . you find out you're wrong."

I knew what she meant—no matter what evils Orissa had wreaked on the Anteros, and there'd been many, I still felt that soar of delight when I came once more upon it.

But neither Irayas nor Orissa should be in our minds now. Our minds and eyes must be on the next step. I asked Rapili where we would moor.

"If you weren't who you are, and if we didn't have orders from the court, you'd be sent to the Trader's Port with the others. But you're the personal guests of the king. Have your captain follow that boat there." He waved at a gondola flying a large black and white striped flag. "*That's* your pilot. I'll take my leave now."

The gondola pulled alongside, and Rapili dropped his pack onto its deck and went after it, with never a word of thanks or farewell.

The boat led our three ships through the maze that was the canal system of Irayas. The city sprawled for miles, with some of the poorer sections on larger peninsulas or strands, and the palaces of the nobility each on its own island or standing alone on pilings driven into the lake bottom. Irayas was laid out in elaborate disarray that was no more accidental than a path winding through a garden built by a master landscaper, and I'd often wondered whether the islands had been magically built by the Old Ones. No one ever answered my queries, though.

Now I was wondering if Janela's theory was correct and the Old Ones had retreated to the fabled Kingdoms of the Night. With a chill, I considered what they might be like. And whether they were as far beyond the wizards of Irayas as those magicians had been beyond all western Evocators when Janos and I first came here.

It was probably an absurd thought, but I wondered what lay beyond gold and diamonds when gold was a simple transmutation and any stone could be given facets and sparkle with a few words of a similarity spell.

Kele broke my thoughts. "What's this Trader's Port that lunkhead spoke of? There wa'n't anything like it last time we dropped our hook here."

That had been no surprise—Hebrus had written to me about it several years earlier. It seemed King Gayyath had become disturbed that his people were being corrupted by overexposure to foreigners, even the few merchants allowed upriver beyond Marinduque, and so he'd ordered an island set aside with a deep-enough anchorage for their ships, a compound for trading, and luxurious villas for them to live in. All outsiders were confined to this area on pain of banishment or even execution.

I'd sent a carefully worded protest through Hebrus to King Gayyath, not only on behalf of all merchants, but also because this was a return to Vacaan's bad old ways when they huddled behind their magic and demonic protectors, reassuring each other that they were the highest beings of creation, and let their culture petrify. I'd never received answer and didn't try again—it had probably been unseemly for me to even think of advising another people on what they might be doing wrong, especially when I considered how blithely my own Orissa was walling itself up with complacency.

We entered a wide canal that went straight into a lagoon, and I started, not able to hold back the cry that left my lips. Ahead was the castle that would be our quarters—and it was the same castle I had occupied when first we came to Vacaan. Here it was that I'd courted Omerye, and for an instant the spires, gardens, and turrets blurred to my eyes. It was here that Janos had begun his betrayal, and from here I'd been kidnapped to be tortured by Raveline's henchman.

"Lord Antero?" Kele was beside me, her arm strong.

I shook my head. "Nothing. Just the sun."

But I turned away from the castle and went to the taffrail, looking back while I regained composure.

Janela's hand touched my shoulder. "This was the place?" She made no more elaboration. I nodded.

"Now," she said, her voice hard, "is someone playing a cruel jest . . . or is he merely paying clumsy respect by showing his knowledge of your past?"

"I don't know."

"Nor do I. But if it's the former . . . one thing that I inherited from my great-grandfather was his long and perfect remembrance for evils done to him and those he loved . . . and his cunning at repaying that debt."

I looked at her. For an instant her hand touched the pommel of her dagger. Then she smiled. "But I think it is better, at least for now, to think we are being honored. Unless the memories would be too terrible?"

I began to answer, then stopped. "No," I said. "Sometimes the echoes of the past, even though they can be harsh, can be comforting." This was true.

Once more Janela looked at me strangely. "That, too," she said, almost to herself, "is something that must be changed."

The moment hung, untouched. I was the first to turn away.

"Captain Kele," I said, formally. "We'll moor at that long dock. And we might want to be leaving quickly. Pass the signal to the other ships, please."

"Aye, sir," and Kele's voice became a bellow. "Turn out, watch below! We'll have a breast and stern rope and springs to port. Shake a leg!"

AS I'D ANTICIPATED we stepped off our ships into silken luxury. There was enough room in the palace for an entire war fleet's contingent, enough so each could have a private room. I was amused to find that most of them preferred to share their quarters with at least a friend or two. I'd expected some complaints when I ordered half of each ship's company to be aboard their craft at all times, weapon racks unlocked and the watch alert, but there were none, thanks to my company's wide experience on foreign and not infrequently hostile shores.

None of us, from myself to the *Firefly's* cabin boy, wanted for anything. New clothes were given if ours were ragged, or else seamstresses were available if we'd rather have them mended. The kitchens were always open, and anything a sailor could imagine would be produced by servants who were either blank-faced or smiling cheerily. There was an even greater abundance of drink, but in this matter I sought the palace's castellan, a cheerful gnome named Lienor, who hardly looked the spy for Gayyath I knew he must be, and ordered all spirits locked up except for mealtimes and two hours after dinner. Sailors, no matter how dedicated and wary they are, will *never* turn away from a cask until it's emptied.

Other needs were met, which I'd always assumed would happen. The people of Vacaan felt happiness could only come when *all* desires were fulfilled. So each chamber had one or more chambermaids, and for the women among us there were serving lads who seemed to have no duties except what was requested of them.

Four women attended my own bedchamber, two very young and beautiful, two middle-aged and buxom, with the experienced smiles of women who knew how *real* pleasure could be given. I was polite to all four of them, but at my age hardly self-deceiving about my abilities, and so I slept alone with Quatervals in the outer chamber. He disappeared for an hour with one of the older women, but after that remained as celibate as I, in spite of my urgings.

Janela was given her own wing on the other side of the mansion in quarters as luxurious as mine. If she had bed companions, I saw none.

Everything seemed placid on the surface, but as the days passed I grew worried.

Where was Hebrus?

*   *   *

ON THE SIXTH DAY after our arrival Lienor requested Janela's and my presence at the main entrance. Waiting there was another Warden, this one in his middle years but just as hard and battle-scarred as Rapili had been. Lienor announced him as Chares, head of all the Wardens. I found it mildly amusing to see Lienor humble himself before the man, as if Chares was his master instead of me.

I asked Chares what his rank was so I could address him properly. Chares said, "We Wardens have no titles and our rank matters only amongst ourselves. We are all equals, all dedicated to the safety of Vacaan."

I asked what service I might do him.

"I have come to take you to the king," Chares said, a note of self-importance ringing in his tone. "He has granted you an audience."

This surprised me. King Gayyath's father, Domas, saw newcomers instantly and then let time pass while he considered his actions. I'd expected Gayyath to continue that same practice.

"That is good news," I said. "I welcome seeing King Gayyath after such a long absence."

"I also," Chares continued on, "bear unfortunate tidings. Your factor Hebrus passed away a week ago." By his voice he might as well have been announcing that the midday meal would be a few minutes late.

That took me hard. At my age, it is uncertain how a death can affect you. By the time you reach my years, you know more people in the graveyard than the street, and so you ought to become accustomed to the event. This is sometimes true, sometimes false. Now, I felt tears fill my eyes. Hebrus had not only been a good man, but with his death, so died the last part of my youth. Chares was staring at me and his look was unsympathetic. No doubt he thought me a weakling.

Janela gave me a gentle pat. I took three deep breaths and set the matter aside. Later, when we returned from the court, we would hold the proper Orissan ceremonies to his memory.

"How did he die?"

Chares appeared uncomfortable. "Perhaps," he said, "we should step into another chamber to discuss that?"

I led Chares into a cloakroom. As I did, I saw a smirk on Lienor's face, as if he was already privy to the matter and had found it a rare matter, indeed.

Without softening his tone, Chares said, "Your factor was murdered."

"By whom?"

"We do not know yet."

"Under what circumstances?" I demanded.

Again Chares looked as if he might be embarrassed. "Lord Hebrus was in the habit of visiting certain areas, certain taverns, for his private amusement. The partners he chose were those noted for, to put it bluntly, their toughness and propensity for violence. Lord Hebrus chose the wrong man, or possibly men, because he was found in his bedchamber, beaten to death. His assailants had stolen what they could before noises woke Hebrus' servants.

"King Gayyath sends his condolences and says that the proper ceremonies were held to receive Lord Hebrus' spirit and that he was also honored in our own ceremonies, being named an honorary citizen of Vacaan, the highest distinction we can grant a foreigner. A suitable public work shall be named after him, and I can personally assure you that his killers will be found and dealt with under the harshest sections of the Royal Code, as if Lord Hebrus were a member of the court."

"Why wasn't I informed of my factor's death on my arrival? He was an important part of my household, and his death may well have an effect on the matter I've come to Vacaan to discuss."

Chares hesitated. "Since Lord Hebrus *was* an important man, it was deemed necessary for a high court official—myself—to convey the message. Unfortunately, I was occupied with the king's business in another district, and was unable to break free as promptly as I wished."

Very thin, I thought. No one else in Gayyath's huge court could have brought the word? Fortunately, I'd regained control and said nothing. Janela, her hand on my arm, must have felt the muscles tense because her eyes flickered over to me, then back to Chares.

The change in Vacaan was worse than I'd thought. I knew that everything that Chares said had been a lie. Hebrus might've fancied younger men, but the types he fell in love with were much like he'd once been—ethereal, gentle sorts, frequently having their first affair. And Hebrus was monogamous, staying faithful to each lover until the affair died a natural death. When he went seeking new companionship, he would frequent libraries, concert halls, or art galleries. Finally, Hebrus *never* drank.

I felt a chill. Vacaan had always been dangerous, its deadliness hidden behind a smile. Those who offended most generally simply disappeared, and it was as if they'd never existed.

Hebrus had been murdered, but not out of any passion. A business difficulty, perhaps. But I thought it interesting that a week ago we would have just been off the coast of Vacaan, and Irayas' magicians would have been sensing our arrival. All my senses were a-tingle. I didn't think I was being an alarmist. Not after the encounter with the demon who called himself Senac and the certainty we would be opposed seeking the Kingdoms of the Night.

I would find time to investigate the death and, if possible, avenge my friend. But that would be later.

Now all there was time for was King Gayyath.

"WHY IS IT," Chares asked Janela smoothly as our gondola coursed down the canals toward the king's palace, "you don't seem to have ever been presented at court before you left Vacaan? Certainly you would grace any gathering. And your family is more than noble enough."

Janela's eyes widened for just a flash, then she recovered. "I thank you for the compliment, Chares. But I was forbidden entry to Vacaan as punishment after I refused a bride-offer because it would have required me to give up my study of magic. I assumed you would have known."

"I pay little attention to small matters like violations of protocol," the soldier said. "These times are too parlous for trivialities."

I interrupted. "Chares, our escort to Vacaan, Rapili, said there had been risings against the king, but he refused to say more."

"Rapili is a good soldier," Chares approved. "It would not have been fitting to discuss such matters with an outlander. He was not, however, aware of your . . . special relationship to the royal family."

I doubted that but said nothing.

"Knowing this will not go beyond your ears," the officer said, "there *have* been some fools deluded enough to think King Gayyath's mercy is unlimited and to blame him for certain misfortunes the gods have visited on us. There have been false prophets, folk leaders, more than enough trouble to satisfy any soldier for several dozen lifetimes."

Chares tried to look human, by which I mean wearied, but I sensed relish for such slaughter. I am too old and too rich to be fooled by men such as he.

He continued: "I fear it's become necessary for certain special measures to be taken and, on occasion, harsh treatment dealt."

"We saw some signs of that as we traveled," Janela said.

"Not really," Chares said. "A ruined city, or an area the king has been forced to embargo from trade—these are but slight examples. We would hardly wish to present the sterner face of our royal master to new arrivals, after all."

"Could you be more specific?" I asked.

Chares' gaze was cold. He held my eyes for a long moment, then looked beyond, across the blue-gleaming water as a fountain rose and gushed gold against the sun.

I remembered examples of the magic of Vacaan—a guardian city on its borders manned entirely by resurrected corpses, and a land blasted bare by sorcery—and the sun's rays suddenly felt icy.

KING GAYYATH'S PALACE showed no signs of the kingdom's troubles. It covered five islands in the center of Irayas and its solid-gold domes still sent the sun's splendor back into the heavens. The gardens were still a marvel of perfection, and the magically tamed animals and birds that wandered and flew through it were as I remembered. The grounds were crowded with richly dressed noblemen and women and their retinues, strolling without a care; others, pacing, worried about the fate of their petitions; the hangers-on native to any court peering about, looking for the scent of scandal. Here was another change, though—in other times there would have been commoners and tradesmen waiting on their petitions. Perhaps King Gayyath had other channels for lesser people's problems, or perhaps this was a day when only the upper classes were permitted the palace.

Janela, I could see, in spite of her obvious efforts to appear worldly, was as awed as I'd been the first time I came here—or, to be honest, as I was at that very moment, still caught in the shining wonder.

Our gondola pulled into a dock and we were greeted by an honor guard. When Janos and I first came to Irayas, the palace guard wore gold and white and their weapons were archaic and ceremonial. Now they were Wardens, immaculate in red and black, weaponry polished, modern, and well-used. I noted the formal but relaxed manner in which they saluted Chares, and even though I'd never been a soldier, thank the gods, knew this was one sign of an elite, war-experienced unit.

As we walked up the broad winding path bordered by multicolored ivory edgings I asked Chares about his Wardens.

"Our purpose is but one—to serve King Gayyath in any manner he wishes and to hold his life and then the kingdom itself more valuable than anything else, including our own beings." Chares sounded as if he were reciting from the oath.

I pretended alarm. "The household guards I saw on previous visits were more ceremonial than your unit. I hope no one has been mad enough to consider any . . . actions against the king himself?"

"Not as yet," Chares said grimly. "But we stand prepared."

"So King Gayyath himself created the Wardens?" Janela asked.

"No. We were chartered by Lord Modin."

Neither Janela nor I knew him, and there'd been no mention of him in any of Hebrus' dispatches.

"Forgive me, Chares," I said, "but I'm embarrassed to say I know nothing of the lord. Would you tell me a bit about him? I despise appearing ignorant, especially about someone as obviously important as the lord must be."

Chares agreed. "Lord Modin is one of King Gayyath's most trusted advisers. He also takes a great interest in our formation. But he has no use for power or panoply, preferring to remain in the background so as to better help Vacaan and our king."

Chares didn't realize it, but he was telling me more than he intended, as he had since arriving at our palace. So Modin was, or at any rate fancied himself, a power behind the throne?

Modin, or that there was someone like Modin, didn't surprise me. King Domas, Gayyath's father, had been all too typical a grand monarch. Too many great kings have an equally great failing: They are unable to realize their mortality and hence unable to ensure a proper succession. Thus it was, I'd learned over the years, with his eldest son. I'd only met the prince once or twice, and sensed that King Domas was deliberately keeping him away from the throne or from learning just how to rule. I don't know why Domas felt as he did, whether Gayyath had somehow offended, or simply by his presence reminded Domas that one day he himself would face the Dark Seeker.

I myself was having problems with Cligus at the time, so, frankly, was wary of judging a man and his son. I avoided thinking of the difficulty, other than feeling some concern for the people of Vacaan and how they would be ruled after Domas' death. I wondered if perhaps Domas, in his last years, had understood his error and realized that Gayyath would need some sort of eminence to rule wisely and well. I doubted that, since I would have heard of Modin before now if that were true. But I chanced asking.

"Lord Modin," Chares answered briefly, "was chief of a remote province until about six or seven years ago. His wisdom and abilities brought him to King Gayyath's attentions, and our king was well-pleased when he found Lord Modin was a wizard of the first order who was also drawn to ruling."

I thought of another being from another remote province I'd faced recently, and then forced my mind into another channel. But the thought that came was no more comforting, as I noted the dots of red and black that were the Wardens moving through the throngs of nobility and their attendees outside the palace.

Red and black . . . add one color, gold, and those were the house colors of Prince Raveline, Janos' corrupter, the monster I'd slain atop the black mountain beyond Irayas.

AS WE NEARED the main palace building I noted something else new: a looming five-story building set apart from the main complex. It was also of gold, elaborately filigreed with what looked like ivory. I remarked on it to Chares.

"No," he said. "You would not have seen that before. It's new and is King Gayyath's seraglio."

I kept my face bland, showing no surprise. Whatever King Domas did for private pleasures had never been known to me—his personal affairs were kept well-concealed from outsiders and even from members of his court.

Chares drew a few steps ahead of us and I looked at Janela, who was staring at the building. Now that we were closer, I could tell that the filigree was not decorative, but served to conceal bars.

"No doubt guarded by eunuchs as well," she murmured. "Castrate a man and prison a woman . . . royal power at its finest."

WHAT I CONSIDERED the greatest single marvel of Irayas was inside the three-tiered audience chamber. On the bottom level were the commoners and the level that was previously most crowded. Now it was nearly empty. Chares led us up steps to the second level, more populous with nobility, and then to the third level, held for wizards and the highest court officials. Above this stretched the great golden throne of the king.

But what took everyone's eye filled most of the depression on this third level: a huge simulacrum of Vacaan itself. Everything was there, from the cities to the farms to the river to the black mountain behind the city. I knew if you examined the model closely you could find boats, animals, even birds. This was not a conceit or work of art, but a powerful tool that was used to govern, observe, and control the realm. What was done to the simulacrum by sorcery would also be brought to the lands beyond, whether flood, rain, or the finest growing weather. The simulacrum could reward and punish from afar and was, I thought, the greatest work of magic I'd ever seen.

Usually it was an area of calm, with the wizards who controlled the model moving unhurriedly around it, their spells firmly in place. Not so this day. It appeared to me as if the spells were slipping, or had been improperly cast, because certain areas of the kingdom would suddenly shimmer and be hard to make out, as if seen through a heat wave, or else would vanish entirely and reveal the intricately carved flooring underneath. Different sections were turning slightly without regard to the others, and the perspective would change, as it might if the simulacrum were on a turntable.

The problems were not being left untreated—there must've been twenty or more sweating magicians, flanked by their acolytes, chanting spells, waving wands or censers. Braziers set along the way let their fragrant smoke waft upward, and there were mystical symbols hastily chalked around the simulacrum.

The chief wizard, or the official in charge, at any rate, was a slender, handsome man not much older than Janela and an inch or two shorter than I am. He reminded me greatly of a fox, and I do not mean this disparagingly, but rather that his sharp face, clean-shaven unlike most in the court, was alert, and his eyes darted constantly around, missing nothing. He moved foxlike as well, quickly, with agility, darting from sorcerer to sorcerer and snapping orders. He was frowning, obviously trying to hold back anger.

The man wore a blue silk tunic and pants and had a bright red sash around his waist that also stretched up over one shoulder. He was the only one in that building wearing red, other than the Wardens, and so I knew him instantly.

"That will be Lord Modin," I guessed.

"It is he," Chares said, and his voice held great respect.

We were drawing near the throne, and I turned my attention to the man who sat, or rather lolled on it. I blinked. King Gayyath had . . . grown since I'd seen him last. His father, Domas, had been large and bearlike, and so too was Gayyath. But where Domas bulked large, dominating by his very presence, Gayyath sprawled, his belly bulging the loose robes he wore, his jowls hanging to either side of his face. His dark hair was cut very short, either for convenience or to encourage it to return quickly to hide his growing baldness. He looked less like a king than like a fabled gourmand at rest. Where his father had worn or more frequently toyed with a simple gold band for his diadem, Gayyath had an elaborately worked crown with jewels and other stones on it. After hearing of his seraglio, I'd half expected him to be surrounded with members of his harem, but he hadn't, at least not yet, let himself slip to *that* level of display.

I'd expected Chares to announce us, but was surprised when the king's voice boomed:

"Lord Amalric Antero of Orissa and Lady Lycus of Vacaan, who now prefers to be known as Lady Janela Kether Greycloak, you may approach us."

Once more I was surprised—either King Gayyath was a ruler who paid more attention to detail than I'd imagined, or else someone believed our arrival was of importance and we should be honored, or, at any rate, set out from the crowd.

His voice was a wonder, a deep, booming sonorous tone that a herald, an Evocator, a Magistrate, or a general would have spent years of servitude to learn. As we later learned, when he spoke, everyone would marvel at what he said—until they tried to find some meaning, of which there was most often none.

Janela bowed and I stood erect as King Domas had told me to behave, long years ago.

"I welcome you to Vacaan," Gayyath went on. "May your stay here be fruitful and pleasant and with the granting of your every wish within our powers."

Out of the corner of my eye I saw a bustle and Lord Modin was beside the throne. His face showed the anger it had a few minutes ago, then he forcibly blanked it and smoothed a courtly smile.

Gayyath nodded to him. "This is Lord Modin, gentle folk. My good friend and most trusted adviser."

Modin bowed slightly. "I thank you, Your Highness. I, too, am delighted to meet our travelers."

We exchanged bows. His eyes swept me, then held on Janela. These at least bore no resemblance to a hedgerow creature, but sent out the strong, burning black stare of a Master Evocator. You were intended to do his bidding, his eyes said, without question or hesitation, and he knew your every secret.

Then he said, "The king and I wish to express our sorrow for the loss of your factor, who was also, I understand, your friend."

"Yes, yes," Gayyath said. "That merchant fellow. I think I remember meeting him, didn't I?"

Now I had the answer—Gayyath was merely well-rehearsed. I wondered why Lord Modin had wanted him to be so courteous, as if our appearance was important.

"You did," Modin said to the king, "but you hadn't seen him for some time and you'd expressed your regrets not long before he met his unhappy fate."

"Of course, of course," Gayyath rumbled. "So how goes Orissa? Well, I hope, and I also hope you haven't brought any problems to us that you want us to solve. Have our own muddles and troubles, as you can see." He waved vaguely at the simulacrum.

"No, Your Majesty. All we want is a favor."

"That's all anyone seems to want," Gayyath went on. "And then those damned favors turn into a small estate and then a bigger estate and some land for the family and perhaps some gold and oh yes could you add in a company or perhaps a regiment of soldiers . . ." He let his voice trail off into what I swear were echoes.

"Actually," Janela said, "what we need is even less than a favor than a simple permission."

Gayyath's eyes held on her and I was reminded that despite his appearance as a vaporing indulgent, he still sat the throne of the most powerful kingdom in the known world and there had been no successful attempts at usurpation.

"You may ask."

"We wish permission," Janela said boldly, "to sail east."

"Why? There's nothing but ocean. The gods don't favor such expeditions. My own father once talked of such an event that'd happened . . . hells, I disremember, but it must have been before his father's father's father's time. Came to some sort of bad end or else just disappeared. Besides, lady, as one from Vacaan you know nothing good comes from looking east. Never has, never shall."

I decided to intervene. "Your Majesty, we wish you to indulge a foreigner, myself, and Lady Greycloak. As you can see, I am drawing on in years and have a deadly fear of dying of boredom in my own bed."

"Not I," Gayyath said. "I hope to pass on in that very place, but not of boredom." He snickered lasciviously.

"I am not a king," I went on, "but a merchant and a traveler and one who's happiest when he's gazing on sights he's never seen before."

"Can't understand that," Gayyath went on. "Likely to be a swamp as anything else. And if the savages who live there aren't trying to carve your liver for breakfast, they're in some sort of dream that they're as civilized as we are. But I suppose it takes all kinds."

He turned his attention to Modin. "Don't your wizards have something to say about that? About going east, I mean? Isn't that forbidden by some gods or other?"

"I know of no such ban for outsiders," Modin said. "Of course, there is one for our citizens, Your Highness. You recollect that is why we maintain a coastal patrol. But for foreigners, which I must say includes Lady Greycloak since she's renounced her birthright, there has been none written into our laws or practiced as part of our customs."

"Don't like it," Gayyath went on. "There's nothing but evil to be found to the east. Everybody knows that."

That was the reaction we'd been expecting, and we had brought many arguments to try to change Gayyath's mind. We'd even considered, if our plea was rejected, to chance going on anyway and risk the distant wrath of Vacaan's sorcerers once they learned of our deceit. The mild interest and lack of concern from Modin was unexpected, and I wondered greatly.

Gayyath suddenly yawned. "Not that it matters," he said. "Like you said, foreigners do things like that. You deal with it, Lord Modin."

"Thank you, Your Highness. I know you have more pressing matters," Modin said.

"Yes, yes." Gayyath said, then smiled at Janela. "Whatever the decision is, lady, I hope to see you again at court. You are most beautiful, and beauty is something I vastly admire."

We bowed, made excuses, said of course we wouldn't leave without bidding farewell to the king and no doubt would be honored in his presence once more, and were escorted to a lower level. I'd expected to be taken to a privy chamber by Lord Modin, at which time the issue would be thoroughly gone into. Instead he drew us aside to a railing.

"East, eh?" he mused. "Would there be any other motive, beyond the purest curiosity, you might wish to tell *me* that might've embarrassed you in front of the king?"

"None . . ." I let the pause grow artfully. "Except, perhaps, one. I may be old but I am still a merchant. If we encounter anything that might be of commercial interest to Orissa . . ."

"Then you must return here to Irayas and discuss the matter with a chamberlain to see if it's proper to open trade and if such commerce is in Vacaan's best interests," Modin finished.

"Of course."

Then came the last surprise—I'd expected him to dismiss us and say he'd give his answer later. Instead:

"As I told the king, I know of no reason you can't be permitted to undertake your voyage, although I do consider it most foolhardy. You are forbidden to take any citizen of our kingdom with you, and any supplies you require must be paid for in gold, not taken in credit. As the king said, no one returns from the east, and I wish to ensure there shall be no outstanding debt to sully the great name of the Anteros. Also, I request you sail within a fortnight."

I frankly gaped, as did Janela, in the purest astonishment. Lord Modin let a smile slip over his lips.

"King Gayyath's father allowed business to take forever," he said. "We have introduced newer methods. When a decision is obvious, there is no reason to not make it immediately.

"So you have our permission. But as the king said, please make sure you attend some of our court events. You'll find them enjoyable, especially when you're long days and weeks at sea with nothing around you but water and emptiness. Now if you'll excuse me, I'll have an escort return you to your quarters." He bowed and hurried back up toward his disintegrating simulacrum.

Janela and I exchanged wide-eyed looks but said nothing as two Wardens approached and bowed.

It was too easy. First King Gayyath had been properly instructed as to our arrival, then the matter was brought up and quickly taken care of. It was almost as if our request was already known and a decision had been reached before our arrival. This boded not well.

There was something most wrong. We had better move fast.

CHAPTER SIX

THE INVISIBLE NOOSE

There was actually little to be done for our ships to ready them for the expedition. The items consumed on the voyage out were made good, and more supplies were high-stacked in any cranny that would hold them. Anything that had broken or was badly worn was replaced and a suitable stock of trading goods was laid in, more to perpetrate the tale that we were on a trading mission than anything else.

We were waiting on one thing: for the proper phase of the moon for a certain ceremony, a ceremony that could confirm our belief in the Kingdoms of the Night . . . or, like all magic, produce nothing but frustration. The proper day was only two weeks distant.

It was just as well we'd brought almost everything we needed with us, since Irayas was seething, dangerous, and it was best for foreigners to stay close to safety. We saw this when we ventured out from our island castle into the commercial areas of the city. I'm not quite sure how to put this—Irayas was still the most magnificent city I'd ever known, where even the lowliest street could be paved in polished porphyry transmuted from humble cobblestones by one of Vacaan's sorcerers, and storefronts could be decorated lavishly with precious and semiprecious materials.

But now it looked as if the city hadn't been maintained, as if the maintenance workmen no longer took their tasks to heart and were content to let a little rust show, a little grime appear, a cracked window to wait awhile before being replaced.

The people were different, as well. They stared more openly and were more likely to comment on anyone wearing expensive dress . . . and weren't unwilling for their jibes to be overheard.

Quatervals put it best: "It's as if they're waitin', for what I'm not sure, but I don't want to be around when it gets here."

We went out in groups, pairs at the least and never alone. Janela, in spite of her protests, was companied by Chons, who seemed to have an entirely different idea than most gardeners about the uses to which cutlery could be put. Frequently, however, she slipped out without him and said innocently, when I chided her, that "One can be invisible, two never."

She was busy on a series of rather mysterious errands, and I was reminded of her great-grandfather's routine many years ago when we set out on my Finding. But Janos' secrecy in Lycanth had been necessary, since he was purchasing magical implements in a time when their possession by anyone other than a licensed Evocator was forbidden. But here in Irayas it didn't seem to matter. Finally I found out she'd been deluged with invitations from Irayas' sorcerers. At first I thought they were eager to hear about what mysteries she'd learned in her studies and travels, but was quickly reminded that magicians here, like other citizens of Vacaan, felt there was nothing but barbarism and ignorance outside its borders. The invitations were primarily out of curiosity and to break the boredom of seeing the same old wizards at the same old gatherings.

Janela fell into the habit of coming by my rooms when she returned from an event, having a final glass of wine or brandy and talking—sometimes about what had happened, sometimes about what we hoped and thought lay ahead, and sometimes just . . . talking. She was, like her grandsire, a good tale-teller and better listener. I found myself talking about things I never had before, things that had happened after the events in my book and which I'd never told anyone other than Omerye, or things that had occurred after her death.

One night Janela came back from a magical conclave a little drunk and a great deal angry. She slid her bag and blade off, poured a full beaker of brandy, and slumped down in a chair.

"I've just spent the dullest blasted evening of my life . . . worse even than when I was a mere acolyte and had to listen to my masters expound on why the stars had more influence over my fate than I myself."

"Who were you guesting?" I wondered.

"Grand Wizard Euboae, who's the wisest and most respected wizard of them all, sitting drooling in his senescence, surrounded by equally dung-brained disciples. None of them know a thing! Janos was right when he said there are no smart fellows in this kingdom. Everyone of them does things by rote, with no change from his grandfather's time to the present."

"You do sound like a Greycloak," I said, grinning.

"Right now I'm so sick of these hidebound fools that I'm beginning to wonder about my great-grandfather. If Janos was so wise, why did he so easily spring Raveline's trap?"

My smile vanished—I saw that Janela wasn't just exercising her temper, but was seriously upset.

"Why single him out?" I asked in my mildest tone.

Janela looked at me, then away at the open window and the lights of Irayas. I thought I could see moisture glisten in her eyes.

"It's just that I feel so damned alone sometimes," she said. "Sometimes I can *feel* these rules Janos was trying to set down, those rules your sister Rali was trying to reach for. And I can *feel* them shaping into one great picture, and then it slips from my mind's fingers like mercury.

"I wish there really *were* some smart ones. Maybe that's what I hope we find when we reach our goal."

"When?" I said. "You sound quite certain."

"Oh, we will, we will," she said. "But I'm afraid when we get there it will be like Janos feared as he studied the spells of the Old

Ones—they'll be working by rote rather than reason, just as they are here in Irayas."

To soothe her, I said, "Janos thought it was possible that not all of the Old Ones were going in circles. That some of them were following the same trail he was on."

"So what happened to them?" Janela said. "Where's our gods-blessed Golden Age covering the earth, sky, and heavens?"

"Maybe that's what we're going to find out," I said.

Janela looked back at me and her anger and insecurity broke as quickly as a summer squall and she laughed that shining laugh I'd grown to love.

"Amalric, I see again why you've been so successful as an adventurer. For you, darkness is only the time between two lights. Dusk and dawn."

I laughed and toasted her. She drained her glass and shook her head when I indicated the decanter. She stood, yawning, anger replaced by fatigue. I got up as well. She put her arms around me and her head against my chest.

We stood like that for a long moment, then she gave me a quick squeeze and stepped away.

"You're right. It will all come clear. In the real Far Kingdoms."

I HAD A DARKER TASK to perform, which required Quatervals to smooth my path. He growled that it was more important to protect me, but I reminded him that I was always armed and, further, had detailed Otavi, J'an's grandson with the butcher's axe, to watch my back. Otavi might not have had the training or the innate caution of my ex–Frontier Scouts, but his mere presence would be enough to make most assailants hesitate.

Quatervals finally reported complete failure, which told me as much as if he'd been successful. I'd asked him to find any servants of Hebrus, to be rewarded for serving their master so long and well. I'd also advertised openly. There'd been no response to my broadsides, and Quatervals had also now been luckless.

"Not one," he muttered. "Not a scullery, not a castellan, not a maid, not a boatman."

I nodded, not surprised. "They've either been well-rewarded to stay away, sent elsewhere by force, or . . ." I didn't finish the sentence, nor did I need to. "Quatervals, tonight, at midnight, you, Chons, and myself will go out."

The three of us, plus Janela, did just that in one of the small ship's boats I'd had lowered and tied up just behind the stairs that led up from our mooring dock. I'd had Janela put a slight spell over my quarters. I'd suggested a fog, or confusion, but she'd gone one better. She took a blotter from the desk, touched it against the walls and chairs, then sprinkled herbs—rosemary, queen of the meadow, rock poppy, belladonna, among others—on the blotter. She then drenched the blotter with a liquid. I asked what it was, and she said, "Elixir of life. I could burn the blotter and herbs, but the elixir will free the substance and join the air more slowly and the spell will last longer.

"It won't stand up to a *real* sorcerer's suspicions longer than one good penetration spell," she said. "But I don't think we're under that kind of suspicion. I hope not, anyway."

She whispered a spell, and fumes rose from the blotter as effectively as if she had, indeed, used a brazier, charcoal, and fire. We went out silently, making sure we didn't disturb Lienor or any of the other servants.

The night was still, calm, and clear. The waters of the lake reflected the shimmering lights of Irayas, which burned all night long, and the crescent moon above. I could still hear touches of music from several places—Irayas was not a city that slept.

Chons and Quatervals rowed us across the lake and down the winding canals. Our destination was Hebrus' mansion. My memory, even after the years and the twists of Irayas' canals, held good—I used the lights from Gayyath's palace as my navigational point, my "north," and within an hour we arrived.

Hebrus' mansion wasn't large by the standards of Irayas, which meant it would be enormous in Orissa. He'd only lived in a quarter of it, being a man who abhorred ostentation and accepted the palace only because he felt the House of Antero required some splendor. It sat at one corner of the large island that was now the Trader's Port, and was built of ornately worked stone.

We'd been about to row directly to it when Quatervals saw a

boat. We feathered our oars and crouched, level with our boat's gunwales, hoping for invisibility. The other craft crossed the moon-path on the water no more than fifty yards away, and I could see it was one of the Wardens' patrol vessels. There were only three heads visible above the rail, two lookouts and a helmsman. Even the Wardens, it seemed, slacked off in boredom when assigned to an area where nothing much ever happened and their only duty was to keep traders in and natives out.

After the boat went out of sight, we rowed swiftly to Hebrus' dock and hurried down the pier toward the mansion. Again, as when we entered Senac's estate, Janela, with all of her sorcerous senses a-tingle, went first, followed by Quatervals, then myself and Chons. None of us had weapons drawn—if discovered, we planned to try to talk our way out.

I could see Janela's form outlined against the stone of the house. Every few steps she'd pause, "listen," and her head would shake. Nothing. No sorcerous wards. Neither Quatervals nor I saw anything, and Chons was also silent. We went up on the stone terrace and to one of the doors, which appeared to be made of solid glass, cunningly grooved with carvings and the grooves stained with myriad colors. It was evident that Hebrus had had no worries about anyone breaking in—we saw no signs of bars or heavy locks. Hardly the habit of a man who prefers goons as bed partners.

Quatervals beckoned to Chons and the two huddled over the door. There came a click, and Quatervals pushed the door open. Chons was beaming proudly. Again I wondered just how my gardener had spent his time away from my estate—he certainly was showing some nonhorticultural talents.

Inside, we stepped away from the door and Janela whispered words over firebeads. I led the way through the house to the part Hebrus had used. The rooms we passed through were almost bare, given only enough furniture to avoid looking abandoned.

I found Hebrus' rooms without difficulty. Janela increased the potency of the firebeads and we looked about. I had expected what I saw: Most of those treasures and curiosities Hebrus had collected over the years, the items that make a house truly a home, were gone. Janela opened her bag and took out a wand that she'd previously touched to a book I had that Hebrus once prepared for Antero traders on the customs of Vacaan—sadly, the only memento I had of one of my most loyal servants.

She let the wand take charge and it turned her; it stretched out like a seeking snake's tongue, looking but never finding.

After some moments she lowered the wand. Nothing. We searched other rooms, including Hebrus' bedroom. Still nothing.

We left the mansion as silently as we had come and returned to our own quarters undiscovered. I dismissed Chons and asked Quatervals and Janela to come to my rooms. She dissipated the still-lingering fumes from the blotter and allowed her senses to reach out. There'd been no "inquiries," no "eyes" looking here. As far as she could tell, she said, the deception had worked.

I explained to Quatervals what we'd been looking for and what we'd not found—someone had not only taken all important physical remnants of Hebrus from the mansion, but, as Janela's magic had revealed, had removed even the ethereal presence a person exudes that clings to all he touches. It was as if an invisible broom had swept any memory of the presence of Hebrus.

"Why?" Quatervals wondered. "Did Hebrus know anything important? Anything that'd bear on our quest?"

"I don't know," I said. "Of course I hadn't time to write him, nor would I have mentioned anything, since all correspondence is read by the king's officials. As far as I know, he'd made no investigations to the lands east."

"Then," Quatervals said, "he must've made an enemy, one that feared you'd begin blood feud when you arrived."

There spoke a true frontiersman. I didn't think so.

"A more plausible explanation," Janela said, "might be that he's been witness to the way Vacaan's changed since you were here last . . . and somebody didn't want Amalric Antero getting *any* information about *anything*."

That was the only conclusion I could reach, vague though it was. I could take it one small step further—the prime instigator was Lord Modin, since the false story of Hebrus' death had been carried by his Wardens. But why?

I did not know . . . but I did know I had an enemy in the king's adviser. Why, then, had he so readily approved our request?

I had questions, but no answers, and so it was time for bed.

OTAVI, QUATERVALS, AND I were picking up some items that Janela needed for the coming ceremony. The shop in question was up a narrow canal, and we left our boat and went down a twisting narrow street, following the instructions Janela had given us.

We found the shop, received a small package from a very old man dressed like one of the desert nomads of my youth, and gave him the somewhat amazing amount of gold he'd wanted.

We started back for the boat, and a mob caught up with us, shouting out of alleys, screaming in rage. But after we'd instinctively put our backs against a solid wall and started to draw our swords, I realized they weren't attacking us. This was an explosion of the purest rage, as I saw a man run out of his own small grocery, look about wildly, shout, and pick up cobblestones to hurl without aim at anything, everything. The rabble grew as sidewalk displays were overturned, the silks used for shade ripped down, and windows smashed. We might not be the targets, but soon the raw violence could well suck us in. I looked for a shop to hide in but at that moment the throng's shouts changed from rage to fear and a solid wall of red exploded at them.

It was a phalanx of Wardens, the front rank armed with truncheons nearly three feet long, the ranks behind carrying reversed spears used for prods. Without giving any orders to disperse, the soldiers waded into the people, clubs swinging like metronomes. I thought I saw steel flash once or twice and saw a dagger in one Warden's hand.

There was nowhere for the mob to run to; then they found exits, just as boiling wine will burst a sealed jar, and the men and women flowed away and the street was suddenly empty.

One of the Wardens noticed us, frowned, then nodded approval, as if he'd just consulted a sheaf of orders and found that these outlanders were not to be bothered.

Two barked orders and the soldiers formed up and were gone.

I counted ten bodies sprawled in the streets, their blood pooling on the turquoise paving, as bright for a moment as the uniforms of the men who'd slain them.

THAT NIGHT too many of our questions were answered. I'd retired early to stock up on sleep before our voyage. Instead I found myself tossing, endlessly wondering what would happen, if there was any chance of our survival, what was going on back in Orissa, and on and on and on.

I finally drifted off and dreamt dreams I care not to remember. I was brought out of that fitful slumber by a tapping at my door. I slid out of bed and found my sword, feeling in the back of my mind a touch of pride that my wanderer's ways and cautions were returning.

I went to the door noiselessly, then jerked it open. Standing there outlined in the dying tapers of the corridors was Janela. Her shoulders were hunched, as if it were winter instead of near-summer. I took her arm and pulled her inside, knowing from her stance and what little I could see of her expression that something was wrong.

She stood in the middle of the floor, motionless, and I uncovered the night-light and blew it into life, then touched it to two of the oil lanterns in the chamber before I realized I was quite naked. Janela didn't seem to notice as I dropped my sword on the table and quickly pulled a towel around my waist.

"What's wrong?"

She licked her lips, looking for the words.

I remembered my manners, and found her a seat and the last of the brandy in the decanter. She but touched it to her lips.

"I know," she said without preamble, "or at any rate can hazard an educated guess why Hebrus was murdered."

I buried an oath, found a cupboard and a fresh bottle of brandy and broke its wax seal and poured for both of us, not worrying about the decanter's niceties.

"Why . . . or," I said, "who, first?"

"Modin. Or one of his Wardens or hirelings."

"Why?"

"Because Modin wanted nothing, absolutely nothing, about

what has happened in Vacaan in the last ten years to be told you when you arrived."

"Go on."

"Modin is afraid of you, Amalric. Afraid of you and afraid of us together. The reason he wants you to go east, without *any* information that Hebrus could've possibly told you, is that he wants you to travel without the armor that's knowledge. He wants you to die out there, Amalric, to die like he believes all travelers from Irayas have died or been destroyed by demons."

"Afraid of *me*?" I was trying to work my way through her spattering words idea by idea, trying to keep from wallowing in this sudden flood. "What threat am I to him? Does he think I plan to destroy him? Or that I am somehow a danger to King Gayyath or to Vacaan itself?"

"He simply doesn't know. He's terrified of what you were, you and Janos Greycloak. Somehow the two of you persisted over all odds and came to Vacaan, and in the doing shook the world from the Western Islands to Irayas itself. Vacaan was drowsing comfortably before you and Janos came, Amalric, just as Orissa was. Now, you've come again with a descendant of Janos' and he's panic-stricken at what upsets we might make in the fabric of this world."

"Obviously," I said, "he doesn't buy the tale that we're simply wanderers looking for new trading opportunities."

"Of course not," she said. "I don't think either one of us thought that—he's not risen to where he is by being a fool. If we were facing him alone, I have no doubt that I could best him in any sorcerous battle he chose. All things being equal. But they are not equal. We are on his ground and he has the resources of all the wizards in Vacaan to support him and strengthen his spells."

I turned the brandy glass between my fingers, thinking about what she'd said and also finding the precise words for my next question.

"This news is not good," I said. "But it's not what's making you shiver like a fawn who's just seen its mother killed by hunters."

"I'm not sure I should tell you more."

"Why not?"

She took a deep breath. "Because you are a man . . . and you might let that interfere with your thinking."

"Janela, you've completely confused me. Just tell me what happened, no matter what. We *are* partners, and I hope friends, aren't we? I'll wager, though, that I can guess at least a part of what you're holding back."

"Can you?"

"Modin either slept with you or wanted to."

"Wanted to is all. Thinking about actually doing it with him . . ." She shivered once more. "But he doesn't want to have sex with me out of lust, not pure lust anyway."

My eyes widened as I caught a flash of what would come next.

"I see you may have guessed it," she said. "A descendant of Janos Greycloak? Sex with her, sex-magic, would bring him great powers, he's sure.

"I learned tonight that he deliberately chose those colors for the Wardens and his house flag out of admiration for Raveline, the man who helped destroy my great-grandfather. When we came here, it was if he had become Raveline himself and now had another chance to own Janos Greycloak, to possess him utterly, and perhaps somehow, in the instant when bodies and souls hang in space together, understand and own the secret Janos sought.

"Your book," she said, in suddenly calm tones, "has obviously traveled beyond Orissa's borders."

I walked to the window and looked out at the night. Janela had been right—part of me responded as a hot-blooded bravo. I wanted to strap on steel, seek out Modin, and challenge him, even though Janela and I weren't lovers. Nor would we ever be. It was not jealousy I felt, but also the rage that Modin wished to drain Janela and her powers with sexual magic. I remembered women used by Janos and cast aside, and suddenly thought of a night long ago in Janos' castle here in Irayas when I'd seen a mother huddled in a boat crying bitterly for her loss, and the smell of something that might have been burnt lamb but wasn't, and a bowl full of a dark liquid being drunk by a thirsty being, not human.

"So one night of passion was supposed to give him all that," I finally managed, and I think my tone was level.

"No. He wants me to stay on here with him. Amalric, perhaps you weren't listening closely when I said he fears *us*. He's more afraid of us, together, than you or I alone."

"We *are* a most hellacious pair," I said, trying to bring a bit of cheer into the room and lift the blood-lust that kept moving my gaze to the sheathed sword on the table. "Heroes of yore and all that."

"It's more than that. One of us is the beaten-together billets of iron and steel. The other is the clay-ash. He thinks there is a great swordsmith waiting in the east and a fiery forge that will turn us into something that can shake this world to its very roots."

"Let him be right about that!" I snarled.

"So now you know as much as I."

I thought hard. "Two days now until we climb the Holy Mountain. We could depart within a week after that. I don't think it would be wise to hurry away the day following the ceremony. *That* would unquestionably send Modin into a frenzy and make him send magic and possibly even warships after us. Do we have that kind of time?"

"I don't know," Janela said.

"Did Modin give you any sort of ultimatum?"

"No. Not specifically."

"Then that's our course. I don't think we can cancel the ceremony and attempt to depart immediately. So we can only hope Modin remains inactive."

There was a very long silence in the room.

"There is one thing we might do," Janela said. I turned to her, and she was looking away at the wall. "Modin knows we aren't . . . aren't familiar with each other. Aren't lovers, I mean. That is one reason he made his offer. He believes that if he sleeps with me before you do . . . it's almost as if he thinks I were still a virgin and he could seize all my powers by having me first."

I felt heat on my cheeks and suddenly the entire situation became a bit funny. "If he is worried about *my* crazed lust and fears the competition, I'm afraid his powers are such that he'd be best qualified for a post guarding King Gayyath's concubines. Isn't he aware of my age?"

"Will you help me, Amalric?" she asked.

"Of course," I said. "Tell me how?"

Janela didn't answer, but stood up, went to first one lantern, then the other, and turned their wicks down until there was no light in the chamber but the night-light and the shine of the moon through the windows.

"He may be a sorcerer," she said. "But he can't know *everything*."

She slipped out of her clothes, and her body was lovely and gleaming in the dim light. Then she blew out the night-light and all was darkness. I heard her whispering, the rustle of bedclothes, and then the creak of the leather bedsprings.

"Lord Modin has seen all that he can," she said. "I've shielded us with a blocking spell and now he's certain to think the worst of me."

I stood there feeling foolish. Janela giggled.

"Don't worry," she said. "Your virtue is safe."

I went to the bed feeling as gawky as a bridegroom and nearly fell over one of her boots. I sat on the bed and wondered if I should try to sleep with the towel around me. Again I saw the humor in my befuddlement, tossed it away and slid under the covers. I did, however, keep very close to the edge of the bed.

It was very quiet in the room. I could hear the lap of the water outside and far away the chime of a gondola's bell. Janela's breathing softened and became regular.

I was almost asleep when she moved close, resting her head against my shoulder and sliding an arm across my chest. She murmured something in her sleep and I felt her soft body pressed against my side.

I felt the stirrings of something awkward and unseemly. She could be my *own* great-granddaughter, after all. What's more, she trusted me enough to use my bed to befuddle Modin.

Then she sighed again and my own eyes grew heavy. And the next thing I knew the sun's rays were flaming in the window, jolting me awake.

THE WAY UP the Holy Mountain was even harder and rockier than I remembered, both in mind and body. The wounds came back, almost as sharp as they'd been those long years ago when I'd cremated Janos' remains and sent his spirit flashing to the east.

It was just false dawn when we reached the ruins of the Old Ones' altar. There were four of us, Otavi, Quatervals, Janela, and myself. I told the two men to set their packs down and go down the mountain, out of sight. This ceremony needed no adulteration from eyes that didn't know its meaning.

Janela took six small jars of paint and a brush from her pack and began marking letters on the altar, letters from no language I ever knew.

I just stood, waiting. Perhaps it was cold atop that mountain. If it was, I don't remember feeling it.

The plateau was deserted. The people of Vacaan were discomforted by the place, reminded of those who'd gone before who had powers beyond their own.

I thought I saw a stain on the altar but I was imagining things—the ashes from the fire that had set Janos free would've been washed away long ago by the storms of winter.

Janela opened the two packs and took out two handfuls of sticks. She positioned them on the altar in an exact pattern. We'd brought these bits of wood all the way from Orissa. I'd gotten a few of them from a jewel case warranted to have been made in Kostroma, Janos Greycloak's birthplace. Others came from a door I'd purchased from the Magistrates' own guard and cut apart, a door that'd been to Janos' room. Another fragment came from one of my father's chairs that Janos had favored when he sat drinking with him. The last came from the dock of the castle he'd stayed in.

Janela poured oil on the sticks and we waited.

The first rays of the sun broke over the horizon, and at that moment Janela said three words and the altar fire caught and roared into life—flame as great as if we were setting a midsummer's eve bonfire alight.

Just as before, the smoke curled above the altar as if waiting. Out of nowhere came a wind into the east and it took the smoke, sending it swirling out over the cliff.

But then the plume hesitated and turned back against the wind and curled to the altar and around us, as if embracing Janela and me.

It did not smell of fire, or of aged wood or the varnishes the woods had been coated with, but instead the salt of the sea, the touch of tar of a ship's rope, and coming through the other odors strange smells, myrrh perhaps, orange blossoms certainly, honey, juniper, sweet calamus.

I was staring directly into the sun's rays but wasn't blinded, didn't see it, but something else.

Once before atop this mountain I'd seen a vision, a vision of a high mountain range, a range that looked like a great clenched fist with snow shining between the fist's covering of snow. I'd seen a mountain almost like that and crossed it with Janos, thinking I'd found the Fist of the Gods. Then, the day I burnt Janos' body, I'd seen the vision that haunted me until Janela came to explain we had been wrong.

And now I knew for certain that she was quite correct.

I was looking beyond Irayas, beyond the land the river curved through to the Eastern Sea. I saw that ocean stretching beyond man's reach, and then I saw land. I saw the mouth of a huge river, greater even than the one leading to Irayas. Beyond the river's mouth my vision fogged, but I could see still farther, and it was as if I were a bird, flying at incomprehensible speed. Land was below but I did not see it.

My vision was fixed on a high mountain range, a range clenched like a giant's fist. A giant . . . or a god.

Now I knew. Yes, I knew to the heart of my soul.

"Look," Janela whispered, and I forced my eyes to the side. She was holding the silver statuette of the dancer, and again it became flesh and again she danced in front of an exotic court, a court of beautiful men and women and demons. The king and queen were still on their thrones, and that wolf-snouted demon still lusted after the dancer. But my eyes went on to where a window opened on the court with gardens and a city below.

Far away in that small tableau against the horizon, I saw mountains, a series of peaks that could only be the other side of the fisted mountain range I'd just envisioned.

In a blink it was gone and my eyes were watering as the sun struck at them.

Neither Janela or I said anything.

Words were not needed.

It was time to leave for the Kingdoms of the Night.

NOW WE WERE READY for a rapid departure, having accomplished the three things necessary in Irayas: confirming Janela's beliefs; resupplying our ships; and, most importantly, securing permission from King Gayyath, no matter how tenuous that permission might be. I'd puzzled on just how to prepare for leaving without word going instantly to Lord Modin and the king through their spy Lienor and the other agents I knew to be part of our household. I did plan to make formal farewells at court, but with such short notice I might forestall whatever Modin might devise against us.

I'd come up with the stratagem of announcing an inspection of all my men and women and the ships, all to be travel-ready. Once the packs were together and the ships' cargoes properly stowed, we could leave on very short notice. To make sure it seemed like no more than an inspection, I'd promised horrendous punishments for dirty equipment or compartments not being shipshape, such as two weeks kitchen duty, a month's worth of night watch, no permission to leave the castle for a week, all indicating that our stay would continue.

Both Janela and myself were shaken by our vision atop the mountain, and I was exhausted from the climb.

Janela sent for me shortly after our return with a request that I make haste. I was sitting in my chambers wanting a nap but having to listen to Pip babble on about how he hadn't known things were going to be like this and he surely wouldn't have contracted under these circumstances and surely the gracious Lord Antero would be willing to discuss the terms of his payment to include benefits in the unlikely event of his not returning to Orissa, and so on and so forth.

It was Pip's old familiar song, which I'd heard on other expeditions. I laughed and said that if he expected more gold, he'd best put out more work and hope there'd be a handsome bonus on our return. Our familiar byplay complete, I went to Janela's chambers, wondering what she needed.

She had her bag open on the table and sorcerous implements spread out. A beaker of some awful-looking and worse-smelling liquid sat in front of her.

"Amalric," she said, without preamble, "we have problems."

"As if I didn't know that."

"*This* you don't know, and I'm afraid I must show it to you, rather than tell you. Sit down. Hold out a finger. I need a bit of your blood."

I obeyed and she nicked me with a tiny scythe—silver, not gold like the ones I'd seen used in spells before. She held my finger over the beaker and squeezed out three drops of blood.

"Perhaps I've been sensitized by the ceremony on the mountain," she said. "Once more I've been feeling that sense of dread, of menace, like unknown enemies have been watching. The last few hours I felt it not just here, which I ascribe to Modin and his sorcery and from whatever we shall face to the east, but behind us, too. From an unexpected place. I'll say no more.

"Now hold out your hands, palms up."

She began smearing a yellowish salve onto them.

"You say you don't have any of the Talent, which I know to be false—hush, I'm tired of the argument. I am now going to send you, in spirit, back down the river to the sea. Then south and east— toward Orissa. I fear I know what you will see. If my incantation doesn't work, I'll tell you what I think is happening and take whatever oaths you require to ensure you believe I'm telling the truth."

I put my hands down, just a bit angry. "Janela. Stop that at once. I need no oaths from you."

"For this . . . you might." She looked at me and her face held infinite sorrow. "I'm sorry, my Amalric. So very sorry."

She held out her palms like a priestess and began chanting:

"Blood finds blood
Blood seeks blood

Blood will find
Blood will see
Blood will find."

In a normal tone: "Now, drink the potion."

I did, holding it awkwardly between the heels of my hands, to the dregs. It tasted sweet, then bitter, then galling, almost making my throat close.

Before I could gag, protest, or even set the beaker down, I was torn from my body and sent reeling into space.

When I was a boy there'd been a brief fascination in Orissa for cycloramas. These were paintings on long strips of canvas. The viewers sat in chairs and the cyclorama was reeled from one cylinder to another in front of them. In this way one could experience a voyage by boat from Orissa to the river's mouth or along the Lemon Coast or by carriage from the city into the mountains. They were prized for their detail and length.

Now it was as if I were hanging over such a cyclorama, one being unreeled at dizzying speed. The river twisted below me like a beheaded snake, and I saw Marinduque and then I was hurtling over the ocean, heading back toward Orissa. Below me on the unrelieved sea I saw dots and I was diving on them. Then the dots became ten ships and I saw the welcome banner of Orissa flying from their main masts.

I recognized the ships—they were mine, part of the Antero merchant fleet. But these had been rigged for war—antiboarding nets were strung from the yards, and catapults or trebuchets were mounted on the forecastles. On their decks were men wearing leather battle dress and practicing with weaponry.

Then I was aboard one ship, the flagship I somehow sensed, and hanging in the air, invisible, above the quarterdeck. Below me stood Cligus! Why was *my son* on his way to Irayas?

Cligus was dressed for war and was in deep conversation with a Guard officer I'd seen before, dancing attendance on him but whose name I couldn't remember. I wanted desperately to hear their conversation and then I could. Not clearly, as if I were next to them, but as if I were halfway down a tunnel, or perhaps hearing them from the depths of a fever, so only an occasional word came clear: "... what we can ... arrest ... a trial, of course ... permits ... explanation ... turncoat ... when I return ... proof ... all Orissa will know ... and then Hermias will be doomed along with him."

Then, most clearly, as Cligus spread a look of mock sorrow that didn't mask the glee in his eyes:

"My own father! In Te-Date's name, how will I ever bear the shame!"

I was smashed back to Irayas, returned to my body, slumped in a chair in Janela's chambers. She looked at me, knew what I'd seen, got up and went to a window, pointedly staring away. I fought for control and failed. Futile tears took me, then rage spread through their midst. In a dull tone I reported precisely what I'd heard and seen. "How could—" I managed to find other words as I spoke. "—Orissa listen to that?"

"Amalric, I know this is a blow, but you *must* keep your wits sharp about you. You told me Cligus said something to the effect that all Orissa will know, once he returns with the evidence or with you. And you said those were your ships. You said before that Cligus had powerful friends. I'd wager that he was able to get an expedition authorized, at his expense, to investigate some charges he concocted. As yet you've not been read out from whatever Orissa uses for a Traitor's Gate. Certainly you still have friends there. Cligus was cursing your heir, Hermias, so he must be standing firm and still be safe. And I can't believe Palmeras would believe anything Cligus told him."

"I know he wouldn't."

"What is important is this thing about bringing you back. Do you believe Cligus is telling the truth about his intent?"

Cligus could not bring me back alive. No matter what evidence or false witnesses Cligus had manufactured, there'd be no way the charges would stand once I returned to Orissa. So Cligus had coldly planned something that could only result in patricide.

"How could he do this?" It was a pointless question on my part, but came from the soul.

"I'll not answer one part of that ... He is what he is, and I won't be the cause of more pain to you. But there is another how—

the practical one. How could Cligus succeed in such an audacious farce that no one capable of thought could listen to? I said I sensed magic, sensed some malevolent force ahead and now behind us, just as I sensed someone I thought to be Cligus pursuing us. The forces are one and the same. Someone . . . something . . . to the east has linked forces with Cligus."

"Forces like Senac?"

"Almost certainly."

"Does Cligus know," I asked, clinging to the straw, "or is he just their pawn?"

"I can't answer that. Perhaps he's but their tool, although that should be of scant comfort since a pure spirit cannot be so corrupted. But openly in league with whoever our enemies are, I'm unsure. He might not be, since there were no great sorcerous forces opposing me when I made my visit. I would think if there were a demon actually aboard those ships, I would have been found out instantly and had to make an immediate escape."

Again grief took me. I buried my head in my hands.

"You're right, I suppose," I managed. "My mind is a muddle. I need some time to clear it."

"We don't *have* time, Amalric. That's why I sent for you in such haste. Cligus' ships are less than two weeks from Irayas, and we'll need at least a week to sail downriver to the sea."

She was right. I sat there like a rock, like a boulder. Then from somewhere I gathered strength. Perhaps Janela was sending me some of her own, which had carried her for so many years through so many realms: I *was* a boulder, a mountain. Power grew within me. What I felt for Cligus I would delve into at another time. What I would do about it must also wait. But I could not sit here sniveling like a dotard. There had been worse pains, such as the deaths of my beloved Deoce and my firstborn daughter Emilie, which nearly caused me to give up, accept the embrace of the river and the Dark Seeker. I'd lived through those.

A dark, cold calm came. I stood.

"I'll make plans for an immediate departure," I said, "and I'll send a message to the king requesting a farewell audience."

Janela reached a hand out to me. But I didn't take it. If I allowed even a crack to appear, the boulder, the mountain, might well crumble.

THERE WAS more to come.

Within the hour a dispatch arrived. It was from Lord Modin, requesting the honor of my presence and that of Lady Lycus, now known as Greycloak, in the king's audience chamber at the fourth hour after sunrise two days hence. We were to be prepared to answer certain questions the Highest might wish to put.

The message was not carried by one of the palace's functionaries but by a Warden, accompanied by two armed fellows.

We were trapped. I had no idea what questions King Gayyath might have or might have been prompted to think of by Modin, but the cold note of the missive, the fact that Janela was referred to by her native name, and the armed soldiery, made me know it was not casual or friendly.

Even if these questions could be answered, it would surely be more than a week before we could conceivably get permission to sail . . . and by that time Cligus would be on us.

Trapped in the vise, feeling it tighten, I had no thoughts, no plans, no ideas. I decided to walk out onto the docks and stare at the water. We Orissans have always used our river to calm us, to bring ideas and peace. Perhaps something would occur to me, or at least I'd feel less like a thick-wit and then I could consult with Janela.

It was dusk when I went out of the castle.

I pretended not to notice Quatervals, who stayed far behind me, trying to appear invisible.

I sat on the edge of the wharf, seeing the small waves lap against the sides of our ships, ships so carefully equipped, which now looked as if they'd never see the usage we'd dreamed.

Something fell from the sky, drifting like a feather, like a snowflake. I reached out a hand and caught an ash.

Then I looked up and saw Irayas explode into flames.

THE SKY was lightening, as if the sun had reversed its course, the birthing of a firestorm. Not fire but fires, I realized, seeing other

flickering glows across the sky. I thought the closest fire was somewhat to the south of the royal palace in what passed in Irayas for
a poor district.

One fire could be accidental . . . but these? I counted three, no,
eight so far. Had an enemy of Irayas somehow crept up on the city
and attacked it? Impossible. There could be but one foe so well-
concealed. The people themselves must have risen.

Quatervals was beside me. I knew exactly what must be done.
The sight of the inferno had seared away all indecision, all
uncertainty.

"Turn the men out," I ordered. "We sail within two hours.
Make sure none of our household spies are able to leave the castle
and spread the word."

A great smile spread across Quatervals' face. "Thank the gods!
Now we'll be shut of these bastards and their scheming." He ran toward the castle doors, bellowing for his sergeants and the ships'
captains.

I went for Janela's quarters. She was already in the courtyard,
bag over her shoulder and her sword belt buckled.

"I see some gods have intervened in our favor," she said, very
calmly. "Shall we seize the moment, my friend?" She sounded exactly like her great-grandfather at the moment of battle, when all
around were panicked, afraid, and Janos grew cooler and more
level-headed.

IT TOOK LESS than an hour to be ready. Lienor and his staff were
locked in one of the inner banquet rooms, the doors into the serving
halls and kitchens nailed shut and furniture piled high against them.
One or two of the men, I found later, importuned their bosuns to let
their ladyloves of the moment aboard, but were refused.

Quatervals had my kit aboard the *Ibis*, but I remained dockside, determined to be the last to board, as much as I wanted to be
safe and away.

I knew for certain now that Irayas had exploded into civil war.
I'd seen one of the Wardens' patrol craft skittering wildly out of a
canal, pursued by several shabby public transport gondolas. The
men and women packing them were shouting and waving torches

and weapons. The gondolas trapped the Wardens' boat and the screams began. When they stopped, I was close enough to see what one woman was waving on the end of a boat hook. It was a man's head, still wearing a red helmet.

My men and women streamed past to the ships and then Quatervals was beside me, saluting and saying something, but it was buried in Kele's bellow: "Single up to the stern rope!" Sailors raced into motion. "We're ready to sail, lord!"

I ran for the gangplank, and as I stepped onto the *Ibis*' deck, it was pulled aboard. The sweeps were out and double-manned.

"Full right rudder," Kele shouted. "Port sweeps . . . pull, damn you!"

One of the *Ibis*' mates began a rowing chant. The steady motion pulled the bow of our ship away from the dock.

"Cast off the stern line," Kele ordered, and the last mooring fell into the water. We were free and moving. "Hold your rudder, mister . . . hold it . . . now midships your helm . . . all sweeps, pull! Steer for that canal mouth. Correct your course as you see fit."

"Ay, ma'am."

The *Firefly* and *Glowworm* followed in our wake.

"Quatervals," I began to order. "I'll want archers—"

His hand swept out, indicating, and I saw armored soldiers on the forecastle. They had bows ready, arrows nocked, and more shafts stuffed in their belts. "Is there any change milord wishes in the battle order . . . poor though it is?"

I managed a smile and wished for just a moment that the *Ibis* was a warship, overmanned with soldiery with no other duties other than battle, a complement no sane merchantman could ever afford. "No, Quatervals. But get you forward and stand by." He touched his forehead and hurried off the quarterdeck.

There were two men on each of the sweeps, sweating their guts out as the mate called for ever faster strokes. The quarterdeck held only Kele, her helmsman, Janela, and myself. The lake was flat and the breeze light.

We rowed into the mouth of the canal and into the abyss. War . . . battle is never pretty, but civil war, when men turn against themselves, is the ugliest. I once saw a lion taken with a spear in his middle, rolling, snapping in agony at his own entrails as they sagged out, actually devouring them in madness. That was Irayas on that night.

Thank Te-Date the canals from our quarters to the river were broad or else we might well have been drawn in. There was fire and destruction on the banks on either side of us.

We went unnoticed at first. The mobs were too busy killing each other and looting to pay much attention to anything other than themselves. I saw a man stumble out of a store proudly waving a wooden rocking horse aloft as if it were the finest prize imaginable. I saw a row of men outside a dramhouse, in line, handing out bottles of wine as the tavern roared up in flame. Each man would take a swallow of a bottle as it reached him, and when it was empty, the next one it reached would cast it aside.

A naked young girl ran screaming out of the darkness, two bellowing louts in pursuit, stripped to the waist. Quatervals shouted, and over the crash and roar two bowstrings twanged and the would-be rapists contorted, gray-goose shafts sprouting from their chests. The girl ran on and disappeared, unaware that she was no longer pursued. Those were arrows we should have husbanded, but thank the gods Quatervals had a soldier's decency.

The sights grew worse as we sailed on. Citizen had turned against citizen, man against his brother. But the enemy they all combined against were the Wardens. I saw other red-helmeted heads on pikes as we passed, and then black-and-red-clad bodies so tormented death would have come as the greatest blessing.

Then we were seen and the chaos reached out to embrace us.

Some that saw us screamed hatred—no one could be allowed to escape this inferno. Rocks, bottles, debris were hurled. There were better-armed men along the banks. The *Glowworm* lost a mate when a spear came from nowhere and pinned her to the deck. One soldier on the *Ibis* took an arrow in the thigh.

We entered a long, straight stretch with a high bridge arcing over the canal. There were men who saw us coming. Working in drunken unison, they tore away a heavy wooden bench and stumbled toward the bridge, intending to drop it on us as we sailed under. Arrows went out and the bench stood alone, surrounded by bodies.

A small fishing smack pushed out from a dock, propelled by poles. I have no idea what intent the men and women aboard had. We hit it full on with our bow and rolled it under. A man jumped from the smack as it was smashed and clung to our railing until a sailor clubbed him away.

Others wanted rescue we could not give. That brought the most terrible sight of the night. A woman ran to a slight promontory as we passed. She was carrying a bundle in her arms and screaming something. Fires roared close, so I couldn't make out what she was saying. She waved the bundle at us, trying to attract our attention, then, before anyone could do anything, she hurled it at us. It struck the water and opened and I had a moment to see that it was an infant wrapped in blankets. I don't know what we could have done, should have done, but before the eye's picture reached the mind, the child was gone.

Again the woman screamed and this time I heard her. Then she jumped straight out into the canal, hair floating above her as she fell. She plunged into the water and was gone.

There were other horrors, but then we came out into the basin and the entrance to the river. We were almost free of Irayas. We had but one foe I yet worried about—the river-patrolling Wardens. But my concern vanished when I saw five boatloads of Wardens rowing into the city. They paid us no attention whatsoever. With Irayas in anarchy, a handful of Orissans were of no concern to anyone.

A strong wind came, blowing away from the city, blowing east.

So, with fire, death, and treachery behind us, we set full sail into the unknown.

BOOK TWO

THE
FAR
SHORE

CHAPTER SEVEN

PIRATES

We reached the river's mouth and the open sea without encountering Cligus' expedition. We set our course east and north toward the tropics as Janela's many-times-revised chart had suggested.

We made no castings, set out no spells, since we didn't want to leave a spoor for Modin and his sorcerers to follow once the riots were suppressed. Even though Janela hadn't encountered any emanations from Cligus' ships showing that magicians were aboard, I knew he would've been able to find a few ambitious Evocators willing to sail with him, no matter how strongly Palmeras would have objected.

We were shaken by what had happened in Irayas. To see such a mighty kingdom shattered was almost as great a blow as if the same thing had happened to Orissa itself. It was even harder on me, since I'd known King Domas and had enjoyed the glories of Vacaan many times over the years.

These were not good days for Orissa or any of the lands I

knew. However, I kept this thought to myself, not wanting to sound like one of those dotards of my own youth, forever going on about how everything was going into the jakes, and that itself needed cleaning and painting.

Quatervals came to me, worried, but I needed no advice from a soldier on what should be done. All three captains were ordered to set continual strenuous drills, from man overboard to fire in the chain locker, day and night, giving no one any time to brood or sulk. Quatervals himself put our soldiery to hard drilling.

I took part as much as I could and slowly began to feel real strength coming back, strength such as I hadn't felt for years.

Janela noted an unusual thing when we were about a week out from Vacaan. It was a golden day with a crisp wind less than two points off our stern, so all our crew had to do was bend on full sail and loll about, hoping Kele, Towra, and Berar would find a little mercy and let them pass the day in ease. I was on the quarterdeck stripped to a loincloth, trying to convince myself to get up and stretch my muscles, but watching the cabin boy check the glasses against each other and playing the old game of: Well, when this minute glass is turned, perhaps this quarter-hour glass . . . and was about to fall asleep.

Janela was sprawled a few feet away waiting to see if the dolphin that had been following us for some hours would surface. She rolled on her side, yawning, and then she said, softly, "Well, bless me. Amalric, I thought your hair was all white."

"And so it is," I murmured, not ready to be brought back from my sopor. "Good thing, too. Makes everybody listen closely to my infinitely sagacious prattlings. One of the privileges of my years."

"I'm serious."

"Must be the light. Or the salt air. Makes everybody look younger."

Janela growled, pulled her bag over and took a small mirror out.

"Look for yourself, Grandfather."

I did, squinting against the glare. It took a moment, but by Te-Date, she was right. Along the sides of my head and above my temples my hair was starting to redden. Not the brilliant crimson of my youth, but it was slowly changing. I scratched my head in some perplexity and felt, along the scalp, stubble. New hair was growing in. I asked Janela to look at it closely, and she said it too was red.

"Now I'm really worried," I said, trying to make light of the matter. "Someone's put a spell of youth on me and soon I'll have to be finding swaddling clothes."

"No such spell exists," Janela snorted. "If it did, no one would give a rat's nose for gold, much less be seeking the Kingdoms of the Night, would they?"

"Actually yes, they would, finding no customer in me," I said, thinking about the matter. "What a horrible fate that would be. I remember the way I was when I was young, ecstatic one day, downcast the next, with never a cause for either state."

"I'll stay close," she said, "to make sure you don't embarrass us with youthful follies."

I truly thought we were imagining things, but my rejuvenation continued as the days passed. Eventually it was noticed by Kele, Quatervals, and then even everyone. Don't mistake me—I hadn't suddenly become the stripling who was about to set out on his Finding, his first trading voyage. Rather I looked as I had ten, perhaps fifteen years earlier. Or perhaps as I had just before Omerye died, not yet two years gone. I had aged quickly since that time, I realized, because I'd given up, had decided my only place was beside the fire, wrapped in a blanket, with nothing better to do but growl about the present, mourn the past, and wait for the Dark Seeker.

A bleak thought crossed my mind—I remembered the dancer that Janos had showed me, a childhood gift. It'd been tarnished and broken at first, but the farther we journeyed east and the closer we came to even the remnants of the Far Kingdoms, the more the statue renewed itself, until it appeared quite new. I also remembered the last time I'd seen it, tarnished and broken, in the last minutes before swords replaced words between us. Perhaps, I thought, this could be a warning to me as well. At one time in my youth, I'd felt incorruptible, and so I had heard some call me. I knew men and myself better and was certain that all of us have a price, and the honest man perhaps has only not been offered what he considers a proper figure.

For Janos it had been knowledge and perhaps the power that would go with it. For me? I didn't know. I wondered just for a moment, and hoped I was merely being cynical, if Janela's heritage included that sinister side of Janos Greycloak; then put the thought away as unworthy. Blood, in spite of the cautions of the priests and fabler, does *not* often run true.

We voyaged on, holding our course. Two weeks out of Vacaan I asked Janela to cast a certain spell. I thought we might be approaching our fishing grounds. This had been one of the few additions I'd been able to make to Janela's plans. At first she'd intended to sail east until she struck land. Then she'd use her sorcery and the various disconnected bits of legend she'd put on her chart to decide whether we should turn north or south until we struck signs of some civilization. If any existed, they might guide us in our search for a mountain range shaped like a fist. If we found the ruins of past greatness, that might prove an even better clue with less likelihood of hostility.

All that sounded vague to me, although Te-Date knows, I've pushed off on trading voyages with less information and more hopes for rich spices and silks than even Janela had for her Kingdoms.

I remembered something she'd told me, and asked: "You said you set sail once for the far shore but were turned back by the coast guard."

"I was," she said.

"I know the people of Vacaan are terribly superstitious about what lies to the east—I saw enough dread of the subject to know for myself over the years. But does this coast guard exist *just* to turn back foolhardy explorers?"

"No," she said. "They also stop fishermen who are intent on finding new grounds to the east, but mainly they are there to suppress the pirates."

"Pirates, eh? I find it hard to believe there are pirates, unless we're talking about a few scoundrels who need no booty but the occasional wanderer or fisherman they can snap up. Such a freebooter, I think, would be *very* thin and hungry."

Janela thought, then got it, grinning.

"If there's pirates," I went on, "there must be victims, just as sharks must have schools of fish to feed on. These victims must live to the east . . ."

Janela finished for me: ". . . and so the pirates would have some familiarity with those lands as well."

"Am I not brilliant, O Lady?" I said, trying to sound as smug as possible.

"Brilliant, lovable, and *most* humble, Lord Antero," she said, and there began our plan.

The spell we began with was, I immodestly thought, equally subtle. We assumed any self-respecting sea robber would have some access to sorcery, rather than sailing hither and yon hoping for victims to sail blindly into range. Having had, I've sometimes felt, more than my share of encounters with pirates over the years, I know that corsairs *never* chance battle with an armed and watchful ship. Pirates, in spite of the romance of the name and all the ballads, are no more than back-alley cutthroats. No footpad will ever consider going after the purse of a man with a sword, but will wait for women, cripples, and drunkards to batten on.

Even though our three ships weren't battlecraft, we still might appear too warlike, so the spell was cast.

Actually, there would be two spells, Janela decided. The first spell was intended for the pirate's seers, if they had any, and the second would ride atop it and was a spell of belief, so no one witnessing the phenomenon we were about to produce could have the slightest doubt. Just as I held the visible weaponry of pirates in contempt, Janela took their sorcerers less than seriously.

"Why," she said, "would any villainous sorcerer of any talent take up a salt-soaked, water-logged trade that generally finishes at the end of a rope when they could practice dry, warm, safe evil as pet wizard for some baron?"

A wide brass bowl was filled with seawater. Into the water Janela sprinkled herbs of vision. The bowl was placed in the center of a circle scribed in blue on the deck, and then a red compass rose drawn over it with symbols at each point.

"This is interesting," Janela said. "I've never had occasion to try this, at least not at sea. I did something like this once when I was, shall we say, leaving a certain kingdom posthaste and wished to convince my pursuers I'd taken a side track."

"Did it work, my lady?" Quatervals asked. We were both helping prepare her magical necessaries.

Janela waggled a hand. "Mostly. Or somewhat, anyway. The count's soldiery thundered up a dead-end canyon just as I'd wished, thinking I was trapped. Unfortunately, the magic also drew some sort of creature down from the heights who decided I must be his. I *hoped* it was just for dinner, but I fear not. It took some interesting . . . convincements before he allowed me to continue on my way."

"Got to watch folks who live in the mountains," Quatervals put in. "Demons or people. Anybody who likes the sort of place where what ain't straight up is straight down probably don't look at things same as others."

"Spoken like a true mountaineer," I said. "Are we ready?"

"I think so."

Janela positioned herself over the brass bowl and pointed to the compass points while reciting an incantation under her breath. She beckoned when she finished.

"Careful you don't step on any of the lines of force," she warned.

I leaned over and looked down into the bowl.

The water had become mirrorlike, and on it sailed three tiny replicas of our ships.

"This is the truth," she said. "Now for the lie."

Beside her on the deck were two tiny ships that'd been carved by the ship's carpenter. They bore no resemblance to ours, but rather to small carracks favored in Vacaan. Janela'd said she had no idea what sort of ships would be favored on the far shores but thought it likely they might be the same as those used by the sailors of Vacaan. The carpenter had cleverly fitted them with tiny mast and sails and then, at Janela's instructions, cut and gouged them.

"They'll appear to be storm-damaged and near-helpless," she explained. "We're using two instead of three, so even the most cautious privateer will slaver at the thought of taking us."

She floated the models on the bowl, then carefully sliced gela-
tin, made from the sun-dried swimming bladder of a fish, and
floated that across the water. It dissolved and the image changed, as
if waves of heat were rising between us and the bowl. She added
more herbs to the water, among them dried bloodroot and rhodo-
dendron. Then she chanted:

"The eyes reach out

Look far
Look long
See this
Just this.

Ships long at sea
Ships off their course
Ships weak and torn.

The eyes reach out
The eyes take in

They see your prey
They see it clear.

You cannot turn
You must not turn
You wish not to turn
Come to us
Come to us."

She beckoned, and again I looked into the bowl. Now I saw
two battered merchant ships crawling through the sea. I fancied I
could see brown, ripped sails, dangling lines, and even helpless sailors sprawled on their decks.

"I'll just seal this," Janela said, looking quite satisfied with her
work, as she should have, "and we can clean up and turn Captain
Kele's deck back to her."

"Then we wait for the pirates, my lady?" Quatervals asked.

"Just so."

"I like this," Quatervals admired. "First ambush I've ever set on the open sea."

"If it works," she said. "If it doesn't . . . we could sail on until we run out of ocean, or else be ambushed ourselves by a fleet of corsairs determined to seize some rich booty that's being flaunted."

"That's what I love most about you, Janela," I murmured. "You're as much a romantic as your great-grandfather."

WE SAILED for another week and a half, seeing no other ships. Kele, the other captains, and I kept sharp ears out for discontent. Too often sailors on unknown seas far from land begin to fret. Worry can turn to mutiny in a instant. Again I was proud of our crews, because there was nothing more than the usual grumble about rations, weather, brackish water, not enough wine, and the rest, generally led by Pip. I was relieved—if there'd been nothing, I would've really worried, since the only sailor who doesn't bewail his present condition is either dead or seriously plotting.

I was especially pleased because these waters were so foreign. We saw things I'd never glimpsed before, nor had any of my mariners.

One day we saw a great mass floating nearby and altered course. It looked like some sort of jellyfish but covered almost fifty square yards, bobbing in the low swell, its loathsome translucency motionless.

"Not jellyfish," Kele opined. "Dead cuttlefish. Kilt by a whale, p'raps, an' floated up from the depths. Never seen one this big, though. Must be fair deep around here."

As we sailed past I looked back and saw a single monstrous eye blink open and then the mass silently sink beneath the surface.

We shouted the watch to stand-to and armed ourselves, but nothing happened. The beast, whatever it was, evidently had been peaceful.

A day or so later, drifting, our sails lowered until the wind changed again to blow toward the east, we encountered real jellyfish, but these were huge, nearly the size of a longboat. They had multicolored combs rising ten feet or more above the water, sails that sent them constantly moving downwind. I counted at least thirty of them before I gave up.

We sailed close enough so I could see, through the crystalline waters, tendrils hanging down into the depths. Tangled in the closest was some sort of fish, perhaps an albacore, but one almost seven feet long, I thought, allowing for the water's distortion. Somehow those tendrils could catch and kill, and so we steered a course well away from them and watched as they sailed on, downwind, west and south toward an undiscovered landfall.

We set out fishing lines, which kept our soldiers happy. The sailors, as always, would try only the most bland of whitefish, and that reluctantly. Any sea creature that was ugly or had dark flesh made them shudder. But that meant more for the rest of us, and let the seamen dine on salt beef from the casks.

One ceremony we did perform for all hands was the Gift of Tongues. When I was a boy, one thing that made a trader's life a bit tedious was the constant study of languages. Janos had taught me the least onerous way to learn a new language: find a bed partner gifted in that speech, and learning came somewhat joyously, especially when it came to naming body parts. Vacaan had removed that excuse for pleasure, though, with the magical Gift that was easily given with a small ceremony and a sorcerously treated clear sponge. One time when I'd done King Domas a particularly good turn, which I don't frankly remember the nature of, I'd begged leave of him for this knowledge. He'd considered well, then told me that since his people journeyed but little beyond their frontiers, he saw no harm, and so Orissan knowledge advanced another step.

Now, to make sure the Gift would work, we Orissans combined the knowledge of Vacaan with the magical elixir Rali had learned to make on her journey to the Kingdom of Konya, which required the addition of some local fruits, meats, or grains to work.

We'd brought the sponges with us from Orissa, and the local addition was provided by the first strange-looking bit of uptorn vegetation we saw that no one could identify, hence we assumed it came from the farther shore.

Then we continued our wait as we traveled on into the East.

* * *

ONE THING I missed was my bed companion. Of course, now far from Modin's leering eyes, Janela slept in her own cabin.

I thought wistfully from time to time of being back in Irayas and drowsing, half awake, in the depths of the night and hearing her soft breathing less than an arm's stretch away, and even of her head pillowed on my shoulder. That produced most unsettling dreams, however, and so when those thoughts intruded I did my best to force my mind into other channels.

Once Janela smiled as we were going below for the night, standing in her open door. "Sometimes," she said softly, "even the most dreadful sorcerer can bring a bit of good, I've learned." She went in and closed the door.

YET ANOTHER WEEK went by, and now we were far into the Eastern Sea.

It was early in the morning and Quatervals had our handful of soldiery and such sailors as were off watch turned out on deck. He'd asked Janela for a favor.

"My lady," he'd said, "I saw how you fought when that demon's tool Palic attacked you in Orissa. Never seen its like before. Maybe you'd show some of your tricks to these wretches I'm trying to batter int'a soldiery?"

Janela had hesitated, then agreed.

Now she stood on deck, assorted weapons lying on the deck beside her, and she'd picked Quatervals as her sparring opponent. The way she demonstrated her skills was unusual. Rather than the usual clash-clang-lunge of the practice yard, she moved very slowly, as if underwater, and asked Quatervals to do the same when he moved.

"It is in the eyes," she tried to explain. "You've got to watch the other man or woman always. Never look away. You'll see the sword stroke clear out of the corner of your eye and have time to counter. You have to *feel* your attacker coming at you. Quatervals, lunge slowly. Now, look, you men. See how his eyes widen as he readies himself. See how his right foot lifts slightly and how he shifts his muscles forward? See how his free arm moves automatically to the outside, both to block and to balance? Seeing that, it's easy to counterstrike or step aside. Watch that, learn that, move swiftly, and you know all I do."

"Damned hard," Maha, another of my crew who had called on the demon Senac, muttered.

"*Dying* is a lot harder."

Otavi looked stubborn, holding his axe in front of him like it was his private amulet. "I'll let 'em come to me. Man never goes wrong lettin' someone else go first."

Janela paid no mind to either comment but picked up a dagger from the deck.

"Quatervals, strike hard and at speed for my heart."

Quatervals considered, nodded, danced briefly sideways and struck. But just as it'd been on the *Ibis* that night some time ago, Janela simply wasn't there. She was turning, spinning like a dancer, and was just outside Quatervals' blocking right hand. She tapped his temple with her free hand, turned once more . . . and the point of the blade touched his neck. Her fist would've sent him sprawling, stunned, or her knife would've sent him to the Seeker.

"You see," she said, a bit impatiently, "the weapon *does not matter*. First is not to be there when the attacker lunges. Then you can take whatever measures you wish. You can fight, flee, or simply knock your enemy on his ass. Now, Quatervals, put them through the paces. Slowly. I'll watch."

She came back and slipped down on the deck beside me.

"Probably not that good an idea," she said softly to me.

"Why not?"

"I studied this technique for two full years before it began to take me. And I'm afraid Quatervals and the others don't understand that the importance is to feel what your enemy intends *and move in that instant as he attacks*. I know of no other way to put it, and the old one who instructed me in this craft told me I'd have the same trouble teaching others as he was in teaching me.

"Two years," she went on, "and then one day it clicked and I *felt* it."

I understood, slightly. "I can't see how any army could teach such a craft."

"No. Soldiers need to spend too much time polishing their armor and being body servants to their officers to actually have enough time for soldiering. Besides, it is near impossible for a soldier to accept that the skill, the art, is what is important, not the choice of weapon. If they learn but a part of what I know, say to prefer a sword or a poignard, they'll have learned less than nothing. Weapons are crutches and can make a man limp and continue their use even after the wound has healed. And another thing: This craft of mine works best when facing a real enemy, someone who intends deadly harm.

"Here, with none of these men meaning real danger, it's no more than a plaything. And even in moments of peril there are times the craft does not evince itself in time."

She touched the bridge of her nose where it'd been broken and never healed properly. Perhaps she was about to go on, but there came a cry from the masthead:

"Sail ho! Three points off the port bow!"

We'd found our pirates.

Or rather, they'd found us.

WE COUNTED ten lug sails, but it wasn't the disaster that might be thought. The sails were small, no larger than a fisherman's smack might raise. We were being attacked by a mosquito fleet. We'd had sufficient warning, since our lookout sat higher than any of their men, and so we had the honor of first sighting. Our hulls were still below their horizon and would be for some minutes.

I seized the advantage and ordered Kele to drop sail on the *Ibis* and for the *Firefly* and *Glowworm* to strike at full speed for our attackers. We knew them to be pirates or warcraft of some type because no one approaches a strange ship without taking due caution unless they intend harm.

Janela had already opened several of our bags of wind and they gusted hard, aided by the already-strong wind blowing from the south that made both our ships and the pirates' tack constantly to hold our converging courses.

Now we were nearly a mile behind our other two ships and had room enough to maneuver. We had the wind's advantage as well, as we changed to a heading of south-southeast, holding that for two turnings of our glass, then set a new course to due east and beat to windward as closely as the *Ibis* could manage. Kele herself had the helm and kept one eye on the tops'l and paid off the helm each time the sail began to back. My intent was to sail around the pirates and attack them on the flank by surprise as they became engaged with the *Firefly* and *Glowworm*.

I knew we'd made two sides of a triangle when we saw sails again, the two from the *Firefly* and *Glowworm* to our left, the sprinkle of time-aged canvas that was the pirates', and then something new. Far behind, to the northeast of the pirate sails, the lookout reported another ship. Dreading a fall but knowing I must see what was there, I chanced going up the ratlines myself.

The ship stood clear. It was larger and looked to be a three-master. That explained something I'd been curious about—just how the tiny pirate ships were able to sail so far from land, although I'd wondered if they'd set out from nearby islands. The larger craft was the mother ship.

I clambered down with care. Adventure isn't best served by slipping on a rope and braining yourself before battle is even mounted.

On deck I issued new orders—sail directly for the mother ship. Then we tried a new device Kele and Janela had developed and tested on the way out—a wonderful device that worked three times out of five.

They'd had the *Firefly*'s sailmaker choose a good piece of light cloth. On it, each of our normal signal flags was painted in miniature three times, duplicates of the full-size signal bunting we used normally to sign from ship to ship. Then these minuscule flags, which might have been intended for a luxury craft on a boat pond, were cut apart, and spells were said over them by Janela. The theory was that they held similarity and to do something with one flag would cause the others to react.

It did. Sometimes.

Now we laid out four of these miniature flags: Full Sail, East, Follow, and Attack. Janela picked each of them up and said:

"Speak now
Speak to your sister
Call her name
Make her heed."

She gently shook each one, then set it down. She sent this message four times.

If Berar and Towra had their wits with them, they would see the matching flags move on the racks that were mounted next to their ships' binnacles, fill in the blanks, and bypass the pirate boats, which shouldn't be too hard if they held full sail and had their boarding nets raised. The pirates were in for a surprise anyway, since our initial plan had armed men hiding under the bulwarks until the last minute. On order, they were to volley into the corsairs, hoping to shatter them on first contact, then destroy them singly while the raiders reeled in dismay at having walked into a trap. But now I wanted my other two ships to follow me and hit the mother craft.

All this might be thought bravado or foolishness since we had but seventy-five men on all three ships. But I didn't think the pirates would have many more—they don't like to increase the number of shares of conquest any more than one of my contract traders does.

We had other advantages as well: Our ships were almost new, with clean bottoms to give us speed and maneuverability; my men were determined to conquer; and, finally, we had surprise on our side. Nothing shocks the ambusher, as Quatervals had known, more than being ambushed himself.

Our ship was hard on its lee as we closed on the mother ship, sails hard in the wind and water smoke curling past our bows, and now we could make out our opponent fair. I nearly laughed aloud, seeing that my opinion was confirmed. The sea rover's ship was dirty, old, barely more than a hulk. It was large, probably once a merchantman, and did have three sails. It resembled a type of ship I'd seen often in Valaroi called a flute, although it was different enough so no one would think it'd ever been constructed in a familiar yard.

It would serve well to berth the small boats the pirates used to board a victim and carry them back to whatever dark port they sailed from, but little more. Again, I was unsurprised—thieves never spend time or money polishing their swords or making sure their clubs are sound. The only time a villain will carry a soldierly kept weapon is when he's stolen it from that poor private's body.

Kele held her course full at the side of the pirate as if intending to ram. Now we were close enough to hear yelps of alarm, and slowly, laboriously, the ship began to come about. I could see but few men on the decks—of course most of them would be off with the raiders. At the last moment Kele put the helm over until we were sailing nearly parallel but still closing course on the vessel. Kele's chief mate Ceram shouted to the men aloft and we dropped sail and pulled level with the pirate. My sword was ready in my hand. I looked at Janela, and she had her blade out, a tight grin without humor on her face.

Quatervals shouted and three men hurled grapnels over, prongs digging deep into the flute's bulwarks. Then they were pulling us together, whipping grapnel lines firm around bollards, and Quatervals led the boarding party over the rails. Janela and I were just behind, and we fanned out on either side of the wedge Quatervals had his few soldiers formed into. Otavi bashed a man with the flat of his axe, and he staggered into the long dagger Pip preferred, and dropped, his guts coming away as he fell. I saw Chons, pulling his blade out of another corpse, then a man poked at me clumsily, not even a thrust, with a halberd, and I brushed the blade away and cut him down as another man slashed with a cutlass. I ducked neatly under it and spitted him.

"The bridge!" I shouted. "Take the bridge!" And we were running, only a few standing against us, and going up the companionway to the quarterdeck. There were two men and a woman there, the woman at the helm; one of the men stood on guard, weaving his blade like the skilled swordsman he was.

"Beg quarter and you'll live," I bellowed, and that made them hold for an instant, as I knew it would. Coast guard ships or naval vessels *never* let captured pirates live, and few of them even see trial before they're dancing on the thinnest of air at the end of a yardarm.

The swordsman spat defiance and came at me, but Janela was between us. Her blade flicked, shone in the now-noon sun, flicked once more, brushing his lunge aside and darting out like a serpent striking, deep into the muscle of the man's arm. He shouted in pain and dropped his blade. Then he stood waiting for Janela's death-blow. Instead:

"Beg quarter, you fool," she snarled, holding, ready to cut him down if he made any motion other than the one he eventually did—holding out both hands, palms up.

Others on the decks saw him and there were shouts and the clatter of weapons falling and a chorus of voices crying "Quarter, quarter" in a medley of languages, and we had the pirates.

Ceram was at the flagstaff, pulling down the banner the pirates called a flag—it was black, of course, with a shark's jaws in white, and I had a moment to wonder who in the hells was still back on the *Ibis*, since everyone seemed to be in the boarding party, and then I saw the *Glowworm* and *Firefly* sailing toward us, hotly pursued by the pirate ships they'd refused to battle.

The discussion that would begin now might be most interesting.

THE PIRATE CAPTAIN, a few years younger than myself, was completely unremarkable and would be taken as a struggling merchant ship officer in any port in the world, with one exception—he had a red scar circling his neck. His proper name was Lerma, but one of his men said he was also known as "Half-hanged," since someone or other in his past had almost rid the seas of a rogue.

He was almost charming for a murderous thief. I had him, his mate, and his helmsman bound and left on the foredeck while we dealt with the others.

The pirates in the small boats hadn't put up much of a struggle, particularly since we not only held the heights by being aboard ships with decks above their small boats, but also since we had the only vessels that stood a chance of weathering the next storm aboard.

I ordered them aboard the flute, which I was told went by the charming name of *Searipper*. I put them in the ship's waist and lined the forecastle and quarterdeck with archers. I told them they were prisoners and since they'd surrendered would be shown quarter. But if any of them even breathed heavily, my mercy, such as it was, would be withdrawn. I asked who their wizard was, and one man told me he'd been killed when we boarded the ship.

I had my men go through the ship's hold and belowdecks and

bring up anything of value or any weapons. There was an amazing pile of death-dealing merchandise but very little in the way of gold or jewels.

"Bein' a pirate's hard cess in these seas, eh," Quatervals observed jovially to Half-hanged Lerma.

Lerma scowled, but his mate, the duelist, a scarred murderer who called himself Feather, glowered and muttered that the gods had been against them for nigh a year and this was just the final stroke.

"Ah, then," I said, seeing an opportunity, "since we happen to be well-blessed by the gods, your willingness to help us will no doubt put you back in their graces."

Both of them gave me a look of utter disbelief. I shrugged—it'd been worthwhile to see if they happened to be superstitious. Even if they weren't, the planting of the idea would do little harm.

Now that there was nothing belowdecks the pirates could use for weaponry to try to retake their ship, we herded them into the hold and nailed the hatchways firmly shut.

That left only Lerma, Feather, and the helmswoman, who squatted nearby, dully waiting for whatever would happen to happen. She might have been decent-looking once; I thought her most likely to be the daughter of some fisherman kidnapped from her village and then promoted for her seafaring abilities and possibly other talents.

I had Feather and the woman sent to the cabins in the stern and kept separated.

While all this was going on, Quatervals was busy. He'd found a small brazier and started a fire in it, adding coal as it built. Whistling merrily, he laid out a selection of implements found on deck— sail needles of various sizes, some metal splicing fids, a pike, a coil of rope, tongs, a cook's cleaver—and then, with Otavi's help, lifted a grating and lashed it to the rail. Janela and I had remained silent, and Lerma's eyes kept following Quatervals. The man wasn't stupid, and it didn't take long for all those implements, the grating that Lerma himself no doubt used for floggings, and the brazier to suggest something:

"You gave me quarter," the pirate captain said hoarsely.

"Quarter means your life," I said casually. "It does not necessarily guarantee you life with a full complement of the usual accessories such as eyes, fingers, or even legs."

"Besides," Janela said, "since when is it wrong to break your word to a murderer and a thief?"

Lerma looked deep into our eyes, and I did my best to look like someone who generally spent dull afternoons at sea torturing pirates—evidently with some success, because he paled, the rope burn on his neck standing out even more vividly.

"Who are you?"

"Seekers of the truth," I said. "Wanderers of the sea. Perhaps if you share some of your seafaring knowledge with us . . . most interesting benefits might come your way."

"Such as," Quatervals put in, "seeing the sun rise on the morrow."

"What do you want to know?" The question was guarded. Lerma wasn't quite broken.

"What lies east? What land? What's it like? What are the landfalls? What are the people like? What about hostile cities? Is it civilized?"

"How'll you know I'll tell you . . . and if I do tell you, that it'll be the truth?"

"Even without my friend there with the convincers," I said, "all we need do, once we've finished with you, is put you in a nice quiet cabin and call your friends up here. If their answers differ from yours, well, we'll be *very* disappointed. So disappointed, shall we say, that each lie will cost a finger, then a toe, and then we'll consider the possibilities when we've run out of digits."

"Even if somehow you and your friend manage to connive at the same lie," Janela put in, "*I* shall know. I am a wizard." And she stretched out a hand toward Lerma, a gentle, caressing woman's hand. She ran her other hand over it, and suddenly that woman's hand became the green-clawed talons of a demon. Lerma shrieked and tried to roll away. Then Janela's hand was quite normal.

"Anything you want," he stammered then. "I'll not lie. I have charts, some charts anyway, in my cabin. I'll show you. Anything you need—all you have to do is ask."

I had Quatervals cut Lerma free and lift him to his feet. "There is no reason," I said, "this discussion cannot be handled in a civilized manner. We'll join you below."

As Quatervals muscled Lerma to the companionway I had a question for Janela.

"How did you do *that*? The hand, I mean."

Janela smiled, a very mysterious, very superior smile. "Don't you remember what your sister wrote? That all magic is smoke and mirrors and fumadiddle?"

I nodded. "Very well, then." And we went after Quatervals.

BY DUSK we'd drained Lerma as thoroughly as a sailor drains his last wineskin. He knew much, which I'd thought likely, since any pirate who's successful must know not the ocean deeps, but the shorelines and inlets where he can hide or lurk and the people he either must avoid or can prey on.

The far shore was peopled, of course. We first asked Lerma about great civilizations. There weren't any that he knew of, at least none that could put out coast patrols as feared as those from Vacaan, which was one reason he preferred to keep his villainy here in the east. The people living along the coast were fishermen, farmers, and some small traders. He'd heard stories of fabulous cities, like any traveler does, but none of the tales had borne out.

Janela nodded. This was as it should be, as her stories had promised.

Next we asked about old ruins, tales of cities stricken by the gods. Lerma said the land was full of these, of how man had once been next to the gods but had fallen mightily for his sins.

"I put no store in those stories," he said, "because if you're a god, who's going to punish you for sinnin'? Other gods? Not a virgin's chance at an orgy, since they'd be too busy dippin' their own wicks an' carryin' on an' stabbin' their own sets of enemies' backs to worry about you. The gods is gods, men is men. What we is, is what we is and what we've allus been."

We ignored his theological lesson and asked specifically about ruins. There were many of these, Lerma said.

"But I never paid 'em mind, since old stone don't spend real well in a tavern. We landed in a couple lookin' for treasure but found nothin'. They'd been looted out clean long afore any of us come squallin' out of our wombs."

A memory came and he hunched his shoulders, as if a chill wind had blown through the cabin.

"There was one different," he said. "We'd heard stories about it, an' one time me an' some other cap'ns thought the tales might bear fruit. We got close enough to see, but somethin' turned us away."

"What? You were attacked? You saw ghosts? Demons?"

"No. Nothin' even *that* real. Not even dreams. Just I knew, an' all of us knew at the same time, that if we went ashore where that great river met the sea, we'd leave our bones."

"Where is it?" Janela was most excited.

"My lady," Lerma said, "we weren't dreamin' nor afeared. What we felt was true. I knew it then, I know it now. I don't wish that on you."

"I asked a question."

Lerma stared at her, shrugged, and went to the table where his charts were laid out. Charts were perhaps the wrong word since that implies they were accurate navigational tools. They were sketchy, imprecise, with long blank areas, scribbles, question marks, and obvious inexactitudes. Lerma muttered for a moment, then his finger stabbed.

" 'Bout here. It don't show on the map but there's a river runs inland. Big river, damned near a day's sail across its mouth. Ain't that navigable, bar's blocking most of its mouth an' it's bad silted up. But here on the north bank there's a stone statue. Sticks straight up like it'd been a lighthouse or something. Man—or demon-built. It's just at the end of a mole. That's where we was gonna sail into and anchor and see what was what.

"Never even got within a mile, though, 'fore we knew we didn't belong here. We sailed on without even sending a boat ashore, and looked for other places for our pleasurin'." He shivered at the memory.

I was about to speak but Janela shook her head and told Quatervals to take Lerma out. Before he was led away she took a bit of his hair, a smear of blood from a small wound, and a dab of saliva.

When Lerma was beyond earshot, Janela got out her own chart.

"Look. Here. Somewhere still north of where we are, see this?"

I read her small writing: *Jayotosha tribe shaman reported dreams. Far shore. River. City. Cursed. Old Ones. Dread of what lies upriver. Something great, beyond good, beyond evil.*

"A river, a city," I said. "Not the heart of the Kingdom, but a port, perhaps? Maybe the Old Ones liked to live upriver, away from the storms and sea raiders? Could that have been their style? When they came across to what we call Vacaan now, did they deliberately look for a navigable river to base themselves on?"

Janela shook her head. "I don't know. But we have one piece of a puzzle that matches another piece of another puzzle very closely."

"And the spell," I said, "assuming Lerma's telling the truth, would be something that could be left hanging over such a ruined city."

"Perhaps. But if there is one, it will hardly be worth concerning ourselves over. It'll be easy to cast a counterspell so we won't even notice such a warning."

Janela paced the deck, barely able to contain her excitement. Then she burst out: "Do we have it, Lord Antero?"

I smiled—I'd been hard-pressed to keep from letting out a whoop like I was fifty years younger, and managed to maintain some degree of stuffiness. That broke and I too did a small dance on the deck.

"After due consideration I think we have it, Lady Greycloak."

Our hands met over the small dot on the chart.

BY FULL DARK we sailed on, having taken measures to ensure that our piratical friends would be harmless, at least for a while. After questioning them we'd taken blood, hair, and sputum samples from both Feather and the helmswoman. The woman knew nothing about this city: it had been before she joined them. Feather knew well and confirmed Lerma's tale.

We assembled the three and showed them the samples. Janela

said if the tales were false or if they'd forgotten to tell us of some hazard, before the demons took us down she'd have more than enough time to cast a spell that would hunt the seas of the world for the three of them. They swore honesty, fidelity, and truth, having to scrabble about in their minds for something to swear on that wouldn't make us chortle in complete disbelief.

We let the pirates out of the hold and bade them watch what we were doing. We sank all of the raiding boats save three which might be needed for lifeboats if their hulk sank. All of the weapons were tossed overside except for four daggers. Those four Quatervals put point first between deck planking and snapped off the points, so they were no longer weapons but sailors' tools. All of the wine, all of the brandy, went overboard. A single set of sails was all I left, enough for them to return to whatever port they called home. There was a low moan when the pirates saw their tiny treasure transferred to our ships. I cared little for such gold, but I wanted these rogues humiliated and broken.

Finally we had each of them pass down a line of armed men. As with their leaders, a bit of hair and blood was taken from each and put in one of our empty windbags. A few of the corsairs tried to fight, but they were quickly clubbed into submission.

That was all. We boarded our own ships. I stood at the rail of the *Ibis* and told the pirates they were in my thrall. I was true to my word and had not only granted them quarter but now their freedom. They were to go and find honest trades. If they did not . . . I waved the bag full of bloodstained tufts above my head. There were mutters and moans. I paid no heed, but turned away and ordered Kele to set a course east-northeast.

We watched the *Searipper* until it was a dot on the horizon.

"Y'think," Otavi said, and I started, since the burly man seldom spoke unless asked a direct question, "*all* of 'em'll take up work, or just some? Figurin' you'll hold true to your oath an' spellbind 'em?"

Janela and I began laughing. She picked up the bag holding the pirates' locks and cast it overside.

Otavi watched it bob away in our wake, then he too grinned.

"I guess, followin' you around, Lord Antero, I'd best not spend much time tryin' to convince myself people're any better'n they are or ever will be, eh?"

THIRTEEN DAYS crawled leadenly past.

The wind held true, blowing into the east, and the seas were fairly calm. But still our voyage seemed to be taking forever. It grew hot, muggy, and I thought I could smell the dark, heavy scent of the jungle. Janela, as promised, did cast a guardian spell over our men to prevent needless worry.

On the fourteenth dawn I awoke to the cry: "Land! Land ho! Land firm dead ahead!"

I pulled on clothing and dashed on deck but even in my haste was still among the last to reach it. Janela wore no more than a wrap, I thought perhaps her bedspread, but neither she nor I nor anyone else paid mind to her near-nakedness.

Beyond our bows was a river's mouth so vast I could not see but one shore to our north. The land ahead was green, tropical, jungled.

Far in the distance, so far it was but a blue presence on the horizon, lifted a monstrous mountain range.

I could make out no details at all, let alone crags that might be the Fist of the Gods.

Closer, though, standing out from the shoaling ocean, was the white finger of the monolith.

CITY OF
THE DOOMED

A s we neared the monolith, an ice storm of recognition blew out of my past. It was an immense statue of a woman warrior. She was remarkably beautiful, even though time's blight had pocked the stone that made her. In her hand she held aloft the stub of a broken sword.

Beside me I heard Janela ask Kele: "Do you suppose it was once a lighthouse?"

The captain made some response but I wasn't listening. Instead I was remembering when I'd first seen that image. It had been in moonlight and I'd been in a carriage, instead of aboard a ship. I had been summoned to Prince Raveline's palace, and as I approached that black wizard's abode I was suddenly confronted with two stone guardians whose visages were so cold and pitiless that they struck dread instead of wonder at their otherworldly beauty. It had been long ago and Raveline was dead, but when I viewed the statue at the harbor's entrance once again, I felt fear buzz a viper's warning in my breast.

We sailed past the monolith, the mole beside us, and I heard the others gasp when they saw the statue's opposite side. I turned, although I didn't need to look to know what they had seen. Like Raveline's guardians, the woman had a second face, looking to the rear, and that face was a leering, fanged demon. And as I had on that long-ago night when conspiracy and betrayal stirred in dank winds, I wondered if the artist who carved the original had worked from imagination—or real life.

I shook off the web of an old man's memory and took stock. The river mouth we were sailing into was truly immense—I saw something in the distance that might have been the blur of the other bank. The channel was honeycombed with sandbars that had built up over the ages, making navigation difficult. I speculated that the original inhabitants had posted guards at the statue so anyone attempting to sail upstream would have had to pay whatever toll those who held it demanded. Some of the bars were so large that the river had long ago given up the fight to breach them and they'd become small islands dotted with clumps of trees and brush.

From the statue a mole stretched toward land. Although the rocks that formed it still stood, in many places time and weather had broken through. The harbor entrance was a funnel with the mole on one side and sandbars on the other, making it not much wider than the statue's hundred-foot height. The channel belled out so it looked like fish traps children set in the shallows to catch bait. The shape had certainly been planned by its builders. A seaborne enemy would have been easily bottled up, then picked off one by one.

The defenders of the harbor, however, were long gone. In most places thick jungle had invaded whatever riverfront had once existed. The delta heat was intense, and a thick mist shimmered up from the water, bearing the odor of rot. Clouds of insects buzzed through the mist, pursued by colorful birds that swooped and shrieked as they snatched up their small prey. Big, heavy-jawed lizards humped up from the mud banks to watch us with yellow eyes, and swarms of monkeys mocked from the trees. Here and there I could make out stone stumps that'd once been the legs of piers, and the bones of old dockside buildings made an ideal trellis for fleshy vines that wormed in and out of the ruins.

Janela nudged me. "Over there," she whispered—it was the sort of place where one instinctively spoke in wary tones.

Some distance inland rose the ruins of an ancient city, strangling in the jungle's grip. Here at the end of the mole would have been the customs and guard posts, I imagined, and on more defensible ground the city itself. It was a grim gateway to the river beyond.

My skin prickled and I saw Janela frown with effort as she pushed out with her magical senses.

"Do you sense any threat?" I asked.

Her frown deepened, then she shook her head. "I can't say with certainty, Amalric," she said. "There was once much suffering here. A battle, perhaps. And magic. Of the blackest kind. But it happened long ago."

"As long ago as the Old Ones?" I asked, thinking of the monolith—and Raveline's guardians.

"Yes," she said after a moment. "Perhaps as long as that."

"Let's give it a miss," Kele said. "Find another landin' place."

I wanted to agree, to give the order that would have us all hoist sail and sniff down the coast for a more pleasant entrance to these eastern shores.

I did not like this place. It seemed a realm of short life spans and vengeful ghosts.

But Janela plucked a set of bones from her purse and knelt to cast them on the deck. I heard their dry rattle and saw the shape they made when they came to rest. Perhaps it was my excited imagination, but to me they did not look unlike the statue's demon face.

She looked up, eyes glittering. "This is where we *must* begin," she said.

Kele growled but went to work with a will as I issued the orders. The people of the Pepper Coast are a fatalistic lot.

"B'sides," I heard her chastise a griping sailor, "only a lummox wi' a boil fer head an' pus fer brains w'd be arguin' wi' a bone caster."

I wished I had her confidence. It *has* occurred to me from time to damp-palmed time to wonder why one would think nothing of checking the dice when a fat purse is at stake, but never question a wizard when one's skin depended on the outcome of the toss.

WE LANDED with caution. Janela and I were to take a small force toward the heart of the city, consisting of Pip, Otavi, three of Quatervals' Scouts, and four tough country lads—the Cyralian brothers—known for their skills as stalkers and bowmen.

We would strike for the city and, I warned Kele and Quatervals, most likely would be forced to remain there until the next day, since I had no intention of discovering what surprises the jungle between us might hold after nightfall.

Our three ships would hold back for any waterborne threat, and Quatervals would stand ready with a landing party. If we had not returned to the beach by mid-morning, or if he heard the sounds of battle in the night, he was to come to our support at first light.

He heatedly disagreed with the arrangement, saying it was his place to be by my side. I said we expected little difficulty—whatever enemies might lurk in the jungle could be subdued with the Cyralian brothers' bows and Janela's magic.

Besides, I wanted the bulk of my fighters to stay on the ships with an experienced leader to command them. I had no desire to be stranded afoot before our journey had truly begun. Quatervals mentioned those small flags that Janela and Kele had devised, but Janela shook her head, saying they wouldn't work in a place seeping with so much ancient sorcery.

He didn't like our arguments and I'm certain he had ample retorts at hand. But I was in no mood to be challenged, and so he wisely held his tongue and did as I wished.

We beached our boat on a narrow, muddy shelf. There was a short, brush-clogged stairwell leading up from the shelf, and from there we could make out what had been a road leading to the city. Quickly, Janela set up a small, brass tripod. I gingerly handed her the decorative pot, filled with smoldering magical embers that I'd juggled on my lap since we left the ship. She slung it from the tripod, swung around, and began gathering bits from the ground:

moss skinned from a rock, a dry leaf that had fallen from a tree, a small, green beetle that scurried from under that leaf when she lifted it.

As she worked I felt a stirring, as if *things* were coming awake from an uneasy sleep. I heard the low mutter of many voices and looked reflexively about, as did the other members of our party. But there was nothing to be seen. To one side something heavy stirred in the thick brush that filled the stairwell. Acting as one, the Cyralian brothers lifted their bows. Meanwhile the others had drawn their swords or raised their spears and moved forward to make certain the brothers had time to practice their deadly skills.

The brush parted violently. An enormous shadow pushed through. It was not a thing of substance or flesh. I could make out the jungle behind it, although dimly, so dark was our visitor. It raised what I could only call a head. A hole opened where a mouth might be. A chorus of voices boomed out, as if the shape were made of many souls.

The form stepped forward—we could see the impressions of huge footprints in the mud.

"Steady," I told the men.

It kept moving forward, mud oozing out from its weight. It came slowly but with steps so large that it could only be moments before it was on us.

The brothers bent their bows.

"Not yet," I said.

Janela was at the tripod, dropping the moss, beetle, and other things into the flaming pot. A bitter-smelling smoke boiled up.

The shape kept coming and the voices were growing louder and louder.

I heard Janela chant:

"Old Ones.
Old Ghosts.
We come for knowledge.
We come to admire.
Wanderers from the West,
Where you once ruled."

The dark shape came to a halt a few feet from our formation. The voices dipped to a low muttering.

Janela dribbled water from a vial into the pot's embers. It was from our river in Orissa.

Flames sheeted up, so bright they hurt my eyes. I rubbed them, then looked about and saw that the shadowy form was gone.

Pip placed his boot in one of the muddy prints. It was swallowed, with room to spare.

An impish smirk glittered through his scraggly beard. "Twice mine, easy," he said. "I'm thinkin' we oughta get double shares for this bit o' work, lads." The men snickered.

The tallest and youngest of the brothers eyed Pip up and down. It wasn't a long journey. "I'd say you was right," he said. "But, *everythin's* twice yer size, Pip! Lord Antero'd be outter coin afore we even started this bitty walk in the green."

Somewhere, a jungle beast howled.

Pip grimaced. "Some walk in the green," he said.

We all laughed, a little more heartily, perhaps, than the jest deserved.

Janela ignored the byplay. She was setting up another spell, dipping into that wondrous purse of hers and laying out vials and small pouches on her cloak, which she'd spread on the ground next to the tripod. The drabber side was turned down so all the bright Evocators' symbols were displayed.

It came to me that she'd acted mere moments before there was even a sign of a threat.

"Did you know what would happen?"

"No," she said. "I only knew *something* would happen. And then I made a most fortunate guess. Thank Te-Date we only had to face a few cranky old ghosts. If it'd been a demon, like the late Lord Senac, we would've been in for it."

"Thank you for setting my mind at ease," I gritted.

Janela laughed, full of youthful daring and confidence. "Never fear," she said. "I'm sure I would have thought of something. I hope."

She pumped a tiny bellows, relighting the embers in the pot. Then a sprinkle of herb, a splash of magical oils, and there was a lively, colorful blaze pleasantly crackling and smoking in the vessel.

I wondered what she was about and surprised myself when I realized I was studying her lithe form and graceful motions with less than grandfatherly interest. Apparently my renewed vigor had revived more than the color of my hair and beard. It embarrassed me, and when I saw her give me an odd look, I covered by asking what she was doing.

"If we're going to investigate the city," she said, "we'll need some sort of a guide."

She crumpled parchment into a ball, chanting:

"The power of the gods
Never dies
But is transformed
And waits for those
Who seek."

Janela dropped the ball into the fire. It exploded into flame and she shouted, "Behold, the Seeker!"

Her arms shot up and the fiery ball rose from the embers until it floated just in front of her face. She blew on it and it began to turn, faster and faster, until it was a blur, like the spindle of a busy yarn maker. Then it shot away, as if it had a life of its own. It darted into the old stairwell, firing the brush, which burned so quickly that in a few blinks of an eye it was nothing but ash. The burning ball hovered over it as if waiting.

"All we need do is follow it," Janela said. She started repacking her things.

"To what end?" I asked.

Janela shook out her cloak. The air stirred and I caught the cool scent of spring blossoms.

"There would have been a seat of power," she said. "A throne or a place where the most important spells were performed. I'm hoping enough of a magical residue is left for us to sniff it out."

She rolled the cloak into a blanket roll, pulled a leather strap from her purse, and slung the cloak across her back.

The parchment ball wiggled back and forth and bobbed up and down, trailing off a fat smoke tail so it looked like an impatient puppy.

I laughed at its antics. Janela grinned. "I thought I'd try something different for a Favorite. My wizard teachers always invoked the same grim little things, with fangs and talons and scales."

"You forgot to mention evil dispositions and even worse body odor," I said.

"That, too," she said. "Mean-souled Favorites have their place, I guess, but in this case it doesn't hurt to have a little fun."

The grins of the men bore her out, and even Pip's grousing was of a light tone as they all formed up and we headed for the city.

The parchment ball shot up over the stairwell and we followed, picking our way through the broken and upturned pavement of what had once been a broad main road leading up from the harbor.

You could still make out the big promenade that had once been a teeming marketplace with fresh food and exotic wares from all over the Old Ones' empire. The road led to an enormous entrance— gates long gone—and the ground and thick walls were smooth black, and buckled as if broken by an enormous force, then fused by intense heat. Our little fiery guide hesitated, then soared above the walls.

"I think it wants us to climb," Janela said.

So, climb we did, scrambling and slipping on the smooth surface as we mounted the wall. At the top it was wide enough for freight wagons to pass with ease, and we could make out the wreckage of towers placed strategically along the wall. The entire city would have been enclosed by this wall, an almost impregnable barrier. It stretched before us, its streets now clogged with vegetation, many of its buildings tumbled off their foundations, while jungle trees had burst through others to tower over the remains. Far away on the opposite side of the city a double-domed structure loomed up. Burnished metal reflected the midmorning sun, glaring at us.

The parchment ball swung toward the domes, and we followed its course, keeping on the top of the walls and curving around the city toward our goal.

* * *

THE CITY had once been a grand metropolis, with broad avenues, pleasant parks, and spacious public baths fed by crisp underground springs. The buildings were made of thick stone faced with white marble. Some were tall, some long and low-slung, but all bore the mark of master builders at their prime. Here and there were the remains of frescoes and wondrous statuary hailing the exploits of a graceful people, people of taste, people of spirit. People who were doomed. Now the city was Hag Misery's corpse. Jungle choked her streets. Vines with spindly brown roots ravaged the marble facing. Beasts stalked the parks, and from the safety of the high walls we saw a troop of baboons warring with a pack of jackals in one of the bathhouses.

The scars of war showed us, as we circumnavigated the city, that she had not died a natural death. Buildings had been blasted, stone crushed and fused by the city's besiegers. Idols of their gods and heroes had been toppled. Inside the barren ground of what had once been an arena we looked down and saw some scattered human bones. For this many to have survived the eons meant there'd been a bleak slaughter that history should well have remembered.

It was frightening to see how the Old Ones—despite all their mythical powers and knowledge—had been humbled. Who had been their enemies? Did they still exist somewhere? And what had been the nature of the wrong the Old Ones had committed, whether real or imaginary, to earn such terrible repayment?

I was roasting those hard nuts in my mind when I heard a hooting erupt from the brush-filled streets below. We all stopped to see, weapons at ready. Another hoot answered the first, but it seemed to come from a greater distance.

"Over there!" Janela said.

I swiveled my head just in time to see a glimpse of a brawny, fur-covered arm.

"Some sort of animal," I guessed.

"Better'n ghosts, my lord," Pip said. "If he 'n' his mates get too close like, I can allus fire a warnin' shot 'tween 'is ooglers."

His jaw snapped shut with a loud click as a whole chorus of hooting broke out, as if in answer to his boasting.

There was thunder of many wings as frightened birds took

flight. The ever-present shrieks of the monkeys suddenly stopped, and we were left in silence broken only by the constant buzz of insects.

"Their cries seem to have come from behind us," Janela said, which might be a threat to an easy retreat if it became necessary.

I pointed to the domes, now only about a fifteen-minute march ahead. "It's just as easy to keep going, then," I said.

We moved on, but with no gawking and at a quicker pace. Off and on the hooting would resume, but always from the rear or to the sides. We didn't catch another glimpse of our stalkers—if that's what they were—although sometimes we heard the sound of running feet and crackling brush.

Finally we came to where we would have to leave the relative safety of the walls. Just below and ahead of us was an overgrown park. Beyond the park—perhaps two hundred feet away—were the domes. They sat upon a still towering structure, with broad, broken steps leading to a gaping dark eye of an entrance. The parchment ball, smoke tail streaming out, dodged across the park. It reached the steps, hovered there for a moment, then flame exploded up and out . . . and our guide disappeared in a puff of smoke.

We'd reached our destination.

We came down from the wall cautiously, one group guarding the other as we descended.

The heat didn't lessen as we went on into the deep shadows of the trees, although the sense of danger grew. My nape prickled and my sword hand ached from clutching the grip so tight. But we crossed the park into the courtyard without incident.

Pip and two men went up the steps and checked the interior of the building while we waited in a protective knot at the bottom. They were gone a long time, but there was no conversation between us, nor did we marvel at the remains of a strange statue that littered the yard, but only looked to see what would make good cover.

Pip hailed us and said all was safe.

Once again, as if mocking him, the hooting erupted. But this time the sound was right on us. We had only time to blink before we were attacked.

They weren't men, they weren't beasts—but the worst of both.

Gray, shambling figures boiled out of the brush, screaming that eerie war cry. They had huge, hunched shoulders, arms the size of a large man's torso, and slope-browed heads with snarling yellow teeth and bloodred eyes. They were armed with stone-headed axes and thick, knobbed clubs. I heard the Cyralian brothers unleash a volley, and four of the creatures died with hoarse cries. But a score or more swarmed over their bodies. Then they were on us. An immense paw reached for me, but I slashed it away with my sword. I heard Janela grunt as she thrust her blade into an attacker. The beasts kept coming, and we retreated up the steps. One monster bounded over the balustrade and met Otavi's axe in full swing.

Wave after hooting wave beat at us, and though we somehow turned back each one, the assaults continued with increasing fury and larger numbers. I nearly slipped a half-dozen times on the broken, blood-slick pavement. Once Janela caught me in mid-stumble, and as I righted myself, red eyes loomed behind her, club upraised. Before I could cry a warning, she swiveled and cut the creature down.

Then we were backing into the building. We made our stand in the corridor, crumbling stone walls shielding us on either side. The Cyralian brothers had dispensed with their bows in such close quarters and were flailing away with their small hand axes. The creatures pressed us, but the narrow corridor was working to our advantage, and gray corpses made a growing pile on the steps outside.

I heard a bellow and spun to see a leather-armored hulk vault over a fallen statue outside, beyond the gray monsters, and run toward us. It was a man—a big bear of a fellow, with a white plaited beard streaming from his chin and long silver hair flowing out from under his helmet. He was being pursued by a dozen beastmen. Shouting defiance, he charged into the group attacking us and hacked his way through, then swung around and joined our line.

Although our numbers had only grown by one, the beastmen seemed to lose spirit from that moment on. Our new ally's presence seemed to spark our flagging strength and we waded in, hammering our attackers down with the ease of a clan of giants.

Then they were gone and we were panting for breath, pounding each other on the back, glorying in the fact that we were still alive.

But there was no question the beastmen might return at any time and with a larger force. I issued orders for the men to make ready for any new assault. While Janela slipped away to investigate the temple—for that is what it was—I turned to interrogate our new comrade.

He'd stripped off his armor and was sprawled on the rubble-covered floor, dabbing at a welter of small wounds with a dirty rag he'd pulled from his helmet. He was big, almost fat, with a keg for a chest, a barrel for a belly, and a hairy melon for a face. A pelt of tight white curls covered his back and chest.

He looked up as I approached, and a grin the size of a ship's main mast was hoisted by the braided ropes that made his beard.

"Cap'n Mithraik's the name, sir," he said, in a voice formed in deep caverns. "Although I ain't got a busted pizzle stick to cap'n just now. And if yuz got a drop of strong drink on yer lordly person, Mithraik's yer man fer life, sir!"

I laughed and handed him the leather-bound flask of brandy I had hanging from my belt.

"It's the least I can do, Captain Mithraik," I said. "We were just about done for when you joined us."

He uncorked the flask. "Looked like yer was doin' fine, sir."

Mithraik let liquor flood into his throat. When he was done he shook the flask to see if it was empty, then looked sheepish and handed the flask back. "Sorry for the greedy beast that's seized me, sir," he said. "But it's been many a day since I last wet me pipes with proper drink."

"No harm done," I said. "We came well-supplied."

He made another wide grin. "I'm hopin' yer kindness will continue, sir," he said. He belched and stretched his arms, tired joints popping like cold fat on a hot hearthstone.

He yawned. "I'm certain yuz got a lot of questions yer'll want answerin', sir," he said. "Seein' as how I'm a stranger and all. But if yuz don't mind, sir, I'll first tuck me up fer a li'l nap. Then yuz can ask away."

I nodded in sympathy, but before I could say another word, Mithraik had curled up into a tubby ball and was emitting snores loud enough to rattle the chamber.

Janela came running up. She was so brimming with excitement that she gave Mithraik only a cursory glance.

"I think I've found what we're looking for," she said. "But I'll need some light and assistance."

I asked what it was she wanted to show me, but she just shook her head and said I needed to see for myself. She dug out a pair of firebeads, whispered the spell that made them glow into life, and handed me a set. I bade one of the men watch Mithraik, having little trust for any stranger in these lands, and followed her along the long, dim corridor.

It spilled into a vast, vaulted room, with gigantic shadows dancing on the walls and floors as we moved, firebeads lifted high. More whispering from Janela and the beads glowed brighter still, chasing the shadows back. She pointed to the center of the room and I saw four stone figures posted in a square—all looking inward. They were smaller duplicates of the double-visaged woman/demon guarding the entrance to the harbor. The figures were undamaged by time, and our light rippled along their black burnished surfaces. Janela pulled me forward to the place the statues seemed to be guarding.

"Look," she said, raising her beads higher still.

In an area about twenty feet wide and a similar measure in length was a pentagram carved into the stone. Within the pentagram were all kinds of strange symbols and drawings and what may have been words in an unknown tongue. Deeply etched within the border they made was a picture of a dancing girl—graceful arms raised high, one hand holding a feather, the other a veil.

My mind reeled. "It's the same figure Janos carried about his neck," I said.

"And mine," Janela said, holding up the silver necklace she'd first shown me in the villa.

Actually, it was closer to hers, since it showed a court scene similar to the one displayed when my touch had brought Janela's talisman to life. There was the monarch and his queen, seated on twin thrones. There were the courtiers—among them were the strange visitors. And yes, there was the demon king leering at the girl. Except now he stood beside the royal thrones. There were other differences, the most marked of which was the aging of the monarchs. The king's face and body had thickened and lines of worry creased his features. The still-beautiful queen had aged as well, more matronly now, and she looked pensive, brooding, as if she had suffered many wrongs.

Only the dancer appeared unchanged.

The demon king appeared more arrogant than ever, his talons stretching toward the dancing girl, so close he could almost touch her; so close I could imagine her flesh crawling in fear.

I shuddered. "I hope you're not thinking of casting some sort of spell," I said, "to bring this scene alive."

"I could, Amalric," Janela said. "But I won't. Black magic has been worked here. That is the purpose of the pentagram. I wouldn't care to see what kind of demon it's meant to contain."

"Why would the Old Ones do such a thing?" I asked.

"They didn't," Janela said. "The original scene is theirs, I'm sure. But the pentagram was carved about it later."

"The ones who destroyed this city?" I ventured.

Janela nodded. "The very ones," she replied. Then she said, "I don't need sorcery for it to serve our purpose."

She showed me one corner of the stone carving. At first all I saw were curving lines and odd-shaped forms. Then I realized it was an ornate map—a map of this region . . . and beyond, into our familiar worlds.

I could identify Orissa and the peninsula Lycanth once sat upon. From that area of familiarity I could trace the path to Irayas or turn to see the route Rali had taken in her great western voyage. There were other areas I could recognize but many more I couldn't, and it was all done in such detail that I hated the man or demon who'd carved this map with such easy familiarity. He knew a world that time—or something else—had stolen from me and my kind.

But that was not what had Janela excited. The map also showed the Eastern Sea we'd just sailed, the benighted coast we stood upon, and beyond that—

"The Kingdoms of the Night," Janela breathed, putting words to my thoughts.

It wasn't exactly that, but it certainly seemed to point the way.

I saw a river curving up from the harbor, winding through many miles of wilderness. It ended in a great lake. Beyond the lake was a road that climbed into high mountains, snaking toward a symbol like a clenched hand, which could only be the Fist of the Gods. The road cut across that formation and then ran straight as an arrow to the miniature towers of a palace—our goal. I whispered a prayer to Te-Date that my wishes were not playing me false.

Janela said something, bumping me into awareness.

"Pardon?" I said.

"I want to make a copy," she answered. "Help me light the carving, if you please."

She gave me her beads, and I held both sets high so she could see. Janela took a small, linen-wrapped object from her purse. When she'd removed the wrapping, I saw it was a charcoal stick, which she rubbed over the portion of the map we needed. She worked carefully, making sure all the etched lines were filled with blackening. The entire charcoal stub was used by the time she was done. Then she spread out the bit of linen that had contained the stick.

She smiled at me. "Well, only a little bit of magic, perhaps," she said.

Janela folded the linen into a square, then squared it again, until it was quite small. She pressed it between her palms, whispered a spell, then undid it. The linen bundle unfolded and unfolded . . . and unfolded—until it was large enough to cover the map. She laid it across the blackened area, pressed it tight, then rubbed the cloth with the haft of her knife. Once again she took her time so every spot got its due.

"I used to do this when I was a girl," she said as she worked. "I had a set of children's illustrations carved in wood. Fantastic things: fire-breathing lizards; people with enormous feet, who stood on one and shaded themselves with the other; wood sprites and fairy queens. You know, silly little stories ·for babes. When I became too old for them—or wanted others to believe I was too old, at least—I made rubbings, just like this. Whenever I gave a gift, I'd wrap it in one of the rubbings."

I looked at her. There was a smear of charcoal on her cheek— and another on her nose.

"I made quite a mess in those days," she said, chortling over a girlhood memory.

"Why, my Lady Greycloak," I said in mock amazement. "I can't imagine such a thing."

She caught my tone. "It's on my nose, isn't it?" she said.

"And your cheek, as well," I said.

Janela sighed, resigned. "So much for wizardly dignity." Then she peeled back the linen and held it up. It was a perfect replica—but in reverse.

"Exactly what we need," I said.

Janela looked for herself and seemed satisfied. And she said, "Now we must concentrate on living long enough to use it."

WHEN WE RETURNED we found that the men had made a low barricade out of the rubble in the corridor. The Cyralian brothers were waxing their bowstrings; Otavi was running a soft stone over his axe blade, while Pip and the others honed their weapons. A campfire had been lit and rations were bubbling in a pot slung over it. Mithraik still snored peacefully.

Outside, night had closed in. The moon was in its first quarter and the light was weak. Fierce jungle noises echoed through the darkness and a swarm of fireflies winked on and off.

Pip was glooming and staring out. "Guess Quatervals ain't chancin' bein' a hero an' wadin' through the muck despite y'r orders."

"I told him when we left that if we encountered difficulty, under no circumstances was he to try to reach us at night," I said. "It would only be begging for ambush and disaster. Besides, we're well forted up."

Pip shook his head. "It's on'y what I deserves fer volunteerin'," he muttered to no one in particular. "I shoulda lissened to me dear muvver. Shoulda taken up a peaceful trade, like me da. Best purse-lifter in all a Cheapside."

I paid no attention, and Janela and I slipped outside to learn more about our opponents. We examined the corpse of a particularly large brute who was sprawled near the entrance. Ignoring his bulk and the club still gripped in his massive paws, he did not look so fierce. He seemed pitiful, actually—eyes wide and staring in final surprise, lips grimacing in pain's last visit. Other than the sloping brow, his face was remarkably human, vulnerable, almost childlike.

"Poor creature," Janela said. "It almost makes one believe there might be some truth to the tales I heard." She shivered. "If so . . . that's what could happen to us."

"What do you mean?" I asked.

"According to some legends," she said, "this is what became of the people who once ruled this city."

I was shocked but said nothing—waiting for her to explain.

"When the Old Ones abandoned the West," she said, "this city became their first line of defense for their eastern empire. At least that is what the mythmakers said. I'm only conjecturing this was the harbor city the tales referred to. Its name has been lost over time. Regardless, a great battle ensued and a siege that lasted many years."

The scars of battle we had seen bore out Janela's guess this was that very city.

She continued: "Then betrayal from within led the walls to be breached. The inhabitants were massacred until only a few remained, all of them women or girls approaching womanhood."

Janela gestured at the corpse. "It's just possible that he is one of their descendants."

"I don't see how that could be," I said, thinking of the graceful figures I'd seen in the frescoes on the way to the temple.

"It's only a story," Janela said. "So you could be right in doubting it. I'd feel more comfortable if you were. For the tale goes on to say the enemy king summoned foul beasts from the ethers and made the women mate with them. The children that resulted were half men, half creature, condemned to live here as brutes for all time."

I looked at the beastman again, but with a mixture of pity and dread. If Janela's tale was history, rather than myth, and if the enemy who doomed these folk was behind the mysterious maladies afflicting Orissa and Vacaan, then I was correct in suspecting that our expedition was more important than an adventurer's whim. Te-Date willing, the answer to that riddle might be found in the Kingdoms of the Night.

An errant firefly floated up between Janela and me, its intermittent light somehow easing my cares. Her hand shot out and she caught it, cupping it delicately between her palms. She made a little opening between her thumbs and I saw light blink. Janela's brow furrowed, then cleared as an idea struck.

"I need to find something to put my little sister in," she said, and started back for the corridor, with me at her heels.

Mithraik was awake and crouched by the fire spooning up food from the pot, so I hoisted up a flask of wine and perched near him on a comfortable stone slab.

"Here's the drink I promised," I said, passing him the flask. "I'll trade it for the details of who you are, and how you came to be here."

Mithraik grasped the flask, rumbling laughter. "Don't need payment fer talkin', sir. Ever'body allas sez, ol' Mithraik loves nothin' better'n jawin'—'specially 'bout himself." He looked at the flask, that wide smile of his flashing white. " 'Course, there's nothin' like a drop t' oil me pipes, sir. And I thankee very much."

He gurgled down a large quantity and passed the flask back. I drank and handed it on to Janela, who'd joined us. I saw her put a tiny box in her boot, guessing it was the firefly's new home. But her full attention was on Mithraik, whose measure she was taking.

She saw the rogue in him and said: "Is this one of those stories that begins with: 'I fell into bad company'?"

Mithraik guffawed and slapped his knee. "Jus' what I was goin' to say, m'lady," he said. "Yuz got ol' Mithraik hammered wi' the first swing a the mallet."

He drank, then grew serious and said to me: "But that be the truth, sir. More's the pity. Me family's been merchantin' these seas since they was nothin' more'n a tear in some god's eye. Honest sailors, sir, doin' honest trade. Was me father's pride, sir, and me mother's as well. Rose to cap'n, I did, and there was a time when it looked like I'd end up ownin' me own ship. Play the owner's pipes, sir, 'n' buy the first round at the inn."

The other men had gathered near. They grinned and shook their heads, empathizing with Mithraik's goals. I saw they were passing their weapons to Janela, who was sprinkling a few drops of some magical oil on each of them and handing them back. Pip stood watch while this was going on, but his large ears pricked to catch our visitor's tale.

Mithraik gulped hugely and passed the flask to the men. "All that mighta come to be, sir, but I was cursed with a wild nature and a quarrelsome tongue. I was al'ays tellin' the owners their business, thinkin' I knew best."

I understood the type. I had captains just like him in my employ. So what he said next was no surprise: "I got fewer berths every year, sir, and poor ones at that. I took to cuttin' corners, if yuz knows what I mean."

I did indeed. Certain cargo items would be stolen, the thefts covered by declaring the goods damaged or lost in a storm. Sometimes the ship might be involved in even more illicit goings on.

"I even went a-piratin', much to me shame, sir," Mithraik said. "Used the owners' ship 'n' a hand-picked crew of lads I knew was bent. But me masters weren't stupid men, sir. They soon caught on and afore I knew it I was runnin' to keep me head on me shoulders, 'n' me arms from bein' stubbed. It was only a matter of time, sir, that I joined the real pirates. 'N' I been a rogue ever since."

"Why the sudden remorse?" I asked. "You sound as if you have seen the error of your ways and want to repent."

Mithraik nodded, solemn. "That I have, sir," he said. "That I have. Yuz see, I was marooned here by me mates many months ago. They 'cused me a holdin' out on 'em, sir. Said I was keepin more'n me share. And that was a bloody lie!" His glare was fierce, as if he meant to prove the truth of his words by its heat. I gave him the flask, and he sighed deeply and calmed himself with a drink.

"But there was no talkin' to 'em, sir," he continued. " 'N' they put me down here, 'mongst the beasts. 'N' I been runnin' and dodgin' 'em ever since. They ain't that smart, yuz know. 'Specially if'n yer on'y one feller, like me. Yuz can keep low, confuse 'em if they spot yuz 'n' gets back to yer hidey-hole afore they knows what's what. So that's what I been doin', sir, since me mates played

me false. 'N' the truth is, sir, for the first months I swore if I ever got
outter this port I'd do 'em right proper. Gets me revenge. 'N' after
that, why I'd become the greatest pirate ever lived, sir. The scourge
o' the seas. But the more time passed, sir, the more I dwelled on me
dear family 'n' how I shamed 'em—honest folk one 'n' all."

He lifted his head and looked at me with big, cow-brown eyes.
"So, what do yer say, sir? Will yuz take ol' Mithraik off this horrid
place? Give him a chance to set things right?"

I nodded. "Fight beside us," I said, "and if we live, you can join
us." Mithraik brightened considerably. So I thought it only fair to
warn him, saying, "You should know, however, that it's no merchant trip we're on. It's more of an expedition . . . to find new
markets."

"Will you be goin' mostly by water, sir?" Mithraik said.

"Yes," I said. "We'll be sailing up yon river as soon as I get
back to my fleet."

"I know the river," Mithraik said. "Even been up it a few
leagues. It's a bit tricky but it shouldn't be much trouble, seein's how
yer shallow-drafted."

My hackles prickled. But before I could speak, Janela said,
sharply: "How did you know the design of our ships? Were you
watching when we came in?"

Mithraik looked puzzled, then smote his head a meaty blow.
"Why, no, I didn't, me lady. So, I ask meself how'd ol' Mithraik
know they was shallow-drafted? 'N' I gots no answer. It just came
to me. Popped inta me head. Like somebody whispered it inta
me ear."

He looked around the temple corridor and shivered. "I gotter
get outta this port, sir. The ghosts 're drivin' me barmy."

Then Pip shouted a warning and those strange, hooting war
cries shattered the night.

We leaped to the barricade and saw a gray mass of beastmen
charging out of the darkness. They came from all sides, and behind
them were a host of others, shambling forward to take the places of
those who would fall.

The Cyralian brothers volleyed arrows anointed with Janela's
sorcery. They exploded just before they reached their marks, and I

heard all-too-human shrieks of agony. But it made no difference to those who lived, and the shaggy wave of gray rolled on, absorbing shock after shock as the brothers rained death into their ranks.

Just before they overran us, Janela pulled the little box from her boot. She opened it, muttered some words of a spell to the firefly, and cast her "little sister" into the air. Then her sword scraped out and she joined us in the hand-to-hand fight.

Our magically aided weapons made it butcher's work, cleaving skulls, splitting torsos, with blood spraying everywhere—and those of us who lived would be cursed with violent dreams from that day on.

I killed until I was gasping, my arms leaden, my legs like stone; and then I killed more. Mithraik proved his mettle in the first wave. One of the beastmen hurdled the barricade before we could tighten our line. But Mithraik wrested the club from his hand and broke his head. Then he fought like a wild thing—a sword in one hand, the stone-headed club in the other. He jumped in wherever he was needed, filling gaps caused by the press of the fight, stabbing over Pip's head in one instance to spear an oncoming beast through the throat.

But there was no relenting. The creatures fought on. Some died just to drag one stone away from the barricade. Others died by deliberately offering their bodies to our swords so a comrade would have time to get us before the sword could be withdrawn. One of the ex-Scouts was killed this way, Otavi avenging him by beheading his slayer. Another was mortally wounded early in the battle but continued fighting as relentlessly as our enemy—his own blood pooling at his feet. Then he slumped over the barricade, sword jutting from his dead hand as if to help stave off the gray horde.

Finally there came a time I realized we wouldn't last another hour, much less the night.

A dry wind blew up and I heard a rustling sound above the din.

I heard Janela shout: "Come little sister!" I looked up to see a black cloud settling over the battlefield—a living cloud—and it was from there that the dry wind blew and made the noise of countless insect wings, a chitinous scratching at the ether itself.

The night turned to golden day as the cloud lit up, making a small sun above us.

It was so bewildering—this magical firefly mass—that I nearly forgot the battle, and dodged just in time as a club hammered the space where my head had been. As I cut my attacker down, the glorious cloud spread out like an enormous net drawn up from fiery, tropical seas.

Janela shouted something in a strange language and the net descended. It settled down and down, falling over the heads and shoulders of our enemies. They howled in agony, flailing helplessly and sinking to the ground to shudder and die.

Few escaped the flaming net, and those who did either scattered into the darkness or were slain by us at the barricade.

Janela clapped her hands . . . and the net vanished . . . leaving a great harvest of gray corpses for the Dark Seeker.

We collapsed on the barricade, exhausted.

But there was no time to rest that night, much less mourn our fallen friends or praise Janela's quick thinking and powerful sorcery.

We wanted to make haste to reach the shore before the beastmen could regroup, and so we had to chance that most dangerous of all retreats—by night and through a jungle. If we hurried and were not ambushed, we would just meet Quatervals when he landed with the rescue party at dawn. As we retraced our steps along the wall, however, I did ponder that in many ways Janela *was* Greycloak's equal at sorcery. And even if she wasn't, she had his same strange turn of mind that would see a magical, death-dealing net in something so small and innocent as a firefly.

Then we were running down the stairwell and out on the muddy shore. The new sun was gleaming on the shields of our comrades from the fleet. Quatervals loomed at their head, and when he saw me, relief flooded his features.

He rushed over, but instead of the expected exclamation of "Thank Te-Date, you're safe," he said, "You must make speed, my lord. The lookouts have spotted an approaching fleet!"

* * *

ABOARD THE *IBIS*, Kele was issuing orders in a violent stream, making sure everything was ready in case the ships were unfriendly.

"What flag do they fly?" I asked, although I suspected I already knew the answer.

She shook her head. "Not close enough to make out as yet, my lord," she said.

"How swift's your pinnace?" I asked.

"It wins its races."

"Your best oarsmen . . . and stand by to lower," I ordered, then took Janela aside.

"If this is who we fear, we'll be trapped in this harbor before we can make our way upriver," I said. "A delaying action is what we need."

Janela nodded. I told her what I hoped her magic could provide.

She frowned. "I don't know," she said slowly. "There's already a very powerful spell in place. It was created to guard against all the storms that have blown against these shores." She sighed. "I don't think much of my chances . . . but we don't have a lot of alternatives, do we?"

"One other thing," I said. "Can you make it happen on command?"

She snorted. "You don't want much," she said.

Janela hurried forward, shouting for the ship's carpenter, and in a few moments she returned, carrying a small balk of wood.

The crew was already standing by their oars. We clambered over the gunwales, Kele shouted orders, and the crew sent our boat dropping into the harbor waters.

The coxswain raised a small spritsail and the oarsmen set to, sending us skimming across the water, tacking alongside the mole with the prevailing east wind until we reached its end, where the monolith stood.

As we sailed, Janela carved on that balk of wood with a small golden scythe. I noted that the wood seemed to have suffered from dry rot. Every now and then she swore, and I heard her mutter once that she was gods-damned if this looked *anything* like it was supposed to.

We pulled up to the mole and scrambled onto the ancient cobbles. Janela ran straight to the statue's base and began her spell.

I went on to the end of the jetty and peered out and saw the ships. It was the same ten Orissan ships I'd seen before in my vision. Except now they flew two banners above our city's flag—the blue coiled serpent set on a golden sunburst that was the emblem of Vacaan, and below that the red and black that were the colors of the Wardens.

The ships were close enough now for me to see the quarterdeck of the flagship. Once again I saw Cligus, but somehow the blow was greater in person. Worse still, beside him stood Lord Modin. My son was hunting me down, and he'd made an ally of a powerful black wizard—a wizard with men and designs of his own.

I imagined I saw my son spot me and lift his eyes in surprise. The distance was too great for such small detail, but he did point in my direction, and Modin turned his head to look. Instantly he threw up his arms and sorcerous lightning forked from the heavens, barely missing the mole and making the seas hiss with the fury of its blast. I smelt the reek of ozone.

I heard a cry from Janela and turned to see her slip back into the pinnace. I ran to join her and we pulled hard for the *Ibis*. I looked at Janela, who was waiting for my order and holding that bit of rotten wood in both hands. I saw that it was a crude model of the monolith.

"Now!" I said.

And Janela snapped the model.

Fire sprayed up from the base of the statue, sheeting above the ghastly head itself. An explosion like a volcano roused from its sleep ripped out, powdering the base of the statue and showering us with stinging small debris.

Slowly, the statue toppled—hesitating a moment in mid-fall— then plunged over, sending up a mass of water that lifted the pinnace high above the distant trees of the jungle as the wave passed under.

Then we were coming down and I saw that the fallen monolith had blocked the entrance. Beyond I saw the sails of our pursuers plunging about on the other side like sea dragons raging to get at their prey.

We didn't give them a second look as we clambered aboard the *Ibis*, and then my three ships were speeding down the channel into the river's mouth.

Within an hour we were sailing up the river that Janela's map said would lead us to our goal. Except now it wasn't a gateway—it was our only means of escape.

CHAPTER NINE

THE RIVER ROAD

I had no doubt that Cligus and his forces would soon find a way to clear the blocked channel, so it was imperative we travel fast. I'd had just two hopes: first, that Cligus wouldn't continue the pursuit beyond Irayas; and second, that if he did, he'd be handicapped by not having an Evocator as skilled as Janela. Those hopes had been dashed when I saw him off the ruined city with Modin.

Our weapons were our wits and our ships. Our shallow-draft, sweep-equipped vessels would have an easier time on the river than Cligus' hastily converted merchantmen, which needed deep water under their keels to keep from running aground. Cligus would also be dependent on the wind's vagaries. At the moment, however, the wind seemed to prefer one direction—directly upriver toward those distant mountains, perfect to fill the sails of Cligus' wallowing ships. I was beginning to regret my prayers for winds blowing constantly east. My seamen naturally didn't share this feeling. They knew that soon enough we'd be unlashing the sweeps from where they were fixed below the railings and the real work would begin.

If we had not entered this gigantic river from the sea it would have been easy to believe we were on but one of many smaller rivers. The waters of the delta were like fingers: twisting, crossing, meeting, or joining into others, and then, quite suddenly, we would be traveling on a current so vast that the farther shores couldn't be glimpsed. An hour later we'd be forcing our way down a waterway so narrow our ships had to travel in a single line. We knew we were on the right course, though, because regularly we saw, set either on islands or driven directly into the riverbed, pillars topped with the same awful double-faced head as the monolith that had marked the river's entrance.

This river *was* the highway to the Kingdoms of the Night.

To confuse our pursuers, I considered landing men to topple the monoliths on land or use a cable from ship to ship to rip the ones in the water away to confuse. I dismissed the notion when I realized it would take too long. Also, something inside me was bothered by destroying monuments this old, especially ones used to help travelers find their way through the wilderness.

The river was alive. Schools of fish frothed on the surface, hunted by unknown enemies below. We kept lines out and frequently had to cut them loose when a fisherman would hook something that seemed more intent on catching *him*. Pip was once nearly pulled overside by a sudden strike, saved only by Otavi grabbing him around the waist and bellowing for the stubborn little fool to let go of the blessed line. After that my diminutive complainer foreswore piscatorial pleasures: "I don't have no truckle wi' anything more innarested in eatin' me than I him."

Once I saw a motion in the water and looked out to see a wedge-shaped creature swimming toward us. I thought it might be a mink or an otter, but then the wedge lifted on a long snakelike neck, became a head, and looked at me curiously. I swear there was at least as much intelligence in its gaze as in any of the awestricken men and women who stared at it. Then it was gone and the water swirled from the great creature's passing.

We spotted another strange animal crossing the river just in front of us. All we could see was a gross head, looking, as Pip said, "uglier nor a fishwife in Cheapside, e'en wi'out the gold teeth."

Mithraik told the men around him it was as ugly out of water with its bulk exposed as it was in. "Great and fat, sir, just like yer fishwife. And movin' as fast when it minds as any peddler seein' someone in the till. Never get 'tween one when he's grazin' ashore and the river, sir, 'less yuz like bein' used as a gangplank.

"Uster hunt 'em from canoes. 'Twas a rare sport. Used harpoons and make the lines fast to the thwart. Give us a tow, sir, faster'n a matched pair'a horses. Unless they turned on yuz." He grimaced. "Saw one of 'em take a canoe and bust it like a paper boat, and then take a man and crunch him like a sweet. But we paid him back in kind, sir, by killin' him and havin' him fer supper."

"Were they good eating?" Otavi wondered.

"Fattish," Mithraik said. "Had to parboil 'em, then grill 'em. Even then, tasted like whale blubber."

"Ne'er could see the point of huntin' somethin'," said Maha, my kitchen apprentice turned cook, "that isn't tryin' to eat you, unless you can eat it or sell the furs for profit." He was someone I'd suspected before of doing a little sedate poaching on some of my neighbors' estates.

"The hide makes decent whips," Mithraik said. "And wet, tied around somethin', it'll dry like iron."

"I'll still let it swim its way," Otavi put in, "and I'll go mine."

There was other life in this delta. Not infrequently, I had the feeling we were being watched. Not by sorcerous means, but by things hidden on the banks. Several times we saw crude canoes pulled up on the riverside, and once, village huts far back in the brush.

Janela chanced casting a few spells to try to determine what progress Cligus was making. I thought they were cleverly laid, being sent out as gently and finely, she said, as a net for bait minnows. But we caught nothing in their strands. Janela said she felt only Modin somewhere behind us, so she knew the wizard had laid counterspells. She could not tell if our pursuers were still struggling with the monolith or were moving. But she did know they hadn't given up. I wondered to myself how Cligus had managed to rationalize *this*—a murderous pursuit to the ends of the world, now companied by a sorcerer with his own nefarious plans.

Janela and I talked about what Modin could be intending. "I doubt," she said dryly, "that it's just fascination with my fair white form or even whatever kind of sex-magic he wants to perform. I can only make two guesses. Possibly, King Gayyath was brought down by the riots or else forced to find a sacrificial lamb for the evils of his regime and chose Modin and his Wardens, which I doubt.

"My best thought—and again, this is truly a guess—is he thinks there could be some benefit to be gained by following us to the Kingdoms of the Night."

"Unless they're hostile and he's made some sort of pact with them," I said. "I keep remembering that demon and his rose in the dancer's scene."

Janela nodded. "That, too, is a possibility. Fortunately, we don't have the choice of being cowards or sensible folk and abandoning our journey."

"Not," I said, "that you'd consider giving up anyway."

"Not I," she said with a smile. "Nor you, either."

She was right.

The delta came to an end and now there were but half a dozen courses. We were traveling through thickly jungled terrain, but unlike any jungle I'd ever seen before. There were high trees reaching up over two hundred feet, which arched out over the water, but I'd never seen trees with trunks of a deep crimson and three-fingered leaves, which were bright red, as big as a man's hand. Green and even blue vines crawled around these trees, stark colors clashing. There were other enormous trees that seemed to consist only of monstrous trunks with many divisions, like knotted ropes, that were as thick as our ship's breadth. Bright red bee-eating birds swarmed the trees, and once, at dusk, a four-winged nightbird dipped and fluttered just in front of me as if in greeting. I saw tulips nearly as big as a man's head, and Mithraik said they could be cut and sucked for their honey.

It was beautiful, if jungle can ever be said to be beautiful instead of what it actually is—cold, calm, neutral, waiting for you to make a single mistake before it kills you. And, like in any other jungle, there were annoyances. It rained almost constantly, and when it didn't, the air swarmed with flies, small creatures barely visible to the eye, which crawled in everywhere and bit like tiny fire-reddened pokers. We'd brought a bale of thin muslin to make mosquito nets and used these to form head coverings to keep from going quite insane with the buzzing, although eating without swallowing at least a dozen of the nasty little creatures was an accomplishment. Chons claimed he held the record of actually getting two mouthfuls under his netting without ingesting anything live, but no one believed him that skilled.

There were other creatures in this jungle, creatures nearly the size of half-grown hogs, which looked like rats but swam like seals. We speared and butchered one and Maha stewed it with onions and potatoes. It was, shall I say, consumable? Once again I realized that for most people good taste is more a matter of familiarity than an actual sensation, since no one said we should kill another.

We saw apes in the trees that were fascinated by our passing, moving swiftly from tree to tree, their eyes always fastened on us, as if they were taking notes for craft they too might build. They were prey for jungle cats, animals smaller than the apes but fiercer, who had mottled coats of dark ocher, maroon, and tan, making them almost impossible to see until they sprang.

Somehow we must have offended the apes, because they began launching missiles at us. This was of little account except when we got close to the banks. They began by throwing fruit with amazing accuracy and range, then progressed to stones. Mithraik wanted to kill a few of them to dissuade the others but I said no. I put the Cyralian brothers in the bows with blunts, flat-tipped arrows used to knock down birds and rabbits, and sailed close to shore for an hour or so. Every now and then a bowstring would twang and an ape would howl and skitter away through the treetops. After that we had no more trouble with hidden snipers.

Now the wind became sporadic and we were forced to use the sweeps on occasion.

Late one evening, the river widened into a lagoon. There was a scattering of islets in the middle of it and we tied up to one for the night. There were some unwary ducks squawking on the lake, and I sent Chons and some sailors out in a small boat with nets. The squawking became outraged and in a few moments we had our dinner. Maha roasted them with milk from nuts, chiles, onions, and other sharp spices, and the vegetable was green bananas cooked with salt pork.

I wandered to the bows, contentedly digesting, and wondering if it was possible to go adventuring and gain weight, as the twilight closed and the last of the hellish flies vanished. I was staring rather idly at the largest of the islands and I thought I saw something in the dying light. It appeared to be a small stone building, a villa, perhaps. Certainly it looked far more sophisticated than any of the rude huts we'd seen beside the river. I wondered if the island was inhabited, and if so, by whom?

A delicious scent crept into my nostrils. I'm not sure how to describe it now, nor was I then. It was not one single smell, but many, and all of them welcoming, desirable. There might have been the smell of a night-blooming flower that grew outside a summer home or the scent of an aromatic fire that blazes up to draw the winter hunter back to his camp. Perhaps there was the perfume of a loved one of long ago weaving through that, like mist fingers across an autumn meadow. And spiced apples, a fragrant punch, a garden that always calmed you after a harried day.

Then the scent was gone and I went back to studying the building, which was rapidly vanishing in the coming night. I wondered what lay there. Certainly something attractive, something worth seeing, something beautiful, or perhaps something important to our expedition. Not that there was any hurry, I thought drowsily.

We were already letting our lines go, I noted, and seamen were readying the sweeps to row us over to that small lovely island where something beyond price awaited us.

I yawned once more and started down from the forecastle to help the men. Then Janela shouted:

"Stop it! There's magic at work!"

I halted, frowning. How could she interrupt what I was about to do? It was important for me, for all of us, to go to that island where something—or someone—waited.

Janela grabbed one of the sailors by the arm as he moved toward the rail with his sweep and sent him spinning away. Again she shouted, "Sorcery!" and I heard someone growl and then I came back to myself.

"Kele!" I shouted, and heard an answering cry from the quarterdeck. "Turn out the watch!"

Silence. And then Kele too began bellowing and the night's soft welcome hesitated, retreated, as sleep retreats when you reach for it. Then something else came back at us.

It was still invisible but now it ordered, not seduced: *The island. You must go to the island. There is someone who needs you. Go to the island.*

I heard Janela chant:

"We are wood
We are steel
We cut
We hold
We do not turn
We are firm
We do not hear
We do not smell
We hold true
We hold firm."

The spell broke and lanterns flared on the ships' quarterdecks and in the waists. Janela stood outlined by one of the lanterns beside our main mast, holding an ordinary marlinspike above her head. All three ships had been cast loose and were drifting in the current before Janela had sensed danger.

We were ourselves once more and in seconds had the sweeps double-manned and were pulling across that lagoon, on up the river. We rowed all that night and into the next day before I chanced allowing a rest.

What was it? A sorcerer, a sorceress, trying to ensnare us? A demon? A sprite? A ghost? Possibly even no more than a lonely earth spirit intending no harm but longing for companionship? I do not know, but I should never linger again in a lagoon that offers peace and welcoming smells in that snake-curling river that leads up from the Eastern Sea, not if I were wise.

As the days passed I noted by the glass that the land rose, yet we never encountered a cascade or rapids. I began watching closely and saw yet again that strange shimmer that crossed the water, and then we would rise to a slightly higher level. This was the same magic used to control the river from the port of Marinduque up to Irayas. I pointed the next magical lock out to Janela and we rejoiced. I wondered if the spell was so potent it was hanging on from the days of the Old Ones or, more hopefully, was constantly renewed, which would suggest we would not find empty ruins suited only for antiquarians.

Then the river broadened into huge swamps and the open waterways became narrower and smaller, twisting even more than in the delta. All we had to navigate by was our compass and those eerie beacons.

Three days into the morass and we were lost. The demon/ woman markers vanished, or else we lost a turning somewhere. Worse, the winds were fickle, either blowing from the wrong direction, no more than zephyrs, or else dying, leaving us in a dead calm with no sound but the lap of the waves against our hull, the rattle of the sails as they hung limp, the buzz of mosquitoes, and then the shouts of the masters' mates to turn out the watch and man the sweeps.

We'd enter an inviting passage only to find it choked with weeds, turn due west, or else see it peter out into marshland or dead-end against a soggy mass barely worth calling an island. Sometimes we'd find the channel blocked with a fallen tree and have to send work parties in boats to cut away the vegetation or, worse yet, to wade waist deep in the brown murk, not wanting to think what else could be swimming there, hidden. All too often we'd exhaust ourselves hacking at these monstrous logs and then have our way blocked around the next bend.

Then we'd have to reverse our course and work our way back to attempt another channel. We went up and down and back and forth, until we doubted our compass. When the rank vegetation allowed, we caught the occasional glimpse from the masthead of the always receding mountains that seemed no closer now than when we had first seen them. No one said anything, but all of us were worried that while we wandered in this labyrinth, Cligus and his forces would catch up. There would be no place to fight other than from ship to ship, and in these narrow waterways no place for cunning or trickery.

It was if we were caught in a nightmare, running from some awful, nameless monster through quicksand pulling at our thighs, holding us, afraid to look back, waiting for the talons to sink into our backs.

Not only were we frequently lost—although lost is not the proper word since it implies there was a correct way through this maze—but we also ran aground at least once or twice a day. Our hulls remained undamaged, and running aground was hardly dramatic, just a slowing of the ship as it nosed into a hidden mud bank. We'd try to use the sweeps to pole off or the boats to tow us free, but frequently we had to kedge off. This was an especially exhausting task. The boats would be launched, carrying one of our anchors, and would row to the full length of the chain. Then the anchor would be dropped and hopefully hold fast. The capstan would be manned and we'd strain against the bars, hearing nothing, feeling the veins bulge on our foreheads and blood roar in our ears, then a *clink* as we won a foot and the capstan pawl locked us. *Clink* . . . then another . . . then *clink, clink, clink* coming faster as we pulled ourselves free again. We'd raise the anchor and sail on until the next grounding.

These days were especially hard on the crew of the *Ibis*. Since we were smaller, handier, and shallower-drafted, it was our duty to take the lead and explore before the hoys would waddle after us.

There were times when all three ships became trapped and all of us had to kedge our way back to what we were calling a main channel, even though it didn't appear much different than the one we'd just gotten stuck in.

The crews' complaints rose to fever pitch, which didn't worry me. It was when they would become quiet that I'd start fretting. Things as yet weren't all that bad—at least we hadn't been stricken with any of the fevers or malaises most tropic rivers carry, and there'd been no serious injuries or deaths. One common lament was what good was magic doing—here we had the great-granddaughter of Janos Greycloak himself, capable of casting spells that destroyed demons and calmed storms, and she couldn't even manage to summon some kind of creature that'd be our guide, or perhaps send herself in spirit high above and direct our progress.

I'd asked Janela about that, and her reply had worried me a bit—she said she'd tried half a dozen times, but none of the spells worked. She said she hadn't lost her powers, but rather there was some sort of preventive spell over the area.

"It's as if," she said, "whoever laid it meant this area to be a trap. Perhaps the absence of those markers was deliberate. Maybe this was a trap set by the Old Ones meant to lure enemies aside, like sugar syrup can distract flies from a table. Or maybe the spell is more recent. I can't tell."

Still worse, she said, was that every time she attempted to cast a spell, she once more felt that looming presence from ahead and its increasing malevolence. Rather than tell the crew this, which I knew *would* terrify them, I merely said we were still worried about being discovered by Modin and the killing magic he might send. This silenced the criticism.

One day we had some good luck: The channel we were following held a true course to the east, was deep enough so we hadn't grounded; and best of all, we chanced on a small solid island in late afternoon. It was little more than a hummock, really, but at least it would let the men sleep ashore for a change. They wanted to clean up, and even though the mucky river would probably make them muddier than before, at least it would wash off the sweat.

I told Quatervals to put out sentries watching both the water and the land and told the crews to go ahead. The men, without waiting, stripped off their clothes and tumbled into the river. I smiled, then noticed our women standing in a disconsolate knot. I was about to order Quatervals to detail four more guards and suggest the women swim on the other side of the islet when Janela found a simpler and better solution.

She'd been wearing nothing but sandals, a pair of tough canvas trousers the sailmaker had made for almost all of us, which were almost guaranteed tear-proof, and a ragged tunic. Without ado, she pulled off the tunic, stepped out of her trousers, ran to the edge of the river and flat-dove in.

There were shouts of glee from the swimming men, who were delighted to see their Evocator gamboling about like any normal maid. The women looked at each other, and Kele was the first to doff her own clothes.

Janela swam a few yards, then came back to shore. She went to her clothes, picked them up, and came to me.

Suddenly I remembered an embarrassment from my youth. It was in my eleventh summer of life, and several of my friends and I had visited a favorite swimming spot and were sporting about when a group of girls came by. Evidently this was also their special bathing area. They'd conferred and then disrobed and joined us. The first thing was that all of us gaped incredulously for half a lifetime. I'm not sure why—there were more than enough nude statues in Orissa, so no one could have any doubts as to the shape of the female form. Nearly all of us had sneaked into one of the neighborhoods set aside for courtesans, some of whom felt dressing and undressing a waste of time when it came to quantity business. And some of us even claimed to have been seduced by older cousins, playmates, or by one of the household's servants. One or two may even have been telling the truth.

At any rate, the second thing that happened was all of us suddenly refused to walk into water any shallower than navel-deep. The third thing, which happened to me, was when a girl I knew from the athletic fields swam up to me and, bolder than brass, stood up and asked me if I wanted to race to the other side. The difficulty I experienced then, which came back to me on that mucky riverbank leagues and leagues beyond Orissa, was a mighty desire to look down, and a neck that was paralyzed and wouldn't let me.

I'm sure I must have flushed, and I'm sure Janela noticed. But all she said was, "You owe me a flagon of wine, Amalric, for smoothing the way."

I made some reply, and she walked away to join the other

women, who were emerging from the water and were recovering their clothes. Janela, moving with the grace of a forest nymph, began dressing.

My neck became unparalyzed.

Janela Greycloak was—is—as lovely and well-formed a woman as I'd ever seen. I rapidly turned away, now completely flustered as I realized that my approval of Janela, beautiful in the dying rays of the sun, was all too obvious.

As I turned, I heard a low laugh. It was feminine. Very bad. Worse, I didn't think it was Janela chortling.

I went to relieve one of the sentries and recover my composure. After some minutes, though, I too found it funny. I guess in some ways none of us become complete adults, and surely that eternal dance between men and women is more likely to turn us into fools and striplings than anything.

The crewmen were coming out of the river, as clean as it was possible to get. There were only three men still sporting in the water. Suddenly there were only two. I thought for an instant that one of them had dived underwater, but then a contorted face surfaced, mouth gaping in a soundless scream, and blood gouted, turning the water black.

I shouted a warning and others were crying out as well and the two in the water were struggling back toward shore. One shrieked and was gone and then his body spun to the surface, ripped asunder. Now there was but one man and he was only a few feet from land. It was Ceram, Kele's chief mate. We were running toward him, hoping to help, shouting, and then he stumbled out of the water, gasping for breath. We'd seen nothing so far and had no clue as to what had taken two of us.

Ceram was a good fifteen feet from the river when we saw the assassin. It was a monstrous crocodile that later I guessed must have been almost twenty feet long. Most people think these lizards of death are slow, supine, stupid, since the most they're likely to see, unless they're terribly unlucky, is a loglike scaly length and a pair of eyes or perhaps a smaller one out of the water sleeping in the sand.

I knew better. I'd seen one leap from the water fully five feet into the air, grab a gazelle that had just been coming to drink on the riverbank, and disappear in an instant.

This beast moved even more quickly. It burst out of the brown water like a striking snake, gray-green with age, standing almost to a man's waist, hurtled across the beach and was on Ceram, its massive jaws gaping. It smashed into him, and the blow most likely killed the sailor, but the reptile had the poor man locked in its jaws and was twisting, turning, almost tearing him in two as a terrier shakes a rat.

It should have turned and raced back into the water with its prey but instead it dropped Ceram's body and roared at us, a strange hissing roar.

Now our wits returned and we looked frantically for weapons. Otavi was the only one among us who'd been thinking, and he stepped forward. But instead of his axe, he'd seized a spear and cast it with all his strength deep into the monster's head, behind his jaws. It screamed, but its scream wasn't that high whistling keen of agony a crocodile should make, but something else, almost like the scream of a man.

None of us could move, and the crocodile put one forepaw on the spear's haft and jerked back, pulling it free. Blood poured on the sand and the animal now turned for the river. But Otavi was blocking his escape, axe raised, and Mithraik crouched beside him, spear butt buried in the ground, ready to take the charge, and then Janela darted in from the side, sent another spear into the animal's side and spun away. I seized a javelin from one of the men and hurled it true. It struck the beast between one of his scales and plunged deep.

Again the crocodile screamed, and then it ran, not for the safety of the water but away, into the scrub brush that covered the hummock. As it raced into shelter, bowstrings twanged and four shafts buried themselves in his back and again the monster cried out, rolling in pain, and then was gone. Men started after it, but Quatervals was shouting "Stop, the bastard'll be turnin' back to ambush."

Another scream and another and brush thrashed as if a great wind was blowing . . . and then there was silence.

Otavi started forward and I stopped him. "No. We wait a full turning of the glass."

And so we did, and then we went after the crocodile, following the wide trail it had crushed with its weight. We found a corpse no more than twenty feet from where the crocodile had vanished.

But it was the corpse of a man.

For a moment the world was chaos, roiling about all of us. Some of us swore, some gasped, some just paled. Then reality, such as it was, returned. I went forward, sword ready, Janela and Quatervals beside me.

The corpse lay facedown and was naked except for wristlets, anklets, and something about its neck. There was no sign of violence. I toed it over. It was a man, clean-shaven, close-cropped hair, with a face that was tattooed in blue from forehead to chin.

"A changeling," Kele said. "I've heard, but never seen."

"Is it?" I wondered. "Look."

I pointed at the body. There was not a mark of violence on it and the face was quite peaceful, as if the man had died in his sleep.

"I've always heard that were-creatures, when taken, would show the wounds they'd taken in their other forms," I said.

Janela knelt beside the body. "That's the story I, too, heard," she said absently. "But I've never seen such a beast, and no one I've ever trusted ever admitted to seeing one, either. But look."

The wristlets, bracelets, and what I now saw was a leathern gorget, were all of crocodile hide.

"T' hell with wounds," Pip said. "I ain't believin' that monsker just happened by where this bastard just happened t' go an' lie down an' die."

"No. Of course not," Janela said. "But it is most curious." She might have been a lycée instructor, sitting in her chambers discussing a strangely marked butterfly a student had brought in.

"We can discuss natural origins later," I said. "We're boarding ship and heading upriver right now."

But it was too late.

It was coming on twilight when we returned to the beach. We'd moored close inshore and used only six boats to land, leaving four men as anchor watches on the ships. The boats were beached near the water's edge. It was no more than a hundred yards, if that, out to our ships. But between us and them now floated a dozen or more ominous shapes. More crocodiles, some almost as large as the one that had attacked us.

"It'll take two trips t' get back t' the ships," Kele said. "An' that'll be packin' the boats to the gunnels. C'n we do that 'fore it's dark?"

"We'd better," Chons said. "What's to stop any of those bastards from just tippin' the boats o'er an' then taking their pick once we're drownin'?"

"You're right," Janela said. "We're safer here on the beach for the night. I can set up wards that should keep them away tonight, and prepare a great spell to guard us in the morrow."

There were mutters of dismay. All of us felt the only safety in this harsh land lay aboard our ships. But Kele and Janela were right. At least we hadn't gone ashore as total numbwits. All of us had brought weapons, and some of us even had some iron rations in belt pouches.

Our companions on the ships had seen some of what had happened, and Kele hand-signaled the rest of the story and our intentions. She told them to maintain a full watch and keep torches burning, although none of us thought the crocodiles could manage to board our ships, not even the *Ibis* with its relatively low freeboard. At Janela's suggestion Kele also signaled that *no one* was to be permitted aboard after dark, not even if it appeared to be Kele herself.

"I'm probably overreacting," Janela said, "but if you can accept shape-changing, why wouldn't it be as simple for someone to appear as you or me as a four-legged river monster?"

Unlikely, but it paid to be cautious.

We set to work, dividing into parties and going inland and cutting brush and the few scraggly trees for our fires. I feared we'd run out of light before morning, but Janela said that, at least, was not a worry. She took supplies from her purse and found a length of wood. She took out two mirrors and held them opposite each other with the wood in the center, reflections echoing. Then she said a spell and ordered Pip to cut the wood into fragments with his dagger.

She separated each splinter from the other and said another spell, and my eyes hurt as the splinters twisted and grew and there was a long line of wood, each length exactly the same as the next. She said the spell twice more and we had wood enough to burn a city.

We made four fires fifty feet apart, just where the brush began and as far from the water as we could get. We buried the torn body of Ceram and said what prayers we knew for the other two seamen, hoping that would be enough to keep their spirits from wandering this horrible country as ghosts for eternity.

None of us were sleepy and few hungry. Quatervals forced a section of jerked beef on me and I gnawed it, tasting nothing. He told me quietly that he knew the crocodiles had to be changelings, native sorcerers who'd traded their souls for the ability to become their totems, for he'd never heard of a crocodile killing and killing again. They'd take their prey, vanish into the depths to let it ripen and rot, feed, and then, when the satiation wore off in days or weeks, look for another victim.

I took Mithraik aside and thanked him for standing so steadfast when that first crocodile came ashore. He looked at me queerly, nodded thanks, and said, "But I'm not for the death here, sir. Not that kind, anyhap." I thought that an odd phrasing but said nothing.

Janela was readying herself for another spell. She drew me aside. "I don't know if this will work, since I have no idea what laws these men or beasts or whatever the hells they are are subject to. But at least saying some words will make the others feel better."

"What about the morning?" I wanted to know. "Could we have the same problems at daybreak trying to get back to the ships?"

"No. That I can guarantee. I can cast a spell using the goodness of the sun to carry my words and devices that nothing on any earth could withstand."

I sighed, relieved, and then Janela had to spoil it by saying, with a wry smile, "Or at least so the man who taught me that spell believed.

"We shall see, we shall see."

Now it was very dark and very quiet. The only lights were those of the shipboard lanterns and from our great fires, at least until you stepped a foot or so beyond the pool of light they made.

Then you could see, across the water, the luminescence of the eyes.

Waiting and watching.

Janela used a length of string to form a fence, burnt some dried twigs she said came from a thornbush, then added some incense that she said had been made from dried cactus flowers and a spell she'd written on a bit of parchment.

I saw a shimmer between us and the river . . . then nothing.

We settled down to wait.

Around midnight I heard a roar from the blackness, as if one of the crocodiles had attempted to slink ashore and had been driven back. Archers sent arrows whispering after the sound but I feared we hit nothing. It looked as if Janela's spell was holding firm.

It lasted until the early hours. In spite of myself I was feeling drowsy, and then we heard splashing.

There came a shout from Towra, who was taking charge of the part of the perimeter facing the river: "They're coming!" And we were on our feet.

The first creature struck out of blackness, and it was as if he rushed into an invisible net, caught, struggling, ripping, trying to come at us. Beside him came another, and I thought they were working together, tearing in unison, and there were others striking all along the sorcerous barrier. I thought the spell might be weakening, and then shafts hummed out. A few struck hard into the unarmored sides of the monsters, but all too many bounced off the thick hide of the beasts' backs. One howled that human scream as an arrow buried itself nearly to its hilt in an eye, then rolled away, snapping and tearing in agony.

Spears pinned others to the sand, and then I saw what must have been the greatest of them all rushing our barricade. I would swear on any god's altar that the brute was half again the size of the one we'd killed, but that cannot be. It came on and I thought the wards were breaking, going down. The crocodile bellowed in expectant triumph just as I grabbed a burning chunk of wood from a fire and pitched it full into the beast's gaping jaws.

It screamed and screamed again, flopping like a beached fish or perhaps a whale, sending other, smaller monsters spinning. As they writhed, their soft underbellies were exposed and my fighters had good aim and the arrow storm struck full, spears driving hard behind them. Sand and water flurried and there were howls and then we were standing, panting, holding weapons, and there was nothing but the night, the flare of the fires and the hum of the mosquitoes. Sometime, perhaps a lifetime later, the sun rose.

Janela cast her spell and ordered the group into the boats. She insisted on being in the lead vessel—she would be the first victim if her spell did not take. I stayed on the beach. I would be the last to leave this hellish islet that had promised a moment's respite and then turned on us. The boats reached the ships and the men scrambled aboard. The boats returned and somehow all of us packed ourselves aboard.

As we drew near the *Ibis* I saw four bodies, floating facedown. All of them wore ornaments, if that was what they were, like the ones we'd seen on the man in the brush. None of them showed any marks of violence.

We got aboard, hoisted up the boats, and manned the sweeps. There was enough of a wind blowing into the east to set the sails, but all of us wanted to do anything, everything, to speed us away from that place.

Kele shouted to look overside. I saw a crocodile surface, take one of the bodies, and vanish, leaving not much more than a swirl.

"Feedin'," Kele said. "Now, Lord Antero, since you're knowin' all things . . . was that lizard feedin' on man . . . or was *man* feedin' on man?"

I shuddered.

CHAPTER TEN

INTO THE GORGE

Quite suddenly the swamp came to an end and the river returned to a common bed, flowing through tree-dotted plains,
thick brush lining its banks. Janela and I speculated about
the area we'd just passed through. The Old Ones wouldn't have
their main thoroughfare suddenly turned into a mire. Something
must have gone wrong. Perhaps a crucial spell had lapsed or maybe
even the crocodile folk had strong earth-magic of their own to overcome the time-weakened ancient sorcery.

"That," Janela said, "or else we stumbled into one of the Old
Ones' traps intended to snare anyone who didn't have the proper
spells or guide with them."

No one cared. It was enough that our passage was fairly easy
now, with no more rowing or kedging, and the wind held firm from
the west. We had to keep men in the bows, however, since there
were sandbars and, every now and again, clotted masses of vegetation that could have snared us.

The land was green and we saw small irrigation ditches leading inland for the river, and not long afterward we saw scattered huts and grazing animals. A small herd came to the water's edge to drink and gave us a chance to look at them closely. They were cattle, but most strange-looking, with high humps, sweeping horns that curled back along their sides, and hair long enough to shear for wool. Every now and then we saw herdsmen, primitive-looking folk wearing skin kilts and tunics and carrying spears. But they weren't that primitive or else traded with people who weren't, because we saw the glint of iron at the spear tips. We waved, and sometimes the herders would signal back, but rather halfheartedly, as if they had little interest in our passage.

"Jus' like a countryman," Berar shouted over to us once, when the *Firefly* sailed nearby. "Been so long since they seen anythin' new, it don't shine through into what little brains they got. Don't it make you want to go farmin', Kele?"

Kele's response was a rather vulgar wave.

One day we lay becalmed for an hour or so and Quatervals spotted one of the herders not far from the bank. The man was seemingly unaware of us, squatting on his haunches in front of one of his animals, staring at it intently. Quatervals asked permission to go ashore and see if he could get any information from him. I told him to take Pip, to give him something new to complain about, and hasten back when we signaled or the wind returned.

We lowered a boat and the two went ashore, taking some beads and fruit from the delta as presents. Pip stayed a few yards back and Quatervals approached the herder. Quatervals' arms waved, and then he squatted and began talking to the man. Evidently, the conversation was unsatisfactory, because he soon got up, motioned to Pip, and returned to the boat. They still carried our gifts.

Everyone swarmed them when they boarded, wanting to know what had happened and who was the man—any bit of news that would break the routine of our journey.

Quatervals had a bemused expression. The man's name was Vindhya, he thought. Or maybe that was his tribe—even with the Gift of Tongues, the herder's speech was hard to understand.

"And," he added, keeping all emotion from his voice, "the cow's name is Soenda. He introduced us."

Janela snickered.

"Why'd he not want the loot?" one of the sailors asked. "Too blasted proud?"

"No. It was"—and I saw Quatervals was trying to keep a solemn expression—"because we were interfering with his worship."

"Pardon?"

"Vindhya, or maybe the Vindhya, worship cattle."

Now there was general mirth, increased when Otavi said, "Now, that's a rare idea. If'n y'r god doesn't do right by you . . . he's dinner. Or she, to put it the way it is here. Guess you could 'milk your faith' for all it's worth out here."

Quatervals waited until the laughter subsided, then continued gamely on. "The reason Vindhya didn't much want to talk," he said, "or even look at what we wanted to give him, is that he was contemplating Soenda. He said it's his favorite cow and if he spends enough time with her, being close and all, he'll completely absorb all of her cowness."

"Cowness?" I repeated incredulously.

"Cowness is what he said."

When the laughter died away again, Pip scratched thoughtfully. "Thank Te-Date we di'n't ask what their *lovelife* mus' be like. Damned strange it'd be, callin' on a man, wantin' the hand of his heifer. Guess we'd best keep a lookout for seein' some half-man, half-moo li'l critters."

That led the conversation, such as it was, into predicted depths of bawdiness. I withdrew, being too much of a gentleman to indulge in such questionable conversation.

Cowness, indeed.

THAT EVENING Janela chanced sending a bit of her spirit back the way we came to spy on Cligus.

She'd asked my assistance in the event she was discovered. She sat cross-legged on the bare deck in the middle of a concentric circle with an eye scribed in it. Four braziers formed a square around her and sent smoke coiling about her like a snake. When she'd completed the spell I could actually *feel* her spirit leave her body. She appeared no different, but I was sitting next to a husk.

Long moments passed, then she stirred and her eyes opened. They weren't looking at me, but rather at some horror. Her hands reached out, grasping, and she tried to speak, but all that came was a grating gargle.

I waited no longer, but cast water across the braziers; they hissed and went out. Before the last of the smoke dissipated I took the dagger that lay beside me and cut sharply across the circle. The spell was broken and Janela returned.

She was pale, shaking. I shouted for brandy and Quatervals brought some. She rinsed her mouth, spat, then swallowed a long mouthful.

"They're coming," she said finally. "Coming fast. They're somewhere below the swamp."

"They saw you," I said.

"Modin did . . . and *reached* for me. He nearly had me and I was prepared to fight him, spirit against flesh on his ground, but you brought me back. Next time—"

"There will not be a next time," I ordered. "Not like that at any rate. This expedition has but one Evocator, and if she can't find another way of reconnoitering, we will travel blind."

"Maybe the crocs'll do for them," Quatervals said.

Janela shook her head. "No. They'll be unharmed. A matter of common background." She managed a weak smile.

She was still shaken by Modin's attack. I guessed the wizard had prepared his trap sometime before. In the future we would have to take better precautions.

I helped Janela to her cabin. I helped her undress, and she tumbled into bed without protest and closed her eyes. I sat holding her hand until her breath came regularly, then touched my finger to my lips and to hers. A smile came and went and I silently withdrew.

THE LAND BECAME drier and rose around us until we entered a deep gorge, the stone walls reaching two or three hundred feet above us. Although the river was nearly a quarter mile wide, the water should have rushed through the gorge like a torrent; instead, ancient magic made it flow smoothly, calmly. The current may have been stronger but so was the wind, channeled up the gorge so our sails creaked and groaned as we sped onward.

There were fish great and small in the waters around us, and birds of prey to hunt them. Fisheagles with wingspans nearly the breadth of our boat dived and swooped. Once I saw a smaller hawk get too close to the water and something leapt up, took the bird, and vanished before I could see if it was fish or reptile. After that, those few of my men who were still fishing when off watch lost interest in the sport and we ate only ship's rations.

In spite of our pursuit, we sailed only by day, not wanting to chance running blind into rocks or hostiles.

The gorge wound on, and I thought if we had no goal and no enemies behind us, the days could have gone on forever. It was always balmy, and what rain fell came in gentle showers. The mornings were soft with mist, and rainbows arced over the gorge ahead of us.

At intervals there were large caves in the rocky wall—caves carved by men. Mooring bits had been cut from the rock and steps led up to where the caves had been built above the spring flood marks. I remembered the road carved into the river rock that Janos and I had traveled on when we sought the Far Kingdoms and knew that the same hands had been at work here. But then there had just been a roadway with occasional bypasses. On this river there were small villages cut into the rock, with cubicles, little roofless houses to sleep in; open areas for markets; benches and tables, all marvelously worked from the gorge's heart, each about a day's sail apart. Travelers in those days could've gone from one encampment to another, never having to either sleep aboard uncomfortable ships nor chance the outdoors.

Kele had asked if we should use them for our overnight landings, but there was a chorus of objections from the men. There was no need to argue with their superstitions, since the river had more than enough islets to tie up to and sleep on firm ground. We posted guards with bows and chanced casting nets for our meals several times without ourselves being fished.

One night, full of a particularly fine whitefish that Maha had baked with wild mushrooms and dried tomatoes, and then covered with a spicy sauce made from river shrimp caught with a bait net, Janela and I sat away from the others, talking idly. She'd taken her boots off and was drawing in the sand with a delicately pointed foot.

"I wonder," she said, "what my great-grandfather would have been thinking if you and he had gone on past Irayas and had sat here on this beach."

"I doubt he would have been relaxing in the sand," I said. "Most likely he'd be trying to cast his vision in front of us, to see what was ahead. He'd be busy trying to come up with a way to travel by night or, failing that, endlessly studying for more clues to the nature of magic. Although Janos had many virtues, appreciating slothful moments wasn't one of them."

"I used to be like that," Janela said. "Then I agreed to study under a master who promised to teach me how to feel one with the world and sense how all things are linked. Since that seemed like part of my great-grandfather's beliefs, I agreed.

"He sat me in the rain with a yellow flower and told me to study it. I saw no sense in it, but did as he commanded. For hours all I could think of was how sore my behind was, how tense my muscles were, and that if I sat much longer I'd catch a chill from the rain. On the next day, I determined to work harder, and did. I concentrated solely on that flower. It may have helped or it may have hurt that the day was fine and sunny. After some hours my mind did clear, though, and I could fill myself with the essence of the flower."

"Thank whatever gods you worshiped you weren't sitting in front of a cow," I joked.

"It might as well have been one." She smiled. "Several weeks passed, during which time I spoke little. My master also spoke little, except to lecture me on the concentration process or, since I had also agreed to be his body servant and cook, to give orders."

"I've heard of such philosophers," I said. "We have a few living in the wilds beyond Orissa. I often thought of visiting them but never quite found the time."

"I don't know whether that was your gain or loss," Janela said. "I learned a bit of patience from this man. I was with him for nearly four months. Then one day I realized something larger and left him that same afternoon. He was angry, saying I'd broken the agreement and I should have been prepared to spend at least five years with him and by then I would have made a choice about the rest of my life.

"But I already had one—to find the Kingdoms of the Night."

"*That* was your greater realization?"

"No. I just wondered why my goal was to have as few thoughts as possible. Stupid people think less than intelligent people, so why would I devote five years to becoming dumber?"

I chuckled. "I'm sure," I said, "your master disagreed."

"Not only that, but he didn't even smile when I told him that. Again I wondered why most of those who choose some sort of spiritual life seem to give up their sense of humor."

"Janos was like that," I remembered, "in the latter days."

"I shouldn't wonder," she said. "Kings and those who would be kings don't seem to laugh a great deal, either, save at the discomfort of others."

I sat, thinking for a while. "You know," I said, "at one time I was concerned about you—that you might be too much like Janos."

"You mean be willing to turn against anyone and anything," she said, "to gain this magical crown of knowledge? Knowledge that gives real temporal power? I don't think I would. I never have held respect for such men or those few women I've encountered who sat a throne.

"Look at those coming behind us. Modin has—or had, at any rate—great powers, and now he's sculling along in our wake after something I doubt he knows much about. Except that it is of value to us. And Cligus? What would Cligus gain if he caught and . . . dealt with you as he plans? Nothing. Orissa will continue on, Cligus will inherit not much more in the way of riches and certainly no more knowledge than what little he possesses now.

"I share all too many of my great-grandfather's faults and have many all my own. I lust after knowledge as badly as Grandsire

Janos did, and long to discover that single law that lays all worlds and all knowledge open to me.

"But then to use that knowledge to gain temporal or even spiritual power? Power for its own sake isn't what I desire. But I'll be honest, Amalric. Such a diadem isn't in my grasp yet. When we reach the Kingdoms of the Night you'd best watch me closely. If I stop making jokes, reach for your dagger." She grinned, then turned serious.

"There was something I gained from that master," she said. "A willingness to be alone with my thoughts. I found that I was able to consider some things I'd never quite known how to handle. Such as what my great-grandfather was. It was most important I deal with this, since he was the one who set a name and a goal for me. But it's hard to accept the reality that my grandsire—my hero, I guess I'd have to name him—was in many ways a monster.

"Do *you* dismiss him, disclaim him because of that? Or do you do what most of us do and paint over his vices and sing loud about his virtues? I was—am—able, or so I honestly believe—to accept Janos Greycloak as a whole man, and still find him great and worth following to a certain degree."

"To be able to do that," I said, "is very hard. I thought when I performed the cremation rites that I had forgiven him. But when I wrote my journal I discovered I still harbored ill feelings toward him, as well as many guilts of my own. There were two journeys in that book. One was the search for the Far Kingdoms. The other was a search for a man I had once called my friend."

"In my view," Janela said, "that was the most successful journey. You may have mistaken Vacaan for the Far Kingdoms. But you did not mistake Janos Greycloak in your final summation of the man."

For reasons I could not fathom, I took her hand. We sat silently in the night for a long time. Finally, a hunting lion roared satisfaction from somewhere on the plateau above us and we made our way past the sentries to our bedrolls stretched on the sand.

TWO NIGHTS LATER we were forced to stay at one of the village caves, since we'd sighted no islands by afternoon. I could lie and say only the more superstitious men were afraid, but shall not, since all of us were apprehensive. After the enticer on the island and the crocodile folk, who knew what strange enchantments lay in this land beyond the seas?

Janela cast a divination when we tied up and said she felt no threat, no jeopardy. But she cautioned us to stay close together since there were many kinds of magics here and her senses weren't yet attuned to all of them. We needed little warning. But nothing happened and we found the small hideaway most cheerful, particularly as it had clouded over and threatened rain. In our nook above the river it could storm as much as it wished.

After we'd eaten, some of the braver men, Chons and the Cyralian brothers, even went exploring. Chons came running back in great excitement and said he'd found a flight of steps that might lead to the land above the gorge.

Janela and I decided to see what lay above us. Quatervals pretended he would have rather napped, but in truth he was glad of some exercise and dug out some torches in case night fell before we returned. The Cyralian brothers, Chons, and three other well-armed men accompanied us in the long climb.

The steps climbed in zigzags, parallel with the gorge. There were high gallery windows cut into the rock, and there was still enough light to see clearly. Centuries of passage had badly worn the middle of the steps, making me realize just how long ago our shelter had been built. When we were just a few flights from the top I whispered a warning and all of us except Janela drew our weapons. There was nothing to fear that I knew of, but it was senseless to play the innocent.

On the last landing lay scattered bones. I studied them closely in the gloom and decided they were those of a horse and rider. Driven into the stairwell to tumble to their deaths by . . . by what? I didn't know. We went on with much more caution.

We came out of a low stone building that might have been easily mistaken for a small rise in the ground. On either side were broken-down hitching rails, and not far away, stone corrals. The hideaway below would've been a connecting point for traders from inland and river merchants.

The land around us was sparse, bare, unwatered. There were strange-looking trees, twisted, reaching up at the heavens for water that came but seldom to this desert. We looked far out into the wasteland and saw no sign of life. Wherever the traders had come from was either destroyed or a far journey.

We crept to the gorge and looked over. Far, far below, like tiny motionless water beetles, lay the *Ibis*, *Glowworm*, and *Firefly*, tied to the dock.

Quatervals muttered in what he possibly imagined to be singing: "*. . . to see what we would see/But all that we did see/But all that we did see/Was more and more to see/Was more and more to see . . .*"

One of the brothers *tss*ed sharply—no doubt one of their secret poaching signals—and pointed off, upriver. I looked but saw nothing.

"At the clouds," he said, his voice in an needless whisper. "See the lights?"

By now it was close to full dark and I craned, seeing nothing, then seeing, very faint, then more discernible, lights reflected off the overcast.

"There's folks over there," he said. " 'Nough of 'em to shine like they're a city. Big village, anyways."

We waited for another hour, and by then it was clear we weren't seeing the moon's reflection, but illumination from some settlement. I couldn't tell how much farther upriver it lay, nor could anyone else make an estimate.

This was producing nothing but a warning for the morrow's travel. We turned back for the stairs and Chons looked puzzled. "I swear—" he said in a murmur. "I swear I can hear music. Coming from where those lights are."

I listened, but heard nothing, nor did anyone else. The Cyralian brothers gently mocked Chons, saying he'd already impressed them and could go a-poaching—beg pardon, Lord Antero, a-hunting—with them when they returned to Orissa. He didn't need to be makin' up tales about what he could see, hear, or smell. Chons looked stubborn, clamped his lips, and said no more.

We lit the torches and crept back downward, minding our way, until we returned to the others.

Janela and I gathered the three captains and told them what we'd seen and asked how we should handle matters. Should we boldly sail up to this city and announce ourselves as peaceful?

Kele grunted and said, "The odds don't favor that, lord, considerin' the closest thing we've had f'r a mate in these parts wa' the steer-shagger back yon."

"By the same token," Towra put in, "isn't that as likely to mean our luck's changin'? Or about to, anyhap?"

I didn't know. Maybe we should break one of our rules and tie up short of the city and try to sail past silently in the depths of the night. I offered this but was argued with—surely any city would have sentries on their waterfront, and anyone who tried to creep past would surely be thought hostile, particularly in these times, when no one was on the river. None of the captains thought we had the slightest chance of not being seen, even if we lowered all sails and used the sweeps—unless the river just happened to broaden out, and there didn't seem to be much chance of that.

Janela was listening and, at the same time, preparing a spell. She lightly chalked a circle with a vee through it, pointing upriver toward what we'd seen, and a curve closing the wide end of the vee. She put a small candle about a foot in front of the arrow and then lit it. She reoutlined the figure with an unguent from her purse, then found an archer and got one of his arrowheads. Grimacing a little, she drew blood from a finger with its tip, touched its point to her eyelids, then laid the arrowhead in the center of the vee and chanted:

"Go now
Go swift
Carry me
To the light
See the light
Find the light."

She cast the arrowhead into the darkness, then sat hastily. An instant later her head snapped back, as if she was mounted on a stallion that had just bounded away, then her head came forward, eyes tightly shut. In a moment her eyes opened and she sucked in air, shaking her head.

"Nothing," she said. "I don't know if the spell didn't take, or if there's wards, but I saw and felt nothing out there, nothing at all." She thought for a moment, then went on. "Very odd, as I come to think, because there was not even the force from animals I should have sensed. I guess the spell just didn't work."

She began putting away her gear, and looked up at us. "I'm sorry. But I don't know any more than anyone else."

"So," Berar put in slowly, "there's nothin' for it but to stick our heads in the noose, eh?"

There wasn't. We doubled the guards that night and roused everyone before dawn. As soon as we could see the water, we cast off our lines and raised our sails.

For the first time the gorge required careful navigation. Pinnacles ripped up from the river's bottom nearly to the top of the canyon's wall or worse, to just a few inches above the water, ready to rip into the hull of a careless sailor's ship. The winds were somewhat fickle and we were forced to tack back and forth, wearing our way upriver slowly and laboriously.

By midday we still hadn't come on the city, or village, or whatever it was, and I determined we'd pull into the next cave village and deal with tomorrow on the morrow. But there was nothing, not a shelter, not an islet, not even rock pinnacles we could tie fast to.

We sailed on and the day grew later.

Sweeping around a bend, we came on the city. The gorge opened into a wide draw, and in this expanse the city had been built. It was large, but there was no sign of life. There were no ships tied up at the waterfront, no boats, no movement on the docks, and not a light to be seen. I ordered the crews into armor and full readiness for battle and we sailed closer.

The city was deserted.

It wasn't ruined and overgrown like the city at the mouth of the

river had been, nor was it empty like the cities of the fables, in perfect order, where food still sits on the tables, kitchen fires smolder,
and clothes hang on their racks, but there's not a living soul to
be seen.

The closer we came, the more damage I could see, as if a storm
had smashed through the town some time ago and the inhabitants
had just given up and moved on. A half-stove-in door hung in an
entryway, and I saw buildings whose roofs had been crushed.

I waited for Janela to say something but she just shook her
head. "Dead," she said. "I feel nothing, no one."

"Should we chance sailing on?" I asked Kele. "Perhaps there's
an island or at any rate a place to tie up farther on."

"I'll do that if you order me, Lord Antero. But we'll have to
ready the boats for ready lowerin', an' I'll tell you firm I advise
against it. I wouldn't fancy our chances all that much, assumin' the
rocks an' shoals're the same on up as they have been. Since Lady
Greycloak felt no evil . . . I can't say, lord. It's y'r decision."

I hesitated long, but the decision was only mine.

Not wanting to do it, but seeing no other logical choice, I told
Kele to order the ships to tie up at the dock I indicated, which was
close to an open square. Use a stern rope and a long head rope so
we faced out, into the current, I ordered, and have seamen standing
by with axes, ready to cut us free on an instant's warning. I wanted
a full watch on deck at all times.

Our three ships pulled in and reluctant seamen went onto the
stone docks and moored us as I'd ordered. Maha sliced smoked
ham, duck, or pork into pocketed bread baked two days earlier by
the *Firefly*'s talented cook, and added an oil/vinegar/spices dressing,
and that, eaten at our posts and washed down with small beer, was
supper. As we ate we stared out at the storm-wracked city and wondered what could have happened. There was damage, more to be
seen now that we were closer, but not enough to have caused the inhabitants to give up and leave.

"Cursed, they was," Pip said.

"What sort of curse?" someone asked in a near-whisper.

"Curses be curses," he said. "Ain't but one kind, several species. Gods, demons, all use the same cloth. Y're cursed, y' run, but it's never no use. Curse pro'ly caught up wi' 'em when they slowed down an' started to build anew. All dead now. No question."

Someone managed a mild curse for that cheeriness—aimed at Pip.

Before dark Quatervals came to me with an idea.

"Meaning no criticism of milord's tactics, but may I offer a suggestion? I think it'd be wiser if we put out sentries in the square, on land, rather than just huddle here with no way of gettin' warnin' if somethin' comes out of those alleyways across. I'd suggest sentries there . . . there . . . and there," he said, pointing.

"And if something does come?"

"We'll pick those who're known for bein' fleet of foot and with good ears and tell 'em to sound the alarm and then scamper for the ships."

I didn't like the idea of setting anyone ashore here, even though there'd been nothing to see or fear and Janela still felt no threat. But . . .

"Very well," I decided. "You pick the men. I'll stand watch-on-watch-off with you from over there, by that dry fountain."

Quatervals came closer and muttered, "*Lord* Antero, meaning no disrespect, *lord*, but there are times, *milord*, when I think Te-Date was feelin' miserly when he put brains in your head. I'm suppose to be keepin' you alive, not these other weasels, which means you're supposed to keep your arse right here on this gods-damned deck and let me worry about the perimeter!"

"Thanks for your opinion and concern, *Citizen* Quatervals," I said. "But my order stands. I'll take first go. Relieve me at midnight."

But Quatervals never made that relief.

The mate aboard the *Ibis* had just rung the midwatch, the ting of the bells resounding into the dead city—and as if that were a signal, the city came alive.

Suddenly there were people in the square, richly dressed, shouting, singing as we scrabbled our weapons out. One man—I had but a second to note that he was ostentatiously drunk—reeled toward me and, as I tried to block him away with the flat of my sword, walked *through* me, and at the same moment I realized I heard no sounds of carnival.

The only noises were the cries of alarm from my ships and the sentries giving the alert.

This was a city of ghosts, ghosts that had come alive, and no sooner did I realize that than the full sounds of a city in mad bacchanal swept over us. Janela, sword in hand, ran up to me.

"Amalric," she said, "this came but seconds ago. I had barely time to feel these spirits and then they were here."

"Can you tell their intents?"

"I cannot. But we must retire to the ships quickly. I fear the worst."

Most of the sentries, following my standing orders, had already retreated to the ships. Quatervals was just coming down the gangplank of the *Ibis* with my rescuing party as we reached the dock. Backs to the ship, we retreated aboard and then marveled.

Now the buildings looked new, brightly painted and draped with banners; the dry fountain I'd been standing next to sent explosions of different-colored light up into the air, and we heard many bands from many parts of the city playing loudly, as if competing for the ears of the city's denizens.

The ghosts continued their revelry, paying us no mind.

"Should we cast off?" Kele asked.

Janela shook her head. "Not yet. Not if we don't have to. I don't feel any malevolence directed toward us. But that could change as quickly as these spirits appeared."

I agreed, and told her to have all men in armor with their weapons ready, although I didn't know what good temporal steel could do against wraiths.

Now we had time to look at the crowd and try to think as to what was going on. It was some sort of special holiday, I thought, because no one, not even the festival-happy people of Irayas, could celebrate so constantly, so frenetically. I could feel the tension aboard ship ebb as sailors looked across the square, identifying the celebrants:

"Look at her. Right naked."

"Aye. Ought to be a law, someone as fat as that. Make 'er wear a tent."

"By the gods, that 'un just drained a double-handed flagon an he's still standin' . . . no . . . there he goes . . . taken aback . . . hung up in irons . . . hard ashore . . . and dismasted," someone said, seeing the ghost in question stagger in circles than collapse.

"Over there. Look at those two, havin' at each other."

"No harm, they're both so drunk they can't see—the hells! He just pulled a dagger! Te-Date, they're both cuttin' . . . an' now they're both down an' dyin'!"

"Damme, damme . . . I've never seen such chaos," Kele muttered. "It's as if this is the last day of the last celebration."

Before I could respond, horns blared over the music and all the ghosts in the square turned. Black-clad crossbowmen doubled into the square and took up positions, their weapons ready. The horns grew louder, and then a wave of men and women poured into sight from a main street. Men, women, and demons, I corrected myself, as I saw something with the body of a woman but the head of a jackal, something crawling behind it like a spider but with a man's head protruding from its midsection. Some of these beings were clothed, some were naked. They were beyond drunk, in an ecstasy I'd only seen in a few lands, during primitive ceremonies aimed at waking the dark gods and demons. These beings coupled indiscriminately, man with man, woman with beast, beast with man. Others slashed at themselves with knives, roaring in glee as the blood flowed. All of them were bellowing, screaming, singing at the top of their lungs.

On deck I heard a sailor mutter a prayer and another one vomit.

I felt a black wave roll toward me, a sea of malevolence from these ghosts. I turned to Janela and saw her expression, which must've matched mine.

Before either of us could speak, something else strode into the square. I don't quite know how to describe it. If it was a demon, it was one such as I'd never heard of. It appeared somewhat like a man in spite of its taloned claws, although Janela told me later she saw it as a woman. But it was constantly changing its shape, and each time it changed it was more obscene, more evil. I don't know why the thought came to me, but I thought that this . . . this presence reflected the evil in us all, reflected and held it. It was huge, towering far over the buildings.

But it was more than just an aspect—this creature was material. There was a line of children, chained together with neck bands, and the monster reached down, howling laughter, and picked them up by the chain, and I could hear the screams as they strangled and died. The being cast them aside like a child abandons a flower chain, reached down and found a woman, lifted her and then smashed her down, her body shattering against the cobbles of the square.

Cages on wheels were rolled into the square, cages full of men, women, children, who saw the demon and screamed for mercy but would find none as the beast lifted one cage, tore the roof away, and took the captives in one hand and squeezed and once more screams resounded.

I came back to alertness and was shouting to cut the lines and cast off when all at once the demon, the presence, became aware of us. As he did, so too did all of the ghastly celebrants in the square. The howls of celebration became shouts of anger, and someone picked up a cobblestone and hurled it at us. Now those ghosts had become real, because the cobblestone crashed solidly against the deck, barely missing Maha. Just behind it thrummed a crossbow bolt that buried itself in a bulwark beside me.

Kele and the other ship captains were shouting commands and axes thudded and lines fell away. Janela looked upstream, pointed, screamed—and I turned.

A huge wave that stretched from wall to wall of the gorge was rushing down on us, its roar now louder than the crowd. The wall of water was enormous, reaching almost to the plateau above, taller than the city's buildings or even the demon, who saw doom coming at him and screamed again, this time a scream of fear and rage.

Other screams came from the ghosts and were echoed by our seamen as doom closed upon us. There was no time, nor would there have been any point in trying, to turn the ships' bows up-stream to somehow take the blow.

I knew the Dark Seeker rode that wave and death had finally come to Amalric Antero, but I was damned if I would give in. I seized Janela and pulled her down, my other arm wrapping around the foremast, in a forlorn hope that somehow we might survive the crushing blow. The wavesound grew louder, louder, filling the world, and it towered over us, over the city, and my eyes were closed and the wave broke, crashing, and the screams were buried in the noise of destruction and I sucked in a deep breath, my last, but I would hold it as long as I could.

But no water poured over us, although it took many seconds for me to realize it. I opened my eyes and the night was peaceful, si-lent, overcast. I sat up in time to see the last of that wave rush across the city, burying the obscene horrors and smashing the build-ings as it went, and then the wave was gone and I was staring out at an abandoned, moonlit city that appeared damaged by what I'd thought to be a storm, but now knew differently.

Janela lifted her head, looked about. My sailors were coming to their feet. Stunned silence lay heavy and then murmurs began as we realized we yet lived.

We were still gaping at the ruins left long ago by that great wave when Janela, quicker than the rest of us, said sharply, "What we just saw happened years and centuries ago. But it was not a dream. Captain Kele, we must set sail at once. The Old Ones, the gods, I don't know, destroyed this city, but the doom still hangs close."

We knew she was right, and moving numbly, as if in a dream, we shook out sails, manned the sweeps, and put men in the chains with torches to watch for rocks. No one cared much about whether or not we might wreck ourselves on unseen obstacles.

It was enough that we lived. None of us would ever forget the horror of that dark carnival, nor of its destruction.

As we rounded a bend and the city fell away downriver, I thought I heard something.

I listened closely.

Music came from behind us and I saw lights flicker against the overcast.

WE HEARD THE ROARING long before we came to it. All of us jumped at the sound, fearing another giant wave's attack, and this one could be real instead of a ghost. Our nerves were on edge now, even though, thank Te-Date, we'd taken few casualties. But there'd been too many horrors which only those far away might term marvels, too much danger, too much blood. Even the gorge's dawn-and-evening beauty was beginning to wear. We needed to see open land, open water, where we might have time to prepare for enemies before they came on us.

Sailing became harder as the current increased and the winds changed direction more often. Again and again we had to use the sweeps, and even then made little headway.

The river angled and our way was blocked.

A wide pool, actually a small lake, opened, and above it boiled the greatest waterfall I'd ever seen. Unimaginable tons of water crashed down into the lake, sending waves washing out across its surface. Mist rolled up almost to the plateau's edge and all was a deadly maelstrom of rocks and water. There was not a break, not a pause where this river fell free hundreds of feet from the plateau down into the gorge.

I ground my teeth in surprise and dismay. Now we'd have to abandon the ships. Worse, I scanned the rocky sides of the gorge for stairs, tunnels that would lead upward, but saw nothing but green-stained dripping rock.

Kele came up, swearing. "E'en somebody wi' their trenails not knocked flush'd know better'n to do this," she said. "A pox on these Old Ones. Maybe they just grew wings an' flew on home carryin' bales an' cargo under their wings?"

"Hardly," Janela said. She closed her eyes and her head swiveled, nostrils flared like a hunting beast. "No," she said. "We can go on."

"Straight up?"

"Look. Over there," she said. "Dead center through the mist."

I peered, and thought I saw something, something dark through the water veil.

"Captain," Janela said, "set your course for the heart of that cataract."

Kele's mouth opened, shut, then she barked commands. I heard protests, but as always, the crew obeyed. There were questions shouted from the *Firefly* and *Glowworm*, and Kele shouted back that they should follow her. I could have sworn the hoys showed reluctance as they fell into line. Tacking back and forth in short reaches, we closed on the falls, and the water bellow grew louder and louder and the mist boiled and took us in its embrace and I waited for the shock of the water to cascade on our deck.

Some did. Perhaps a dozen bucketsful, and then we were through the portal where Janela's eyes and other-worldly senses had seen the way, through where the water fell but lightly, and in an enormous cavern behind the waterfall.

There was no way to talk here with the roaring of the falls behind and beside us; we could only signal, as if we were in a storm at sea. We rowed on across the cavern, toward its far end. I'd thought it would grow darker and darker, but it stayed an even twilight. I don't know if there were cunning portals to let in the sun or magical illumination, but saw no signs of either.

Not that I looked for long. My eyes were taken and held by a true marvel.

Sorcery is normally a construct or a spell, and most of us do not think in terms of magic being connected to engines. But it can be done by very skilled Evocators working with the most handy mechanics. I suspect the model of Vacaan that occupied the center of King Gayyath's palace was such a device; and my sister Rali had destroyed the doom machine built by the Last Archon, which was intended to destroy Orissa and make him into a god. Those were indeed marvelous, but in some ways this was a greater feat, even though it showed a debt more to cleverness than wizardry.

A huge wheel rose out of the water before us, a cogged wheel that a huge, endless chain ran on, a chain with links almost the size of that sea chain that had once closed off Lycanth's harbor. The chain ran below the water in one direction, I guessed, and just at water level in the other.

As we approached, the roaring became louder, and with a screech the wheel began turning, the links of the chain clanking up from underwater, over the gears and away into the distance, very slowly. I was certain sorcery worked these engines because in spite of their age, neither the iron wheel nor the chain showed the slightest rust, but were as new as when they'd been hammered out in some unimaginably huge foundry.

I saw a sailor drop to his knees and begin praying; he was jerked up and backhanded back to his duties by a mate.

Janela leaned close, shouting in my ear, "The magic of the Old Ones still senses us. This, I wager, will take us to the top."

I didn't know how and so peered ahead.

The chain rose a bit as it traveled, and then I could see it followed a huge trough that went upward, wide enough for the biggest merchantman in my fleet, and vanished into the distance. The trough was set at almost a ten-degree angle and water ran down it, but not in the torrent it should've. Again, water-magic at work.

Janela went to Kele and pointed and spoke, but Kele was already nodding, as if she knew what was to be done. She bustled about the deck, grabbing men and shoving them into motion, shouting inaudible commands into their ears. I could hear nothing, but saw them obey, unshackling the anchor chain from the anchor, laying it on deck, then, from the chain locker below, breaking out the spare chain and laying that out as well. Other seamen took down the forecastle rails as if we were entering harbor. Still others ran halyards from the foremast's yards to the ends of the chains, set to, and lifted the chains until they dangled clear of the deck, just overside.

Kele came up, saying, "Just like a toy L'ur bought me as a wee one, my lord."

I still hadn't a clue, but she had no time for me. Three of the *Ibis*'s best seamen were detailed, and Kele ordered the sweeps to bring us close alongside that chain. At least *someone* knew what she was doing. Waiting for their moment, the seamen went overside, until they were standing on that huge chain as it clanked along. Our own anchor chains were lowered and made fast, first with rope, then with cables, and we were secured to that chain and carried on, toward that enormous flume.

Then it dawned on me that the enormous apparatus was no more than an endless bucket such as farmers use to water their fields; or a funicular, like one an Orissan speculator had once rigged with cables and boxes to carry those too lazy, old, or infirm to the peak of Mount Aephens, which had lasted one entire summer until the winter winds ripped it away. But by Te-Date, the magnificence of this magic and machine! This was yet another device the Old Ones had to guard their heartland well.

There would be no need to fight an enemy trying to come against them upriver. All that would be necessary would be to cancel the spell working the gears and shut the engine down, or lay a simple vision-blocking conjuration so the slight gap in the waterfall wouldn't be seen. Into my mind flashed something Janos had once said: "The greatest warrior I've known was one who fought never a battle but won all his country's wars by subtlety and subterfuge."

No doubt the spell would sense a ship going downstream above, and the gears automatically reverse and send the chain the other way, working as a brake, although we'd have to design some sort of chain-rigging if we returned by this route, no doubt. I grinned. Was I becoming so self-confident I actually believed any of us would survive this? A day ago I'd been locked in gloom and fear, and now, with something that appeared to be going to design, was suddenly as bubbling and happy-go-lucky as a bumpkin who has finally been allowed to win a toss of the dice.

Kele was on the quarterdeck, hand-signaling, Janela beside her, working with those tiny signaling flags, and then we were in the channel, being taken up toward the land above.

I saw working parties scurrying on the decks of the *Firefly* and *Glowworm*, so knew Towra and Berar had understood what was needed.

The chain lifted us slowly up and up, into another pool, where another toothed wheel and chain went up a second flume, just exactly like stairs. We had more than enough time to free ourselves from the chain before it went underwater and back down. There were two more channels and again we journeyed upward hour after hour and then came out of a high-arched tunnel into the clear sunlight and were back out on the river as it flowed across the plateau. We unshackled the chains for the last time and rejoiced as our other two ships came out of the darkness.

Downstream we heard the roar of the waterfalls that fell into the gorge we'd left some hours earlier.

I swore that now I could *smell* the real Far Kingdoms.

WE SAILED ON, the land around us as barren and sere as it had been when we climbed the stairs at the trader's shelter far behind us. There was nothing to see, nothing to do but the few duties required to hold our course, since the wind blew steadily in the direction we wanted, and lie on the deck panting like hounds and sweating. We rigged awnings but the wind came hot and dry, bringing sand from the desert across our decks and into our food.

But we were all cheerful, knowing we'd finished another stage of our journey. Perhaps there'd be another gorge or another swamp around the bend, but we would deal with that, just as we had dealt with the others and would, in time, deal with Cligus and Modin if we were unlucky and they caught up to us.

Such is man, always reeling from elation to despair. But then, if those of us who were out here, far beyond the known world, had wanted it any other way, we could have snuggled down in that warm sty of contentment and boredom that was civilization.

One night we sighted a glow on the horizon. We became nervous, remembering that city of ghosts behind us. But it was still there when the sun rose and, as we closed on it, hour after hour, became a vertical pillar of fire, rising out of the bare desert.

"Magic," one of the sailors said.

"Not necessarily," Janela said. "Haven't you ever seen when the earth bleeds sticky oil or where tar covers a swamp? If that could be lighted, I'd wager it'd look like what we're seeing."

As we came up on it we saw a scatter of huts along the riverbank, no more than a league from the column of fire. We saw people standing near them, watching us.

We chanced drawing close but kept our weapons at hand, ready to fire back and return to midstream if we encountered hostility, but there was none.

There was a rude dock, and we moored not far from it and lowered a boat. Janela, Quatervals, Pip, and I went ashore, more to stretch our legs than in the hopes of getting information or finding anything.

It was well we had no expectations because the people were a poor lot. Unsurprisingly, they called themselves the People of the Flame, and claimed they were the last of a once-mighty people who'd ruled this wasteland with sword and fire. But their mounts had been taken from them by the gods.

Gods? we asked.

Those who live up there—and they pointed on, up the river.

Who are they? What did they look like? How far away were they? Had anyone of this generation or the one before *seen* these gods?

No to all questions. What had happened to them had happened in their grandfather's grandfather's grandfather's and so forth time.

They had little to trade except water from a sweet well, but more out of pity than anything else, we filled our barrels and left these miserable folks with some play-pretties and candies.

I gave a sugar stick to one boy who would have been above seven. He was quite naked, and it was evident from his and the others' smells that they didn't consider swimming a worthwhile avocation. I noted he had a pet, a lizard about the length of my arm, on a string. I asked him if it had a name and he shook his head, no.

He said it would be bad to name it since it was a great one, descended from those steeds the gods had taken away. I blinked at that and reached down to examine the little creature.

It opened tiny fanged jaws and spat at me, and its spittle smoked and burnt like fire. I jerked my hand back and swore.

The boy nodded. "Does that to me, too."

He sucked hard on his sugar stick and his expression grew dreamy, finding tastes he'd most likely never known.

I looked at the lizard and wondered a bit, but knew I'd never know more.

We reboarded and sailed onward.

ON THE SIXTH DAY after that we saw a shimmer on the land ahead of us, crossing from horizon to horizon.

Hardly daring to hope or even to pray, we sailed closer and closer, and then a great lake opened before us.

Just beyond rose the mountains.

CHAPTER ELEVEN

THE PEOPLE
OF THE
LAKE

All river folk have a fascination for where a thing might begin or end. We sit by the banks of our river and watch the endless coming and going, dreaming of what it would be like to join such grand processions. Some of us are so afflicted that we become wanderers, always seeking the source of all things; praying, even, that we might be the first to see such wonders. It's a glorious if childish feeling that allows you to briefly imagine that instead of a puny mortal looking up at a mountain you are that haughty, ageless range looking down. I've enjoyed such fleeting moments many times in my life. But never so much that the pleasure grew stale. And so when we came into the great lake where the river was born, one part of me was wary, sniffing the heavy air for new dangers, while the other was drunk with the heady wine of discovery; for while the Old Ones might have reigned here a millennium or more ago, it was a place no one from my world had ever seen.

The lake seemed nearly as broad as a sea. Janela's map showed we needed to sail for its most distant shore, out of sight to the east.

Plumes of mist ribboned up from the lake's cool surface and the air shimmered under a bright sun, giving the view the cast of a magical mirror. The water was low that time of year, and near the shore trees grew right up from the bottom—singly or clotted together like small woodlots. Lily pads the size of serving platters at a palace table floated their blossoms across the shallows, filling the air with fragrance. Fabulous dragonflies with dazzling wings darted here and there in search of mates, while emerald-feathered birds half as tall as a man stalked the water on stilted legs, necks as graceful as swans, scarlet beaks long, slender poniards prodding among the lilies for dinner.

There was a faint breeze carrying the cool, damp scent of the feather ferns that fanned out under trees that grew amazingly tall and straight toward the sky. Fat-fisted clouds knuckled under that vaulted course, giving everything an ethereal, peaceful look—as if we were at the entrance of a realm where all was clean and kind and good.

From this lake the river flowed, bringing life to those who dwelled below. After the Months of Cold, when the snow from the mountains melted, wondrous falls would thunder from craggy cliffs and countless streams would burst their narrow banks, filling the lake to the brim until it spilled out and made the river a glorious beast, rushing along all those weary miles we had traversed until it met the sea. In happier eras villages and towns would have held festivals to thank the gods for such bounty; there would be music and love-struck couples and clucking grannies shaking their heads at such goings on.

I smiled, chuckling to myself in memory of those lusty years when my own loins were as bursting as a reborn river and there had been many a maid to dally with and fuel the gossip of those finger-wagging grannies.

"What amuses you so, Amalric?" Janela asked.

When I told her, she smiled and said, "Are you certain those years are lost to you, my friend?"

I felt my cheeks flush, which made her smile wider and her eyes dance in humor at my discomfort. There was no denying I'd changed greatly since she'd first set eyes on me in my villa. I'd grown stronger, sleeker—limbs heavy with new muscle, waist narrow, chest no longer sagging with age. My old man's stoop was gone and I stood tall and straight again; easy in my boots, confident in my stride. I didn't need a mirror to know the marks of age had been erased from my features as well or that my white locks had been replaced by a shock of red hair that shone like hearth fire. I only had to see the occasional looks of wonder from my companions to realize that I appeared a man in his fourth decade rather than a fellow who'd seen nearly seventy summers.

Their wonderment, however, was never expressed in words. At first this mystified me almost as much as the change itself. I later realized, however, that they saw it as merely another facet of the mystique of Lord Amalric Antero—a mystique that in their view had already led me to make great, previously unthought of discoveries.

But instead of glorying in my regained youth I was now stricken by odd guilts after Janela had reminded me of my appearance. Age had taken my friends, as well as my dear Omerye. Why should I be spared? If spared I was—for I was not certain the gods were cursing me instead of bestowing a blessing. Sometimes I felt a stranger, an intruder in disguise among my companions: Their talk was the talk of youth, full of yet-to-be-realized dreams and untainted by harsh disappointment.

"What is happening to me, Janela?" I asked.

She placed a comforting hand on my arm. "I'm not certain," she said. "But I wouldn't worry that the change is an evil thing."

I looked at her, wondering how she could have guessed my bleaker thoughts.

"I've made castings," she went on, "and searched my memory for similar occurrences of men and women who might have had similar experiences. I've heard of people becoming old before their time; witches, even, who became hags overnight and nothing but a hank of hair and pile of dust by the next day. But I've never read of age being reversed, although it is certainly a long-sought goal of many a sorcerer. All I can say is, the closer we come to our goal, the younger you seem to become. Although your progress has seemed to slow of late. I very much doubt you'll continue until you become a mewling babe trying to use his sword for a teething ring."

I laughed. "I hadn't thought of that," I said. "Now you've given me something new to worry about."

"Well, don't," she said. "Think of it as that figurine my great-grandfather carried and how it became newer and more whole the closer you came to realizing your dreams."

I saw the development in a more cheery light. I thought how happy I would be if Omerye were with me now and we could grow younger together and pleasure each other every night until the break of dawn.

My reverie was broken. Up ahead was one of the Old Ones' demon/woman markers jutting at the channel's edge. The beauteous side was turned toward me, peering down coldly, regally, as if mocking my foolish dreams. I didn't need to see its demon side to be reminded that life's sweetest promises can be its greatest lies.

The first lie was the lake, which proved to be nothing but a skim of water over mud so deep that our longest poles could not reach the bottom. The demon/woman markers showed us the channel the Old Ones' ships must have taken long ago. Only a few, however, remained whole after so much time. The majority were broken off near the base, but even though those stone stumps were as snaggly as a crone's teeth, they rose higher than our rails, and from the crusted shellfish on their rough surfaces it was apparent that in other times the water was high enough for easy sailing. Now, however, the water was so low even our shallow-bottomed ships would find the way difficult, if not impossible.

I sent out scouts in small boats to investigate, and they returned to say it was much the same no matter how far they probed, although there were clear, deep patches along the way where we could make good progress.

I called everyone together—including Quatervals, Berar from the *Firefly*, and Towra from the *Glowworm*, to decide what we should do next.

"Maybe it's time we got off the water," Quatervals said. "Lady Greycloak's map shows we'll be needin' to strike out overland by and by. What's stoppin' us from doin' it now?"

Kele snorted. "Just like a lubber," she said. "All muscle-swole from walkin' 'n' no brains from lack of use. Sees a spot a trouble an' it's back to trompin' on the hides a poor animals again."

Quatervals bristled. "Don't take much wit to see we're in a fix," he said. "Ship can't sail on mud. Even you've got to admit that, Cap'n. I say we leave the damned things and circle the lake afoot."

I turned to Janela, who was poring over her map rubbing. "What's the terrain around the lake like?" I asked.

"There is no way to tell," she said. "The map this was made from was more for ceremony than anything else. All it really showed was the traditional route, the easiest way for the Old Ones to travel with their goods."

Quatervals broke in. "But there must've been some kind of road around it," he insisted. "With cities and villages and such." He glared at Kele. "Folks can't live on the water, leastwise not permanent like."

Before the defenders of sea travel versus land could fling more missiles, I stepped in.

"Why don't we send a party to see?" I asked. "We could use some fresh meat, so we could make it a hunting party. To make doubly sure no time is wasted, we could press ahead with the ships as best we can. Looking at the swamp ahead of us, the ships won't be able to go far enough to lose the land party, and it appears from the Old Ones' markers that the channel lies not far offshore, so Quatervals can track us down and signal or shout for a boat."

Eyebrows were raised and dark looks exchanged at my mention of wasted time, but no one commented. No more of a reminder was necessary that among our other difficulties we had an enemy on our heels whose demon prayers would be answered if they came upon us stranded on mud flats.

I tried to lighten the mood, grinning at Kele and saying, "Besides, my friend, how many shares in this venture would you trade for a fresh haunch of venison crackling over a fire?"

Kele chortled and slapped Quatervals on the back. "Bring us some wild mint with it, lad, 'n' I might even forgive yer lubber ways."

It was agreed to take the middle course, pressing ahead as best we could with the fleet while Quatervals set out with a party to hunt and, more importantly, to seek a route by land. He was gone five days—days that for us were burdened with labor so filthy, so horrid, that in the end even Kele admitted that two legs were not necessarily the worst means of locomotion.

To move the ships we had to drag them one by one, while our oarsmen heaved on the sweeps as if a demon strode among them, cracking his black whip. To aid the sweeps we first lightened each ship—piling all its goods into the one that waited behind. Then we ran lines to the ships' boats, and each of us took turns rowing those boats—straining with every muscle to tow the ship a few feet at a time, as we had back in the delta. Even the slow progress we made wouldn't have been possible if we hadn't also used the stone channel markers to help pull us along. A line would be made fast to the pillar, many-sheaved blocks would be tied to it, and lines would be woven back and forth through the blocks to the ship, men pulling hard to winch us toward our goal. The air was filled with groans and curses and cracking bone and sinew as we all pulled or rowed. And then when the ship reached the marker, we had to do it all over again—shifting cargo and goods and then muscling the next craft onward along the muddy channel.

When the blessed time came to be spelled, we'd collapse on the deck—too tired, even, to remove the leeches that made the mud a home and seemed to have waited all eternity for the leech gods to bless them with a tasty feast such as ourselves. Our mates had to rub them off with handfuls of salt or torture them with a burning splinter so they'd withdraw.

Once in a rare while we'd come to a deep place, and then we'd croak cheers as the fleet got properly under way again, sweeps carrying us easily for perhaps a mile or more. Then the mud-clotted lead would be hauled and the depth announced in a harsh cry that would have us cursing our mothers for bearing such unlucky children, and it was back into the boats again, or joining the men at the capstans, to drag the wooden mountains over the mud.

The fifth day broke gray and dismal, with a cold rain to add to our misery. We worked all morning, the light growing dimmer, the rain sleeting harder, but then our spirits lifted about midday when the channel suddenly deepened enough to bear up the ships and we could make slow, but less laborious progress.

Mud flats stretched on either side of us, and soon we saw first a few, then scores of mud cones rising up twelve feet or more. I didn't know what to make of them except to observe that they looked a bit like the large mounds I'd once seen on a wild plain. But those had been homes of a kind of wood-eating insect, and I couldn't imagine such creatures ever favoring mud flats for nests. Then instead of scores I saw hundreds of the things stippling the flats, their surfaces bubbling with moisture, popping, then pustuling to a head again in a steady rhythm—almost as if they breathed.

The channel carried the *Ibis* close to one of the cones, and as I leaned to get a closer view, a large, flat, diamond-shaped head shot up, hissing like an angry lizard. The head was albino-white with a single black bead for an eye. Four sharp mandibles framed a mouth of mottled pink and they clacked ferociously. I drew back in surprise and no little fear—just in time, because the creature reared back and spit a stream of putrid yellow liquid which spattered on the rails and deck. The surface of the wood blistered and smoked and I heard a cry of pain as the creature spat again and a hapless sailor was hit. He clutched his bare breast, which had turned a fiery red, as if seared by fire, and he fell to the deck, writhing in agony.

An arrow fired by a guard buried its head into the creature. It gurgled and shot back into its mud lair.

Just ahead, the channel widened into a deep pool. I shouted for Kele to make haste and ordered the signaler to flag the other to do the same. But then the lookout cried a warning, and his warning was echoed all down the line as others spotted the same threat.

Thousands of the creatures swarmed out of their nests and churned toward us from all sides. They were perhaps the length of a child, but you would never mistake them for such an innocent thing. Their bodies—a glistening gray-brown behind the white heads—were half again as thick and tubular, so they resembled a huge garden slug; but they had stubby legs with paddlelike feet—ten to a side, so they could move with alarming speed across the flats.

A score or more reached the channel and plunged into the water toward our ships, so incredibly agile that they could leap higher than our rails—bursting from the channel like blunt-tipped spears and raining their deadly spittle as their legs scrabbled at the rails for purchase. Two of them plopped down on the deck on either side of me, and I cut one in half with my sword, but before I could turn to dispatch the other, my whole side lit up in agony as it spewed thick yellow glop on me.

As I reeled in pain, Otavi chopped the creature in two with his axe, then he, too, was shrieking as one of the creatures reared up from the deck and caught him full in the face. Chons speared it, pinning it to the deck, where it wriggled mightily to get at him, but then Janela stepped in to lop off its head. Mithraik, who'd proved to be an uncommonly good fighter, laid about him with his sword, hacking at any of the gross creatures who came near him. All over the ship I could hear men shouting and cursing or crying in pain as they battled to keep the creatures from boarding. I recovered enough to slash one of our attackers, and it fell off the rail and into the water where five or more of its companions raced to devour it. Every one we killed and kicked over the side seemed to divert the attention of its none too fussy friends, who'd eat their own as easily as us. It was probably the only thing that saved us. The deck was slippery with rain and stinging mucus, and it was difficult for even the best of us to keep our feet, much less our wits.

The *Ibis* broke from the narrow channel and into the pool. Behind us our comrades were still fighting their way out. I saw one man go over the side, a slug-thing fixed to his throat. The others struggled to reach him but were driven back by a shower of venom.

The man's cries were terrible, and just before they stopped, I thought I heard him scream my name.

Then all three ships were in the clear, but the danger wasn't over. The creatures seemed only to pause for a moment at the channel's edge, then plunged after us, fanning out in a long half-circle many slug-bodies deep. They swam like the big flightless birds that favor the frozen Southern Seas, diving downward a body length then bursting up to break the surface and curling over for another dive.

Janela called to me and I saw her muscling an empty oil keg to the side. She slashed her arm with a knife, letting blood spill into the keg. I steadied myself as she reached for me with that knife, but she veered at the last instant, cutting off a bit of my hair. Quickly she stuffed the red hank into a small bag with a long sling. And she whirled the bag about her head, chanting:

"Demon Dreamer,
Who sleeps in the deep;
Awake onto me!
Demon Dreamer,
Hear my plea:
Awake!
Awake!"

The bag burst into flame and Janela flung it into the barrel. The oil residue caught and an unholy flame sheeted up.

Janela shouted to me for help and reached for the burning barrel.

I steeled myself and the two of us grabbed the keg—the intense heat of the fire nearly impossible to bear—and threw it over the side.

I had barely time to marvel that despite the heat, my hands were unscathed, when there came an unearthly shriek, as if from the bowels of the earth, and the surface of the water spumed and boiled.

The flaming keg exploded upward and a wave caught the *Ibis*, flinging us to one side.

Out of the depths rose an immense demon whose like I had never seen. It had the form of a woman—lush as any courtesan's—but covered with scales like a lizard. Her hair was long and dripping and the color was a foul green. Her face was that of a hag but with long, filed teeth. She had the hands of a corpse, bony and long, with needle talons for nails.

The demon turned this way and that, eyes black, flecked with yellow. Fear gripped me when I thought her gaze had fallen on me, but they swept on—until she saw the swimming mass of slug-things.

She gave another shriek—so loud that my ears rang with the horror of it for many hours—and plunged toward the creatures. Our attackers immediately swerved to meet her.

The demon gurgled in glee, scooping up a score or more in her huge hands. Chortling, she swallowed them whole and reached for more. The slug-things were unfazed, flinging themselves at the demon. Soon she was covered with them, screaming in pain as they ripped at her scaly flesh; but even then she scooped up more and gulped them down.

We were the unwilling audience for longer than I care to dwell on. And it was a fight without an apparent victor, for in the end the demon, with the last of the slug-things clinging to her, finally sank beneath the water. And as we fled, the water's surface continued to boil.

Eventually we thought it safe enough to stop. The rain had finally ceased and the sun made so bold as to peep out to swab filth from the decks and salve us with an ointment Janela conjured up to heal the burns made by the creatures' venom.

I was helping her work on Otavi, who'd narrowly escaped blinding, and she was commenting that it didn't look like his surly looks would be spoiled by a scar, when the lookout shouted that he saw signals from Quatervals' party on the shore. The hunting party had returned, and from the fatness of their burden, it looked like all had gone well.

When we'd fetched them, the first thing Kele asked was: "Did ye, perchance, find us that road?"

Quatervals shook his head. "Not a sign of one," he said. "And although there's game aplenty, the forest's so thick it'd take us a month to get where we're goin'."

"Now there's a great pity," Kele said. Quatervals goggled at her, amazed at such a swift change of mind. "And here I was prayin'," Kele continued, "that we'd finally get off this damned lake."

QUATERVALS had come across more than just difficult terrain in his journey.

"It was a lucky thing for us, my lady," he said to Janela, "you had the foresight to prepare us for the worst."

Before his group had left, Janela had cast a protective spell over each man, blowing bone dust in their faces and giving each a ring woven from the black fur of an apelike animal known for its ability to move through the forest without being seen.

"I can't make you invisible," she'd told Quatervals, "but if you practice your woodsman's skills well enough, I can make it harder for you to be noticed. You'll emanate the peaceful aura of something harmless but foul-tasting. It'll make you seem dull-witted as well, so if there are any witches or demons about, they'll pass you by as not being worth their notice."

"So there's something out there?" I asked Quatervals.

His face grew dark. "Indeed there is, my lord," he said. "And if it weren't for the spell Lady Greycloak cast, I wouldn't be standin' here tellin' the tale."

Quatervals had struck out to find a land route first and to hunt for fresh meat on their return.

"All went well for the first two days and nights, my lord," he said. "Although we didn't find anythin' like a road, there's game trails aplenty, cuttin' every this way and that." He shook his head. "I've never seen such a forest. Trees're so tall and thick it's nearly black as night on the floor. So dark some of the plants make their own light—big things, lookin' like mushrooms a witch'd conjure up. All glowin' red or blue and makin' the nastiest smell when you'd tread on them. And some of them favor meat, 'stead of good earth and water. Saw one catch a rabbit sort of animal. The poor sod got too close and the damned mushroom burst open like an umbrella. Had big fangs ringin' it, and a red, hairy sort of throat. It gobbled up its snack quicker'n it takes to tell, then went back to bein' an innocent-lookin' mushroom again."

Quatervals said some of the trees grew their fruit right out of the bark instead of from branches. "It gave us the shivers," he said. "The fruit was large and a sick-lookin' green. Made the trees look more like plague sufferers, all covered with boils. And I've never seen so many bats. Hangin' down from the branches in the day like they grew there, then goin' off to feed at night. Seemed to favor the tree fruit I mentioned, so I wasn't worried they'd want to make a meal of us. Still, the sight of them was enough to make a man's skin crawl."

He shivered at the memory. "Especially since the trees they

lived in were the safest place to sleep at night. All sorts of huntin'
things came out then, just like you'd expect. Saw a tiger once, but
he didn't give us any trouble. Thanks to Lady Greycloak's spell, he
just looked up in the direction of where we were perched, then decided to ignore us and move on. Same with the bears we saw. Two
of them, size of a small house, it seemed. 'Course we were pretty
nervous, so it might have been me thinkin' what it'd be like if they
took it into their heads to climb. But the worst thing was a fella
who resembled a big damned lizard, but with fur. And he rose up on
his two hind legs to spy out his prey. Seemed to favor those rabbity
things I mentioned. When he'd see one, he'd scream like blazes.
Froze your blood in its veins and your mind as well, so you couldn't
make a thought no matter how hard you tried. At least, that's how
we felt, and the rabbity critters must have done the same, because
they just stood there like they were stone and were snapped up by
the lizard with no trouble at all."

Kele sniffed. "So far," she said, "yer tale sounds like a pleasant
walk 'n the woods next to what's been goin' on here."

Quatervals nodded. He'd heard our story and had made proper
noises of commiseration and shock at our ordeal.

"And you'd be right to think that," he said. "Because that's all
it was . . . mostly. We were even gettin' used to it as time went by.
But that all changed on the third day."

Quatervals and the others had clambered out of the trees that
morning, eaten, made their ablutions, and were discussing the day's
travel ahead when it happened.

"It sounded kind of like a horn," Quatervals said. "Except it
was the loudest horn to be heard since the gods thumped us together
out of muck. It was deep as thunder and it hit us like a wind in the
Month of Storms. First blast nearly bowled us over, and the trees
shook so hard we were pelted with branches and leaves. Second
blast was deeper'n the other. Made your bones tremble. But the
wind wasn't so fierce. And the third call—for that's what it turned
out to be, and I'll get to that in a minute—was . . . gentler, is the
only way I can describe it. Seemed more like music, sort of. Made
you feel nice. Made you think how much nicer it'd be if you went
to listen to that horn up close."

Janela's eyes narrowed. She'd guessed a small portion of what was coming. "My spell should have protected you from that," she said.

Quatervals nodded. "That it did, my lady," he said. "It wasn't like we *had* to go. More like ... well ... that it'd be *nice*, that's all."

He looked at me. "My mother didn't breed a fool, my lord," he said. "So I knew straight off it was some kind of sorcery we were dealin' with. Talked to the others and they said the same. We talked about it an hour or more, and the whole time that horn kept playin'. Nearly decided then and there to head back, pick up a little meat on the way, and report what we'd heard. But the more we talked, the more we'd known that you'd want more'n just that. As scouts, our duty was to get a look-see, and it ought to come from as close as we could get."

"You thought correctly," I said, congratulating myself once again for picking a man like Quatervals, who could reason so coolly. "Go on."

"We tracked the sound half the day," Quatervals said. "Usin' game trails when we could and cuttin' our own path when we had to. All the critters knew somethin' was up. Didn't hear even a bird stirrin'. When we looked up we could see them sittin' in the trees, not even peckin' at a feather to get at a flea. We stumbled on some animals hidin' in the brush or behind fallen logs. They didn't bolt or threaten if they were a size to do so, but slunk off to find another place to hide.

"We were climbin' the whole time. Sent a man to shinny up a tree once, and he said the lake was at least a couple hundred feet below us. So I wasn't surprised when we reached a ridge crest and the ground dropped away and the trees opened up. Down the bottom of that hill is where the sound of the horn was comin' from. We eased about and found a rocky clearin' with boulders stacked nice and convenient for spyin'. So I reared up and did just that."

Quatervals' voice had grown hoarse, whether from weariness in the telling of the tale or in reliving the experience, I couldn't say. I sent for some wine to ease both, then urged him to continue.

"I was lookin' down into a canyon," he said. "Maybe twice as wide as the Grand Amphitheater in Orissa. There was a creek runnin' down the middle and the ground around it was bald of everythin' except rock. First thing that got my attention was all the people. Couldn't say how many because they were comin' from everywhere. Scamperin' out of the woods on every side except the one we were on—thank the gods. They were scramblin' down into the canyon, then runnin' in the creek or alongside it—didn't seem to matter to them. Nothin' mattered, in fact. Saw them fall, saw them stub their toes on rocks, saw them skin themselves on boulders. Didn't matter. Just got up or brushed away the blood if their head was hurt and it got in their eyes. And kept goin' to the sound of that horn.

"There were all kinds of them, too. Long-legged men and women wearin' nothin' but bark loincloths. Little fellows, maybe as high as my waist and dressed head-to-toe in animal skins. Some were black as night. Some a dirty white. And some were painted all over in all kinds of colors so I couldn't see their skin. Anyway, you could tell they weren't from one tribe. But from all over the forest, carryin' nothin' but the babes in their arms."

The wine had arrived. Quatervals gave me a thin smile of thanks, drank, then plunged on.

"I looked to see where they were goin'," he said, "and right where the canyon ended and the creek spilled into the lake I saw the horn. It was maybe twenty feet long, or more, with a huge bell at one end, cradled on a framework of logs. The tube came out from there, gettin' narrower as it went until it came to the fellow puffin' on it. He was fat as an ox, with a chest nearly as big around. Two men were holdin' him up while others held the horn for him, so all he had to do was blow. And blow he did. Puffin' up till it seemed he'd float away, then bearin' down to blow. And out came that sound we'd been trackin' all mornin.' Except now we were so close I could understand what all those people were doin'. Because I wanted to join them in the worst way. Throw off my clothes, kick off my boots and go runnin' down the canyon to that music.

"But just when I thought I couldn't stand it any longer, my finger started to burn. Underneath the ring Lady Greycloak gave me. And then I got scared and it came to me that something awful was about to happen."

Quatervals shuddered in a deep breath, wiped sweat from his eyes, and took another drink of wine, steadying himself for what was coming.

"I looked closer," he said, "and saw maybe a hundred more people like the man blowin' the horn. They weren't fat like him but they were wide-shouldered, with thick muscles and kind of stocky. They were wearin' some sort of armor, made of leather and wood with metal studs and nails. They had helmets, fanned out wide and at the neck and steeplin' in to a point on top. Weapons were spears, swords, clubs, bows . . . that kind of thing. But only a few of them seemed to be made of metal. And what skin showed was dyed real red, like the color of your hair, Lord Antero, if you'll forgive the comparison. Their faces were painted red as well, except for the eyes and lips, which were daubed with black.

"Most of them were tendin' this corral they'd thrown up. The horn was set just outside and behind it—and the gates were open so the people had to run into the corral to get close to the horn. Some of the warriors, which is what I thought of them as, were pushin' everybody who hesitated inside. A score or so others were mannin' a smaller gate to the side. Pullin' folks out, whippin' some into line to be chained. Pullin' others over to . . ." Quatervals licked dry lips and shook his head.

"It was some kind of stone oven, I guess. In the shape of a demon. Two holes for eyes, with smoke pourin' out. And an opening wider than three spears for its mouth. With fangs carved all around it. Anyway, that's where they were takin' the second group to. Don't know how they picked them, poor souls. Some of them they threw in alive. To roast. Others had their brains bashed in. Butchered them on the spot." Quatervals coughed. "Cut them thin and stretched the meat out on frames for jerkin'.

He stopped a moment. Janela patted his knee. He seemed to take comfort and moved on.

"The ones in chains," he said, "they put neck irons on, and chained 'em together, then marched 'em off into the forest in groups. I don't know how many. They kept comin' and goin' the whole time I watched. About two hours, was all I could bear."

"Did there seem to be anyone in charge?" I asked. "A chief? A shaman?"

Quatervals reflected, then nodded. "Over by the oven," he said, "they had an . . . altar, I guess. There was a man there they all treated as if he were important. And he was dressed like it, too. He had on a robe, all golden and long. It looked like it was made out of feathers, although I've never seen such a bird. And he was bare-legged, with sandals that laced up around his legs all the way to his knees, and he had a kind of breechcloth wrapped about his waist. Woven out of every color yarn you could think of and decorated with gold hoops and things hanging off. Above that a breastplate, the ribbed kind, worn over bare skin. And on his head, comin' out of the high neck of the robe, he had an animal's head for a hat. Couldn't tell what sort but it was spotted and had long fangs."

Quatervals sighed. "It was somethin' fierce, I suppose. Although its wearer was the meanest thing I've ever seen, so maybe it was lost to me. All I know is I thought of it as a crown."

"I wonder why we didn't hear the horn," I said.

"P'raps," Quatervals said, "you weren't meant to. P'raps it only *calls* to those who're prime for the pluckin'."

A long, uncomfortable silence set in, each of us lost in private dread. Janela and I exchanged glances. She nodded grimly, knowing what I was thinking: that sooner or later we were going to have to meet the man in the gold-feathered robe and snarling crown.

TE-DATE SMILED on us the following day. The channel remained deep, and turned away from shore into the middle of the lake. A fresh eastering wind filled our sails and eased our labors. Even the demon/woman markers didn't seem so forbidding as we skimmed smoothly along for several hours, winding around small wooden islands and vast stands of tall reeds. We could even occasionally glimpse our goal—the thin smear of blue that was the far shore.

I was straining to catch another glimpse of it when I was startled to see a tiny canoe racing toward us, a small figure paddling furiously and shrieking in fear. It was a child, a naked little girl of perhaps eight or ten summers. Her canoe was nothing more than skin stretched over a fragile frame and so small that there was barely room for the kneeling child, and with so little freeboard the water came within scant inches of the top. The child glanced behind her, shrieked again, and plied the paddle with all her strength.

She had good reason to scream: Following her was an enormous serpent, swimming effortlessly in her wake. The girl was so frightened she didn't notice us, and before we could shout a warning, her canoe struck the side of the *Ibis* and flipped over, spilling the child almost into the serpent's maw.

Without a thought, I grabbed up a spear from the forward weapons' rack. A few months before, my effort would have been for naught, and the spear, powered only by my wizened old muscles, would certainly have struck weakly, if at all. But now I felt a surge of my new, youthful strength as I threw, and the blade struck home with a meaty thunk, transfixing the creature's body.

The water boiled from the serpent's death throes, but to our horror we saw no sign of the child. Janela cried out and we saw the girl's body rise to the surface and float there, unconscious. Out of the reeds came two gaping-jawed lizards, anxious to enjoy what had been the serpent's intended dinner. Janela plunged over the side and caught the child by the hair. The brothers' bowstrings twanged in unison and four arrows arced out to intercept the lizards. As they shrilled in agony, Pip and Chons dove in to help Janela lift her small burden.

A few moments later all were back on deck and the crew cheered as the child opened her eyes to gaze in wonder about her, then vomited water.

Pip shook his head, saying, "T'ain't right fer a child like this t' be about without her mother."

Later, after Janela had tended the child in her cabin, wrapping her in a warm blanket and feeding her a restorative broth, we tried to find an answer to Pip's unspoken question. What was the girl doing here and where was her family?

At first she was too frightened to say, shivering and shaking her head as if she didn't understand. I thought it was because we were strangers and therefore suspect, but Janela knew better.

"She's afraid of being punished," she told me with a small

smile. Then, to the child: "Your mother doesn't know you're out here does she, dear?"

The girl shook her head, solemn.

"Don't you want to go home?" Janela asked.

The child nodded.

"Well, how can we take you home, dear," Janela said, "if you don't tell us where you live?"

The girl thought about this a moment, then shrugged. She sipped the broth as if she were satisfied with the standoff. The child was a pretty little thing, with a small, shield-shaped face and long black tresses, wet from her adventure in the lake. Janela sat down beside her, toweling her hair, and the girl curled up to her as natural as could be, clutching the cup of broth in both hands.

"Will you tell your name, my sweet?" Janela asked.

The child thought again, then nodded. But she didn't answer.

"Well?" Janela said gently, "what is it?"

"Shofyan," the child said, but so low I could barely hear.

Janela stroked her cheeks. "Shofyan," she repeated. "That's a pretty name."

The child nodded, confident this was so.

"I imagine your mother is very worried about you," Janela said. "She wouldn't give a little girl such a nice name if she didn't love her very much."

"Yes," Shofyan said, a little louder. "I think she is. Probably."

"I have a thought, my sweet," Janela said. "How about if we take you home and tell your mother that we were lost and had no place to go, but then you found us and said we could come home with you and stay for a little while."

Shofyan brightened. "You mean *I* saved *you*?"

"That's right," Janela said. "You saved us."

"Let's go," Shofyan said, anxious to proceed now that the danger of parental displeasure seemed to have been lessened. "I'll show you the way."

And show us she did: wrapped in a blanket and perched on Pip's shoulders—pointing out the direction as imperiously as the grandest pilot who had ever trod a deck.

Before we reached her village we neared an island surrounded by thick reeds. Shofyan recognized it, cheered up considerably, and said her home was "only a little farther." But before we rounded the island six canoes shot out of the reeds. They were large vessels carrying ten warriors each, all armed with heavy bows. Five of them sped toward us, the warriors' high-pitched, ululating war cry raising bumps on our spines. The other sped away, no doubt to raise the alarm. As they came closer I saw with amazement that all the warriors were women, bare to the waist and with short kilts of soft lake grass, dyed with bright colors and woven into intricate patterns.

I heard weapons scraping out and Mithraik—who was near my side—growled, "We're in for it now," and raised his bow.

I knocked it aside, snapping, "You know better than that! Do nothing until I order it." He grumbled something but I paid him no mind, for just then one of the women in the lead canoe saw the child on Pip's shoulders and cried out to the others: "They've got Shofyan!"

Their fierce cries became fiercer still. Some raised their bows. But the woman shouted, "Don't! You might hurt her."

Before I could act, Janela stepped forward, plucking Shofyan from Pip and holding the girl up for all to see.

"We mean her no harm," she shouted to the woman, who was young and comely, with a small, shield-shaped face like Shofyan's. The little girl cried out in delight when she saw her mother.

"Look what I found, Mother!" she shouted, making a wide gesture that took in our three ships. "They were lost and I found them."

The lead canoe bumped against the *Ibis*'s side and Shofyan's mother swarmed up and pounced on the deck like a big cat. She showed no fear as she stalked over to Janela and plucked the child from her arms. Shofyan threw her arms around her neck, clutching her tightly.

"I'm all right, Mother," she said.

Her mother patted her gently but still glared at us with fierce eyes. Other women were boarding now, and although they seemed ready to fight, I signaled for my people to make no threatening gestures.

The child's mother, assuming Janela was in charge, said: "Who are you? What do you want?"

"Don't be mean, Mother," Shofyan wailed. "She's really nice. And I didn't really find them. Her name is Janela and she saved me. She jumped in the water and killed the snake before it could eat me."

"Is that what happened?" the woman asked.

Janela shrugged. "It was something like that," she said. She waved at the rest of us. "The others deserve as much credit as I."

The woman looked us over a bit disdainfully, as if she grudged thanking mere men.

She turned back to Janela, saying, "I am Taisha, mother of this disobedient little wretch." She stroked Shofyan's locks as she scolded her. "I owe you thanks. But I can do nothing without first speaking to Queen Badryia—my mother. It is she who rules the People of the Lake. You will come with me and see what the queen decides." She graced the rest of us with another sneer. "These . . . men . . . must stay here."

I stepped forward. "Forgive me, Lady Greycloak," I said to Janela in my most obsequious tones—playing to the woman's assumption that Janela was our commander. "May I accompany you?"

Janela nodded, going along with the act. "Would that be permitted?" she asked Taisha. "This man is Amalric Antero, my, uh, maternal grandfather."

She winked at Taisha. "Actually, he's not really my grandfather, but to explain further would tell more about my grandmother's love life than I'm sure she'd care for me to reveal."

Taisha snickered knowingly.

Janela continued. "He is wise . . . for a man . . . also, I promised my grandmother I would look after him."

Taisha hesitated, then said, "If you wish. But only so you won't have to tell your grandmother that it was Taisha who made you break your pledge."

Janela thanked her, then turned to Kele, who was looking at me with amusement. "This is Captain Kele," she said to Taisha. "She commands the ship—and these men—in my absence."

"Greetings, sister," Taisha said to Kele. "More of our warriors will arrive soon to guard you. But they will do nothing to harm these men if you make certain they do not let their weak natures cause us trouble."

Kele buried laughter. "Rest assured, sister," she said. "Not a man here'll do more'n take a breath wi'out my orders."

Taisha nodded, satisfied. Behind her I could see dozens more canoes filled with warrior women approaching. They fanned out, ringing the fleet.

"This is good," she said. "You must come from a wise people to make your men so obedient." Then she motioned to Janela. "Come," she said. "Queen Badryia awaits."

I joined Janela in Taisha's canoe. We rowed swiftly for a time, leaving the main channel after about a mile and curving around many small, wooded islands. We entered a large lagoon with scores of huge, round huts perched above the lake on towering stilts, with rope ladders dangling down for access. The huts, all gaily decorated, had thatched conical roofs and walls made of woven reed that could be rolled up to catch the breeze or down for shade or to keep out a winter's chill. People stared out from their stilted homes as we passed, and I noticed the only males among them were boys or infants.

Shofyan called to some of the children—obviously her favorite playmates—as we paddled by, boasting loudly of her adventures and her new friends. They all laughed and clapped and urged her to visit them soon so they could hear more.

We made for the largest platform—which seemed nearly as big as a merchant ship. The roof of the conical structure that sat upon it was even more colorful than the others, and as we drew close I could see that the bottom of the platform was painted with glorious scenes of women engaged in many activities: spearing great fish, fighting off attackers—both human and lake-dwelling—or merely in repose—with children playing, or suckling at their breasts. When we came to the ladder dangling under what I guessed was the queen's home, women grasped the stilts to steady the canoe, while others held the rope so we could ascend.

Janela started toward it but Taisha admonished her to wait.

"There's a saying among my people," she said, "that beauty should proceed the stronger-willed." Taisha grinned at me. "And if you don't mind me saying so, sister, your companion is quite comely—for a grandfather, that is."

Janela hesitated, then laughed, agreeing. "We have a similar saying," she said, casting me a sly look. "And I must admit I was surprised when my grandmother allowed Amalric to accompany me." She nudged Taisha, then whispered in her ear. Taisha's eyes widened as she whispered, plainly shocked.

"What a waste of good seed," Taisha said aloud. "How could she permit it?"

Janela shrugged. "Although Amalric is her favorite, she has other husbands to please her," she said. "Besides, she hopes this journey will satisfy him so he can get such silliness out of his head."

"A wise woman, your grandmother," Taisha said. "I for one would be tempted to take a stick to him. But I'm not noted for my calm temperament." Then she motioned to me. "You first, my sweet."

Blushing furiously and wondering what Janela had whispered, I mounted the ladder. Someone gave my rear an appreciative pinch, but despite roars of laughter from the other women in the canoe, I managed to climb with some dignity intact.

Once at the top, we were told to wait while Taisha saw that Shofyan was cared for, then sought an audience with the queen.

I took the opportunity to question Janela as to what had been said.

Janela chortled. "I was only protecting you from lustful advances," she said. "These women seem a randy lot."

I blushed again, remembering the pinch. "So I gather," I said dryly.

"I don't know what sort of traditions they practice," she continued, "but it's easy to guess that here things are reversed and men are considered the weaker sex, so hot-tempered they are not permitted to stay in the village."

I made note of the many children running about. "But not completely banned," I said. "Else where did the children come from."

Janela grinned. "Oh, they'll let them visit irregularly, I suppose," she said. "Fertility festivals or such. And unless you want to be the object of an impromptu celebration, I'd suggest you go along with what I told Taisha."

"Which was?" I gritted out.

"That you believed you had been blessed with a visit by our goddess and had taken a vow of celibacy at her behest," Janela said. "Furthermore, that your patient wife, my grandmother, allowed you to join in this voyage with me, hoping that you'd return cured of your male foolishness."

I was shocked. "They must think I'm crazy!" I hissed.

Janela nodded. "Most probably."

I started to object, then noticed several of the warrior women leering at me, whispering amongst themselves and making suggestive gestures.

I sighed. Odd how . . . nasty . . . one felt when put to the same stresses that women undergo in Orissa. "Then mad I shall be," I said.

A tall woman strode out of the yawning doorway of the thatched palace.

"Queen Badryia bids you welcome," she said to Janela. "You and your companion are to be honored with an audience."

Janela bowed her thanks, as did I.

"Come," the woman said, beckoning.

The interior was dim, lit by ropes of some sort of shell that glowed like firebeads, as well as by the central fire pit where a large earth pot bubbled and filled the air with rich smells. The circular chamber seemed empty of furniture—but over the heads of the curious women crowding around us I could see stools and grass mattresses dangling from rafters that snaked off into the gloom, as well as weapons and fishing implements. Against the walls were cane trunks I supposed held the belongings of those who lived here with the queen. Despite the gloom, it seemed a happy place, with women speculating freely about our presence and children running all around, shrieking in glee.

About fifty feet beyond the fire, netting draped down in a wide arch. Glowing shells dangled from that netting, making a glistening bower for the woman who waited.

Queen Badryia lifted her regal head as we approached. She was sprawled on an immense, fur-covered couch. Even lying down she was one of the most imposing monarchs I have ever met. She was tall, easily seven feet. She was dark like the other women, perhaps in her late fifties, with a shield-shaped face like Shofyan and Taisha. She had the kind of beauty that defies age, with high cheekbones and a noble brow. As we came close and she sat up, her blue and green robe fell away, exposing large, supple breasts as firm as a maid's. Her hair was piled high into a crown, and fixed in it were all sorts of dazzling gems and rare metals, as well as a few of the glowing shells. She had fan-shaped earrings that dangled nearly to her shoulders and seemed to be made of colorful feathers and bits of jewels. A dozen bracelets graced each arm, and thick ropes of what seemed like pearls decorated her neck.

We bowed low and I heard her jewelry clatter as the queen leaned forward to get a better look at the ones who had been so bold as to intrude upon her watery kingdom.

We said nothing. In such circumstances, royalty always speaks first.

I heard whispers and chanced a look to see Taisha perched next to her mother and whispering in her ear. I thought I heard Janela's name passed on. When Taisha was done, the queen nodded.

Then she said: "I understand I owe you thanks for keeping my granddaughter from fattening up a serpent."

I started to answer but remembered my role as lowly male adviser.

"You are most gracious, Your Majesty," Janela said. "But we don't deserve thanks for doing what is any mortal's duty when she sees a child in danger."

And I thought: Good woman!

The queen laughed, rich and deep. Then her tones turned colder as she said: "It is fortunate for you, Lady Greycloak, that little Shofyan was naughty today. Else you might not be treated so gently by *this* queen!"

Janela answered: "Fortunate indeed, Your Majesty. The goddess smiled on us all this day. On the child for encountering friends when she most needed them. And on us for discovering the same."

I thought: Well said!

Queen Badryia must have thought the same for she rewarded us with another rich chuckle. "Your mother taught you well, little sister," she said. "Now, tell me, and answer me honestly if you value my continued good nature."

"I'll do my best, Your Majesty," Janela said.

The queen leaned closer, jewelry rattling. "Are you a witch?"

"Yes," Janela said. "I have been blessed with such powers."

Badryia nodded in satisfaction. "I thought so."

She turned to Taisha. "Didn't I say, earlier . . . before Shofyan turned up missing . . . that I sensed sorcery about?"

"You did indeed, Your Majesty," her daughter said.

The queen turned back. "I have a little talent of my own," she said. "Enough to keep a few nasty things about at that end of the lake." She was obviously referring to the slug-things and the demon. Badryia sniffed. "Sorry if they inconvenienced you, my dear," she said. "But we lake dwellers try to discourage surprise visits as best we can."

"And fearful things they were," Janela said.

The queen smiled hugely, pleased at the flattery.

"It was only by chance that I sensed the Demon of the Lake you have posted there." Janela shuddered, whether for real or as part of the flattery, I wasn't certain. "What gave her away was her hunger. It was so great it set my own belly to growling, even though I was in fear of my life . . . and the lives of my companions. Then, once I suspected her presence, I tried to turn that hunger on our attackers instead of us."

I listened as closely as the others, for I had wondered as well how Janela had pulled off her life-saving trick.

Another deep laugh from the queen. "Poor Salamsi," she said, obviously meaning the demon. "It was well past her regular feeding, but I've been so busy I hadn't time to tend to it."

"I hope she wasn't injured," Janela said.

The queen shrugged. "By those little nasties? Not hardly. Rest assured, only her dignity was harmed for being fooled. But if I were you I'd not pass by her watery lair again if you return that way."

We accepted her advice in silence, for the queen's face had

turned thoughtful. While she considered, she called for stools so we could make ourselves comfortable and food and drink so we could break our fast. We nibbled on delicacies such as fresh shellfish with a dollop of hot spice on each and sipped a light wine that had the tangy taste of a morning breeze and made one feel alert and at ease with the company.

Finally the queen broke off her thinking and addressed her concerns. "You haven't said what you are doing here," she pointed out.

"We are on a holy mission," Janela said. "We live in a land far to the west. And we have suffered many evils of late."

The queen made a gesture with her hand. "You mean, plagues and demons and such?"

"Yes, Your Majesty," Janela said. "Plagues and demons and such. Things became so critical that at last our witches gathered in a great council. And that council prayed to our goddess, who graced us with her presence in a vision."

Janela hesitated a moment, no doubt inventing a few more palatable twists in her highly altered account of the doings in Orissa. But the queen had been swept up by the drama of her tale, and she motioned to her most impatiently.

"Yes, yes," Badryia said. "The vision. Do go on."

"Well," Janela said, "the goddess appeared and she told the witches that the answer to our troubles was in a distant land—far to the east. A kingdom where the Old Ones still reign."

"You mean, Tyrenia," the queen said.

"Tyrenia?" I blurted, forgetting myself. "Would that perchance be the realm we call the 'Kingdoms of the Night'?"

Shocked silence greeted my indiscretion. The queen studied me for a long moment. Then she turned to Taisha. "You are right," she said. "He *is* a pretty thing. Although I like my meat a little younger."

Then she said to me, "I understand you've taken a vow of celibacy, my sweet."

I nodded, bobbing my head like a fool so I could fit easily back into my role as a pampered, slightly mad plaything of a rich and powerful woman.

"Yes I have, Your Majesty," I said. "My wife nearly took a

switch to me after I made the vow. But when I told her the goddess bade it—and said I had to go find the place of the Old Ones along with Janela—she only slapped me a little, then commanded Janela to take me with her so I could get over my silliness." Then I suddenly made myself haughty. "Silliness, indeed," I said in a deeply injured tone. "Our great goddess came to me and said that I—Amalric Antero of Orissa—must seek that realm in my purest state and that I was to let no man or demon or woman stand in my way."

The queen laughed, slapping her thigh. "He has spirit!" she said to Janela. "I like a little spirit to spice up my bed. Pity he's mad."

Janela's finger made a circular motion about her temple. "My grandmother said the same thing, Your Majesty."

"You should adopt our practice," the queen said. "We send our males away as soon as they show the first signs of leaving childhood behind. They must dwell on the islands, making their way as best they can until we allow them to visit us on the lake during certain times when it is known that we are fertile. It's a difficult life for them, to be sure. But they do well enough, even if we do lose a few now and then. We keep them sweet with little gifts and we have a few other festivals, which to tell the truth I make up on the spot. There's nothing like a little tumble with no thought of child-bearing duties in mind to keep a glow in a woman's cheeks."

Janela glanced at me, made a thin smile and said: "I quite *like* that system, Your Majesty. You can be assured I'll suggest it to my grandmother when we return to Orissa."

Badryia nodded in great satisfaction. "Tell my sister in Orissa that it's really the only sensible way to keep them in their place, poor things. It's a pity, really, that the goddess made them that way. I am a woman wise in the ways of the world as well as the heavens, and I still don't understand how men can turn from such lovable little things as children to such great boors as men, causing us women no end of grief, if you let them, and still behaving as if they were children, who have unformed minds, after all, so they can be forgiven. But as men they swagger about as if what they had between their legs was anything more than what the goddess gave them to pleasure us. Getting in quarrels with one another and wanting to solve it with a fight instead of talk. And they can be such sour creatures, don't you think? Taking offense at the slightest thing and supposing that the goddess herself plots against them. And pout! Why, they pout more than any babe!"

The queen laughed at some memory. Then she said, "My grandmother had a man once who took offense at some nonsensical thing he believed she'd overlooked on purpose. This on their bridal journey, mind you, when she was doing her best to please him. And do you know he didn't speak to her for an entire day? He only rattled about the canoe in a great dark mood, pushing her with his silence. He even boasted about his treatment of her to his friends when they returned."

"What did she do to set him straight, Your Majesty?" Janela asked, shooting me another amused look.

"Why, she cut out his tongue," the queen said. "Then he had good reason to keep his silence."

"I wish you could return with me yourself, Your Majesty," Janela said, quite fervently. "Every woman in the West would praise your name to the skies."

The queen nodded—this was a royal truth that needed no further comment.

"Then you should listen to me closely on another matter, little sister," she said. "This journey of yours . . . to Tyrenia? I believe it to be the same place you seek, although I am not familiar with the name you use—what was it?"

"The Kingdoms of the Night, Your Majesty," Janela said.

"Yes, that's it. Kingdoms of the Night, indeed! What drama! What silliness! Must have been a man that called it that."

Janela nodded and smiled that, yes, this was so.

The queen continued: "I know the tale well. We tell it to our children to ease winter's drear. It is a myth of never-ending sunlight and warm breezes that the people of Tyrenia enjoy the year 'round, thanks to wizards who are as wise as they are kind. And it is also said that the city sits atop a glorious mountain with emerald spires glittering in the sun."

"That is the same story we have heard," Janela acknowledged. "But in our land it's also said the city is besieged by dark forces that grow stronger by the year, and if that city falls, those evil forces will engulf us all."

"Yes, yes," the queen chortled. "We speak of the same place. For all I know there really was such a city long ago. But I strongly doubt it still exists."

She waved a royal arm, taking in her thatched palace—and beyond. "We have evidence enough of the Old Ones all about us," she said. "Ruins of the ancients in such plenitude it is no wonder our imaginations are fired. We—the People of the Lake—have dwelt here amongst those symbols of the Old Ones' former greatness longer than any other. We have found the wrecks of their mighty ships that once plied these waters. We have dredged up their weapons in our nets. We have even come across bits of their magical knowledge that we have incorporated into our own.

"But I tell you this, little sister. The Old Ones—whoever was their enemy—were destroyed. Their glory is a thing of the distant past, and who is to say that it's a pity? We made a place here. And we live well. It is our time now. Theirs is past. Let us all praise the goddess and take pleasure in that simple fact."

"You are very wise, O Queen," Janela said, "so I question your thinking only with the greatest of reluctance. However, may I ask you this: Is all really that well in your kingdom? Have any new difficulties arisen—difficulties that might have been caused by black magic?"

Queen Badryia's brow furrowed. She was not used to having her word questioned. But I could see something else in those imperious eyes: a small but growing light of awareness.

She said, very slowly, "Yes. There have been things happening of late that puzzle me."

"Such as the wizard with the great horn," Janela said, "whose music casts such a powerful spell that people willingly scramble to their deaths?"

The queen suddenly seemed furious. "Azbaas," she hissed. Her guards clasped the hilts of their long knives, as if waiting for her to order our throats slit. Then she asked: "How do you know of King Azbaas?"

THE PEOPLE OF THE LAKE   265

"One of our hunting parties encountered him," Janela said, quite calm. "Fortunately, they were not seen, and equally as fortunately, the protective spell I'd cast shielded them from the effects of the horn."

Badryia nodded, soothed—if only slightly. "As I observed before, little sister," she said, "you are a very lucky woman. You would not have liked to have fallen into Azbaas' clutches."

"He is your enemy, Majesty?" Janela asked.

The queen shrugged, relaxing slightly. "Enemy? Not really. Let's just say we've agreed to be wary of one another." She sipped her wine, reflecting. "He is a new king. He's ruled the Epheznuns for ten years or more. They are the largest of the savage forest tribes, but until his reign they were in disarray, always squabbling amongst themselves. Azbaas was a minor shaman but with a great talent of making folk fear him. He used that talent so well that over time all his opponents were quelled, one way or another. Now he's unified the Epheznuns so they answer only to him."

"Using black magic I assume, Majesty?" Janela asked.

Badryia sighed. "I fear so. It's said he's made a bargain with demons. I don't normally listen to such things, but with Azbaas ... who can say? He is the sort of king one tends to suspect of such things, even if they might not be true. We get on well enough, however. He has no power on the lake, as I have no power in the forest. We trade at times, and if any of my people stray into his realm, he returns them without injury. And I do the same."

"But you don't trust him, Majesty?" Janela said.

"In addition to being a man and having habits more disgusting than is common with his sex," she said, "he's an ambitious king. I doubt if he's satisfied merely ruling the Epheznuns. Witness his attacks on the other forest dwellers. You may have noticed that many races are represented in these parts."

I nodded along with Janela, remembering Quatervals' description of the vastly different types of folk they'd seen scurrying mindlessly to their fate.

"It's said," Badryia continued, "all of us in this region were brought here by the Old Ones from across their kingdom, and that our ancestors did their labor for them—many, perhaps, as slaves. I've always believed this, for how else do you account for our many differences?"

"How else indeed, Majesty?" Janela murmured.

"By any course," she continued, "one would come to the same conclusion. However, before Azbaas, we all seemed content to stay in our own lands—with the occasional blood feud erupting, of course. But they were easily settled, for this is a difficult place to live, and wars sap one's strength for doing more important things— like staving off starvation."

"But after King Azbaas came along," Janela said, "things were not so sanguine."

"No," Badryia said. "They were not." She peered at Janela. "Do you think, little sister, that his growing power has something to do with what you fear afflicts your own land?"

"I can't say, Majesty," Janela said. "But I also can't deny the likelihood."

"If you persist with your journey," the queen said, "I fear your budding theory may be tested. Because—save the way you came— there is no route away from the lake that Azbaas does not control."

Janela and I glanced at one another. Another barrier had been set in our way.

"I suppose we'll have to find out, Majesty," Janela finally said. "If you will let us pass, we must seek an audience with King Azbaas and pray to the goddess he will look upon us as kindly as you have."

The queen snorted. "Not likely."

She turned to Taisha to confer in whispers. After a long discussion she reached a decision.

"I must confess I don't like what I'm about to do," the queen said. "Which is to use a woman who has won my respect to further my own purposes. However, I hope you understand I have my own people to think of, and that one way I can assure their future is to permit you to risk your own life and the lives of your companions."

"Then you'll let us continue, Majesty?" Janela said.

The queen nodded. "Yes, you may pass. And I'll alert my spies to keep close watch on what transpires. I can learn much more about Azbaas when I see how he treats you." She paused to consider more, then said: "I shall also supply you with a document written in my own hand," she said. "It will be a letter to my"—and her tone turned sarcastic—"good friend and brother monarch." She gave us a thin smile, then went on. "I'll tell him I owe you all a great service and that it would be a kindness to me if he greeted you warmly and assisted you any way that he can."

"Thank you, Majesty," Janela said for both of us. "The people of Orissa will be forever in your debt."

The queen shook her head. "I doubt it," she said. "More than likely they'll curse me for letting you fall into Azbaas' clutches."

She raised a royal hand to signal that our audience was at an end.

But as her guards hastened us from her presence, she called out one final thing:

"If you live, and if Tyrenia really does exist . . . tell the Old Ones that Queen Badryia sends her warmest greetings. And that the People of the Lake wish them good fortune—now and forever more."

CHAPTER TWELVE

KING AZBAAS

A cold wind hastened our departure from Queen Badryia's realm. The skies were gray, the air heavy with moisture, and although it did not rain, the distant mountain peaks were obscured by black storm clouds. Lightning flared in those clouds, picking out the sort of fearful images that bring prayers to the lips and reminders of past indiscretions to the soul.

It was weather for contemplation, and the only talk aboard the *Ibis* was of the most necessary kind: orders from Kele and the mates, or the men mumbling to one another about the tasks at hand. Even that rogue Mithraik seemed affected. I saw him leaning over a rail fumbling with what appeared to be some sort of amulet. His eyes were closed and he was muttering as if in prayer. I smiled, wondering what sort of gods a pirate prayed to.

The nearer we came to the region Badryia said was King Azbaas' domain, the more the mountains hugged the shore. The weather became colder and windier, and the chop of the water sorely tested the guts of the lubbers among us. I could see that the storms in the hills were growing fiercer. The creeks leading down to the lake were swollen to the size of small rivers, and in places waterfalls appeared, filling the air with the sound of their thunderous release. The lake was visibly rising—lapping near the tops of marks old floods had made on the banks.

Kele was relieved, saying it made it unlikely that we'd have to return to our labors in the mud.

Janela, however, was not so sanguine. "It will make it easier for Cligus and Modin, as well," she said.

The same thought had been nagging me. "Do you suppose those storms have anything to do with Modin's wizardry?" I asked.

"I have no doubts at all," she said, "that they are Modin's work."

I asked her if there was anything she could do.

"I've already tried," she said. "Unfortunately, his spells are so strong that to overcome them I'd have to give away our position. Instead I made spells of confusion. When he makes his magical soundings, he'll receive all sorts of conflicting information. Weak trails, showing we could be any number of places on the lake."

I relaxed. The lake was enormous. We'd be well on our way before he ferreted us out.

But what Janela said next burst that peaceful bubble.

"One thing that troubles me," she said, "is that Modin's powers seem to have grown stronger as each day passes. As if someone or something were aiding him. I'm not worried that he'll outstrip *me*. To my delight, I've grown stronger, as well. But my improvement has come naturally, from constant practice and, I believe, from deeper understanding."

"We've known from the beginning," I said, trying to soothe her, "we have powerful enemies opposing us. Just as we've known the closer we come to our goal, the more dangerous they would become. The possibility they'd be in league with Cligus and Modin has also not escaped us. Still, we've progressed. Quicker, actually, than I had hoped. Never forget that it took Janos and me three attempts to reach Irayas. If the gods continue to favor us, we'll only need this one."

Janela's worried features smoothed. "Sometimes I forget who I

am with," she said. "It's comforting to know that you've faced—
and conquered—much worse."

I blushed, mumbling some suitably humble nonsense. Janela
placed her hand on my arm.

"Am I as much a help to you as my great-grandfather?" she
asked.

"More so," I said. "To begin with, I have no doubts about the
honesty of your intentions."

Janela squeezed my arm. "Then you trust me?"

I looked into her dark eyes. Once again I saw their resemblance
to Janos'. The strength. The intelligence. The burning curiosity.
What I didn't see was that glint of madness that was both Janos'
curse and blessing. Then the faint musk of her perfume rose up and
I saw perhaps more than she wanted to reveal.

She lowered her eyes. "I see that you do." She removed her
hand and the moment passed.

Just before night swallowed the grayness of the day, we came
upon a small island, a large, wooded hill climbing steeply out of the
lake. The top was bare save for an enormous tree with branches
that seemed to shade the entire summit. Steps were cut into the
rocky base of the island, which led to a path that curved around
to the top.

Janela became excited, saying, "We need to stop here, if you
please."

When I asked her why, she said it was a magical place. "But it's
not the magic of men or demons. It has an aura of the earth—and
of much peace. I have a feeling it may prove very helpful to us if we
investigate."

"We have time," I said. "I was thinking it might be wise to stop
for the night. We should reach Azbaas' kingdom soon, and I'd prefer to deal with him in the light of day."

I issued the orders, and as Kele and the other captains an-
chored, Janela and I took a small boat and rowed to the islet. The
weather had moderated, wind turning to light breeze, the cold to
just a slight nip. As we tied up at the remains of an old dock, a
bright moon broke through to light our way. We mounted the steps
and found the path. It was rough and broken in many places but its

rise was gentle, so although it took nearly an hour to reach the top, it was an easy climb. A spring's runoff spilled across the path the final few feet; Janela stooped down to scoop up a handful of water to drink. Her eyebrows lifted in surprise.

"Taste it," she said.

I did so and the first surprise was how cold the water was when I dipped my hand in. It quite numbed my fingers, and when I drank it pained my teeth. But the taste was as pure as melted snow off the highest peak. I wondered how that could be. We were in the middle of a vast lake, and the mountains were many leagues away. Janela had moved on, so I didn't comment but only followed her.

The tree at the top was even larger than we'd thought, with thick sprawling roots humping up nearly as tall as the woods near my villa in Orissa. Its leaves were shaped somewhat like an oak's, gleaming silver in the moonlight. They rustled softly in the breeze, making a pleasing, peaceful music like brushes against brass temple bowls. The tree had broad, sturdy branches, placed so neatly it made one wonder if a master gardener had lovingly pruned them for a thousand years. Near the edge, the roots had flung up a large, flat rock; the spring burst out from under it. I raised my firebeads and saw markings on the rock.

The marks were quite faint, and Janela rubbed a hand across them, frowning. "I can't make them out," she said, "although I have no doubt they are magical symbols."

I spotted an indentation in the center of the rock and said, "Hello. What's this?"

We looked closer. There, carved deep enough to suffer centuries of wind battering, was the figure of the dancer. It was set within a square, with a beveled channel cut around it. Janela blew away debris, clearing the channel.

"It looks like some sort of box," she said. "A box fitted into the stone."

Off came the purse from her shoulder and she rummaged around for a moment, then drew out a slender piece of metal.

Janela laughed when she saw how curiously I looked at it. "It's nothing magical," she said. "Just something to use as a pry."

She worked at the box for a time, chipping away grime and

blowing out more debris. Finally she got out her knife and popped the box out of its nest. It was about the width of my palm, perhaps twice as deep, and it was made of smooth milky stone—like the walls of the royal court where the dancer twirled for the demon audience. Janela fingered the box this way and that, found the secret to opening it, and lifted the lid. We both looked inside.

A single rose petal peeped out at us. It was a deep, rich red and so perfectly formed I felt compelled to touch it. I lifted it out and was surprised to find it was made of fine, spun glass. I held it up and the moonlight prickled over the surface, sending up small sparks of light.

The music of the rustling leaves grew louder, sounding like faint, chanting voices. I found myself smiling, turning my head this way and that to make out what the voices might be saying. I thought I heard my name and I thought I heard Janela's, but I couldn't be certain because the voices seemed like they were coming from a distance. I felt light-headed but pleasantly so—as if I'd just sipped a strong wine. Then I was *certain* I'd heard my name and I took a step forward so I could hear more clearly. But as I did so, it felt like I separated from my body. I felt free and light and glad to be rid of that earthly burden. I looked at Janela, who was staring at me in amazement. Silver leaves showered from the tree, wafting in the breeze. They fell like a warm summer rain and I felt clean and fresh and as innocent of avarice or sorrow as a babe. Then I lifted up the hand holding the petal and saw my flesh was pale and luminescent—as if it had no substance. I laughed; the sound was like the wind chimes in my garden, so I laughed again just to hear that delightful noise.

Janela reached out and plucked the petal from my fingers. I saw her place it back in the box and close the lid. Instantly my hand became just a hand again. I felt heavy and plodding and thick-witted. I groaned aloud at my loss and the sound was grating agony to my ears.

I wept, not knowing why, and Janela held me until the tears came to a chest-shuddering stop. Brandy bit my lips and rasped my tongue as she forced me to drink from her small flask. It must have been spiced with one of her restoratives, for I soon felt well again.

I told her all that had happened after I touched the rose. "It was as if I'd become a spirit," I said. "Not a ghost, for that would be a dead thing. But a spirit of such vibrant life and form that the Dark Seeker himself would have fled the light it cast."

"And that is how you looked, Amalric," Janela said. "Actually, there were two of you. Your body, made of ordinary flesh and blood. And then your . . . spirit self . . . stepped out of it. That self gave off the most glorious light. And I thought you were laughing, but what I heard was . . ." Her voice trailed off as she sought a comparison.

"Chimes?" I said. "Did the laughter sound like wind chimes?"

"That's it exactly," she said. "Wondrous chimes, like I've never heard before. I'm so sorry I had to make you stop. I could tell it would hurt you, but I wasn't certain what would happen next."

"I didn't care," I said gloomily.

She patted me. "I know you didn't," she said. "But what was happening was not necessarily a good thing. Evil doesn't always wear a black cloak. Demons are not always ugly. And the greatest pleasure I've ever known would have killed me—or worse—if I hadn't drawn back before it was too late."

I looked at her, wondering what that could have been.

She lightened the mood with a grin. "Don't ask," she said. "It's a wizard thing, and I'm sure you'd understand more than my self-respect could bear."

She held up the little stone box. "May I keep this?" she asked. "Because of what happened I feel that it's rightfully yours. But I'd like to investigate its purpose—with all the safeguards I can muster."

I said yes, of course she could—but as she dropped it into a silk drawstring bag and tucked it away in her purse I wanted to shout: *I lied! Give it here!* I held my tongue until the feeling faded into a faint but lingering loss. It joined many others: a lifetime of all the small agonies we suffer on the wandering road the gods set before our feet. If I have more than most, it is only because I'm older than most. Sometimes when I look in the mirror and see how much time's ravages have been erased from my features, I miss the scars of age that I'd worked so hard to earn.

We left that island without further discussion, pausing only to once again sample the sweet cold springwater. I slept heavily but not well. And the following morning we set sail again under skies of slate and a sun as dismal as my mood.

Our first sight of King Azbaas' capital was as foreboding as the chill winds that blew us to it. We were enveloped in mist so we had no warning: We burst out of the greasy fog into a long, narrow bay. The city sat in a valley between two high bluffs, with wooden-walled castles on those bluffs to guard the bay. Long, low docks fronted the city, and those docks played service to scores of rafts manned by naked slaves of both sexes, who were pinned to the rafts by bolts and chains. Only a few primitive boats plied the waters, evidence of Queen Badryia's insistence that Azbaas had little power on the lake. The city—which we learned later was called Kahdja—was more of a wooden fortress than a thriving town of industrious souls. A high log palisade ran from bluff to bluff, with watchtowers set every fifty feet. A branchless forest of log buildings stretched out behind the palisade, rising slightly in the valley's climb from the lake. The valley itself, we later were told, was an ancient river-bed that had silted over long ago, with city after city being constructed on the abandoned riverbed, until there was little evidence of its former grand purpose. After I'd met Azbaas it seemed fitting that any river he commanded would be such a poor, dead thing.

As we drew closer I could see that the bluffs, yellow as the smile of a gap-toothed hag, were pocked with many caves. I saw movement in the mouths of those caves and the small figures of spear-carrying soldiers sentry-walking along paths and steps carved into the bluffs.

I called for our least-worn flags to be hoisted, and coaxed a little group of volunteer musicians to play a ragged air of greetings on pipes and drums. We waited, but not for long. The palisades' gates swung open and a small retinue of important-looking men bustled out. They climbed aboard what I first took to be a dock, but before my eyes a colorful tented pavilion rose up on that dock and a multitude of slaves groaned under the lash, heaving and pushing, until the dock separated from the shore and I realized it was a great royal barge moving out to meet us.

Three men boarded the *Ibis*, and I did my best to convince them I was a genial man of innocent purpose and powerful friends who pined for my return. We had all changed into our best clothes, and the crew made a respectful aisle for Janela and me to walk between as we strode to welcome our visitors.

Their red-painted faces were striated with fierce, ceremonial scars. Their eyes were black-painted holes, and streaks of black flared from the corners of their lips. Long leather capes, worn over wood and leather armor, hung from their shoulders, and they had helmets with high pinnacles that made them seem taller than they were. This was the same stocky, muscular breed of men Quatervals had seen in the ravine.

The man in the center, who had a large, golden badge of office dangling from his neck, stretched his tribal scars into a smile.

"I am Lord Fizain," he said. "I bring you greetings and a warm welcome from King Azbaas." He had a thin, high-pitched voice. Even so, it was the voice of one comfortable with command.

I hid my surprise at their quick acceptance of us. "And I am Lord Amalric Antero," I said, "and this is Lady Greycloak, my—"

Fizain broke in. "Introductions aren't necessary," he said. "We know of you, my lord, just as we know that Lady Greycloak is a sorcerer of much renown."

He bowed low to both of us. "I believe you have a missive from our good friend, Queen Badryia." He stretched out a hand. Numbly, I handed him the rolled-up parchment letter from the queen.

"I must confess, my lord," I said, "you have the advantage of us. We are merely weary travelers on a sacred mission for our homeland. How did we earn the attention of your most gracious majesty?"

Fizain squeaked laughter. It was an unnerving sound from such a fierce, muscular man. "Did you not know our king is the mightiest shaman in the history of the Epheznuns? There is nothing in his domain that escapes him. And little in the regions beyond."

Janela shook her head as if in wonder. "I am most anxious to meet the king," she said. "Perhaps we might exchange a magical tidbit or two."

Fizain made a sorrowful face. "That meeting," he said, "would be welcome to his majesty. But I fear that it must be delayed a few days. He is busy with important affairs of state."

"Naturally," I said. "Such a rich and mighty kingdom must be a burden on your king's time. Although we were so hoping to steal a small moment of it, alas, we must be content with his greetings, which you so ably delivered. Our only real business with him, however, was to seek permission to pass peacefully through his realm. Perhaps on our return he will gift us with a moment or two of his presence."

Fizain shook his head. "I have little doubt our king will grant your request of passage," he said. "Unfortunately, he gave me no such instructions. He only begged you to accept his hospitality for a day or two, and as soon as duty permits, he'd be pleased to meet you in person."

I had little choice but to accept. It is not wise to argue with a king. If you do, you must make very certain that the distance between you and his throne is greater than your defiance. So I bowed low—as did Janela—and made many lies of gracious acceptance of the king's will.

And with those bows we became prisoners of the king.

I'VE HAD the dubious pleasure of such confinement before. I've paced luxurious dungeon suites as well as vermin-ridden cells within hearing of the torturer's song. The quarters Azbaas reserved for Janela and me were somewhere in between. They put us in the highest tower of one of the bluff-top castles. We had three spacious rooms, all with cheery fires to stave off the damp chill blowing up from the lake. The center room overlooked the bay, and we could see our ships tied up in a narrow inlet. Our crew were confined to those ships, which were under heavy guard—to protect them from certain unruly factions among the Epheznuns, Lord Fizain had said. Naturally, similar protective measures were necessary for us, and we had sentries posted day and night at our door.

"Although our kingdom is most peace-loving," Fizain had said, "there are certain outside elements who hate our dear king and do everything they can to upset his citizens. They have even infiltrated

witches among us—witches who possess our weaker-natured brothers and sisters and cause them to do evil things. Therefore, constant
vigilance must be kept. And all must be suspect—until the innocence
of their purpose is shown beyond any doubt."

In short, he said we were being quarantined—not imprisoned
like all those unfortunates who were crammed into the caves in the
bluffs below us. I saw them when we were taken ashore in Azbaas'
royal barge. The motion in the cave mouths I had noticed earlier
proved to be hundreds, if not thousands, of the kingdom's supposed
felons. The cave entrances were barred and I could hear the moans
of the prisoners and the curses of the soldiers guarding them as we
passed under.

They gave us several slaves to tend our needs, which rankled
me almost more than our forced circumstance. I used my lordly
privilege to complain I missed the tender care of my own servants.
I was allowed to exchange them for Quatervals and Mithraik—
who'd impressed me mightily as a man who could get out of a tight
scrape. They were quartered in rooms below us, and since they were
deemed nothing more than lowly servants, they had a bit more freedom of movement in the castle.

Mithraik immediately proved his worth by pointing out several
likely if chancy avenues of escape.

The most ingenious involved the fireplaces, which we were continuously feeding and stoking to keep off the chill.

"A seaman's life ain't always fresh breezes 'n' good salt beef,
sir," he pointed out one day. "Ol' Mithraik's been marooned in
town now 'n' ag'n. Indeedy I has sir. 'Specially when I was a barefooted lad with no brains in me head 'n' only a willin'ness to climb
a mast in any sort of weather to recommend me t' the captain. Spent
a bad season as a chimley sweep's mate with the meanest, laziest
skipper of the broom 'n' ash that yuz ever laid eyes on. So I knows
a thing, sir—or even three or four 'bout chimleys, I do."

I puzzled a moment, then realized that by "chimleys" he meant
chimney—such as the one servicing the large fireplace in the center room.

"Go on," I said.

"Well, sir," he continued, "thing about chimleys is they gots to get the smoke out, sir. But they also gots to let the air in, if yuz sees what I mean."

I didn't but I had him go on anyway, and soon it became quite clear. If more than one fireplace existed, he explained, they usually shared a common shaft that was not only large, but constructed in such a way that smoke could easily pass out while the fire drew air in to feed upon.

"I was outside on'y yestidy, sir," he said. "Made 'em let me go t' market wi' the quartermaster's mate so's I could fetch yuz a proper supper. 'N' first thing old Mithraik noticed, sir, was there may be lots a fireplaces in this here castle. But I on'y spied a couple a places where the smoke was comin' out. Didn't take much in the way of wits, sir, to see that the fireplaces gotter be connected t' a shaft big enough to sail a ship through."

He was proposing we use that shaft to reach the roof of the castle. From there, we could climb down, work our way to the palisades and through a gate or over the wall, no problem, Mithraik said, with a seaman like himself to aid us, " 'though," he said politely, "I hain't doubtin' there'll be little need t' help spry folks like you two an' Quatervals." From there we could flee into the forests surrounding the city and hide out until danger passed.

It wasn't that bad of a plan. However, it meant we'd have to abandon our comrades in the ships.

Mithraik grinned. "Didn't figger yuz would, sir," he said. "Not that kinda skipper, I says to meself. But old Mithraik woulda been neglectin' his duty, sir, if he didn't point it out."

Just the same, I congratulated him on the keenness of his weather eye and the sharpness of his wit and encouraged him to favor me with any other ideas he came up with.

Quatervals, on the other hand, proved his worth in bed. He'd impressed a kitchen wench who was round of form and possessed a vivid imagination concerning the delights that a stranger from a distant land might be concealing in his breeches. Her sister was a servant in the king's dining hall, while her mother was one of his many cooks.

He must not have disappointed, for over the days, she supplied

him with invaluable gossip about what was going on in the house of
the good King Azbaas.

It seemed Azbaas had not learned of our presence until shortly
before our arrival. When he did, there'd been a flurry of meetings of
the king and his advisers, with all sorts of late night sorcery that required the kitchen staff to work long after their normal hours sup-
plying those worthies with refreshment.

"They're still burnin' the oil lamps late, my lord," Quatervals
said. "Seems the king is mightily impressed with himself. Figures
he's got a rare opportunity in us. But he ain't quite sure what yet."

"If it's ransom he wants," I said, "I'll promise him enough to
buy his whole army as well as our parole, and then we'll see what
surprises we can work up for Lord Modin and my errant son."

Quatervals shook his head. "Don't know about that, my lord,"
he said. "But it seems to me it'll take more'n gold coin for the likes
of King Azbaas."

I knew that as well, but I had decades of merchant's tricks up
my sleeve that had sweetened the view of many a gimlet-eyed prince.

It was from Quatervals that we learned Azbaas' antecedents. As
well as the history of his capital, Kahdja.

Like Queen Badryia had said, the king had once been one of
many shamans who served the scattered tribes that made up the
Epheznuns. But it wasn't Azbaas who had first unified those tribes.

"He was chief shaman to the biggest, strongest tribe," Quatervals said. "King of that group was a greedy sort who trusted nobody, but nobody, except Azbaas. Azbaas, bein' no fool, and havin'
lots of practice takin' out all the other shamans to get so high,
played on that king like he was a temple drum. Kept him suspicious
of everybody. Any smart fellas who caught the king's eye was
branded as traitors, an' it's said Azbaas took personal pleasure
seein' they was punished for their ways."

In a series of wars, the prince that Azbaas served carved a kingdom for himself. But shortly after the savage ceremonies he staged
to mark his assumption to the throne, the king went mad and became such a useless, gibbering hulk that he had no means to defend
himself when Azbaas led a revolt and had the king put to death.
From there it was an easy if bloody reach to the crown.

Quatervals shook his head. "It's no secret he made a bargain with a demon to drive that poor fella mad," he said. "And it was that demon's idol I saw in the ravine."

I turned to Janela. "In my experience," I said, "a wizard who makes a bargain with a demon usually loses more than he gains."

Janela nodded. "Especially one who is lured into dining on human flesh."

I asked her what she meant, and she said: "The wizard is led to believe he's consuming the strength of his enemies. Actually, he weakens himself—and his people, if they are made to follow suit, and their hunger grows with each passing day. The end result can only be madness and chaos. It is only the demon who gains power."

"That may be so," I said glumly. "But at the moment we are at Azbaas' mercy. We don't have time to await his eventual demise."

Janela didn't answer. She just busied herself sorting the contents of her purse as if that work were the most important and absorbing thing in the world.

Later, however, when Quatervals and Mithraik had returned to their quarters, she said: "We won't have to wait much longer to confront the king. He's been probing us since our arrival, but I've blocked his every effort." She smiled. "Right now we have a very frustrated, supremely curious wizard-king. And unless I've gone soft-headed, he'll be summoning us soon."

She lifted up the drawstring bag that contained the stone box we found on the island. "It's time we prepared ourselves for such an encounter," she said.

I eyed the small box as she drew it out, shivering in memory of my experience. "I thought you were worried about the source of its power," I said. "Or have you unraveled its purpose?"

"No, I haven't," she said. "My instincts now say it is a force for good. Good for us, that is. But that could be a trap. A spell to lull us into thinking all is well. However, the sorcery used to make this talisman—which is what I believe it is—was so strong, I can use it to magnify my own magic, without fear of tripping such a trap."

She set the box between us. I stared at it, lips dry with a sudden desire to open it. The feeling vanished as Janela anointed me with a sweet-smelling oil—dabbing my temples and the pulse point of each wrist. She did the same for herself, then dribbled oil on the box until it filled the carving of the dancing girl. She lit the oil with a golden candle. A blue flame shimmered up, taking on the wavering form of the maid. My skin grew warm where Janela had daubed me with oil—but not unpleasantly so.

Janela chanted:

"She who dances
In the demon hall;
And never falters
Or loses grace;
Never ages
Or tires
Or weeps.
The demon's lust
Will be our power;
The demon's heart
Enclosed by stone."

The fire flickered out and the mild warmth on my skin vanished.

"Are you sure the spell worked?" I asked. "I felt almost nothing."

Janela laughed. "Are you one who thinks the best medicine is the most foul-tasting? Or has the most unpleasant effect on the body?" I must have looked confused, for she patted my hand. "That spell was necessarily mild so we don't warn the king—and especially his demon friend."

Janela returned the box to its pouch and tucked it into her purse. "It also has a double purpose," she continued. "I've grown quite interested, you see, in the king's demon."

"Why is that?" I asked.

"I sense he is a very raw, very primitive force," she said. "He reminds me of the demon lord Elam, whom your sister encountered in the Western Sea. He claimed to have been summoned by a wizard, if you recall, and when the wizard was slain by his enemies, Elam was unable to return to his own sphere."

"I hear doubt in your tone," I said.

"I had doubts when I first read it," Janela replied. "Nothing can be truly lost. Forgotten, perhaps. Misdirected. Beyond reach. Or even barred. But not lost. When a sorcerer wants a thing, she imagines its placement, its home. She might use a chant to heighten her imagination, and magical elixirs or objects to magnify her power. My great-grandfather believed in order above all else—that there were basic laws governing all things—in this world as well as the spheres where demons such as Elam dwell.

"There are wizards, as you know, who doubt those spheres exist. But your sister proved that part of Janos' theories when she pursued the Archon into the ethers. She described several different worlds she passed through during her final chase.

"She was quite careful in her account to separate her opinions from the facts. In her description of Elam, for example, she made certain we knew that it was Chahar, the demon's Favorite, who said her master was lost. Rali had no other evidence beyond that simpleton's word."

"What do you think happened?" I asked.

"I believe Elam was an outcast," she said. "Otherwise how could such a powerful demon come under a wizard's thrall? I believe he was barred by his own kind from returning to his natural home."

"Do you mean he was so evil—even for a demon—that he was exiled?" I asked.

Janela chuckled. "I mean nothing of the kind," she said. "I part company with my great-grandfather on the issue of good and evil. Both states exist—and demons are definitely evil. Of this I have no doubt. But there is no doubt that many demons have a common purpose, and an orderly view on how to achieve that purpose."

"Such as those who oppose us?" I asked.

"Exactly," she said. "We must never doubt the keenness of the intellects of our enemies. Because they are evil, they are likely to consider means of defeating us we'd be loath to think of. They are great seducers, great carnivores of human weakness. They also have whole legions of lesser spirits at their command. Many, however, have yet to come under their rule. Which is why we can sometimes bend those wild demons to our own purposes. Or make a bargain—

like Azbaas has—with a powerful creature who has either defied his masters or has yet to come to their attention."

"Elam was such a demon?" I asked.

"So I believe," Janela said. "And he was exiled—not lost—in punishment for his defiance. King Azbaas' demon, however, has too little power—and intelligence—to be an Elam. He's not an outcast, but a savage, forgotten force in this long-abandoned region."

"What do you plan?" I asked.

"It isn't necessarily a plan," she said. "Call it a notion, my dear Amalric, nothing more."

I was going to press her, but before I could, the door to our chamber was flung open and Fizain stepped inside.

"I'm most sorry to inconvenience you, my lord and my lady," he said. "But you must make haste to prepare yourself. For you have been honored with a summons from the king."

THEY PUT JANELA and me in a large gilded chair borne by eight brawny slaves. Quatervals and Mithraik trotted behind as we raced through the city under heavy guard. Fizain sat stiff and tall in a similar chair, which led the way. It was midday and the city was oddly empty and silent. Doors hung open and windows were unbarred and the only sign of life we saw were a few dogs and maimed beggars lolling in the alleys. The marketplaces were empty, as well, but their stalls were heaped with goods, as if merchants and customers had fled. The main street ended at large wooden gates which were flung open at Fizain's shout, and we emerged at the rear of the city, trotting along a broad road paved with rough timbers. The road wound through heavy forest for an hour or more. The slaves slowed as we came to a steep hill, but cracking whips and vicious curses spurred them into a faster pace.

When we came to the top I looked down and saw our destination. Spread out in a barren valley was an immense wooden amphitheater. In the center of the amphitheater was a huge red and yellow pavilion, its sides drawn up to let in the breeze. Beside that pavilion—and towering over it—was a massive statue of a demon. Janela nudged me but said nothing. The idol had the body of a crouching dog but its head was more human. Like the much smaller idol Quatervals had seen, the statue seemed to also serve as an oven. Black smoke poured out its eyeholes and flame sheeted from its stone mouth.

When we reached the amphitheater, gates were again flung open at Fizain's command. Whips cracked, but this time to slow the pace. We trotted onto the field, moving toward the pavilion. All around us the stands were packed with what seemed to be every citizen of Kahdja. They were silent and, except for an errant child or two, there was no motion in the crowd except heads swiveling to watch our progress.

As we passed the idol, it belched foul smoke and flame and my eyes burned and I found it difficult to breathe. My will weakened and I felt small and unworthy to come into the presence of such majesty as King Azbaas'. Janela's hand flashed under my nose and I shuddered in drafts of sweet air tinged with the scent of pine. I felt strong and confident again. I also had the measure of this king. Such trickery, in my experience, is used by princes who have much to fear, and if you don't keep them under your feet they will be at your throat. There is no in-between.

I whispered to Janela: "Follow my lead."

She whispered back: "Keep me close, so I can help."

Fizain barked orders and the chair came to a halt in front of a high platform. Without being asked, Janela and I slid out of the chairs. Fizain looked surprised as I ignored him and motioned imperiously to Quatervals and Mithraik to join us.

I brushed past Fizain and mounted the platform steps as if it were I who ruled here.

Azbaas sat upon a barbaric throne made from the bones of mighty forest animals. Their skins were his cushions and their fierce heads his decorative vanity. The king was a big man whose golden robe had consumed the feathers of a wondrous bird, and it pained me to think such a creature should be slaughtered for this purpose. Pride made him leave his torso bare, and his muscles rippled under a sheen of red paint. Rings hung from the skin of his flesh, as did the tiny bejeweled skulls of fanged animals. He had the head of a big forest cat for a crown, its canines leering down over his brow.

I paid no mind to this savage display, only drawing myself up higher, treading more heavily on the platform boards, my face a haughty mask.

When the king saw me, he hid his amazement well—betrayed only by a flickering glance at Fizain.

His black-painted eyes narrowed as he peered at us. His lips sneered into a smile.

He nearly got the better of me when he spoke, for his voice was magically amplified and his words boomed across the massive amphitheater.

"It was gracious of you to come so quickly, Lord Antero," he said. "I hope my hasty summons didn't inconvenience you."

He snickered as if it were a jest. Fizain and his other aides jerked into life like marionettes and guffawed loudly at their master's humor.

Janela plucked at my sleeve and I made my most courtly leg, bowing with exaggerated flourish. I felt wetness as Janela pressed something into my palm. As I came up I rubbed it against my lips. It was a small, oily pebble, and I popped it into my mouth.

When I spoke, my voice was his equal. "I was only slightly put out, Your Majesty," I said. "I was engaged in a game of naughts and crosses with my wizard." I nodded at Janela. "For a change I was winning."

I heard Fizain and the other courtiers hiss surprise at my sorcerous parry. Mithraik whispered: "He'll get us killed!" And Quatervals said: "Quiet, fool!" He laughed as loudly as the aides who'd jollied the king.

Once again Azbaas was forced to hide amazement. "Naughts and crosses?" he chortled. "I think we have better amusements than that to offer, Lord Antero."

I made a slight bow. "Then I am at your service, Majesty," I said. "I've grown weary whiling away my time in your guest chambers—magnificent as they may be." I turned to Janela. "Although they are a trifle chilly, don't you think?"

"Quite so, my lord," she agreed.

Azbaas stared at Janela, ignoring my small sally. "I've heard you were a most powerful sorcerer, Lady Greycloak," he said. "Is this true or have you merely blinded your admirers with your beauty?"

"Perhaps both are true, Your Highness," Janela said. "I'd be most interested in your opinion on the latter. After all, who better to judge one wizard than another?"

"I was thinking that might be part of today's amusements," Azbaas said with another of his black-lipped sneers.

I looked about the broad arena. "Is this crowd for us, Majesty?" I asked. "I fear we'd be taxed to supply entertainment for so many."

"Actually," Azbaas said, "I've invited you to witness a witch sniffing. We have trouble with witches on occasion, and I've found the best way to deal with it is to regularly purge them from our midst."

He motioned for Fizain to fetch us two stools. I noted they would put our heads well below his. I waved to Quatervals and Mithraik to sit in them instead.

"If you don't mind, Majesty," I said. "I'd rather stand. I fear my behind has become numb from so much sitting in our quarters. A goblet of wine, however, would go quite well—if you would be so kind to offer it."

More hisses from the courtiers at my rudeness. In the stands the crowd was whispering to one another at my audacity.

The king and I locked eyes for a moment. One word from him and we would be cut down as easily as a washerwoman's line. But he knew as well as I the cost to his image would be most dear. A prince may rule with the cruelest of hands, he may keep his subjects cowering before him night and day. But let them once spy weakness and his reign is over—no matter how many spears or demons he has at his command. Azbaas was angry, to be sure. His anger, however, was turned inward for making this contest so public. I saw his jawline firm as he determined that he would bend us to his will. Once again we were blessed with a kingly smile.

He settled back in his throne and nodded to Fizain. His aid shouted orders, and drums thundered across the arena. Gates swung open beneath the stands and a horde of men and women stumbled into the light, kicked and lashed by soldiers.

They were a most pitiful lot, half-naked and starved, so their bones jutted out alarmingly. I heard cries for mercy and the king laughed, his laughter echoed first by his court and then by the suddenly jeering crowd.

Over by the idol I saw half a dozen priests unveil an immense horn, such as the one Quatervals had described. Several of the priests steadied it as a squat mountain of a man approached—thick rolls of fat jostling as he walked.

"That is Bilat," King Azbaas murmured. "My chief shaman."

I said nothing but watched in horrified fascination as Bilat put his lips to the horn and blew.

The sound was deep, penetrating to the very bone. It stirred an animal in me, a fearful animal that suddenly wanted to run to his master and ask forgiveness. I heard Quatervals curse and glanced to see him straining mightily against a powerful force. Mithraik, however, showed no emotion—other than an odd gleam of curiosity. Bilat blew again and my desire to bow and scrape and please made tears well up in my eyes.

Azbaas laughed—harshly.

Janela stepped forward, hand coming up to pluck the feather decoration from her cap. I remember it was green, like the tunic she wore over her black leggings. She placed it on her palm and blew. The feather floated up and Janela blew again and the feather shot across the arena like a spear. She made motions with her hands, muttering a spell I couldn't hear, and then the feather became a great, ugly black bird that swooped above the shaman, squawking: "Bilat! Bilat!"

Then it shat and the shaman jumped away from the horn, howling in angry humiliation. The crowd burst into laughter, which made him madder still. He shook his fist at the bird, which squirted white feces on him again.

Janela clapped her hands and the bird vanished—after one final squawk of "Bilat!"

She turned to Azbaas, whose own lips jerked in amusement.

The king was a man who immensely enjoyed the humiliation of others. Janela pulled off her cap and her mouth rounded into an O of surprise.

"Where'd that feather get off to?" she asked, scowling. Then she snapped her fingers and Azbaas jolted as one of the golden feathers from his robe leaped off and flew into Janela's hands. "Do you mind terribly, Majesty?" she asked with a pretty pout. "This hat desperately needs a bit of color."

The king was still amused and laughed his permission. Janela stabbed the feather into her cap and turned back, her face smoothly innocent as she watched Bilat snarl at the priests and slap one of them on the head for laughing.

Finally, the king tired of Bilat's antics. "Tell the fool to get on with it," he said to Fizain. He sighed impatiently as Fizain rushed to do his bidding.

Somehow Bilat regained his composure. He gestured, and magical drums renewed their thunder. Another gesture and rattles joined the drums, sounding like a nest of disturbed vipers. He reared back and howled like an animal, and suddenly he and the priests were clutching the jawbones of direwolves mounted on ebony sticks with scarlet ribbons streaming from the black handles. Bilat began to dance and weave across the arena, shaking the jawbone this way and that. He moved lightly, no more the comical figure, but a wizard on the stalk. His priests danced around him as he moved toward the mass of prisoners. As he came closer men shouted in terror, women screamed, and I saw children clutch their parents and weep.

Bilat chanted:

"Witch . . . witch . . .
You cannot hide.
Witch . . . witch . . .
You cannot sleep.
Witch . . . witch . . ."

The crowd took up the chant:

"Witch . . . witch . . .
You cannot hide.
Witch . . . witch . . .
You cannot sleep.
Witch . . . witch . . ."

Bilat and the priests circled the prisoners, drawing that circle tighter and tighter as the crowd pinched in to avoid contact. People fainted and were crushed under the heels of their fellow victims. One man dashed out and fell to his knees in front of Bilat, begging to be released.

Bilat struck at him with the jawbone, crushing his face. Soldiers swept in, hoisted up the moaning figure and dragged him to the idol.

There, more priests were at work, stripped to the waist and streaming sweat. A grate set in the belly of the crouching stone beast had been flung open, and the priests were throwing logs into the furnace. The soldiers pushed by them and hurled the man inside. He made no sound, and I thanked any gods who might be watching for making certain the poor man was dead before the flames touched him.

Bilat was worked up to a fury, dancing like a demon on fire, his voice wailing over the chanting crowd:

"Witch . . . witch . . .
Where is the witch?
Witch . . . witch . . .
Come to me, witch.
Witch . . . witch . . .
Azbaas awaits . . .
Witch . . . witch . . ."

Bilat stopped. He threw up his arms and the crowd hushed.

"My king," he said, his words rolling across the arena. "All are witches! All are traitors!"

The prisoners screamed frightened denials, but soldiers hammered them into silence.

Azbaas rose from his throne. I saw he had a direwolf staff like Bilat, only his was gold and encrusted with rare gems. He turned to the demon idol.

"O Great Mitel," he intoned. "Once again your subjects have failed thee. Once again we have found witches walking among us. Help us, O Great Mitel. Rid us of this plague of disbelievers."

He shook his staff at the idol, then drew a figure in the air.

"Take them, Mitel," he shouted. "Remove them from our sight."

Fire and smoke boiled from the idol's mouth; then it came to life, rearing up taller than a building and roaring in fury. It leaped across the arena, reaching the prisoners in two great bounds. The soldiers scattered as the idol leaped into the mass of people.

I turned away from the carnage, not caring when I saw Azbaas' sneers at my display of weakness.

"Now, are you amused, my dear Lord Antero?" he asked.

My fury vanished, to be replaced by a sudden awareness of what was to be done. My temples and wrists grew warm and the delicate odor of a rose graced the air about me.

I looked at the king and made a sneer of my own. "Such a display might dazzle your subjects, Majesty," I said. "But as for me, it only made me glad I had no time for breakfast."

Then I said to Janela, "I usually find travel more broadening than this. But I suppose one can't expect much more from a savage."

Janela took my cue, adding, "Especially a savage whose master is a dog."

"Master?" Azbaas shouted, his enraged voice echoing across the arena. "I have no master! Only Azbaas rules here!"

I yawned. "I won't argue," I said. "It's impolite to disagree with one's host."

Azbaas turned toward the demon, who was slaking his hunger on the bodies of the accused. "Mitel!" he roared. "Come to me!"

Janela and I looked to see how the demon was taking such rude orders. He lifted up his head, fangs drooling blood. Then he lowered it again to return to his gory work.

I snickered, driving Azbaas to greater fury. He screamed: "Did you hear, Mitel? Come to your master at once!"

Once more the demon lifted his head. Azbaas swiftly changed his tactics. "More disbelievers await thee, O Great Mitel," he implored. "Come see what a tasty feast I've prepared for you."

We didn't wait to see who'd win the battle of wills. Instead, Janela took my hand and we descended the platform and strode toward the demon. Behind us Azbaas shrieked for our blood.

The demon saw us. He howled in delight and trotted forward, the ground shaking under his paws. But I knew no fear and whispered to Janela: "The box. Get out the box!"

She was already pulling the drawstring bag from her purse. Calmly, she withdrew the stone box and motioned for me to halt. Then she removed the lid and placed the box on the sand. I saw the delicate glass petal peeping up from the stone confines.

We stood our ground as the demon bounded toward us. Its breath was hot foulness, its eyes boiling smoke and flame.

Janela raised her arms, chanting:

"The demon's lust
Is our power;
The demon's heart
Enclosed by stone."

The demon gathered himself for a final leap. But as he did so, rose-colored smoke spewed from the box. The smoke became a thick swirling cloud of enchanting sweetness. It took on the slender form of the dancer, whirling in time to the most beguiling music.

The demon froze. His bloody jaws snapped shut and his eyes seemed to grow larger and larger as he watched the ghostly figure dance.

Janela whispered. A soft breeze blew and the rosy smoke drifted over the demon. It moaned in pleasure or perhaps in pain . . . I wasn't certain. That moan became a bubble of light floating out of its maw. The light hovered in the smoke, sinking lower and lower until it was scant inches over the box. Janela leaped forward, the lid in her hand. She slammed it down, trapping the light inside the box.

I looked up and saw that the demon had become a mere stone idol once more. Somewhere in the heavens I thought I heard a mournful howl.

All was deathly silence as we strolled back to the pavilion to confront the king—not a murmur from the crowd, not a cry from a babe.

Azbaas didn't wait. He was striding across the arena, flanked by his aides. Behind them, soldiers hustled Quatervals and Mithraik along at spear point.

When the king reached us his features were so drawn, his eyes so blazing with madness, I thought for a moment I had miscalculated and he would have us killed before I could complete my plan. He opened his mouth as if to issue the orders. But Janela held up the box and his jaws snapped shut.

"There is your power, King," she said. "Without your demon you are nothing but a poor shaman. And a weak one at that."

Azbaas looked at the stone idol, then at the box, and licked dry lips. His hand rose as if to snatch it away, but Janela gestured and the box vanished.

The crowds sighed and Azbaas shivered.

"I have in mind a bargain," I said. "Free passage through your kingdom. And if you are very kind to us, perhaps we can be persuaded to return your demon."

The king was a crafty prince. He made no empty threats of torture, knowing Janela would have loaded the magical dice so that his demon would be lost to him forever. Nor did he sputter or rage, further damaging his image in the eyes of his subjects.

Instead he said, quite mildly, "Very well, you have the better of me. You shall leave at once. And we can arrange the exchange at my borders."

Then he turned and stalked away.

A very humble Fizain had us returned to the docks where our companions waited.

I quickly explained what had happened to Kele and the others.

Within the hour we had unloaded the most necessary items from the ships and were preparing for the long overland journey. A troop of our former guards stood by, glowering as I ordered Fizain to open the armory where our seized weapons were kept. Then I made him supply us with maps of Azbaas' kingdom, and we pored over likely routes for our march while the others completed the preparations.

It was nearly dark before we were ready. But I had no desire to test my hold on the king, and sent Fizain to tell him that we would soon depart. A storm blew up as we waited, but we were so glad to be nearly free that we didn't mind the wet and cold. Thunder blasted from the west and I saw an eerie glow of light on the horizon.

Janela called to me, her voice anxious. "Amalric," she said. "They're coming!"

I thought she meant the king. I was even more certain of it when I turned to see Azbaas and his minions coming out of the night. Fizain held a broad animal-skin umbrella over the king's head to protect him from the weather.

When he reached us, Azbaas looked all around, lips twisting in amusement. "I see you are ready, my dear Lord Antero," he said.

"Ready enough," I replied. "Now, here's what I propose we do when we reach your borders—"

The king waved me to silence with a lazy hand. "Oh, that won't be necessary," he said. "It appears you'll be my guest a bit longer."

Magical thunder blasted again from the west, and now I knew what Janela's warning had meant.

The king laughed. It was a most evil sound. "Your son was right," Azbaas said, "when he told me you were old and weak."

My heart wrenched. The king said, "We've been in communication, you see. Lord Modin of Vacaan and your son, Cligus Antero." He shook his head. "At first I didn't trust them. They made such wild claims. I thought I'd have my fun with you and your pretty little witch. Then, when they arrived, I'd have new guests to entertain."

He made a mournful face. "But such was not to be." Another chuckle. "However, after your display in the arena, their offer sounded much more real—and attractive. Also, the more I pondered, the more it was apparent I had nothing to fear from a man who cannot control his own son."

Azbaas sneered. "As for the demon—keep him. I don't have such a great need for him now. Your friends have offered me a much better trade. If I turn you both over to them, they've vowed to deliver what I desire most. And that, of course, is power. More power than any wizard has ever held in this wilderness. Power over all my enemies." He looked me full in the face. "Power," he continued, "from fair Tyrenia. From the Kingdoms of the Night."

He pointed to the glow on the horizon. "Cligus and Modin are sweetening the bargain as we speak. To show good faith they are attacking that great soggy bitch Queen Badryia. They've promised to deliver her to me by morning.

"Then you can join me on my royal barge and sail out to congratulate your son."

In my rage I imagined Azbaas had miscalculated by allowing us to rearm. Very well, I thought. If I am to be a corpse, the king could join me on my pyre. I signaled the attack and drew my dirk. I launched myself at Azbaas. But the king laughed and lightning crashed between us. I found myself on my knees in the mud. I had been robbed of all strength, and the rain became hot needles of fire in my flesh. I heard moans of pain as Azbaas' spell overwhelmed my companions.

The king spoke, his voice a great roaring in my ears: "As you can see, they've granted me a few more powers already. To show their generosity, they said. Actually, we both knew better. The real reason was to make certain I could hold you captive."

He stooped and plucked my dirk from the mud. He touched the tip next to one of my eyes. "I wonder if they'd object to my delivering you blind?" he mused.

Nearby I heard Janela moan. The sound was as piteous as the others, and I knew we had lost. She moaned again—and this time I realized it wasn't a mindless gasp I heard but words meant for me.

"Think of the feather, Amalric," she was saying. "Think of the feather!"

The king heard her as well. The dirk was withdrawn as he turned to ask, "Feather? What feather?"

And I remembered the golden plume Janela had snatched from Azbaas' robe. The image shimmered up in my mind and I felt Janela's spirit joining me, weakened by the spell at first but growing stronger as we bore down with our combined wills.

We thought of the rare creature that was the victim of the king's vanity. With that the feather became a small golden bird. And then we made it larger—large as an eagle, with an eagle's hooked beak and an eagle's sharp talons. It gave an angry shriek and spread its wings, and I heard Azbaas shout in surprise as the bird leaped from our minds and sped toward him.

The king's spell vanished and I struggled up to see him grappling with a huge golden bird. Azbaas screamed for help, but Fizain and the soldiers were too stunned to move. The bird became twice the size of a man. Its wings were thunder as it rose in the air, carrying the king in its claws. Higher and higher it soared, Azbaas' cries growing weaker. The bird suddenly let loose, and the king screamed his last and plunged to the ground.

The soldiers scattered as the bird dived after the corpse, caught it once more in its talons, and soared off into the storm.

NO ONE OPPOSED US as we marched through the city. All the king's soldiers had vanished, and his citizens slammed their shutters and barred their doors when we passed their homes. The storm had ceased, and a bright moon lit our way. There was only the creak of harness and the stomp of our boots to hint of human life, although when we left the docks the people in the caves broke out of their prisons and swarmed down the rocky paths to freedom.

Before we set out we'd fired our ships and Janela had used a few drops of my blood to cast a seeking spell. When last we'd seen the *Ibis* and her sisters, they had been fully engulfed in flame and sailing away—manned only by the spell—to confront, and hopefully cause much grief to, Cligus' and Modin's fleet.

There was no one at the city's rear gates when we reached them. They were sealed by sorcery, so we fired them and then dragged them off their hinges.

We marched along the rough board road that led past the amphitheater where we had confronted Azbaas. We followed it all night, followed it until it became a wagon track, and followed the track until morning.

We camped where the track intersected a broad, rubble-strewn road. Posted along the road were the demon head markers.

Somewhere ahead, we prayed, that road ended at Tyrenia.

CHAPTER THIRTEEN

THE ROAD TO TYRENIA

For the first time I wished I'd been traveling with just a handful of men, even though I knew a small party could not have made it so far. But a dozen or so would have been easier to disappear with into the countryside, instead of the nearly seventy I had to worry about.

We'd found the demon-marked way that led to Tyrenia—but that would increase the likelihood of discovery. Once Cligus and Modin found that track, they would assume we were on it and wouldn't have to waste time sweeping the land for our traces.

I estimated our pursuers numbered between three and five hundred men, although I hoped they'd been decimated in their journey upriver by the crocodiles and every species of plague imaginable. That many troops would move more slowly than mine, even though I knew they were elite forces, and I also assumed there'd be some confusion and delay passing through Azbaas' city.

Quatervals exercised what craft he could to conceal our travel,

including having everyone travel barefoot for a few leagues, since
he'd observed that most folk in this country went unshod, so our
tracks wouldn't stand out. Beyond that, all we could do was travel
as fast as possible, always heading toward the mountains.

The way was overgrown—it had been some time since many
people had traveled this way. But clearly the road had been built by
skilled engineers with much time, workmen, and resources. It ran
nearly straight for the mountains, not curving around foothills or
taking the easiest path. They had carved into the hills and crossed
rivers with either low, arched stone bridges or paved fords built up
from the river bottom so water rushed over them no more than a
foot deep. Several times the road disappeared into tunnels, but I refused to chance them, fearing not only cave-ins but confrontations
with creatures who might have chosen them for dens. Since we were
afoot, it was a simple matter to find our way cross-country to where
the track emerged into the open once more.

The forest thinned as we climbed up into the foothills, but it
continued to block more than a momentary view of the mountains
ahead—and there were still no signs of the rocky formation we so
desperately wanted to sight.

Five days from King Azbaas' city Janela chanced a passive sensing spell that required little more than anointing her eyelids and ears
with an unguent and putting herself into a light trance. In a few
minutes she returned to us and reported.

There was dark magic behind us, she said, but it still seemed
distant—as if Cligus and Modin had stopped in the city. That was
good news, although she cautioned me not to rely upon it too heavily. What simultaneously concerned and drew her was the feeling of
dangerous forces ahead, swirling, waiting. Dangerous or not, we all
hoped and prayed they were a sign that we were nearing Tyrenia.
We pressed on.

The land around us was barren and uninhabited, laid to waste
either in the forest tribes' internecine warfare or by Azbaas' relent-
less raiding for sacrifices. But even though the few huts we saw were
deserted, showing the marks of fire and axe, I kept flankers out to
the sides and front. The term barren, I should add, is the usual ar-

rogant description people have for land they do not occupy. Truthfully, there was much life abroad, animals seeming to rejoice where the killers on two legs came no more. Birds flocked heavy in the trees, and squirrels and chipmunks raced about gathering stores of food for the winter. Deer bounded across the road and sometimes peered curiously from the brush as we passed. Both Maha and Chons returned their intent interest—not out of curiosity, but appetite.

At a rest stop one of the Cyralian brothers said he wished to show me something and led me a dozen yards off the track to a small stone arch. It rose over a low altar, with a small statue on it. The statue, aged by years of wind and rain, was unusual: Most gods, including our own beloved Te-Date, are pictured as looming, horrible of visage, threatening. This was different. I didn't know what kind of animal was represented, but assuming the statue was life-size, it would have come to just below my waist. It was fat and squatted on its haunches, holding out its paws palms up as if it were begging—or making an offering. It had pointed ears and a full face with almond, slanted eyes. A long bushy tail curled around it.

These lands were deserted—but placed on the altar were flowers and a piece of fruit that looked like a green peach. I started to pick the fruit up, then stopped and knelt to examine the offerings without desecrating them. Both the flowers and fruit were freshly picked, the petals and flesh not yet having begun to wither.

Quatervals spoke from behind me and I started. "Now, who'd be makin' offerings all the way out here?"

I said I didn't know.

"Animals don't have gods," he went on quietly. "Do they?"

I started to reply but said nothing. Again I did not—do not—know. We quietly withdrew, leaving the small god to its worshipers and peace.

We climbed higher and the forest thinned even more. I heard a halloo and hurried to the front of the formation. Chons was pointing excitedly up. Looming above us was a mountain range whose shape took my breath away.

The Fist of the Gods appeared exactly as Janos and I had

viewed it so many years ago in the vision we had glimpsed in the Palace of the Evocators. I saw the four black peaks and clenched thumb all dusted with snow, with white drifts picking out each digit. I saw the valley rising between the thumb and forefinger and knew it afforded passage to the other side.

I thought I heard Janos' voice whispering in my ear: "Beyond, lie the Far Kingdoms."

I shivered, and then Janela was at my side. She took my hand and we looked deep into each other's eyes. We kissed for the first time—no more than a touching of lips to convey feelings that mere words could not do justice to. Then we pressed closer—only for an instant—and the kiss became something more. My mind swirled as we parted, and Janela smiled at me and I thought I saw a hint of a promise in her eyes.

I steadied myself. We both laughed as emotion piled on emotion. Ahead was the pass. Ahead was Tyrenia. Ahead lay the Kingdoms of the Night.

We moved on. Now there was little but scrub brush and twisted pines on the increasingly steep hills. The road held true, due east. The rivers we crossed were far below us—in near-vertical chasms the sun would illuminate for only a few minutes a day—and we could hear the roar and echo of the cascades. Again I admired the builders who had managed such a marvelous bridge that worked no matter whether the water was a foot or half a mile below. All were single arches with never a pier. It was fortunate the canyons were narrow enough to allow this, although a few times it had been necessary to lay stone out from either side and reinforce the landing with a buttress braced into the rock before the arch was set. It seemed as if the bridges would hold for another epoch, but we took no chances, crossing in small groups and moving swiftly.

The hills, now small mountains, had stood firm against even the intentions of the Old Ones who built the road, and so it lost its arrow-flight directness and curved and wound as it climbed, always toward the Fist, always beyond the next summit. Then we crested a butte and came down the other side to find that the road had stopped.

A bridge had collapsed and there was a gap of nearly thirty feet where the rock fell away for perhaps four hundred feet.

There was cursing and mutters of disappointment and worry that we could be trapped here. But not from Quatervals or some of the other ex-Frontier Scouts he'd enlisted. Now we were in their element.

Janela and I stood there, ignored at first, as Quatervals and his team went into what was to them a very familiar drill.

He took a small roll from his pack. He handed it to Janela. It consisted of a handful of straight dowels and small pieces of one-inch rope that had been carefully cut apart. He gave lengths of the rope and two of the pieces of wood to Janela.

"We need to do the 'lesser is part of the greater' spell, my lady," he said. "I know the words and was given the blessin' to say them when I was in the Scouts. But it'd be more potent if you'd do us the honor of makin' the castin'."

Janela smiled. "I'm familiar with the spell," she said. "And I'd be proud to assist you."

He handed her two of the dowels, considered, then gave her half a dozen of the bits of rope. "More'n we'll need, my lady, but it's best to be safe." He reached back in his pack and fished for more equipment. "I'm too old to be doin' this," he said.

But there was a broad smile on the mountain man's lips as he pulled out forty feet of carefully treasured climbing rope made of cotton and silk that appeared too weak to support a man's weight. I knew, however, that the line had been specially blessed with a spell of cohesion and three men could hang from it without it stretching or snapping. He slung it in a coil over his shoulder, stripped to a loincloth, took off his boots, and tied a drawstring-equipped bag on a light cord around his waist. Into that went some narrow steel wedges with holes drilled in their ends and little rope loops through them, a hammer, a small grapnel, some rope fragments, two more of the dowels, and a tiny pouch containing ground materials for the spell.

"I'm away," he announced, and without further ado went straight down the cliff's edge.

We crept to the edge and watched him as he went down, moving deftly from rock to crag toward the bottom. Watching him was fascinating—at no time did any of us feel that he was in the slightest danger of falling or even slipping.

As much as I wanted to keep watching him, I was just as interested in Janela's task. I knew the bits of wood had been cut from fully shaped logs and the pieces of rope were fragments from other, far longer lines.

She turned each piece of wood in an intricate series of movements, as if they were wands, and the same with the line.

"This isn't the traditional way of doing things," she explained, "but one that takes a lot less work and no real materials."

She drew a bit of red chalk from her bag and marked a single symbol on the wood, then simply touched the chalk to the rope ends. Janela placed the wood on the ground, each piece about three feet apart.

"Stand clear," she warned, and began chanting. As she did, she moved her hands in a pattern that looked identical to the motions she'd made with the wood.

> "Children you listen
> As you were
> So shall you be
> Stretch out
> Stretch far
> You are the whole
> You are your fathers
> Stretch far now."

Although I knew what would happen, I was startled to see the transformation. Now lying on the roadway were large coils of rope, and in front of them two perfectly smoothed logs of the clearest pine that might've been cut, aged, smoothed, and shaped for a boat's mast. They were about a foot in diameter and twenty-five feet long.

Without orders, some of the former Scouts busied themselves

tying the logs into an X shape and lugging them out to where the bridge had fallen away.

One of them grinned at me and said, "Damned sure better doin' it like this, me lord, than havin' to leg it back down to the closest tall trees—which, I rec'lect, were a couple days distant."

Mithraik was looking about nervously, and I reassured him that I'd sent scouts back and we'd have plenty of warning if Cligus' soldiers came into view.

"It's not him I'm worried about, my lord," he said. " 'Tis this road itself, sir—and its builders. Stinks of demons and their works, it does."

Janela eyed him. "You needn't worry," she said. "The magic worked on these stones was cast before your ancestors' ancestors drew their first breath."

"I feel different, my lady," he persisted. "I still feel 'em about."

Janela eyed him. "I didn't know you had such talent," she said. "You've never spoken of it before."

Mithraik looked at her and I swear his expression was almost contemptuous for a flash. Then his look turned humble. "Beggin' yer pardon, my lady," he said. "It's just a feelin' in Mithraik's old bones."

I sensed he was lying. I had no doubt he was afraid. But exactly what caused that fear was another matter.

"He's at the bottom," someone shouted, and the moment was broken.

We all went to the edge to look.

Quatervals had reached the base of the cliff and was fording the small river. Now we *did* hold our breath, as he was caught and nearly swept away twice by the racing current. But then he was across and climbing once more.

Here the rock was less striated than the cliff on our side, and twice he had to tap in wedges and tie himself securely into the rope before venturing off on seemingly blank rock. Once he fell and we gasped as he dropped about eight feet before the rope caught and held him. Undismayed, he instantly found a handhold and tried once more. When he'd made his passage, again he pounded a wedge in, tied the rope to that, and went back down to free the wedge and rope below.

Watching Quatervals work, I could see it was more than just skill. His abilities came from years of experience. Added to that was his superb physical conditioning. Without showing any strain, he could reach his foot above his waist, find a toehold, then hang by that and a hand *below* his body and stretch upward for another purchase. He looked like a spider, placidly moving across the wall of a room.

With no further problems he reached the top. He didn't even seem to be winded. He tied the grapnel to one end of his climbing rope, coiled the rest at his feet except for a long loop that he held in one hand, and took the grapnel in the other, letting it hang almost to the ground. Underhand, he swung it around until it was a blur. At some chosen instant he let go and sent the hook spinning out across the gorge. Not only did it make the distance in his first cast, but it fell just at the feet of Levu, another ex-Scout, who had it firm before it could skitter back over the edge. Quatervals allowed himself to look mildly pleased.

Levu tied the rope to a close boulder, and across the way Quatervals secured his end to a massive chunk of the fallen bridge's springing. Levu took off his own boots, held up crossed fingers to the heavens, muttered a prayer, and slipped out onto the rope, hand-over-handing across to the other side like a lemur. After him went other men.

Quatervals was paying no mind to them, no doubt assuming if they were stupid enough to fall, they didn't deserve recognition from him, and was laying out his own sticks and rope. He sprinkled what was in the pouch over them and whispered the spell he'd been taught as a Scout, and as on our side, the wood and ropes writhed and grew. I noted that the growth was much slower than when Janela had used her own magic and wondered if her spell was better, or, which I thought more likely, if it was just that an experienced Evocator would have greater powers than a nonwizard—no matter if he'd been blessed and given permission to use minor tactical magic, as were all officers and most senior warrants in our army.

Those logs were also X-tied and carried to the verge. Meanwhile three larger ropes were laid out, and small ropes, about four feet long, fastened them together at six-foot intervals. The climbing rope was used to pull those heavier ropes across, and now three-inch-thick lines stretched across the chasm. These were tied to the notched ends of the X-tied logs and to the center, and then the two wooden X's were lifted to the vertical. All that remained was to brace the logs' feet and to lash them to secure moorings and we had a bridge.

It was *interesting*, to say the least—walking splayfooted on the single line that ran from the center of the X to its opposite, hands bracing on the upper lines, especially carrying the heavy packs and our weaponry.

But without incident we reached the far side.

"Not bad," I complimented Quatervals.

"Not good either," he snorted, and pointed at the sky.

I was jolted to see almost a full day had been lost, a full day that Cligus would have to close the distance between us. That day we traveled no more than a mile before long shadows began to crawl toward us.

We found a small grassy vale with a spring and a pool and set that for our camp.

I heard the rattle of stones and turned in time to see half a dozen antelope clatter over a rise.

"And there goes dinner," Maha muttered.

Since I'd done nothing but watch all day, I found a bow and quiver and determined to put a little work in. Janela asked if she could go along, and borrowed a light bow from one of the men. Quatervals said something about coming along and I flatly ordered him not to. My spiderman had done enough. He muttered, but indicated to Chons that he should accompany us, not as assistant poacher, but bodyguard. The Cyralian brothers, even though they'd labored mightily helping build the X-bridge, protested about not being allowed to go—huntsmen to the end.

Whether in mountains or plains, there are only two ways to stalk antelope. The first is to come on them while they're unawares, and the second is to play to their only weakness—besides tasting so wonderful when grilled with butter and served with a butter sauce of salt, pepper, parsley, lemon juice, and a splash of sweet wine, I mean.

Antelope are insatiably curious, as much or more so than cats. I proposed to use this against them, borrowing a red handkerchief from Otavi for my chief weapon. We slipped out of the vale, and within moments the world of the hunt took me and all else fell away. I've always enjoyed stalking. It was one of the few legitimate excuses a rich old merchant such as myself could use to get out into the country away from the stress of business. I have no particular liking for killing the poor creatures I stalk—although as one who likes meat as much as the next man, I feel mildly hypocritical about such squeamishness.

Antelope are among the most skittish of creatures, so we crept along as silently as we could, using every scrap of cover that presented itself. Rather than peer over the rocks, which is guaranteed to stampede the wary beasts into the next county, we peered around them. Unsurprisingly, since this was country man had penetrated but little, we saw three of them: small, longhaired beasts, grazing in a meadow not five minutes' walk away. We were downwind, so all was well.

I cut a stick from a bush and tied Otavi's handkerchief to it. We waited until the antelope had their backs turned and were intent on their dinner, and then Chons moved into the open, stuck the long twig into a crack in the rocks, and returned.

We didn't have to wait for more than a few seconds, peering through a crack in the rocks, when one of the animals looked up and spotted the handkerchief moving in the breeze.

All three were instantly alert, about to flee. But nothing threatened, and that handkerchief's waving became hypnotic, irresistibly attractive. They walked toward it, stopping often when a wisp of wind made the cloth flutter a bit more strongly. They came closer . . . closer . . . we nocked the arrows we held ready on our bowstrings . . . closer . . . and they were but a dozen paces from the handkerchief when I nodded and all three of us rose from the sheltering rocks and fired.

The antelope sprang to escape but it was too late. Two leapt high and fell, Janela's and Chon's arrows buried in their chests. My own arrow struck the third victim, as I'd intended, in the lungs. The animal shrilled, turned and bounded away. But I'd struck it fair and knew it would only go a few dozen yards before falling. We waited a few minutes, then went in pursuit.

There was a blood trail to follow and we came around a rock and found, as I'd expected, my antelope, stretched dead on the rocks.

What we hadn't expected was the enormous tiger standing over the buck's body. We froze. The tawny beast stood equally motionless, staring at us. Then a low growl came from its throat as it announced its intentions.

Although arrows had somehow, reflexively, found their ways to our bowstrings, none of us were so foolish as to lift them. The tiger was a female, and I noted from her sagging belly that she had borne cubs this season.

The tiger's growl grew louder and she stepped toward us. I saw that she was limping badly and noticed a barely healed wound streaking one rear leg.

I signaled a retreat and we slithered away, our eyes never leaving the huge cat. We kept backing until we'd reached open ground. We exchanged glances.

"I wasn't going to say anything, but your buck looked old," Janela opined. "Certainly would've been no tastier than the soles of my boots. Otherwise, I wouldn't have hesitated to run that tiger off."

"No doubt about it," Chons said. "Certs, none of *us* fear tigers, eh? Sides, wi' two the men'd be gettin' full fat, an' we need to be slim to travel at speed, right, Lord Antero?"

I grinned. "I can tell," I said dryly, "that both of you are more experienced at the hunt than I, since your lies came faster than mine.

"*My* reasoning was simple: I've always been a *great* fancier of pussycats, and—"

Janela made a rude noise and we cleaned our trophies and

started back for the vale, leaving the field and the other, largest antelope for our friend.

THE NEXT DAY we saw our first snow, beside the road in a sheltered nook. The Fist of the Gods reached above us now, and the road climbed for that gap between the thumb and forefinger, curving back and forth and back again past gigantic boulders that could almost be called hillocks in their own right.

It grew colder and we were shivering in our light clothing. It was time to shift into winter kit. Again I was grateful for the benefits of sorcery, which had kept us from having to carry an impossibly great burden.

Before we'd left Orissa I'd had all of the men outfitted for the coldest conditions, with silk undergarments, two-piece suits knitted of wool with wide gaps between each strand to trap and hold the warm air, and the finest tailor-fitted furs for outerwear, the jackets hanging to mid-thigh and hooded, the pants equipped with suspenders so they'd stay up, and boots reaching almost to the knee. Naturally, these suits were bulky and would completely fill a man's pack, so he could carry no more than that. But our cleverness went on from there.

I'd hired seamstresses who specialized in making very expensive dolls for rich children. Each garment had some fur or cloth cut from it, and the doll-weavers set to work, using that cloth to make a minuscule duplicate of the full-size piece of apparel. These doll-size copies were sealed in a pouch and the pouch given to its owner with orders that the direst penalties would be wreaked for losing it. Since I was under no illusions about travelers being able to misplace anything not immediately needed so as to lighten their loads, Janela also cast a conjunction spell on the men's packs so that anything tossed aside or honestly forgotten would send worry cascading through the owner's mind for a long enough time to be annoying.

All that was needed now was to open the pouch, lay out the new garments, and have Janela say the few words necessary to activate the preparatory spell she'd cast in Orissa. As she did, the doll clothes grew and I felt I was in the midst of an expeditionary tailor shop.

Some of the men protested about having to put on clothes as fine as these when they were so filthy, and so we went on until we reached an icy mountain stream. I forced myself to strip bare and sluice the dirt of the road from my body, although the soap would barely lather.

Others felt differently, such as Quatervals. "By the gods," he said, pulling on his trousers a few feet away, but keeping his face decently turned away, "you'd never have made a good Scout, my lord, insistin' on being clean and all. Here you've got a fine shelterin' coat of oil the gods have given you as we've been walking, nearly as warm a coat as this fur, and you're casting it away. Tsk."

"I prefer not to be able to smell myself," I said.

"More proof you'd never make a Scout, my lord," he said. "You only smell yourself three days without bathin' and your mates but three or four beyond that. Then the nose quits, out of pure self-respect as aught else."

I saw Pip nodding full agreement and chuckled—it was hard enough to get *him* to bathe in the heart of the city without offering a few silver coins.

Janela had suggested I have half a dozen extra sets made in varying sizes, since we might hire a guide or guides from local tribesmen. Mithraik was hardly anyone's idea of a guide, but he, too, was outfitted warmly before we climbed on.

The journey wasn't that wearisome, more like walking up an endless ramp that zigged back and forth up the mountains. But it was tiring for the mind, especially when we would reach a peak, look down past the monstrous boulders, glimpse a section of the road below, which we'd been on two days earlier, and feel drained from all that effort that seemed to have accomplished so little. Then we'd crest the hill, move down a slight valley, and start up the next one.

At last the enormous fingers of the Fist loomed high, and became more ominous with each step we took. It looked as if the range was one big rock or a single polished casting. Snow covered the road, almost thigh deep, even though we were still shy of winter.

We were just about to round the Fist's thumb and enter the pass when the tiger repaid her debt and saved our lives.

CHAPTER FOURTEEN

BATTLE IN THE MIST

We were approaching the pass entrance at a slight angle, since the road had been torn by a landslide sometime in the past, and the open country, even though deep in snow, was easier going, which also helped to save us.

The tiger was crouched not more than thirty feet above us, where the rocky formation that was the Fist's "thumb" was born from the mountain's base. She paid us no mind, her attention fixed on something just inside the pass entrance. The tip of her tail was flickering back and forth. My archers had arrows nocked and their bows lifted, but I waved them down. As yet the creature was no threat. I thought it best to wait until she finished whatever business she had in the pass before going onward; I was about to shout for a rest when the tiger sprang.

She roared as she jumped, a scream intended to freeze her victims' bones to the marrow, and as she leaped I heard an answering scream—the scream of a terrified man. I heard shouts from the pass

☞ 311

just on the other side of the rocky outcropping, and then the tiger came back into view.

In her jaws was clenched the limp body of a man. I thought the tiger had torn through his jugular when she killed him but then realized that the deep red I saw was the man's tunic.

He was a Warden from Vacaan.

Somehow Cligus and Modin had slipped ahead of us and laid the perfect ambush, an ambush spoiled only by the tiger.

She stood triumphant for just an instant, then bounded away, on up the thumb's crest and out of sight.

Despite the shock, my mind was very clear and examining the options. We could not—would not—retreat. Nor could we conceivably walk into the pass. The only option was . . .

Quatervals was pointing. We must go on, on up, *outside* the pass entrance. We forced ourselves upward, always upward. Quatervals used the Scout hand-signaling to put half his mountain-experienced men, five of them, in front to break a trail, and five to the rear, both as a guard and hopefully to help anyone who fell. As the slope steepened, a fall could mean more than a faceful of snow and a cascade of soaking powder down your furs. It would be a long tumble down the slope to the road behind us—a rolling fall that would maim or kill.

In Orissa when my party was first training, we'd had lectures and demonstrations from Quatervals' men on how to move and what to do when we entered the mountains, and even two afternoons of practice on the snow-barren Mount Aephens. However, a speech is hardly the equivalent of years or, in Quatervals' case, a lifetime of mountaineering.

We should have taken rope bits from our packs, said the words over them, and tied ourselves together. But there was no time and so we pressed on.

The sky was clear and the sun scorching. I was sweating as badly as I had in the swamps and pulled my jacket open. This could be deadly—when we stopped, sweat would freeze. Not that I concerned myself about living that long: Before then, Cligus would send out a reconnoitering patrol and see our tracks and the people who made them laboring on above.

The mountain rose yet again, and now we were climbing on our hands and knees. The snow was less deep, but frequently it had turned to ice. I used my dagger as a pick to dig in and make a hold.

We could not continue much longer. I had to stop; my lungs were screaming for air. Not far ahead the slope rose again into a sheer rock face. We were blocked.

Quatervals, who never seemed to tire, moved cautiously to the side, to the rock wall of the thumb. He'd seen what I now spotted: a tiny cleft rising toward the ridge crest, a crevice that we might—we must—force ourselves into and up.

I heard moans of despair as others saw the cliff ahead and chanced low orders: Follow Quatervals. We clambered and crawled after him. Now we forced the time to find rope bits and have Janela cast the spells. Quatervals tied himself into a line and started up, hands and feet on either side of the crack, stair-stepping steadily upward, carrying a second rope with him. He tied off to a rock outcropping and motioned Levu to come up. The rest of us roped up and followed, creeping our way upward. I looked down once, saw Janela's white face looking at me and nothing but air below her, gulped, and looked in that direction no more.

I'd climbed in the midpoint of the party, so when I reached the crest there were nearly forty men and women stretched prone on the icy rock. Quatervals beckoned me to join him but—hand held palm down, pressing repeatedly—keep low. I slithered like a serpent until I was beside him. I slowly raised my head, looking over the edge and then down to where the pass began. Below, concealed behind rocks, our ambushers waited. They were dotted in outposts at the mouth of the pass and the rest drawn up in an attack formation in a small vale. Farther up the road there was a tight knot of men in red tunics looking like a bloody dot on the stone. There would be Cligus and Modin. Son or not, I wished for the powers of a great Evocator and the ability to cast one single lightning bolt.

"How in the hells did they get ahead of us?" I muttered aloud.

"Blasted if I know, my lord," Quatervals said. "Not that it matters none, now, does it? P'raps they used magic, or more like there's more'n one route. Orissa's got more'n one highway to *its* gates, now, don't it?"

It was as good an explanation as any. We crawled back to where Janela waited. We quickly held a war council as to what our plans should be. We must move quickly. I asked Janela why Modin's magic hadn't spotted us, and she looked worried.

"Again I've sensed some great presence over these mountains, enough so I feel my magical senses somewhat befuddled. My guess is that Modin's powers have also been reduced."

"My lady," Quatervals said, "then that would mean this presence is friendly? If it's keepin' Modin from kenning us out, I'd certainly name it so."

"I'm not sure I'd use that word," Janela said. "Nor would I call it an enemy. Someone . . . is watching us with interest, is the best assessment I can make."

We had no time to debate whether this aspect was good or evil, having definite enemies not a mile below. I looked along the ridge crest. Could we follow that, staying clear of the pass, until we passed out of view?

I didn't need to ask Quatervals or send out scouts, since I saw several rifts that cut through the mountain range's thumb. We could go no more than another quarter mile or so before we'd have to descend and use the pass.

"Are there any spells you *could* attempt?" I asked.

Janela considered. "No . . . Wait. Perhaps yes. An earth spell, something that would call to local phenomena." And she muttered on, pulling her purse around and fishing for materials. She took out two small mirrors, tinder, steel, and a bit of powder that she sprinkled on the tinder.

"Yarrow," she explained, half smiling. "It's for fertility. A multiplier. I think it'll work like that, anyway."

She found an indent in the rock where an ice pool had formed perhaps a quarter of an inch deep and put the tinder on that. She made certain arcane motions over the tinder, then struck the steel, and sparks flew into the tinder. She blew the tinder into a flame, and as it flared up, she held one mirror so it reflected the flame and the second near her mouth. Then she chanted:

"Feel the warmth
Feel the spring
Water rise
Whence you came
Lift and grow
Spread and roll
Then follow the earth
Follow it down
Follow it down."

Obediently, the ice melted and steam rose. As it did, she exhaled into the mirror, fogging it completely.

"One reflects the other and back and forth," she murmured. "Now we should do whatever comes next because there's little point in waiting for a spell that may not work."

She considered a minute, looking up at the range that rose above us and the pass, then went back into her purse and brought out some more items.

"These," she said, "might help later, so I'll have them ready." She grinned. "Let's go, Amalric. I'm freezing on these rocks."

Her apparent unconcern was another thing she had in common with Janos, who had seldom showed dismay when trapped by a seemingly overwhelming enemy.

We went along the crestline as far as we could until the crevasse blocked our way. As yet there was no sign that Janela's spell was working. I thought to ask her what exactly it was supposed to do, then reconsidered. If there was some force blocking magic here, it would do little good to bring attention to it, either by words or thoughts, and so I tried to think of other problems. Unfortunately, there were more than enough of those.

One more time ropes went down the side of the rocks and we slithered back to the road's level. We tried to hide in the crevasse as much as possible, but it wasn't big enough for more than sixty people. I bade the others to crawl out and lie still along the rocks until the order was given to move. Luckily, our furs had been chosen for their mottled appearance, drably fitting in with the stones and snow. Once more Te-Date smiled and we were undiscovered. Our best chance now was to move as quickly as possible on up the pass until we'd be lost to sight. At that point we'd drop off rear scouts and travel on, knowing that sooner or later our evasion would be discovered.

But it did not happen that handily. The way was hard, breaking through virgin snow almost to the waist. And we'd gone but half a hundred yards when I heard a dim commotion from behind and we were discovered.

There was no point in silence now so I began issuing commands, keeping my voice calm and controlled.

Quatervals and the others followed suit: "All right now . . . Don't waste energy looking back . . . We're movin' as fast as they are . . . Pay 'tention t' yer footin' an' help yer mate . . . There's no cause t' fret, we've got a long lead on 'em."

But we did not have much of a lead. I stopped and let the column stumble past. My duty was to be at the rear of the formation, facing the Wardens, Modin, Cligus and his Orissans. Quatervals saw me, and he and Otavi fell out of line as well. Janela and Towra stayed at the head of the column, setting as fast a pace as possible.

I desperately wanted to see some curve in this pass or places where fallen debris could be used for shelter to fight a holding action that might give us time to break free. But the Old Ones had built well: The pass ran straight as an arrow's flight nearly halfway to the summit before it curved left at the first knuckle. There were but few boulders that'd fallen—the road had been cut cleanly through the rock, as if a red-hot blade were making a deep vee slice in butter. There was no shelter, nor could we even dream of fleeing up the sides of the cut for safety.

The others went past, gasping with effort as they forced themselves onward a step at a time. I doubt if many of them noticed me. Their eyes saw no more than a patch of snow . . . a foot lift . . . come down . . . and come up again, trying to carry on, trying to keep from falling. I saw with dismay that the sailors, the least experienced at moving on land, were beginning to drop back. I shouted for Janela to slow the pace and ordered Quatervals to name the rear guard.

He bellowed commands as the last man, Mithraik, came even with me. I noticed the look on the pirate's face, pale, terrified, although he didn't even seem to be breathing hard. I wondered why he wasn't at the front where it would be the safest for the longest time. I wondered what had broken him on our long journey—he'd seemed more than brave fighting the half-men back in the jungle city or the crocodiles of the river.

"Hold, you," I ordered, trying to shock him out of his fear. "Stand and fight with us."

His eyes widened and he seemed about to protest, but then he firmed up his lip.

"Aye, Antero," he said, and there was no pretense of humility in his voice. "As you say. If here's the place, then here's where I'll leave my mark."

I was looking past him toward Cligus' army. It's all too easy to sneer at soldiers in pretty uniforms and say they probably know nothing more than bashing the parade square or shining their brass, and assume so-called elite formations are such in name only. But Modin's Wardens deserved their reputation, no matter how murderous and criminal their behavior had been in Irayas. In the few minutes since we'd been sighted, they'd broken out of their ambush positions, formed up, and started up the snowy road after us. They marched in three ranks with flankers in front, and I heard the shouting of their warrants and officers for more speed to catch those damned renegades.

They were climbing faster than we were, even though there were several hundred of them.

"Quatervals, you're the expert. What can we do?"

" 'Tisn't but one thing," he said. "We'll split the party. I'll stay with, say, a third of the men and we'll hold 'em as long as we can. Meantimes you an' Lady Greycloak streak for the pass. Once over, try to go to ground. Move on when you're sure you've evaded 'em."

I started to protest and Quatervals shook his head. "And I don't want to be hearin' any gods-damned bleedin' about how you should stand here an' fight. You an' the lady make a pair an' it'll take the both of you to win through. Now don't be six kinds of a fool, my *lord*, and kindly get your arse forward and keep on movin'. Put up a plaque or somethin' in Orissa for us when you make it through."

Otavi had come up beside him and was listening. He nodded in agreement. "He's right, m'lord. An' this appears to be as good a place to die as any." He spat on his hands and swung his huge axe back and forth, warming up.

There were others coming back down the mountain to join him and my eyes blurred as I saw they were my best: Kele; Chons and Maha, my other two stalwarts who'd battled the demon that was Lord Senac; the Cyralian brothers; and others I'd known and traveled beside for years. Even Pip stood among them.

He saw I'd noted him and looked abashed. "Times a wee lad'd rather do *anythin'* but wear his footers out on these demon-bless't rocks. An' I'm hopin' you pays death benefits prompt like y' promised, or m' old bitch'll be on yer like stink on shit."

Brave men and women all.

Then there was a windrush and I saw a blur out of the corner of my eye. I flung myself flat, heard a loud crunching thud—and blood spattered the snow. I lifted my head to see Chons' body tumble, nearly cut in two by a monstrous iron bolt.

Quatervals swore. "They've brought engines!"

And they had. I saw small groups of men winding large pedestal-mounted crossbows, lifting iron darts nearly the length of a man into their troughs. They were firing over the heads of the advancing infantry. Another bolt hummed in and shattered against the rock wall, and yet another. Archers below chanced their first volleys, but they fell yards short of us.

"Lord Antero," Quatervals ordered. "Get you gone, sir! Now!"

I turned to obey, feeling like a coward but knowing Quatervals was right. The enemy was now only a hundred yards or so away and their arrows were beginning to land among us, even though they weren't aimed well by those hard-breathing men in red below us.

A man shouted in agony and one of the Cyralian brothers stumbled forward, hands feebly plucking at the arrow that stood out from his lungs. Blood frothed, and he fell facedown.

We still had the advantage of height, and our own arrows volleyed up and then dropped full into their forward ranks. It was impossible for any of my people to miss, firing into the packed mass of Cligus' still-charging troops.

They were close enough for me to hear one of their sergeants bellow, "Take the old man alive! Lord Cligus wants him for hisself," and found a moment for a wry grin: If he did capture me, which I had no intent of allowing, he'd certainly not recognize his father, who now looked some years younger.

If I didn't manage to escape, most certainly I'd be slain by one of the soldiery in ignorance. I slogged away to rejoin the rest of my retreating party, suddenly aware that I had a great duty to Janela. If we did not escape, I must not allow her to fall into Modin's hands.

Just behind me came an animal bellow, and despite myself I spun.

It was Mithraik, roaring like a beast.

"Antero! Antero!" and I could barely distinguish the words. "Here is the place! You're sealed to me! You and yer cow!" And he began changing, writhing, growing until he reared tall, as tall or taller than Lord Senac, and his furs ripped, revealing a body that was red, raw, like a flayed man, slime oozing from its pores.

The demon that had been Mithraik, the demon that had been set to betray us from within, roared defiance at all men—Cligus' as well as my own. Otavi hurled his axe but the demon brushed it aside. The beast was nearly twenty feet tall, and I could smell its stink from where I stood. It had clawed feet and two arms, each pincered like those of a marine animal. But its face was the worst, a protruding forehead with bulging eyes like those of a man strangling, skin pulled back over its cheeks to reveal gross fangs that reached up almost to its nose slits and down to where a chin should have been. Hair hung in clumps from the monster's face, and roaring, roaring incoherently as it completed its transformation, it started toward me.

An arrow hummed past, cutting deep into its cheek, sending ichor flying, and the creature turned, screaming anger and no doubt a promise to kill its attacker as soon as it finished me. Not ten feet away, just below it, was Quatervals. He held the bow of the fallen Cyralian, aiming upward. His stance was perfect, as if he were shooting for range or perhaps demonstrating how to fire over a foe's front line. An arrow was full-drawn, broad head just touching the rest, and he made his shot.

The shaft flew true and buried itself in one of the demon's eyes. It screamed once more and the rocks around us shook with its pain and anger and then it stumbled forward, staggered and fell, rolling, tumbling down the slope, still struggling for its feet. Then it was up, trying to stop its momentum, blinded, the horrid fluid that must have been its blood spraying into the middle of Cligus' men.

Blind with agony, it cared not who it slew, and slashed about. Wardens and Orissan soldiers howled and fell, and now they had no time for us as the monster savaged their ranks.

Perhaps the awful magic that had been worked by the demon's transformation freed Janela's spell, or perhaps that presence was taken by surprise, because suddenly a mist rose around us and from behind us, a thick summer mist that could take a mountain traveler by surprise and make him lose his way, no matter how familiar a path he might be on, and fall to his death into a hidden crevasse.

But we had no such worries. Quatervals and I shouted orders: Move, move, move, damn your eyes! Uphill! You can't get lost, you can't go wrong—and we were stumbling away, the sounds of battle behind us, the demon's shrieks louder than ever as it did our slaughter for us.

Fear and the blood-rush of battle transferred to our feet and we waded on and on, each of us alone in a private world of white and gray, and then we broke free of the mist.

Two dozen yards in front of us waited Janela and the others. They were in battle formation, but Janela was some feet in front, crouched in the snow.

"I saw," she said, without lifting her eyes from her work. "The bastards set a spy on us and I never sensed a thing. Amalric, tell me when you think everybody's safe and I'll see if my second trick works."

I did, counting as they passed, and blessed the gods for that tally sheet that was always a part of my merchant's brain. There'd been twenty-six people who'd chosen to stand with the rear guard, and now came eighteen . . . nineteen, which was Otavi, who'd managed to recover his axe; one more . . . and then Quatervals.

"I'm the last," he croaked, finally showing some signs of human exhaustion.

I still waited for another half minute, hoping there'd be some others come out of the roiling mist. But no one appeared. We'd lost five friends down there and my heart whispered pain to me, even though my head told me true that we were unbelievably lucky to have suffered that few deaths.

Below, Mithraik's demon howls were growing fainter. Even a monster like it would eventually be taken down by that many men.

"That's all," Janela said, a bit of impatience in her tone. "Get behind me, Amalric. This one might be a bit spectacular."

She'd rolled half a dozen small balls of snow and held them in her palm together with some pebbles she'd picked up on the rocks. I don't know whether she'd already said words over them or doused them with some potion, but she began snapping them away down the road as she simply chanted:

"Move away
Roll on
You have brothers
You are great
Now grow
Now roll
Gather as you go."

Most of us have made snowballs as children and rolled them down steep slopes in the hopes of creating an avalanche. It never worked for me, but I never lost hope of one day creating a truly monstrous slide that would wipe an entire slope clean. Janela's spell fulfilled my finest dreams as the tiny snowballs rolled, gathering snow as if they were lodestones, rolling even faster than the road's steep slope would warrant. From the high slopes above the road came other rumblings as snowbanks high above us let go. None of us could see what happened, but the road was swept clean and we heard the roar as the avalanche crashed down on Cligus and his men.

Janela rose, her expression startled.

"I didn't plan for *that*," she said. "The best I'd hoped for was to pitch the snow in front of us down on the bastards. I wonder if . . ." She looked around thoughtfully. "No. I've got to be wrong. I wondered if somehow that presence was helping us, which makes no sense at all.

"I guess somehow my measurement was off and I managed to create a thousandfold snowball instead of tens or hundreds. Or perhaps Cligus and that pox-ridden Modin are finally getting a share of bad luck."

"We can theorize later," I said. "You, or the gods or the demons or whoever, have given us more time than I could dream of. Call it luck if you want. We'll make the correct sacrifices at a better time."

She slung her bag and we moved out.

Perhaps it was luck or maybe the degree of the slope did lessen, but travel seemed easier now, and in half an hour we rounded the bend of the knuckle.

It was growing dark, but we could not stop. I put men out front with firebeads and pushed on. We stopped once at midnight, melted snow, and ate jerked meat, dried fish, and boiled sweets we'd carried with us. Then we went on. If there was an ambush or an enemy ahead, we'd rather chance the unknown than what was coming hard behind us—I knew better than to dream that Mithraik could have destroyed the entire pursuing army.

Just at dawn we reached the summit and a great, drear plateau spread out below us with a fog-shrouded mountain range in the dim distance.

We took a break, and now, feeling no sign of pursuit, had time to feel the fatigue that was sucking the marrow from our souls and bones.

"Why is't," Quatervals wondered, staring out over the steppes we would be crossing, "the romances never tell you that beyond the great hill's most likely going to be another damned great hill, vaster'n the one before?"

There wasn't any answer, so we pressed on.

We stopped after another hour and I ordered two hours sleep.

Only four of us stood guard, Quatervals not among them. My entire body moaned for sleep, cried out to lie down just for one minute on that welcoming ground, but I dared not even lean against a rock. I finally found a shortspear and propped its point just under the skin of my chin. Twice I awoke with blood trickling down my neck, but at least I stayed conscious.

We marched on for another six hours, then chanced two hours rest. This time I slept, letting Quatervals have the watch.

We went on like that for two full days and nights, never daring to stop for more than two hours, not until we would reach some sort of safety.

On this side of the Fist of the Gods the road was in better repair, cutting almost straight toward the sere flatlands below.

By the end of the second day we had reached the last of the snow, but the barren foothills offered no sign of shelter.

We could hold my torturous schedule no longer. We were now so groggy that the most minor danger we might stumble into could allow the party to be wiped out. We sheltered just off the road and allowed a full six hours for sleep. Then up and on. After this longer break I felt worse than I had before, with every bone creaking, every muscle begging for relief.

I pushed my company harder than I'd ever pushed any expedition. They glared at me, hating me but not having the strength to swear. Not even Pip complained, and I knew we were close to the end of our powers.

A day and a half later we were on the flatlands. It remained cold and some of the men found energy to curse, but I was grateful. Men travel better in cold than heat. The road still shot ahead, never turning, never rising, regularly marked by the two-faced woman/ demon head toward its unseen end against the distant mountains that must be Tyrenia.

We could go no farther without rest. We turned aside and marched for three hours at a sharp angle away from the road. Quatervals and his Scouts were at the rear, calling on every bit of their cunning to mask our trail, and Janela was with them, using her sorcery to keep anyone from being able to follow our path.

We found a cleft in the seemingly featureless plain that was nearly a valley, almost a hundred feet deep, with two springs, a pool, and trees.

Someone, Quatervals most likely, lifted my pack off and laid out my bedroll. I fell across it, not bothering to take off my boots or crawl in, and slept for a full day with no memory of having come to the end of this march.

I AWOKE to a truly monstrous noise.

> "Back an' side go bare, go bare
> Both foot an' hand go cold
> I'll see no more ale in my life
> This road goes on so bold.
>
> It stretches far
> It stretches long
> Antero drives us hard
> I fear I'll be naught but bones
> Before I reach the . . ."

The voice—Pip's—broke out of what he imagined to be song and asked, plaintively, "An' what's rhymin' wi' hard?"

Janela's voice came: "Go back three lines and try, instead of 'Antero drives us hard,'

> "I'll stumble like a bum
> I fear I'll be naught but bones
> Still whining, never dumb."

"Better stay wi' magic, me lady," Pip came back. "Yer don't 'ave t' make the words stick so tight."

At this point I sat up and opened my eyes.

Pip, a few feet away, reluctantly splashed water on his face from a basin and pretended he'd just noticed me.

"Lord Antero, sir, an' how did yer lordship sleep? We all recked yer throat'd been seized by a demon, f'r the rattlin' an' groanin' comin' out."

I pulled myself out of my bedroll to my feet, trying to ignore each and every muscle's scream.

"Quatervals, doesn't this troubadour have some duties?"

"I'm thinking of them right now," he said. "Dark, dangerous, an' deadly."

"An' what else is new," Pip said, undiscouraged. "Bad enow yer makes me wash. Almost rather get m'self kilt."

"How long have I slept?" I asked Quatervals.

"A full day, sir."

I cursed. "You should've woken me!"

"Why? I sent scouts back to watch the road and they've seen no trace of Cligus and his toady. P'raps Mithraik put paid to 'em all."

I doubted that but said nothing. I looked around our encampment. All appeared in order: my people busy with the maintenance tasks of travel, sharpening weapons, mending torn garments, cleaning, and eating. There were sentries posted at the top of the cleft, and I knew, even from the fog I'd been in when we stumbled into this haven, that no one could approach us by surprise—at least not in earthly form. I also knew Janela would have her own wards out, so we were as secure as we could be in the magical sector, as well.

Ideally, we should have remained in this quiet place for three or four days to recover, but we had to keep moving.

There were two matters that had to be dealt with before we could travel, though.

The first was with Janela. I took her aside and asked what she thought about Mithraik. Did she have any ideas about who his master was? Who was he working for? What was his mission? How much did he know about us? Why had he chosen that moment to expose himself?

Janela considered her answer carefully. "As to whose employ he was in, I can't answer that. I'd suspect, though, someone ahead of us. Our yet-unknown enemy. If we assume the demon that took on the role of Lord Senac was in this enemy's hire, wouldn't it be logical for Mithraik to be the same? He was shielded with powerful magic of his own or I would have sensed him.

"I'm willing to say with a great deal of certainty that he was not in the thrall of Modin or one of his familiars—they've spent too much time wandering aimlessly in pursuit to have had a lodestone in the heart of what they seek.

"As for what his task was, I'd suspect as you said: a spy, someone who could keep track of exactly where we were at any time. Maybe once we reached the mountains his master didn't need him anymore.

"Maybe that was why he started behaving as a mortal and a coward—perhaps he sensed this and felt his master no longer cared if he lived or died, if that phrase even applies to those beings from his realms.

"As for what he'd learned about us, if we assume he had no mind-reading abilities, then we must think he learned everything any of the men know, no more and no less. How much that weakens us I cannot say.

"Why he chose to unmask himself when he did, again, this I can't answer. It could be his master decided he wanted you to die in the pass. Or since there are twists within twists in this matter, perhaps this presence who sometimes almost seems to be aiding us might have caused him to behave as he did.

"I don't know, Amalric." She smiled. "You see what the study of magic gives you? It can and frequently does make the adept more confused than the person who sees no more than what is around him."

She considered. "A wonderment just came to me about the study of magic. Do you suppose that if we *do* find this single binding secret of sorcery, ordinary people will be able to quietly attend lycées to learn how to become Evocators? And no one will have to hunt spider-haunted ruins for demoniac secrets or bind themselves to evil masters to learn their secrets?"

For a change, I had a ready answer. "There's not a chance that would happen," I said briskly.

"And why not?"

"I could offer many reasons, but will give you only one. Magic shall never be a subject like history or the music of the past taught by bone-dead tutors, for one reason: There's too great a profit for rogues in it.

"Be honest, Janela. If you could have learned everything just by dancing close attendance on some wizened stick of a man prattling lessons, would you now be a thaumaturge? Don't you and all the others who aspire to this wisdom beyond the seen *want* to be climbing the steps of dark towers and making great stinks with alembics and incense?"

Janela grinned.

"Besides," I finished in triumph, "I doubt wizardry could *ever* be learned in a classroom, even if Janela Greycloak's Warranted System of Thaumaturgy could be written. Why, that would be as absurd as . . . as believing you could teach trade and the art of being a merchant in a lycée!"

The second matter I had to deal with was most unpleasant: giving rest to the ghosts of our dead. We may have had to abandon the bodies of our friends in the pass, but we could hopefully guarantee that their spirits wouldn't wander this wasteland for all eternity. I sought around for any scrap, any memento they might have left or given another of our men, and all of them had. Even though no one said anything to me, I gathered this was a precaution most had taken in the not unlikely event their bodies would not be available for the correct ceremonies.

Janela made a small ritual over the mementoes, burnt incense, and prayed, sending their spirits on to Te-Date. I said a few words after that, meaningless to the dead, intended for the living, as to how these men had served not just me, but all of us and Orissa and all of mankind to boot. I could only hope I was correct.

While I spoke I noted the expressions on the three surviving Cyralian brothers. They looked solemn, but hardly as if they'd lost one of their own. Actually, I thought they were forcing sobriety out of respect for the friends of the others we'd lost.

After the ceremony I asked them to accompany me on a walk and we went to the far side of one of the ponds and I inquired as gently as I knew what was wrong.

The elder brother smiled. "There's naught wrong, my lord. But the four of us went t' a seer ere we left Orissa, payin' good coppers f'r a spring lamb t' sacrifice, an' the ol' hag said one of us'd die out here but the other three'd return safe wi' riches."

"It's nae we didn't love Daf," another one put in, "but like all men, our own lives're loved best."

I thanked them, apologized for intruding, and had something else to talk to Janela about.

She grimaced. "If, and that is a very big if, the damned seer had any of the Talent and saw anything resembling the truth, there's no harm. But if she was wrong or merely taking their money and another of them dies . . . you'll have two shattered young men to deal with. Don't set this aside, Amalric, because very few sorcerers are given any true glimpse of the Dark Seeker's intent, even though all of them prattle on about being able to give you the day you'll meet your loved one, the day you'll marry, your children and their fates, and the death-hour of all you wish to ask about.

"This is one of the few things that make me think maybe gods do exist. If you were a deity, wouldn't you want your subjects to live in blessed ignorance instead of having that awful knowledge of just when the candle will be snuffed out?"

I thought about it and nodded. As I readied my pack to travel on, I realized that in many ways Janela was wiser than her great-grandfather, even though she would have laughed if I'd suggested it. Janos Greycloak had knowledge in many areas, but all too often his erudition fell short in real life, in spite of his years of wandering and time spent as an officer in the military. I suppose some people are gifted at being able to understand their fellow men, and others, in spite of their boastings, are as thick-eared as any tone-deaf bumpkin sneering at a lyre player.

IT IS VERY HARD for those who have never traveled on great plains to envision them. The hardest thing to picture is how they go on forever. People who have grown up in normal lands shrink down when they walk out on these endless sweeps where it appears there is nothing but flat land and windswept grasses that sprawl to a distant horizon. The sky stretches huge around them, and at night, when the stars appear, it as if the gods are just overhead, almost visible, and all thoughts, dreams, and sins are very tiny indeed.

Some find these lands depressing, swearing that such a land with no life to be seen anywhere is soul-destroying.

I am no bred-to-the-tent nomad, so I admit to some of these feelings, wanting to hunch down a little in my soul when I come out on these steppes. But I know a bit about them from having traveled on high lands when I went a-trading above Luangu, looking for new cattlemen to do business with.

These are lands to traverse with caution, since they are far from the tablelike flatness most think. Instead, they're riven with clefts such as the one we'd hidden in, valleys that can support an entire tribe, and gullies perfect for raiders to lurk in and spring out in ambush on a caravan.

They appear waterless but are not completely arid. There are springs to be found that sometimes produce oases such as the one we'd hidden in, or wets to be dug out that'll give enough water for a man and his horse. Sometimes there are rivers or creeks to follow.

Also, they aren't desolate—the skilled and experienced traveler can generally find water within a day or two's travel. As for life— the high plains are well-populated with animals, from ground-burrowing owls to small predatory cats to antelope and other grass eaters. There are predators as well, two-legged and four.

We traveled cautiously, moving away from the road on a ninety-degree course until we'd found the oasis. We'd kept track of our paces. Three men were responsible for this, each counting independently, and each time they reached a hundred paces, they tied a knot in a small length of twine they kept in a pocket. At a hundred hundreds they tied another knot in a second piece of woven cord, woven so it would feel different at night to the fingers. That gave us the distance traveled.

When we left the cleft, we set our course by compass in the same azimuth as the road had gone. Once more we kept count of our distance in paces. When we would decide it was safe to return to the road or when it became too difficult to travel, it would be simple to turn another ninety degrees and, when we'd made the same number of steps we had going out, be back on the road to Tyrenia.

We traveled in spread-out order, keeping flankers distant, barely within visibility, ringing us to the front, sides, and back. We moved as quickly as we could but no longer forced the pace. When people travel too quickly they become tired and easily stumble into danger. Also, we wished to raise no dust to signal our presence.

The weather continued cold and windy, the gusts coming from the chill mountains we were traveling toward, making the endless miles of grass ripple like ocean waves. Our sailors saw the similarity and were cheered.

We encountered herds of antelope, and the Cyralian brothers brought down three. Maha butchered them and cooked them over low, smokeless fires.

While we were gathering wood for these fires, we spotted a herd of animals I'd never seen before. There were perhaps twenty of them and they looked like oxen but with longer and sharper horns that jutted forward like lances and long shaggy coats. They showed no fear of us whatsoever, and so we approached them curiously.

As we grew near, they showed signs of alarm, the bulls snorting and signaling. Then, marvelously, they formed a closed square, putting the nearly grown calves in the center of the formation, the bulls facing out, horns lowered. Now the snorts became threatening. I thought they might charge us, but these wise beasts would not be drawn out of their self-made fortress.

As we returned to the camp, Janela saw a strand of hair dangling from a prickly bush, hair that'd been pulled off one of these oxen. She gathered it up.

"An' what's your intent wi' that, my lady?" Pip wondered. "You'll be startin' a sweater, p'raps?"

"Or a winding sheet," she said. "For a *very* short man."

Pip snorted as if unconcerned. But he looked worried and I chuckled. Janela tucked the hair into her purse with no explanations, and I thought no more about it.

A day later we saw motion along the horizon. It came closer, and we made out a pair of direwolves, moving parallel with us as if tracking our journey. They were enormous, larger than any of the others had ever seen. I said nothing about the giant beasts I had once been unfortunate enough to witness. They had been Prince Raveline's estate guards, standing almost eight feet at the shoulder, dark intelligence in their eyes and death in their every move. I told Quatervals to move the flankers in closer and pair them up. Direwolves are among the cleverest of man's enemies, and except in unusual circumstances, aren't known to attack a man if he is alert and well-armed. The problem we had is that no one knows what unusual circumstances are to a direwolf.

We saw several mirages as we went on. Once, there was a lake that reached from horizon to horizon, a lake with boats, islands, and running water. It moved steadily away from us, and when we came to where it had first appeared, we saw the boats—more of the longhaired oxen, placidly grazing.

Twice we saw the mountains that were our destination hanging inverted in the sky.

The third illusion was different. About midday we saw a city to the north. It was beautiful, golden, spired. We were concerned, wondering if it was real and if haze had obscured it previously. But then we noticed that it was traveling with us and began admiring its illusory detail. Strangely enough, it lasted all through that day. I expected to see it vanish at dusk but it didn't. I forgot about it as we cooked our supper and then put out our fires before full dark.

When the night's blackness was complete, I happened to glance out. There, appearing not more than ten or twenty miles distant, was the city, all gleaming lights and shining minarets. I had never known an illusion to last so long, let alone illuminate itself, and when the others noticed it, they became upset, talking in low murmurs. About midnight it suddenly vanished and was seen no more.

Four days later we saw our first men. It was by the grace of Te-Date that they did not see us first.

THE TERRAIN BECAME more broken, cut with gullies and ravines and made up of small rolling hills. Because of this we moved more slowly and cautiously than before. One of the flankers signaled, and we took up covered positions while Quatervals went out to see what he'd found. He came back and reported finding a trail, a trail that most likely led to the road we were paralleling, which lay to our south.

"More'n just a trail," he said. "Almost a roadway. Hard-packed dirt, grass beaten down and chewed short to either side of the track. Caravan route, most likely. I saw some old dung, dried, been there a spell. No hoofprints, though. I'd guess the last travelers would've been through a few weeks ago or longer. Hard tellin' for sure, since I don't know the last time it rained."

We went on, crossing the track and keeping our heading of almost due east. The trail changed direction to our north and for a time ran east along with us.

Then came another warning from the flanker, a shrill double whistle that meant danger. We found cover, dips in the ground we could fight from, before sending someone out to learn what the problem was. I saw what had brought the alert before Quatervals came back to report.

A caravan was moving down the trail toward us. It wasn't very big, no more than two or three dozen horses, and was still in the distance. Quatervals sent us back, moving in short dashes, keeping low to the ground, to a dry watercourse we'd crossed a few minutes earlier. This would serve to keep us hidden from the travelers. In these lands no one but a fool would wander into an unknown encounter unless forced.

They came closer and I scanned them with an experienced eye. As I'd thought, it was a very small caravan, and I guessed trading prospects in these lands were poor. Or else they carried goods of inestimable worth but little bulk, such as jewels or spices. There were half a dozen outriders, heavily armed, and behind them the main group. There were four important folk, or so I guessed from the richly colored clothing they wore. Beyond them were packhorses and the rear guard. I frowned. This was not the most secure way to move in dangerous lands—there should have been more outriders and at least two squads of foot soldiers accompanying them. But perhaps I was wrong: Just because we had enemies in this wasteland didn't mean it wasn't perfectly safe for the natives.

That thought had but touched my mind when I saw other movement—this near a deep gully but a hundred feet or so from the trail. It was a man hiding behind a bush. He lifted himself up, his back to us, and scanned the approaching travelers. He was wearing armor. Quatervals had been intent on the caravan and hadn't noticed—I felt a flash of pride that for once, and I knew it would be one time only, I'd outscouted the mountaineer. I pointed out the bush that hid the soldier, and Quatervals swept the area with his experienced eyes.

"Five . . . no, ten or more," he whispered. "They're lyin' in wait for the traders." For so Quatervals had also decided the caravan to be. "Bandits."

He looked at me, hope shining in his eyes for a moment. "For once we'll just sit here and watch the slaughter, right, Lord Antero? Think neutral and all?"

I stared at him.

"We've got our own troubles here, sir," he tried next. "If we go and start takin' sides, we could be gettin' into somethin' we know nothin' about that'll make sure we have more enemies on our plate."

I said nothing.

"My lord, we don't even know if they're a member of your guild or not, so how'll we know what price to ask for the rescue?" he joked feebly.

"Now," I said softly, "now *we* are the tiger and it's our turn to give the warning."

Quatervals had known better than to expect me to sit and watch. Damned to all the hells if I would, seeing travelers who looked peaceable cut down as they rode. I've been attacked too many times by brigands and lost too many fine people to have any use for highwaymen except to measure a rope that's suspended from a tall tree with their necks.

Quatervals warbled a whistle that sounded like some sort of bird or perhaps a hunting lizard, and all around the wash my people slid out of their packs and readied their weapons. Janela, crouching a few yards away, looked at me askance, then grinned, shrugged, and set her own pack aside. The gods *never* favor those who take no side but their own, and even if they did, who would want to be counted as such?

"They'll hit them just . . . there," Quatervals said, pointing. "Four minutes, perhaps."

"Bowing to the judgment of a man who knows more about highway robbery than I ever shall," I said, "would you give them a warning just before they're hit?"

Quatervals smiled at my chaffing and found a bit of cloth in his kit, tied it around an arrow, unraveled the end a bit and struck flint and steel until sparks smoldered up. It flamed, and he nocked the arrow, drew, and fired high into the air just seconds before the ambush would be sprung.

The arrow, trailing a wisp of smoke, lifted across the ravine the ambuscade was mounted in and sailed over the heads of the caravan riders.

It was seen and horses reared and I heard shouts in the still air, and then the bandits attacked. The men in the bushes fired a volley of arrows at the travelers, intended to shock rather than kill, just as the raiding party rode out of the gully. There were thirty men on horseback and they were whooping and shouting. They spattered arrows, then abandoned their bows and charged forward. They brandished javelins, ready to throw, and their intent would have been to close on the caravan without warning, launch their spears, then close in the confusion and destroy the travelers in the first shock of battle.

But Quatervals' arrow had given a few seconds for the riders to ready their weapons. Better-aimed arrows went whistling out and there were empty bandit saddles.

I could no longer speculate, as Quatervals shouted and we charged forward into the rear of the brigands. They'd turned from their first charge and were regrouping when they saw us. Now they were caught between the two forces.

They may have been careless in setting the ambush with no rear watch, but they weren't inexperienced soldiers. Their leader cried orders and they charged directly at us. The best way to survive an ambush is to attack straight into it.

"Kill their horses," I cried, knowing this would be unexpected and terrifying.

On the plains, horses or whatever the mount may be, are life itself. Men fight and die but take great pains to keep their horses alive, both for safety and for trading purposes. We cared nothing about such customs, and arrows thudded home and horses reared, screaming, and other arrows went into them and they fell, sending their riders tumbling.

"On them," Quatervals shouted, and we ran on.

A man wearing some sort of dirty cloth tunic that camouflaged his mail came to his feet in front of me, still wheezing from the fall from his horse. He blocked my lunge and we closed, hilt to hilt, and I shoved him away, booting him hard in the stomach as he stumbled back. He staggered and I drove my sword into his side, wrenching it free as he fell.

I saw Otavi, rumbling on with his axe in both hands, as unstoppable a force as one of the oxen we'd seen. A lithe man darted at him, swinging a morningstar. Otavi held out his axe, let the star's chain wrap itself around his axe haft and pulled the star, handle and all, from the man's grasp, then crushed his attacker's skull with his weapon's point.

The caravan's guards were firing arrows rather promiscuously, one skittering across the ground not far from where I was, and I cursed at the thought of being slain by those we were trying to rescue.

The bandits reformed and attempted another charge, trying to break past us into open country, no doubt willing to abandon their brothers on foot. They rode close together, forcing their mounts into the gallop, spears leveled.

There can be little more fearsome a sight for a person on the ground, feeling very small, particularly if he isn't—like most of my party—*really* a soldier, when a horseman rides down on him intent on the kill. But Quatervals had trained us for that.

"Spearmen forward!" he shouted. "Stand firm! Stand firm!"

And my people did, gritting their teeth and setting their spear butts firm against the ground, kneeling to brace the shafts. The bandits' horses raced on, as if they would overrun us. But in some ways a horse is smarter than a man. A man will charge a spear wall and spit himself bravely in the doing. A horse will either try to leap over such a barrier or, more likely, balk or turn.

So these robbers' mounts did, and there was a milling and a falling and then the horde was fleeing for their lives. The men afoot ran after them, screaming for succor, and some of the braver robbers pulled their fellows up beside them before riding on. But others were left in the dust.

We reformed and moved toward the caravan. As we did, I heard shouts of pain and saw that the travelers were showing no more mercy to the freebooters' wounded and abandoned than they themselves would've been shown.

We'd taken but one casualty—one of the Cyralian brothers had been pinked in the arm by an arrow. But since it wouldn't be near-fatal, he was laughing and singing as foolishly as a young blood on the town with his father's purse as he broke the shaft off at the head and pulled it free. Another brother, just as cheery, tore off a strip of his tunic to bind the wound. Other than that we were unscathed—the shock of our presence and immediate attack had been the best armor imaginable.

The caravan hadn't been so lucky—at least half of their men were down, all too many of them not stirring where they lay. There was a flurry of dust and shouts as they regrouped and calmed or put their horses out of their pain.

Janela joined me, and I called for Quatervals, Kele, Otavi, and Pip and we went to meet the travelers.

Four people came away from the others to meet us. The foremost was a man my age—I mean a man who appeared to be my actual age in years, not as I now looked. He had a weather-seamed face, a yellowing beard that was plaited in two long ropes that hung to either side of his chest. On his head he had a stiff leather cap that would have served as armor. He wore a leather tunic stripped with metal, an elaborately embroidered shirt under it, tight leather breeches, and knee boots. A long curved sword was sheathed on one side of his belt and a matching dagger on the other. The second man was dressed similarly, although he carried a strung bow with a quiver of war arrows at his belt as well as a knife.

The other two were women. The rearmost was very old but carried herself rigidly, as if she were royalty. She wore a black blouse that fit closely, buttoning high on the neck, and a skirt split for riding, with dark undergarments visible when she walked. Her white hair was tied back in a queue and on her head she wore a leather tiara. Her expression was sour, unforgiving, and I sensed it had been that way since she'd first realized what a man's intent might be with her when he lowered his breeches.

The third caught and held the eye. She was very pretty and quite young—no more, I guessed, than sixteen, likely less. Pert breasts pushed a low-cut leather vest out, and a silk high-necked blouse in turquoise showed under it. She wore flaring pants, which narrowed at mid-calf and were bloused into riding boots. She had a silver belt buckled about a slender waist and a small dagger that looked like a toy, but I suspected could be used quite effectively. She had a small, pointed face with all of the intelligence and wit of a fox. Her dark blond hair was braided and then bound in a ring around the back of her head.

"I greet you, strangers," said the older man, and his rumbling voice was exactly what his imposing bulk deserved. "You are truly wolves, having driven off the jackals of Ismid who thought themselves rulers of the steppe.

"We are thine."

He knelt, holding out both hands palms up, his head bowed. The others followed, the younger man first, the old woman last, after giving me a look that suggested this certainly wasn't *her* idea. The young woman flickered a smile at me before kneeling.

"Please stand," I said. "We are your equals, not your conquerors."

The man looked up, complete puzzlement in his face. He started to speak but shut his mouth.

The younger man looked amazed. "You're foreign," he said, "but speak our tongue." The older one looked aghast, as if he expected me to put the other to the sword for daring to speak.

"Our wizard"—and I indicated Janela—"has given us the power to speak as those we meet."

"We are honored to be the slaves of so gifted a group of men . . . and women," he added hastily.

"What makes you think you are my slaves?"

Before the old man could answer, the young woman stepped forward.

"I am Sa'ib, of the Res Weynh." She paused, expecting me to know one or another name and be impressed. Not wishing to show ignorance yet, I smiled politely but made no answer. "My father, Suiyan, sent me to be schooled by the courtesans of Tacna in the skills a wife should bring to her wedding bed. A wonderful time it was. I finished and was honored a month ago and am returning to the tent of my father, where he will seek a proper husband for me, knowing what a fine brideprice I shall bring."

"No doubt," I said as neutrally as I could.

"That slime-eating eunuch Ismid, that bent-cocked barbarian who honors not his father—who begat him on a wandering mongrel—that bandy-legged lizard of a man who knows not the laws of the gods or men, learned of my departure from Tacna and determined he would have me to bed as his slave.

"But you saved me. So now I am yours, to do with as you wish. I can only ask that you extend mercy to my fellow slaves and allow them to serve you as well or, if you decide to sell them, to find mild masters." Once more she knelt, and the others followed suit.

I stepped forward and lifted her and then the old man by the hand.

"I said before we are your equals. I do not take slaves, I do not own them. All of us are free."

The four travelers goggled at us. It was as if I had announced that the three score of us were desert demons.

"You do not take slaves," the young man managed. "Then how do you live? How do you prosper?"

"I prosper by my own hand," I said. "Those who work for me are paid for their work in gold and silver. No man can serve another well if he is property, nor can that slave's master ever be free himself so long as he permits such bondage to endure."

I felt, just for an instant, a flash of shame from the distant past; for when I was a youth, Orissa had held slaves and it was only Janos Greycloak bringing the light to me that had made me the tinder that set the torch of freedom alight in my lands. I also felt a bit like a pompous ass for my speech.

The old man was perplexed. A bit of what I'd said sunk into the younger man.

"I am Ziv," he said. "My captain, here, is Diu. If we are not your slaves, then what *are* we?"

"Men and women whom I've been fortunate enough to help and who are now free to go their way," I said. "I ask only that you give us what information you have about these regions we travel through."

Now there was a babble of joy and we were embraced by three of the four. I thought that Sa'ib held the embrace longer than the others, but perhaps, being youngest, was the happiest and least restrained. As we returned to the other travelers and Quatervals beckoned our party to follow, giving secret signals for them to maintain their alertness, I learned that Diu was the officer sent by Suiyan to bring his daughter back, Ziv was his son, and the old glowering woman was Tanis, who'd been Sa'ib's nursemaid since birth. I wondered idly what *she* had thought when Sa'ib flung herself into that "wonderful time" in the brothel.

We asked many questions of them and discovered a great deal, but not nearly enough. The steppe we were crossing was the home of at least a dozen always-warring nomad tribes, the Res Weynh being the mightiest. Or so we were told by Ziv, and naturally agreed with him. They did but little trading with the other inhabitants of this land, and that mostly for weapons and jewels, the tribes living on their sheep and by hunting. No one could enter this region, they boasted, even if they wished to pay tribute. It was the will of the gods that they remain as they had been created. None of the People, for so they called themselves, needed any more than the animals, water, and sheep they'd been granted when the gods created them, and it would be terrible sacrilege to allow anyone to farm here, let alone build villages or cities.

I asked Sa'ib how they would find her father's tents, and she told me, with some surprise, that of course they'd know where they'd be and go straight to them. Janela later said that perhaps the tribal shamans had given their people a homing spell, or perhaps it came naturally over the centuries as a survival trait.

My main interest was the Kingdoms of the Night—Tyrenia. They didn't know it by either name. They said there were gods living in the mountains and pointed toward the cloud-obscured peaks that were our goal. They told me there was a road not a day's journey south that ran due east like a spearcast, which had been built by these gods. Naturally, they never used the road. Janela asked why, and Ziv explained that it did not pay to deal too closely with the gods or their works. It was best that they were worshiped from afar.

"So," Janela said, "none of the Res Weynh have ever seen any of these gods of yours?"

"Of course not. Except our shamans, and they say the vision is too terrible to ever talk about."

So the Old Ones who dwelt in Tyrenia held to themselves and had nothing to do with these nomads, but used them as unknowing guardians.

I asked Ziv if Suiyan would object to our passage through his kingdom, and he said he did not think so. Naturally, he added hastily, he could not deem to speak for such a great monarch as Suiyan, but no doubt the service I'd rendered him by saving his daughter from that pig Ismid would make him grant us such a boon.

I noted that both Ziv and his son were looking increasingly worried as they considered what Suiyan might think of them for nearly allowing his daughter to be kidnapped or even killed. If Suiyan was as other nomad leaders I'd encountered, I fancied their chances of seeing another birthday were exceedingly slender. But that was not our concern.

They offered us anything we wished from their goods, but we took little except some sweetmeats, some unfamiliar spices that Maha said would enliven the menu, and some dried delicacies.

We helped them reassemble their horses and cargoes and make ready to leave. I pitched in on this. One of my great areas of expertise, and one I unutterably loathe, is loading unruly, biting, neighing, bastardly pack animals for a journey so the ropes don't slacken, the hitches come untied, or the most creative bucker manage to send his burden flying in all directions.

While I was doing this I heard shrill voices and looked across to see Sa'ib arguing with Tanis. She ended the debate conclusively by slapping the old woman.

I'd been remembering Deoce, my first love. On our initial attempt to find the Far Kingdoms, we'd saved her, a young nomad woman, from slavers. In the journey she'd become my lover, and when we returned to Orissa, she became my wife. Save for spirit, there wasn't much resemblance between her and this nomad princess who now came stamping toward me.

As she approached, her face smoothed and she spread a smile across it. Her walk became more seductive and I noted that she'd rearranged her clothing so more of her bosom was bared.

"Lord Antero," she greeted me. "You might make one of us, working with your hands like you are. I've never heard of a great lord who actually labored."

"Titles are given by other people," I said, again feeling like a stodgy old man in the face of youth. "I'm really just a merchant, a caravan owner."

"I'll wager," she said, "that you have many caravans in your land and your tents reach for days, although I know you live in those cold, bare, fearsome buildings of stone like those in Tacna. I know you have other wives, but that doesn't matter."

I didn't answer. She came much closer, put her hand on my arm, and leaned so there was no way I could not see the rise of her breasts and the erect roseate nipples. Her breath smelt sweet, of cardamom and spice.

"You know," she said, voice throaty, "when I realized I was your slave, I felt a thrill go through me."

"Ah?"

"I doubt my father will find me such a fine-looking man as you, a warrior who always leads."

"I'm sure he'll do well for you if he went to all the trouble to have you, um, so well-schooled."

"Perhaps," she said. "Or perhaps not."

She touched my beard with the back of a finger.

"I've always preferred older men," she said. "They have more staying power. Young men . . . boys . . . it's in, out, and gone.

They're like rabbits playing in their burrows. And older men have other ways of giving pleasure." She smiled dreamily. "I know. And I like them all."

She opened her mouth and ran the pointed tip of her tongue over her lips. Then she said, "I, too, know some ways of love even a great warrior and traveler like yourself might be pleasured to learn."

She reached between her breasts and took out a silk cord, knotted at intervals. She ran it through her fingers, smiling at me. "In my tribe," she said, "a man or woman might choose to be bonded to a greater one. For safety, for happiness, for . . . love. All that she has to say is 'I take thee for master' three times."

Sa'ib waited for my response. I was trying to find the right words, and looked around. I saw Janela, busy helping Otavi reload a horse. Sa'ib saw who I was looking at and hissed with rage, and I looked back at her pretty little fox face, lips now pressed together.

"I understand," she said, and the coo was gone from her tone. "You're in thrall to the sorceress. I should have guessed!"

She actually stamped her foot, something I'd never actually seen anyone do other than in a pantomime.

"Yes," I said hastily. "That's it."

She nodded twice, jerkily, turned, and bustled away.

Half an hour later Ziv had his riders ready. The caravan moved off, following the trail. Sa'ib glanced at me once, quickly, then away, her face cold with anger.

We waited until they were no more than dots on the horizon, then set out. For the first hour we traveled on a false azimuth in a direction we'd told Ziv we were heading, before changing back to our real track. There was no harm in being overly cautious.

We fell back easily into the rhythm of the march. Janela came up beside me. I saw a sparkle of merriment in her eyes.

"Amalric," she said sadly. "How could a great chieftain such as you turn down something like that?"

She'd guessed what the exchange must have been. Some women might have been angered. Janela thought it was funny.

"You're right," I agreed. "Someone like that would add sparkle to my life. At least until I didn't give her whatever bauble she wanted and found myself suddenly qualified for a post guarding someone's harem."

"I do pity whoever Suiyan finds for her husband," Janela agreed. "No doubt he'll discover reason, once the first pleasures of the couch wear away, to make many great raids. As far away from her as it's possible to ride."

She turned serious. "I do have a question, though. I was reminded you were the prime cause for Orissa freeing its slaves. Now there's been a generation, perhaps two, of freemen who remember you as their liberator."

"Possibly," I said. "Although they probably think I'm long dead, made into some kind of minor deity with a statue on the Street of the Gods that's covered with pigeon droppings."

"You could have used that popularity to seek office, couldn't you?" she asked. "There's no reason you couldn't have become a Magistrate. Perhaps even Chief Magistrate."

I looked at her in honest bewilderment and blurted, "Now why in all the names of the gods would I want something like that?"

Her laugh pealed like temple chimes across the windy plains.

"That, Amalric Antero, is one reason I love you."

She took hold of my beard, pulled me closer, and kissed me.

The men marching beside us cheered.

And I?

I blushed like a schoolboy.

CHAPTER FIFTEEN

THE DIREWOLVES

It was just dawn when Modin came to us.

I'd been sleeping fitfully, my blankets spread next to Janela's when a roaring voice brought me to my feet. I was still half asleep, but as I rose, my blade came whipping from beneath its sheath where it had lain beside me.

Modin loomed over our campsite. He stood almost twenty feet high, and one foot rested, unscathed, in the ruins of our fire.

Janela rolled up, her dagger in her hand, and my brain came aware enough to decipher the last of Modin's voice:

". . . summon you, my own, my prey. You must obey. You must call me to you."

For an instant I thought Modin had used sorcery to sneak up on us. But if that were so, how had he gotten so huge? Then I realized I could dimly see the plain's grass through his legs and knew he was but a projection—although I didn't knew what powers he could have in such a form.

"I must obey no one but myself," Janela said. "Don't waste time prattling. If you've cast some sort of summoning spell, save your powers. It isn't working."

"I cast no spell," Modin said. "I need none and am using my sorcery merely to ward off your feeble attempts to slay me."

Janela looked startled, then quickly covered her puzzlement. I noticed Modin's arm was bulky, as if bandaged, and I saw he held it very stiffly.

"I am using," the sorcerer went on, "the real powers of my Wardens and my newfound friend and ally Cligus' own soldiers to hunt you down, with but small aid from my seeing.

"You think you've eluded us, but actually I've let you run and run, letting your blood run hard and fresh. Don't you know game is sweeter when it's been tormented before the kill?"

"What happened to your arm, Modin?" I shouted up at him.

"The demon you sent down among us tried his best but was no contest for my powers, Janela Greycloak," he said, trying to ignore me. "It took less than an hour for me to kill him."

Now it was both our turns to puzzle before we realized that Modin thought the Mithraik-demon was Janela's creation. For a moment I wondered if it might shake Modin's arrogance to tell him the demon came from another place, from the *real* Far Kingdoms of Tyrenia. But then I thought better. In spite of his bluster, it must have shaken him to think Janela could summon such a creature— even I knew there were few Evocators who could not only call up such a creature, but force its bidding. Best we allow him to continue to believe in the greatness of her powers.

Evidently, Janela reached the same conclusion because she laughed, mockingly. "An hour, Modin? How many Wardens did my pet kill before you brought him down?"

"We still have more than enough to deal with your poor party, Janela," he said. "In a few days I'll have ripped apart those puny concealment spells and will be on you. Just from their presence I have sensed the area where you and Antero lie, licking your wounds." Again a perplexing statement.

I noted a change in his behavior from the time we'd met him in

Irayas. Then there'd been at least the pretense that he was King Gayyath's most loyal servant and no more. I decided to put in another barb.

"We, Modin? Is that the royal we? Didn't King Gayyath live through the riots?"

"Antero," he said, "you were not supposed to be awakened by my presence, but to slumber on like the others were commanded. But I see you have a bond more close with Greycloak than I knew. No matter that. It matters but little when I bring her to my bed how many lovers she's taken.

"Perhaps it'll even increase the potency, being where an Antero has been." He smiled.

"You did not answer my question about King Gayyath, wizard," I said. "Or perhaps you did by not doing so."

"King Gayyath still sits the throne quiet easily," Modin hissed. "The serfs who dared question his rule have been destroyed. Gayyath's dynasty will continue, even if I have to obliterate every man and woman in Irayas and repopulate the city from the outermost provinces."

"Spoken," I said, "like a true patriarch."

All that elicited was a glower, and I wished that I'd been able to devise a better insult, having determined to use this appearance of Modin's to our advantage, hopefully to anger him, knowing an enraged man sees poorly through the mist of his own blood-fury.

"What do you hope to gain, Modin?" Janela said. "You pursue us hard, even unto our destination. What bodes it for you if those ahead of us, those in the *real* Far Kingdoms, sense your presence and find it unwelcome?"

"I doubt that," Modin said. "I've heard much about what lay beyond the Eastern Sea, but when I found it necessary to cross, I found nothing but savages and beasts. If there is anything ahead, which I doubt, it will be mere barbaric shamans, practicing by rote what they learned epochs ago. The Old Ones are long, long gone from this plane.

"No, Janela, you are in for disappointment when you realize the real power of sorcery rests in only one place: Vacaan."

"Is that why your little kingdom-model doesn't work?" I asked.

Not waiting for a response, I went on. "Is that why the people are crying their woes, willing to rise up against the only rule they've known, choosing anarchy over order? Is that why your gods-damned river spells don't work like they used to? Is that why the power that Gayyath's father Domas wielded with never a question is bursting at the seams?"

Modin started to answer, then decided not to. His image blurred, danced, and then, standing behind him, normally sized, was my son, Cligus. Perhaps he'd been permitted to listen or even watch, invisibly, when Modin cast out for Janela. I doubted this. It was more likely that his appearance had not been planned.

I knew I was right when I saw his eyes widen as two shocks struck him. First at being in this place, even in spirit form; then seeing me and how much I'd changed. But he still recognized me, blood calling to blood. He flinched for an instant, as if he were still a mischievous boy trembling in my study, expecting his father to step forward and punish him for his crimes. Then his face firmed as he recovered.

I attacked first:

"Cligus, I am surprised to see you. But it gives me an opportunity to put some questions to you as well. What sort of face are you putting on your actions? What do you plan to tell Orissa when you return with my head? Do you think the citizens of our city will announce a triumph for you for patricide? Do you think Palmeras will nod and accept your version of events without inquiring, sorcerously, into what really happened?"

He answered defiantly: "I plan to return with full proof of your treason."

"Very good, boy," I said, putting as much sarcasm into my voice as possible. "You've managed to convince yourself I'm a real villain. That's always the best step.

"But you've had much practice, haven't you? I recollect that poor serving girl you got with child when you were what, fourteen, and she was a year younger. You tried to tell me it was her fault for not cleansing herself with vinegar. Do you remember how you raged when I forced you to sell your stallion so you could have a sum to set aside for the child's upbringing?"

"I do not have to listen to this!"

"Yes, you do," I said. "Listen . . . or vanish. Modin, is *this* the best you can do for an ally? Or do you think you can stand against an Antero and a Greycloak alone? You had better be careful, wizard, for you're committing the crime of great pride, and are most likely to be brought down for it."

"Oh," Modin said, and I noted he'd recovered control. "I am supposed to listen to the words of a merchant, a cloth-peddler, and shake in my boots? Listen to me, Antero." He rose again, almost doubling his size, and I barely noted that Cligus' form had vanished. "Listen well. Janela Greycloak and her powers are fated to be mine. I said that her doom will be especially sweet the more she twists and wriggles trying to escape it.

"But there shall be a fillip. I'll let her watch your death, and it shall be slow and as painful as I can arrange. You do not know what it is like to have a great mage such as myself punish you, but there are pains beyond the pains of this world, and your soul can be tormented through many worlds before it's finally destroyed to the last bit of its existence.

"That death beyond death I promise you, Amalric Antero of Orissa. And I have never broken such an oath."

Then there was nothing but the wind and the blowing grass and the endless plains.

Janela and I looked at each other for a long time before either of us said a word. I was the first.

"So we're licking our wounds, eh? Did you cast some sort of spell when we left the road that you sort of forgot to mention? That would maybe give out all sorts of hints that somewhere around or about there a bunch of broken-down Orissans got stuck, doing nothing more than licking their wounds and waiting for the butcher to call?"

"I might have."

"You *are* good. First that demon, then this." A serious question occurred to me. "When I met Modin I saw him as a powerful wizard, the equivalent of Lord Raveline. Was I mistaken?"

"I doubt if he was ever deadly as Raveline. He came not from the royal bloodline, and I don't think he had all those decades of bloodbaths Raveline had brought about to feed his dark powers on. Perhaps that's why he wished to . . . ally himself with me.

"Or possibly he *was* that great. Maybe being in these lands, where there is truly awful magic being worked," she said, indicating with a motion of her hand the mountains where Tyrenia lay, "perhaps he's lost some of his own strength. Maybe that presence I've been feeling is helping us."

"Or maybe we're just getting used to having eminent enchanters standing in line to pummel us," I said.

"That is the only true explanation, I warrant." Janela's smile died. "But we can't ever treat Modin with contempt. He is what he is, and he'll pursue us to the gates of Tyrenia before he'll give up. And the temporal power of his army cannot be denied."

I nodded but said nothing, because just then Quatervals stirred from his sleep, eyes opening, and then he sat up.

"Lord Antero," he said in surprise. "You're wakin' early. Got the trots—sorry, lady, I didn't realize you were up as well."

We said nothing about the magical visit, but as I began helping break camp I felt strangely cheery. Perhaps it was having won a few meaningless exchanges with Modin, or as likely seeing that Cligus, even in his murderous intent, was as weak a man as I'd finally realized him to be.

But somehow I knew we would have the best of Modin and Cligus, no matter how many soldiers they had, and was quite cheerful.

Of course I was being a fool.

WE SAW THE DIREWOLF in the late afternoon of that same day. It trotted directly toward us from the south as if we'd called it, then swerved about two hundred yards from the nearest flanker and slowed his pace to a walk, moving with us at the same speed we did. As before, I ordered Quatervals to bring the scouts in closer to the main formation and double up their strength.

Direwolves are interesting creatures. If someone were to ask me for a career entailing the greatest amount of hazard for the smallest returns, I'd set them to studying these beasts.

They are wickedly intelligent, normally hunting in packs; when they have young, the mother hunts alone with her cubs safely in her pouch. Like all hunters, they prefer to take down the weak, hungry, or old, and will go well out of their way to avoid a battle with an animal in the fullness of strength.

They have few enemies who can stand against them, and even those, but with one exception, will leave them to hunt in peace if left undisturbed. The exception is man, and the direwolves sense that, taking almost any opportunity to kill their two-legged foe. Farmers in the cold South have gone to work their fields and have never been seen again, searchers finding only the plow's iron and wood; the man, his draft animal, and even the leather lines gone without a trace. They've attacked outlying houses, waiting until the man is gone and then smashing through the door or a window to savage his babes and wife.

But even in this unrelenting hatred for man they are clever. Like the crow, they can recognize a man with weapons and will sheer away from him. They'll never attack an armed group, although they'll harry its flanks just as they do a herd of elk, hoping for a straggler.

That single animal sent a chill through me. Perhaps it was the deliberate way it paced us. We usually sought camp an hour or so before dusk so we could build cook-fires without giving ourselves away. This day I told Quatervals to push on until we found a safer place than usual.

By the grace of Te-Date we were lucky, finding one of the few rivers, actually little more than a shallow stream, that wound its way through the steppe. A wide, flat-topped knoll rose next to the river, an eminently defensible position that seemed perfect.

After we'd set our packs down I asked Quatervals, since he was the soldier, what criticisms he had of the place. He looked about and admitted to few. If this were war, he'd prefer that the scrub brush around the river be cut down so the view was unobstructed. He also said if he were a god, he'd move that small islet across from us farther downstream—an enemy might be able to use that to ford the river more readily.

This proves what my sister Rali had preached, that soldiers are good for many things, but their fortune-telling ability is, as she put it, somewhere between slim and rotten. That island saved our lives.

We'd barely set down our packs when one of the pickets reported two more direwolves, these to our rear. They'd appeared as if from nowhere, he reported. Wondering if these beasts might be unaware of some of man's talents, I sent for one of the Cyralian brothers and ordered him to try a shot with our heaviest bow. But before he could bend it, the creatures turned and trotted just beyond bowshot, then continued staring at us.

Quatervals sent working parties, closely guarded, along the banks of the river to cut the straightest saplings from the scrub brush. These saplings were pointed at each end and then driven into the ground at a close angle to the earth. They should have been heavier but that was the best we could find.

As it grew dark we heard howls from the distance. The scouts were summoning the rest of the pack. Other yowls answered, sounding across the steppes, coming from all directions. We were surrounded.

I decided to the hells with worrying about being sighted by Cligus and Modin—we had enemies even closer; and so I ordered fires built and brush tied together for torches and laid close to them.

Then we waited.

The night dragged on.

Just before dawn, when man's hopes and dreams are drowned in blackness, the direwolves attacked. I'd never heard of such bravado, but perhaps these monsters were far more savage than any I'd experienced.

They came at us from two directions, tearing in from the night. We were most fortunate in two ways: I'd half expected something to happen just around dawn and had everyone awake, in battle gear, and my best men standing sentry. Also, one of the directions they came from was guarded by another of the Cyralian brothers. An experienced poacher, he kept lookout flat on the ground, looking out and up, his eyes able to distinguish silhouettes even against the blackness of the sky. Possibly the first wolf didn't see him as well, as he charged forward at full bound.

Taking down a dog or wolf is relatively simple: You feed it your arm and cut its throat or gut it with your knife before it can do any real harm; or else, if unarmed, you toss it to the ground and crush its rib cage with your knees. But not when the wolf is nearly the size of a horse. As the direwolf leapt, the Cyralian rolled to his back, flat on the ground, and drove straight up with his blade, letting the beast gut itself with its momentum.

The wolf screamed and the night was alive with echoes as the others in the pack ran in on us. There was a flurry of shouts, blades flashing in the dimness, then the torches flared and our camp was a flailing battlefield of steel and fangs. Men shouted death agony and fell, and wolves yapped and howled, some impaled on our stakes, and then they fell back. They should have stayed close among us, continuing their savaging, because as they retreated my people seized bows and sent arrows whipping after them. Otavi rumbled forward and cleft one retreating beast's spine with his axe, then, on the backswing, struck its head from its body. Mad with blood, he would've gone on, into the darkness and his death, if Pip hadn't grabbed him by the belt and pulled him back.

Otavi glared madly, blood drenching him, and for an instant I thought he might cut Pip down. But then he came back to himself, grunted something like thanks, and was ready for the next onslaught.

Once more they came, but this time we were ready and spears flew and broke their charge. Baying as madly as we were shouting, they whirled just beyond the low flare from our fires. Quatervals ripped up a dead bush from the ground, passed it over the fire, and then, as it caught, pitched it out toward them.

The direwolves howled defiance but held their ground—they were no more afraid of fire than a man would be. I sensed they were going to charge in a moment and shouted, "Back, back! To the island!"

My company heard and obeyed, but none of them turned and ran. Instead, like experienced fighters, they moved slowly and or- derly, backing down the knoll toward the stream, weapons ready as the wolves, growling, closed on us. Archers stepped between swords- and spearmen and thudded their goose quills home. A wounded wolf snapped at the arrow sticking out of his ribs and rolled into a mate, and the two snarled and began tearing at each other.

We splashed backward through the shallows onto the sandy island. It was thick with brush, which in normal circumstances would have been a threat. But here it served as a screen.

The animals attacked once more, and I realized I could see them, dimly, as the day began to grow on the horizon. I expected the wolves to give up, but they redoubled their efforts. Their red eyes gleamed, matching the red of their tongues and mouths and our dripping wounds. But the brush slowed them enough so spearmen could lunge with deadly accuracy and bowmen or crossbowmen had time to pick their shots with full skill.

The direwolves retreated across the stream. But they weren't intending to give up this war. On the knoll were our packs, and I counted five, no, seven bodies. Now the wolves would savage our dead and rip into our rations, I thought. But they didn't, seemingly having no interest in anything but the complete destruction of our party.

I saw Janela busy on her knees, her purse beside her, and was grateful that she almost never let that carryall more than an arm's reach from her.

"Look at them," Quatervals said. He finished knotting a cloth tie around his lower leg, where one of the wolves had ripped at him. "They're like warriors, plottin' their next move."

And so they were, grouping in knots of five or ten beasts—packs, I suppose. There was enough light to see clearly, but I wished we had not that blessing for I saw almost fifty of the huge animals gathered on both sides of this river.

"What," Pip said in mock anger, "we're the only bassids worth eatin' in this whole blest desert? The gods're no dealin' justice."

"So what's new about *that*, little man?" Otavi growled.

Quatervals and I looked at each other, sharing a common thought but not putting it into words. One pack or perhaps two should have been all that would have attacked us, and they should have waited until we were moving and then tried to cut off any stragglers. Other packs would have gone on, looking for their own victims. Both of us were wondering if these wasteland beasts were brighter than any we'd heard of or—and this was the unspoken thought—if they had been *sent*, if they had been *directed* against us. If Raveline could use direwolves for his watchmen, couldn't Modin use them, as well? Or, if not Modin, that still-unknown presence that lay ahead?

If that were the case, I hoped Janela could devise some strong sorcery, that being our only hope.

"Look yon," Pip pointed. "Beyon' the knoll, atop that rise."

I saw where he was pointing. Beyond the ringing animals, on that low hillock, stood one single animal. There was enough light to distinguish color, and I could see that he was old, his pelt graying, turning toward white. If these creatures were huge, he was the largest. Even allowing for our fear and the natural tendency to exaggerate the size of an enemy, I would make a blood-oath at the temple of any god that this direwolf would have been over ten feet high at the head, taller than a man at the shoulders.

"Perhaps they were sent," Quatervals said in a low voice, "as I'm thinkin'. But mayhap they've found leaders of their own."

"Why not?" I agreed, hoping he was right, preferring any degree of animal cunning to magic. "Other beasts have leaders—elephants, lions."

Quatervals was measuring the distance with his fingers. "Mmmph," he grunted. "Beyond the reach of *my* bow. The bastard knows where he's safe."

"Maybe," I said, "or maybe not. Janela."

She looked up from her work, frowning. "Amalric, can you hold for a moment?"

"No," I said. "I'm sorry . . . look. Over there."

She was annoyed, but stood. I pointed. Janela understood instantly what might be done. She looked around, saw a longbow, and picked it up. She drew her dagger and touched the two together, her lips moving. I heard just the end of her spell:

". . . take hold, take change
Once live, now dead
Take strength, take power
Take hold, take change."

The bow changed as she chanted, and instead of the live glow of yew, it took on the dull hue of metal. Next she touched her hair to the bowstring and cast another spell. This one I didn't hear at all, but the string changed to woven black, like the women's tresses the greatest catapults use.

"Here's your bow, Amalric. You must find the archer."

But that was the easiest.

"Otavi. On your back. Quatervals, you help him aim."

Otavi dropped onto his back and, holding the bow level with the ground, put both his boot heels on either side of the grip.

Janela had taken a handful of arrows and went to a direwolf's corpse that sprawled half in and half out of the water. She pricked the body in the center of its chest, allowing a little blood to flow on the arrowpoint. Then she touched the arrowhead to her eyelid:

"See what I see
Hunt what I hunt
Kill what I kill
Fly fast
Fly true."

She handed the arrows to Quatervals. "With luck that'll serve better than your best aim. Now, let me go back to my own casting." I saw she had some long strands of some kind of string and was dragging them over the sand. But our plan required my full attention.

Quatervals knelt beside Otavi. "Pull back, lad."

Otavi grabbed the human-hair bowstring with both hands and heaved mightily, veins standing on his forehead. The steel bow drew slowly, coming back and back. Quatervals nocked an arrow.

"Can you turn a bit . . . right . . . aye, that's it . . . now bring your legs down . . ." Otavi's legs were beginning to shake with the strain of pulling the metal bow.

"Loose!"

The bowstring twanged and Otavi yelped as it thrummed against his ankles and the arrow shot away. I saw it climb then whip past the direwolves' chieftain. We missed him by at least five feet.

I cursed, but the beast still stood, hesitating. Before he could realize he was within range, Otavi had the bow pulled back once more, there was an arrow ready, and Quatervals squinted once more.

"There . . . down just a slack . . . arrow, take the damned spell to heart . . . *loose*!" Once more the bowstring thwacked and the arrow hurtled away.

This time it sped true, just as that monstrous direwolf was realizing his danger. But as he turned, the bolt took him, full in the chest. He was dead before he realized he'd been shot, collapsing bonelessly where he stood.

A moment later a low moan came from the opposite bank. The moan grew into a long howl as one direwolf, then another, saw their elder had been slain. The howl rose to the skies, crying sorrow and loss. Even I foolishly felt a note of sadness, as one must when a great leader, no matter if he is your enemy, is gone from this earth.

An instant later the howls of mourning became signals and once more the direwolves rushed us. If they had been human, I would have said they had desperation and hatred on their side now. But we had daylight on ours, and our archers could fire well and true.

Direwolves stumbled away, or fell, but there were still more of them coming on, and then I realized we were doomed, because the earth itself was shaking. Maha was looking at me, and if my face was as pale and frightened as his, I was a poor war leader.

Then we saw what was making the ground shake.

A herd, perhaps thirty, perhaps a few more, of the great oxen came bellowing over the rise. Janela was beaming: Her spell had worked. I took a moment to look at her casting. In the sand she'd drawn not figures or arcane symbology, but a model of the river and the island we stood on. There were bits of fur around it, I guessed cut from one of the dead direwolves. Those strands she'd been running over the ground I realized were some of the ox hair she'd plucked from a bush when we'd first encountered the beasts. Indeed it had become useful.

How she managed to devise a spell that would call those beasts I don't know. But she had and they came. They saw their ancient enemy and for some reason, perhaps some more of Janela's magic, ignored their traditional behavior of defense and attacked.

They rushed down on the wolves with their long horns lancing out. The direwolves tried to hold for a moment, tried to duck around, but three, then four of them were impaled, cast down, and trampled by the herd, and then the direwolves were fleeing as if they had a pack of demons at their heels. But I never doubted their courage. It was magic that was their undoing, not us.

The direwolves were over the far bank of the river, up over the rise and disappearing into the tall steppe grass. The oxen thundered across the river, then their pace slowed and they were walking, snorting, I swear like a pack of boasting warriors after their foe has fled the battleground.

Then they remembered they'd just crossed water, and they were no longer warriors but cattle, lowing for the stream. One or two of them glared at us and *whuffed*, telling us they, by the gods, had taken this land and we were not welcome here.

We left them victorious on their field and went back across to the knoll. We bound up our wounds, gathered our dead, and once more said a burial ceremony and laid them under. After that we were ready for the march once more.

I missed Quatervals and Otavi and looked about for them. I saw them on that low rise, standing over the huge direwolf's corpse. Their heads were bowed for a moment, and I thought I saw Quatervals sprinkle a bit of sand over the corpse as if giving a burial so its ghost would rest.

They came back but said nothing, and I respected their silence.

We continued our march.

At the top of the hill I looked back. Five killed at the Fist of the Gods, seven more here . . . I prayed to the gods I no longer believed in that these would be the last.

Because now I knew we would, we must, meet Cligus and Modin before we reached Tyrenia.

WE WERE CLOSING on the mountains and the steppe was rougher, corrugated with gullies and canyons. We were forced to detour so many times I feared we'd lose our bearings to the road, and so Quatervals and I decided it was time to return and take our chances.

We turned due south and began keeping track of our paces. As the distance grew greater we began craning ahead, eager to be the first to sight the paved track.

I admit to another desire: to see whether our navigational skills were well-honed, since I've never actually believed in my abilities to do anything other than become thoroughly and completely lost. Each time my compass or map or reckoning abilities have proven true, I've been hard-pressed to appear as if such achievements were commonplace. How sea navigators are able to find a harbor dead on after days and weeks of seeing nothing but the sun and the stars and then pretending boredom when complimented is beyond me. If I'd been able to do such a thing one single time, I would have cast aside my navigating tools, taken up the robes of a priest, and spent the rest of my life on my knees thanking whatever deity I believed responsible.

So when the correct thousand thousand paces were made and we saw no sign of the road, I was not alarmed at all, feeling it perfectly natural that we were lost once more.

Then the lead scout sighted something. Not the road but a settlement. Quatervals and I went forward on our bellies to look at it. It was a sprawling village that stretched straight across our course. It consisted of nearly a hundred low stone buildings of various sizes. The village looked long-abandoned and so we chanced moving forward, through it rather than around.

The closer we got the more eerie the village appeared. We were closer to it than we'd thought when we realized the houses were low, no more than five feet high. They were windowless with curved roofs, and looked like various lengths of gray bread loaves positioned haphazardly on the sand.

Strangeness grew as we closed in and saw the doorways. They were also low, less than two feet high but almost four feet wide. No human would ever build such a door for a shelter and I wondered what sort of beings had built and lived in this village.

Quatervals, who had stayed in front with the lead scout, motioned for a halt and beckoned me forward. He was no more than thirty feet or so from one of the huts.

I trotted up to him. He said nothing but pointed. I looked at the nearest hut. It and all the others were covered with bas-reliefs cut into the stone walls. I went a bit closer trying to make out what the inscriptions were, and a chill ran hard down my back.

I will not describe the creatures depicted on those walls. Suffice it to say they were not men, nor any earthly creature I have ever seen or heard described. Nor were they like any demon seen or described by any Evocator I've known, but were rather liquid, flowing, plastic creatures like jellyfish, yet capable of holding strange weapons and fighting dark battles with other creatures equally fabulous.

My skin crawled as I looked at them, and something told me it was unhealthy to stare too long at these murals. Nor did I dare creep through any of those eldritch doorways, fearing this village might not be dead, but sleeping. I told Quatervals to move the men through at the double and he merely nodded, not saying a word.

We left that village of the unknown hastily and none of us looked back until it was gone.

We found the road half a day's journey later, and followed it east. We also learned why our navigation appeared to be in error—it wasn't. The road—which I thought ran perfectly straight across the steppes—curved to arc around the village, as if even the Old Ones of Tyrenia feared it and wished no reminder of their existence.

I suppose I should have been frightened at that, but instead felt heartened that there was *something* even the Old Ones dreaded.

THREE DAYS FARTHER and the mountains were rearing above us, the road beginning its long climb toward their crests. We looked often for some sign of our goal but the clouds hung so close about the fog-shrouded peaks that we saw nothing.

Ahead of us on the road was a small dark blot. As we grew closer we saw it was three horsemen, sitting their mounts and waiting. The land was very open here and we saw no place an ambush could have been laid, so we continued on.

I knew one of them. It was Sa'ib, beautiful in fur robes and silk, but her face as hard and cold as the peaks behind her. She sat to the rear.

In front of her was a small, old man. His hair wisped out from under his helmet, which was the top half-skull of a direwolf, neck cape still attached so it hung down across his back. He wore a fur loincloth, sandals, and a many-colored coat of feathers that must have been made from many birdskins from faraway jungles—no doubt his most prized possession. He did not seem to notice the cold. I guessed him to be a shaman or perhaps war councillor.

The man in front was large, nearly six and a half feet. He was in his fifties and at one time would have been a perfectly muscled warrior. Now he'd begun to grow heavy, but still would have been the foremost fighter in any army. He wore breeches of the finest red leather, with gold thread embroidering them, black knee-boots, and a tunic of the same color but with brass armoring. On his head was a half-helm set with gold and gems, almost a crown. His beard was long and carefully combed. Over his shoulder was slung a long, wide-bladed sword. Its grip was darkened with long use. There were two stained leather bags tied to the front of his saddle.

I halted my party and walked forward to the three. I stopped before him and waited. The windsound was heavy in my ears.

"You are Amalric Antero. Lord Amalric Antero, from a far place called Orissa." His voice rumbled like the sound of the steppe oxen as they charged. It was not a question.

"And you are Suiyan, lord of the Res Weynh," I said.

"I am. You rescued my daughter from Ismid's dogs."

"I did."

"Yet you refused to take her and the others as slaves. Or to use them as is the right of the victor."

"That is true."

"Had you heard the terror of my name? Were you afraid of my vengeance?"

I stared at him, not answering.

"I thought not," he said.

"I do not believe in slaves," I said. "And I don't believe the sword gives anyone any right, no matter what it may seize."

"That is what a weak man believes," Suiyan snorted. "But you are not weak." He stared at me for a very long time.

"Perhaps, one of these years," he concluded, "I should journey to your land, or to a city, at any rate, and attempt to understand such thinking."

"If you so decide, you would be welcome in Orissa as the guest of my family." I half smiled, thinking what conniptions he and the outriders he'd no doubt think necessary for such a journey would rouse in the streets of Orissa. He saw my expression and nodded, as if I'd spoken aloud and he, too, had seen the humor.

"Without serving me, you served me well," he said. "Here is the fate of those who serve me poorly." He opened his saddlebags, reached inside, and lifted out a human head. He cast it down and it rolled nearly to my feet. It was the head of Diu, the old man in charge of taking Sa'ib safely home. A second head thudded beside it. Ziv, his son.

"As you served me, one chief to another, so I have served you."

He stopped and I realized he would say no more. I began to ask, but the look on his face discouraged my question. He spoke once more then:

"I have but one regret and that is you are in thrall to that sorceress my daughter told me about. Perhaps the boon I should have granted you is to slay her, but my chief shaman advised me to interfere not in the magic of foreign lands, for perhaps it is linked to those in the mountains beyond, those who not even I can stand against. But it is a pity.

"You would have made a good husband for Sa'ib, or at least a man worthy to father children from her loins.

"Travel on, Lord Antero."

He wheeled his horse and galloped off the road. In his wake rode the other two, neither of them looking back.

Janela trotted up beside me, followed by the others. She looked down at the heads, then at the vanishing dots of the three Res Weynh.

"Fine friends *you* have," was all she said.

ON THE NEXT day's journey an immovable force, the road, finally hit its irresistible object, the mountains. Now the road was forced to wind in and around foothill peaks as we went on.

Now we were especially alert for ambush.

Just where the road entered a narrow cleft we came on the first two Wardens. Or rather their heads.

They were on either side of the road, stuck on spears. From their expressions it looked as if neither one of them had died easily.

Quatervals went to one of them and touched the ragged cut in the neck. He came back rubbing his fingers together. "The blood's clotted but not dried. They were killed no later than yesterday."

We continued on, waiting for battle. But all we found were more heads. They were stuck on spears set on either side of the road at regular intervals, ghastly mileposts. We counted as we went past, and I ordered a halt to the numbering when we reached one hundred fifty. Finally there was an end to the red-helmeted ghastliness, but only to have it replaced after another hundred yards by another display of heads. These wore more motley headgear I recognized as Orissan.

They lined the road as far as we could see ahead. Some of our men had been jesting a bit, seeing hated enemies who'd gotten what they deserved. But now the jests stopped as some of the men recognized fellow Orissans.

Quatervals pointed. "That was Captain Jamot. Right shit he was. They broke him out of the Scouts for cutting down a truce party under a white flag." I thought I recognized him, having seen him as part of Cligus' contingent.

Now I knew what service Suiyan had performed for me. Janela, her face grim, was a few paces behind me. I began to ask her if she sensed sorcery, not knowing how Cligus' entire army could have been trapped and destroyed, but now was not the time to speak.

Without being aware of it I found my pace quickening, looking at each head as we passed but not wanting to see what I knew I would.

We came to a meadow that at one time would have been a delightful waystop on this long road. But now it was a horror of blood. Its delicate highland grasses and flowers were drenched in gore and bodies, hundreds of bodies lay high-piled. It was a slaughterhouse's killing floor and it was as if Cligus' army had been caught in a sorcerous web that made them march up to the headsman's axe and kneel quietly, awaiting their fate more meekly than any sheep.

The wind had stopped and there was complete silence.

Then we heard a moan. It came from the road ahead of us, where bodies had been laid in a ghastly star pattern, each torso meeting.

In the center writhed two yet-living men. They were both naked.

The first man was unconscious. Janela gasped when she saw what had been done to him. There was a red sear across his forehead where a red hot blade had been laid, burning out his eyes.

Blood pooled between his thighs where he'd been castrated.

That was Modin.

The second man was just conscious. He had been slightly wounded in the side, but the wound had been treated and bandaged.

After that someone had sliced through his leg tendons, as a cruel farmer cripples a fence-leaping goat.

It was Cligus.

Suiyan had repaid his debt a hundred times over, leaving full proof of his honor. But as my guts roiled within me I half wished it had not been done, and even that we had left Sa'ib to be taken by Ismid's riders.

I knelt over Cligus, wondering how, naked, he and Modin had

survived the night and why no scavengers had come to the feast. The shaman of the Res Weynh, I decided, was truly mighty.

Cligus opened his eyes and they unglazed from horror and saw me. "Father?"

He looked about, reassuring himself that he was not in delirium. His face twisted in pain.

"So you have won."

His head lolled back and he blacked out.

PERHAPS I SHOULD HAVE gone on, but I could not leave my son to die, no matter what he would have done to me. I asked Janela if she wished me to kill Modin. She shook her head.

"I've never yet murdered. He's blind and unmanned, with no powers, no danger. I'll not be the one to say yes to his death."

I ordered the men to improvise litters—we would carry them with us. Quatervals seemed about to object but saw the look in my eyes and said nothing.

I walked out of the meadow beyond the spear row of heads and sat, looking out at nothing. I found myself crying, crying for my son, crying for what he might have been, crying for what was, crying for myself as well.

Footsteps came up and Janela sat beside me.

She waited until I was through, then handed me a handkerchief. I wiped my eyes.

"I could be a fool," she said gently, "and say some such ending was inevitable for either you or him."

I nodded. Of course she was right.

But at the moment I dreaded any sympathy. She stood up.

After a long moment she said, "Shit!" and then walked away.

I sat there for a long time feeling very old, very used up. Then I brought myself back.

Sometime later we marched on.

THE ROAD WOUND on and up. We could feel the thin air strain in our lungs as we climbed.

"I vow," Pip said, "if we top this hill an' there's another bastardly valley an' another mountain, I'm desertin' an' joinin' up wi' the headloppers."

Then the clouds lifted and the fog blew away.

TYRENIA

The castle was dazzling white, with domed turrets of jade and mighty gates of glittering gold. I rubbed my eyes and the colors shimmered and shifted until the white was a glowing pink, the jade a pale blue, and the gold became the silver of crystal held near pure flowing water.

A dark cloud blew across its face and the castle became as gray and bleak as cold granite. I could see that its walls were impenetrable by any force, and I could feel sorcerous weapons bristling on and above those walls, and I could hear the ghostly screams and clashing weapons of ancient armies who fought and died to breach them. The cloud passed and I had to lift a hand to shield my eyes from the brightness of the walls.

"Tyrenia!" I heard Janela gasp in wonder.

I knew she was right, because there could be no other place like it in all existence.

As we gaped, the gates swung open and a fleet of immense chariots thundered out. They flew down the mountain road at an amazing speed. The chariots were red and trimmed in gold with sharp whirling scythes set in their hubs. They were drawn by fierce white stallions—made fiercer still by studded-black armor—and they seemed half-again larger than a normal steed. The lead chariot bore a banner that undulated furiously in the rushing air, but I could make out a golden crown set in a field of blue.

We were too bedazzled to move as they roared up to us—the lead chariot skittering in a wide arc, hurling up a shower of sparks and settling a few paces away. There were six or so armored men aboard it, but only one leaped down and approached me, sweeping off a gilded helmet with a graceful white plume and letting golden curls tumble to his wide, mailed shoulders. He was a tall and handsome prince with fair, sharply defined features and a beard as gold as the curls on his head. For a jolting moment I thought the impossible: that he was the king in the ancient court scene revealed by the dancing maiden. But although the similarity was strong, he was much younger—barely into early manhood.

He smiled at me with fine white teeth and spoke in a most melodious voice. "I am Prince Solaros, son of King Ignati, who has given me the honor of greeting you, Lord Antero," he said. "Many of our subjects have waited long years for your arrival."

Solaros made a gracious bow to Janela. "All Tyrenia is at your feet, my Lady Greycloak. For if you had not picked up your great ancestor's fallen banner, this blessed day would have never occurred."

Then he flung his arms wide as if to embrace our whole company and said in a loud, rich voice: "Welcome! Welcome all! Welcome to the realm you know as . . . the Kingdoms of the Night."

THERE ARE FEW men and women, either living or dead, who have rolled the gods' dice and come up with sacred sevens twice in a row. I first rattled that cup in my youth and entered a land few believed existed, and those who did said was impossible to find. At the far end of that life—with the Dark Seeker's shadow hovering near—I'd tossed the bones once more and captured a still greater prize. That prize wasn't only the discovery of a mythical land. It was knowing those childhood myths were true, that the songs we piped in the nursery of fabled realms and golden folk and flowered paths were more than a charming rhyme.

And so for the second time in my life I entered the Far Kingdoms. The name was different. My motives more desperate. And many shames and many regrets scarred my soul.

But oh, the swelling in my breast, the spiced wine of victory coursing my veins, and the sparkling visions dancing before my eyes were as fresh and glorious now as they were then.

We came to Tyrenia as pilgrims weary and soiled from the road. We came ignorant and humble to seek wisdom in the most ancient city in all of Te-Date's creation. We came in awe of the Old Ones whose descendants these folk were. We came with trembling hopes and no little fear; for what if they were to spurn us or, worse, mock our savagery? I was especially vulnerable. Failure, whose name was Cligus, groaned on a litter nearby me as we rode the prince's chariot up to the gates of Tyrenia.

The first thing I saw when I entered Tyrenia was a multitude that had gathered to fling praises and kisses into the air and flowers and gifts in our path.

The first thing I heard was my name and Janela's shouted to the highest vaults of the heavens.

The first thing I felt was the otherworldly bewilderment of a man declared Hero by strangers when he knew best of all he was but a man.

I rode on Prince Solaros' left, Janela on his right, and he guided the chariot one-handed—waving at the cheering crowd with the other. He was evidently a popular prince, and before long his subjects began to chant his name, as well. His face was rosy with delight, his hair tousled by the breeze, his rich white cloak thrown back carelessly over his shoulder to reveal a broad chest clad in silver chain mail and a slender figure that drew longing looks from the women in the crowd.

We rolled along a wide smooth avenue paved with a pearly surfaced stone that seemed to give under the stallions' hooves like wet, hard-packed sand on an ocean's shore. The chariot's springs were magically enhanced, absorbing all motion that might be a discomfort, so I felt almost as if we were flying. Above us colorful kites soared, trailing long tails of sorcerous smoke that filled the air with the essence of cool gardens and fruited orchards. There was music, such wondrous music that I shed a tear for Omerye because she wasn't alive to hear it. It came from the clouds, it came from the parks beyond the avenue, it rose around us from the very stones we rode upon.

The castle covered the entire mountaintop and was linked to smaller fortresses on distant peaks by magical bridges that were slung on slender cables. It wasn't one castle but many castles, each set inside the other, with gracious homes, rich windowed shops, and bountiful marketplaces edged between each succession of walls and turrets. But even as I marveled I could see knots of wary soldiers manning the walls and knew that if ultimate danger threatened, the homes, shops, and marketplaces would be abandoned as the Tyrenian forces made a fighting retreat to the next defensible position.

Gate after gate was flung open, and beyond each gate was another crowd to praise us.

Finally the last gates loomed before us—more massive than all the others. When they were parted I knew I was looking at Tyrenia's ancient seat of power. The stone was a greenish-gray and shot with lines of age. Sorcerous smoke boiled from the high towers, and the triple domes of the central building glowed with an eerie light.

Sturdy grooms and servants rushed out to greet us. The prince leaped from the chariot and issued a stream of orders concerning our care.

He turned to Janela and myself, a wry smile on his lips. "My father is an impatient man and he ordered me to bring you to him forthwith. I fear I must beg your forbearance and ask you not to take the time to freshen up. Your company will be placed in commodious quarters, so you needn't worry about their comfort."

Janela nodded acceptance and quickly dug out a few items from her purse to make herself more presentable. I hesitated and Solaros caught my quick, worried glance at Cligus and Modin.

The prince lowered his voice. "I'll see they are well guarded . . . until you make your own arrangements," he said in sympathetic tones. "I'll have the royal physician tend their injuries." He paused, then said: "You are a charitable man, Amalric Antero. My father thinks it a weakness. I disagree, but . . . as you shall see, our opinions . . . differ . . . on many things. Still, I'm not so certain I would have had the grace to do the same if I had been in your place."

I suddenly became unreasonably angry, but bit my lip to stem any outburst and merely shook my head as I summoned self-control.

When the emotional shield had once more been set in place, I said: "Thank you, Your Highness. Now if you please, lead the way. The king, as you say, awaits."

Once again the prince hesitated. Then: "I must warn you to guard yourselves. The glad greetings you received from our subjects will not be matched in my father's court. It's a complicated situation which I will explain later in detail. But know there are those who are greatly unsettled by your presence, while others see it as a great blessing that may reverse the tide against our common enemy."

Janela nodded. "I sensed as much, Your Highness. Would I be too bold if I speculated that you and the king are on opposite sides of that dispute?"

The prince sighed. "As opposite as can be. But please, have patience. I'm certain I can win him over . . . Although I fear there's not much time." He straightened his shoulders. "I mustn't dwell on such things now. When we've had a chance to talk, all will become clear."

And then he led us into the bleak fortress that was the palace of King Ignati.

I WAS SURPRISED when we entered the throne room, although I'm not certain what I had expected—except to say that as the royal court of the last of the fabled Old Ones, it was a chilling disappointment.

The chamber was vast, poorly lit, and filled with gloomy statues and fierce-visaged idols of strange gods. The high walls were frescoed with scenes marking ancient wars between the Tyrenians and demon armies. It was sword against talon, wizard against devil, and sorcerous siege engines battering ungiving walls. Interspersed with the frescoes were the royal portraits of Tyrenia's kings and queens, many of them so faded by time that I could barely make out the features. Thousands of names were carved into the floor, and I

soon realized that interred beneath the stone were the remains of
Tyrenia's rulers and greatest heroes. It was like walking on a field of
ghosts.

There was light at the far end of the chamber where shadowy
figures moved about. As we neared it a dozen young lords stepped
from a recess to join the prince. Solaros introduced us in whispers,
saying this fellow was Lord Emerle and that one was Lord Thrade
and so on. I had to struggle hard to glue each name to a face for de-
posit in my memory.

Janela plucked my sleeve when we were introduced to one
young man—who was tall, exceedingly slender, and uncommonly
pale. His face was long and horselike, with wide-set eyes and overly
large teeth that stretched his mouth. His name was Lord Vakram.
As we touched palms in the Tyrenian manner of greeting, my skin
tingled with magical energy. I wasn't surprised when I later learned
he was the prince's wizard.

The king's throne area was a wide, curved vault that was softly
lit by some magical source. The walls were draped by earth-colored
tapestries, and the floor was thickly carpeted with material of a similar color. Scattered about were scores of low tables and seats padded with dark, heavy cushions. Most were empty, their potential
occupants knotting about the throne.

King Ignati raised his head as we approached, barely acknowl-
edging our bows.

"Your Majesty," his son said, "I have the honor of presenting
to you Lord Amalric Antero and Lady Janela Greycloak."

The king said nothing, but leaned forward to peer at us through
cold, narrow eyes.

He seemed to be middle-aged, with still-blond hair under his
wide crown and a thick blond beard that fell nearly to his chest,
then curled up to a point. His skin was fair but mottled with dark
spots, and his fingers were thin and long with sharp, polished nails.
I couldn't make out the color of his eyes, but they seemed rheumy
and old. The closer I looked the more I thought his age had been
magically arrested. A fine network of lines etched his face; and his
cheeks, which I had first thought flushed with health, had the faint
purplish tinge of someone whose heart is greatly stressed.

He gave me but a cursory glance, spending most of his time on Janela—although I didn't sense lust in that look.

"You're prettier than I was told," he finally said to her. His voice was high and full of irritability.

"Thank you, Your Majesty," Janela said.

The king shook his head. "Didn't mean it as a compliment." He turned to a dark man in wizard's robes. "I don't trust pretty people, Tobray."

The wizard smiled, bowing once to the king and then to Janela. "King Ignati meant no offense, my lady," he said.

"Don't tell people what I mean and what I don't, Tobray," the king said to the wizard. Then, to Janela: "But it's true, I meant no offense. Only speaking my mind."

"None taken, Your Highness," Janela said.

The king waved, uncaring, then turned to me. "So you're the great Amalric Antero?" he said. His tone was thick with sarcasm.

"I plead guilty to the name, Majesty," I said, "but not to any greatness."

Ignati chortled. For a sign of humor, it made an unpleasant sound. "Clever. Very clever." His head swiveled to Lord Tobray. "Always said he was a clever fellow, haven't I, Tobray."

"Indeed you have, Your Majesty," Tobray said. Then to me: "The king has often expressed his admiration of your intellect, sir."

Ignati's fingernails tapped impatiently on the arm of his throne. "Not *that* often, Tobray," he said. "Only from time to time."

"As you say, Your Majesty," Tobray soothed. "Only from time to time."

"Don't want these two getting the idea I'm so admiring," the king said. "I'm not like that rabble in the streets that the gods have cursed me to govern. Mob fever, I call it. They think times are bleak when the fact is they've never been better. I give them peace, they think it's surrender." He glared at Tobray. "Don't argue with me. I *know* what they think."

Tobray, who'd given no sign of disputing his sovereign, kept that maddening smile on his face and shook his head. "Of course you do, Your Majesty," he said.

The king's eyes swept back to us. "Mob fever," he said again.

"They see an ordinary mortal like themselves accomplish a wondrous feat—and I admit your expeditions match that definition—and they blow it all out of proportion. Start believing you might save them from the demons when the gods know very well I have that matter well in hand. *Very* well in hand."

"I was as surprised as you, Majesty," I said. "I know nothing of your situation here, but it was apparent the moment Prince Solaros escorted us into your city that your subjects are blessed with the wisest of rulers."

Another chortle from the king. "Clever, *clever* fellow! No wonder you're such a success."

"We are fortune's fools, Your Highness," Janela broke in. "The gods have smiled more often on us than on our enemies."

Ignati hawked laughter, pausing to spit into a handkerchief before he spoke. "You're clever, too," he said. "Just like your great-grandfather Janos Greycloak." His features darkened. He wagged a bony finger at Janela. "But you're just as dangerous as he was, although now that I've met you, I'm sure you don't mean it."

Janela looked concerned. "What have I done that is so dangerous, Your Highness?" she asked.

"Oh, all that sorcerous meddling," Ignati said. "Why couldn't you be satisfied with curing boils, or making it rain when it ought and making it stop when it oughtn't?"

"Simple curiosity, Your Highness," Janela said.

The king dismissed this with an impatient wave. "Yes, yes. I've heard that before. Well, I suppose you can't be blamed, considering your dubious heritage."

Janela only bowed, wisely saying nothing.

Now it was my turn to again enjoy the king's scrutiny. "I suppose you know that your family has given us nothing but trouble."

I spread my hands. "In what way, Majesty?" I said.

"All that adventuring and demon bashing is what I mean," he said. "Expeditions here and there. Supporting these Greycloaks in their silliness. I don't blame your sister so much. She was fighting a war. But I must say if you hadn't gone riding wildly off to Vacaan, the war never would have started. And yes, I know you had trouble with Raveline, who made his own bargain with the demons. But what of it? I was willing to concede a little more in the West. Nothing but barbarians there, anyway. Why couldn't you do the same?"

The prince cleared his throat to catch his father's attention. "You'll forgive me, Father," he said. "But his people are among those barbarians you seem so willing to give up."

"Yes, yes . . . of course they are," the king admitted. "I suppose their actions were to be expected—considering the circumstances. I'm only trying to explain to them what an awful lot of trouble they've caused us."

"In the view of many, Father," the prince said, "the only trouble they've caused is to the demons."

"Same thing," Ignati said. "If I've said it once, I've said it a thousand times. My duty is to be as much a juggler as a king. We've made war too long, and the only way to stop it is to try to see the other fellow's view. Which in this case happens to be the demons'. What do they want? What do I want? Somewhere in the middle we find common ground. Without a damned war, mind you!"

I could see that the young prince—our benefactor—was becoming angry as he and his father picked over an old, painful argument. I tried to intervene.

"Might I ask what you intend for us, Majesty?" I asked. "We came seeking knowledge. And more than that, to beg your assistance. Our homeland is threatened. We witnessed the collapse of Vacaan, and I fear the same will happen to Orissa if we do not find a solution."

"If you want wisdom, hear it from these lips," the king said. "Make your peace with the demons. You're a merchant. You can bargain. Give a little of this for a little of that. Then trust in the gods that all will end well if your intentions are pure."

It was all I could do not to first gape at his insanity, then condemn him as a fool and a coward. To hear such mewling cant from the king of the Old Ones rocked me to the core.

"As for the rest," Ignati continued, "I suppose I have no objection to Lady Greycloak dipping into our books of sorcery. For purely scholarly purposes, mind you. It will pass the time while I consider the consequences of your arrival. To be quite frank, if it weren't for the acclaim you received from my subjects, I'd feed you dinner, call you brave to your faces and fools behind your backs, and then send you on your way. But I find it wiser to keep the rabble happy when I can. At the moment they are so elated by your presence that I'd prefer for you to remain my guests until they've settled down. It shouldn't be too great an inconvenience for you. Like children, they forget quickly."

The prince hid a smile. "May I oversee their stay with us, Father?"

Ignati snorted. "I knew he'd ask that, Tobray," he said to his wizard. "If he were a normal lad he'd be putting mothers in fear for their daughters and making tavern keepers happy with their profits. But he's a serious sort, like his mother—may she be resting peacefully with the gods. He's got a band of similar-thinking young bravos to praise his right-thinking, and on bad days I think I ought to let them have their war. Let a few demons have at 'em to show them the way of the world."

"Gladly, Father," Solaros said hotly.

Ignati made that disgusting sound he meant as laughter. "Don't tempt me, my son," he said. "I'd rather keep things as they are. You're only young. You'll see the right of it soon enough. Meanwhile, have your fun. Play with your new toys. And when someday *you* are king you'll know your father was not such a fool after all."

The prince may have been young, but he was wise enough to allow his father and monarch have the final word. He assumed dismissal, bowed low, and led us out of the court room.

"You see how it is?" Solaros said when we'd reached the hallway.

"I think we do," Janela said dryly.

I was glad she'd answered for both of us. My diplomatic skills felt blunted at the moment.

"Don't think it's hopeless," he said. "My father's mind can be changed."

"And you're just the one to do it, Your Highness," one of his bravos said. It was the horse-faced wizard—Lord Vakram. "Isn't that right, my friends?"

The prince's bravos rumbled agreement and told Solaros what a mighty influence he had on the king.

"Now we've got Lord Antero and Lady Greycloak with us," Vakram continued, "the convincing will come easier still. I say push on, my prince! And before you know it, we'll be telling those demons where they can put those demands. Then we'll see how much of a stomach they have for a fight!"

The prince flushed with pleasure. Then he said to us: "If I can beg your time just a little longer. I know how weary you must be. And hungry as well, although I can fix that as soon as we reach my chambers."

"We are yours to command, Highness," I said.

"Actually, I was thinking more of a partnership," the prince said. "Now if you'll come with me, I'll give you the explanations I promised."

He dismissed his friends and we followed him through a maze of corridors that seemed to grow more ancient with each bend.

Sounds of workmen greeted us as we came to what I took to be the rear end of the fortress. The prince pulled aside a large tarp and we saw laborers chiseling out squares of crumbling stone while others mortared new ones into place. The air was thick with dust, and the prince shrugged apology, opened a heavy door, and beckoned us to follow.

"These are my chambers," he said with a touch of pride. He shut the door and the sounds of labor vanished. "This whole wing is part of the original palace. It's fallen into disuse over time, with rooms being boarded up as new ones were added. I've become quite interested in my ancestors, so I've won permission and funds from my father to restore this area as it was—and turn the rooms into my quarters."

We were in what appeared to be the large receiving room of the wing. It was pleasantly lit and artfully decorated with bright colors and comfortable furniture. In the center of the room was a table with chairs drawn around it, and in the middle was a small, swirling globe.

Solaros bade us sit and whispered instructions to a servant to bring us food and drink. Janela and I studied the globe while he did so, seeing quickly that it was a miniature of our world. Although the scale was small we could make out the distant islands of the West that Rali explored, and, closer in, the familiar coastlines and sea surrounding Orissa. From there it was easy to trace the route we took to Irayas, the perilous Eastern Sea we'd crossed to this land, and the river and ruined roads we'd traveled to reach Tyrenia.

"Our journey doesn't seem so difficult when you look at something like this," Janela said with a wry smile. "And think how much easier it would have been if we had its twin instead of my battered old chart."

The servant had brought refreshments, and Solaros sat between us, graciously serving up delicacies onto two platters and pouring wine.

"Its twin," he said with a laugh, "occupies six floors of a large tower. It gives us a view of the entire world and allows our wizards to manipulate the weather. And keep watch on important events—and the people involved."

"Such as the Greycloaks and the Anteros, Your Highness?" Janela said.

"Exactly," the prince said. Then, to me: "Do you know how excited all Tyrenia was when you and Janos Greycloak set out on your expeditions?"

"As it turned out," I said, "we failed."

Solaros smiled and sipped his wine. "You didn't fail so much as stop too soon. Of course that was long before I was born, but I'm told the whole city went into mourning when it became apparent that Lord Greycloak had missed the vital clues to our presence in the vaults of Irayas. Still, it was a marvelous achievement and gave many hope."

"Including your father, Your Highness?" I asked, hiding sarcasm.

"Actually, yes," the prince said—to my surprise. He paused, struggling for words. "It's easier if I start at the beginning. And please bear with me if I sometimes sound like an old schoolmaster."

He refilled our goblets and began.

"As you have long suspected, a good deal of this world you see before you"—he waved at the globe—"was once a great civilization that we nurtured and controlled. How this came to be is not so certain, for time has made the picture dim. However, most of our scholars agree that we Tyrenians were as savage and ignorant as all the rest. But we had a talent for organization, and when writing became known to us, we quickly turned this talent into records which we meticulously studied and maintained."

The prince laughed. "In short, we were wondrous scribes. But the result was that over time our wizards had organized all that was known of magic, which they added to greatly over the centuries. This made them the superiors of the sorcerers of our enemies— or those whose lands we coveted. I must be honest and tell you that we were, and are, no different than other people in such matters. The second thing this dry talent for organization gave us was a disciplined army which easily defeated the poor savages who dared oppose us and kept them permanently under our rule."

He made a sour face. "In many cases, I suppose," he said, "this meant they were enslaved." Then he shrugged. "But who am I to judge the ancients? They were hard men and women to match the times."

I sipped my wine to cover my feelings. In my view, as you know, there is no excuse for such treatment of your fellows. And as for harder times, what pray tell did the prince call these? Ah, well. At least I had to credit him with some delicate feelings that his father evidently did not share.

"But there were not so many wars as you might expect," the prince continued. "There were few large settlements under single rule. Mainly we achieved our empire through trade and attrition. People naturally came under our sway. Some because they feared us, some because they saw all the wonders our wizards were creating. Toil was lessened, hunger nearly banished, nature gentled. There was time for pleasure. For art and music. For the writing and reading of books and poems for the sake of the words alone. That is how things were when the first attack came."

"The demons, Your Highness?" Janela murmured.

"Yes, the demons," the prince said. "But you should know such creatures were nothing new to us. We encountered them wherever we settled, and either made them our Favorites or killed them if they were too powerful and dangerous. But they were wild things. More canny than intelligent, and with no other purpose than immediate gratification."

"Like Azbaas' demon, Your Highness?" I asked.

Solaros nodded. "Most of our great wizards thought they were as natural to this world as evil kings like Azbaas. That they were merely dangerous nuisances such as the were-tigers who prey on distant villages or sea beasts who attack the far-seeking mariner. We didn't know they came from other worlds . . . attracted to us like leeches to the scent of hot blood."

"In other words," Janela said, "the more successful humanity became, the more we drew their notice."

The prince frowned. "I suppose so," he said. "Although no one I know has ever put it that way."

I saw Janela jolt back as if she'd had a sudden shock. Her eyes glazed over for a moment, then flashed back to life—glittering with realization.

"Actually, Your Highness," she said, "I believe there's more to it than that. But never mind just now. Please, go on."

"It wasn't a single attack," the prince said, "but many attacks launched simultaneously. To say we were caught by surprise has to be one of the great understatements in history. For we weren't aware such an enemy even existed. And here we were confronted by demon legions who appeared from the blue, and at their head was the most cunning and powerful king anyone could ever have imagined. His name is Ba'land, and he seemingly lives forever, for he commands the demons still.

"No matter how hard we fought, no matter how many lives were sacrificed, we could not stop King Ba'land's hordes. Not only was their sorcery greater than ours, but we had never been confronted with a superior army. In the past, as I said, our only opponents had been savages. Even so, it took many centuries for them to drive us back. Many centuries for us to be forced to abandon an empire—until only Tyrenia remained. Here we have held them, praying that someday a time would come when we could rid the land of King Ba'land's influences."

"Excuse me, Your Highness," I said, "but I must ask a bold question."

"Please do," the prince said. "I'm no scholar and I'm sure I've left out much."

"Tell me this, if you will," I said. "If Tyrenia has fought continuously over the ages, why is it no one in the West has had any indications of those wars? Not just in my time, but my father's time and his father's, as well? Our wizards in those days may not have been near the equal of yours, but surely they would have noted such mighty forces locked in battle."

The prince blushed. "I exaggerated our boldness," he said. "And I'm sorry for that."

I admired the prince for making such a confession. It is very difficult for anyone to admit he is wrong, much less a man who would someday be king.

"First off," he said, "we made a stand in the land you know as Vacaan. There we lost half our forces. The agony we suffered in that defeat was so terrible, so soul-shattering, that few are willing to bring up the subject to this day. We made a second and final stand on our eastern shore." I nodded, remembering the ruined city and beastmen. "Once again we were defeated. But we fought more desperately and managed to inflict grave losses on the demons. For a while their attacks ceased. During that time the demons made their first diplomatic contact."

The young prince sighed. "What happened then is a shameful incident in my family's history. The king who ruled at that time—King Farsun—was a weak man. A coward, if you will. Over many years he negotiated with King Ba'land. Little by little he gave up the remainder of our kingdom. During his reign the demons even had free run of Tyrenia, debauching themselves at our expense and including themselves in even our most sacred celebrations.

"One of our legends, in fact, tells the sad tale of a dancer King Ba'land became enamored with. It is only a myth, but like most myths paints a telling picture of what might have been. The dancer, it is said, was the most beautiful and talented woman in all Tyrenia. Her art was not just natural, but imbued with a magical force that made her dances a wonder to behold. According to that legend, King Ba'land pressed his attentions on her but she refused. He increased his unwanted wooing, and when the dancer begged our king to help her, he refused. In the end the demon took possession of her. Made her his captive. His slave. The end of the tale, however, claims that she was so spirited that the demon could never fully possess her, that no matter how much he promised or tormented her, she held on . . . and retained her soul."

I looked at Janela. She crooked a finger to beg my silence. For some reason, she didn't want me to tell the prince what we knew of the dancer.

The prince plunged on. "Finally, King Farsun died. His successor ordered the demons out, retook the region around us, and fought a series of battles that showed Ba'land our resolve. They were small wars, sieges really, since we've proved to be better at defending what we have than gaining more. Other kings followed who maintained that warlike policy. And over time the demons seemed to lose interest. They seemed mostly satisfied with leaving Tyrenia alone as long as the rest of humanity remained frozen in barbarism."

I made so bold as to comment, "It seems to me it was more than we barbarians who were frozen."

Once more the prince took the criticism of his people calmly. He started to say something, hesitated, then stared at us for a long moment, as if deciding whether we were worthy of more. He nodded once, satisfied.

"It may have appeared a truce to outsiders, but it was not. In fact, we were losing slowly but surely, and from within. Now, what I am about to tell you is barely remembered legend. I did some digging in our archives, much like Janos Greycloak did in those of Irayas, and, unfortunately, discovered the legend to be truth.

"In this unnatural false peace, certain Old Ones, our finest leaders, our greatest philosophers, thinkers, wizards . . . left us."

"I don't understand," Janela said.

"Nor do I, exactly, but that is the best I can put it. One of them said, in a farewell letter, that it was 'time and past time to move on, to see other worlds.' "

"Like the demons have the power to do?"

"No. Something entirely different. First, it meant the death of the body. Suicide in one of several forms. But it was not the real death as we know it. This destruction of the physical self, when accompanied with certain drugs, or rituals, or spells, made something else happen, or so the wizards our kings ordered to investigate reported, not understanding themselves.

"The best explanation that was offered was by a man who was more of a poet, really, than a sorcerer, and he wrote a short note to his ruler that this moving on meant going to an entirely different place, a place beyond men, beyond women, beyond demons, beyond the gods themselves and even beyond death.

"Then he, too, killed himself." The prince smiled wryly. "This information, of course, was kept not only from the people at large, but from the demons, as well. The first would have been sent into despair when they found there appeared to be some goal, some golden place they themselves would never be able to reach. As for the demons, surely it would have driven them into a frenzy to learn there might be a place even their evil could not reach, and they would require us to provide the knowledge on how to reach it.

"But we lost this knowledge as the years passed—it vanished with our best, as well as ideas on how to smash the demons or at least end the war with a permanent victory. And so time drowsed on."

Janela leaned forward. "Then Janos Greycloak and Amalric Antero appeared," she said.

The prince seemed surprised at her guess. Then he smiled. "Yes, that is when the demons became . . . interested again. Here in Tyrenia, I am told, everyone took comfort in the evidence that our brothers and sisters in the old kingdoms were gradually throwing off the mantle of savagery. We delighted at the successes of places like Orissa and especially Vacaan—where they discovered our old books and pretended to the world that they were the Old Ones. It made Tyrenians hope that one day the world would be as before.

But we dared not show ourselves to you at that time because we didn't want to draw the attention of Ba'land.

"When Greycloak and Antero joined together, it was as if some great force had been released. Our wizards said the very ethers were astir with forces they could not explain. Some said it appeared Janos Greycloak was on the verge of a great discovery. But he died before he could make it. Then Lord Antero's sister Rali made her voyage to the West. Once again the ethers were full of sorcerous storms as she pursued the Archon into the very worlds the demons commanded.

"King Ba'land became very angry when he realized what was happening. But for some reason, he couldn't or wouldn't or feared to launch attacks on your regions as he had done with us ages ago. He was forced to use subterfuge, infiltrating Orissa and Vacaan, making bargains with men of evil intent. He also came to fear our presence here in Tyrenia again."

The prince had become pale and disturbed. He drank down his wine, filled the goblet, and drained it again.

"He came to my father and threatened full-scale war. He said he would crush us, wipe the mountaintop of our very presence. My father resisted at first. But plagues were sent that killed many, including my mother. Small but very bloody assaults were made on our defenses. Gradually, my father . . . gave in. He abandoned long-held plans to expand the kingdom to our old borders on the Eastern Sea. He relinquished the few gains we had made over the years."

The prince gave Janela an anguished look. "When you took your great-grandfather's place and persuaded Lord Antero to once more seek us out, King Ba'land approached my father again. While all Tyrenia cheered you, and the ballad of the dancer who refused the demon king was sung in all our taverns, my father did nothing to help. Instead he turned surly and cursed the names of Greycloak and Antero."

Solaros wiped an eye. "I did what I could," he said to Janela. "I have very quietly used my influence to help you when it was possible."

"I know you have," Janela said gently. "I have sensed an assisting hand from time to time. Always when we needed it most."

The prince nodded his gratitude. "My view is that now is the time to fight. We should attack the demons in full force as they attacked us long ago. Most of the army agrees with me. And I believe the people want the same. I'm hoping that with you here it will be easier to persuade my father to see I am right."

"We are at your disposal, Your Highness," I said, although I knew he was too green to know what would be required to mount such a war.

I was feeling a bit hopeless. After traveling so far, overcoming so much, and suffering the loss of my son's very soul, we had found a kingdom of legendary greatness. In reality, however, that magical realm was hollow to the core.

Perhaps Solaros caught some of my mood. For next he said, "My father hasn't always been this way. When he was young he was a great dreamer. But Ba'land bled him little by little. Now he fears Tyrenia is tottering on the edge of disaster. We have fought the demons for thousands of years. And it has taken a great toll on all our spirits. You must know this if you are to understand my father's dilemma."

He rose and walked toward the far wall, motioning for us to follow. A heavy curtain blanketed the wall. The prince tugged a cord and the curtain was swept aside.

"Look," he said.

And we did. Instead of stone, the wall proved to be an enormous window looking down on the terrain on the far side of Tyrenia.

It was like viewing another world. The sky was a veil of cold darkness, with unfamiliar stars peering out like the hungry eyes that gather near a wilderness campsite. A bleak moon glared over barren hills in the distance. But it was not the graceful goddess we know at home. This moon was red as blood, and I could feel it tugging at the dark things I keep hidden in my mind. I had to fight hard to stop it from unleashing a nightmare tide. The plain beneath us was pitted and scarred from thousands of years of warfare. Wind blew clouds of ashes across the bleak landscape, and my imagination made them ghosts crying out in soundless agony.

It was such a terrible sight that I finally had to turn away. I looked at Janela and she seemed as shaken as me. The prince pulled the curtain shut.

"Now perhaps you understand," he said softly, "why they call this the 'Kingdoms of the Night.' "

CHAPTER SEVENTEEN

THE WITCH AND THE QUEEN

The Heavens, they say, are the realms of the high gods. And the gods, it is claimed, are glorious, all-knowing beings who do not know pain or want or fear. Most are said to have taken such a kindly view of our affairs that they have permitted us to become their subjects—poor mortals though we be. However, a multitude of vanities must scurry about in the gods' hair the way lice plague a savage, for we are also taught their favor must be purchased and their kindness leased through continuous payments at the altar.

That last remark aside, in the past I have normally not been a cynic about such things. When Janos spoke of his doubts concerning the gods, my childhood teachings made me worry for him and gave me no little shock. Like most gods-fearing men and women, I keep a small temple in my head whose four pillars are Faith, Fear, Myth, and Ignorance. And I imagine Godhome to be like the legends of the Far Kingdoms, except even more glorious because the mystery is even greater.

But when we came to Tyrenia and saw its cowardly king, its brave but foolish crown prince, and the too-pretty people who were their subjects, those pillars collapsed one by one until only Fear remained. Janos once said he was always seeking the wise men of the world; but each time he thought he'd finally come into their company, he was sorely disappointed because it always turned out they knew less than he. This made Janos despair, for as the wisest man of *my* time, at least, he knew best how shallow was the well of human knowledge.

What I saw in Tyrenia made me finally grasp that despair which was the engine of Janos' destruction. The prince's dramatic plea for understanding lifted a veil he did not intend. I suddenly thought all must be chaos. There were no gods—or if there were, they must be as hollow as the Old Ones. There was no grand design for a heavenly palace which the gods continually improve for our eventual spiritual residence.

I never thought of myself as one who leaned too heavily on religion. I did my work, trusted the gods did theirs, and in the end we would see what we would see. So it surprised me when the crutch was kicked away and I had to struggle for balance. In the days that followed, that precarious balance became more difficult to maintain.

Part of my difficulty was the sudden great absence of Janela. Like her great-grandfather, she flung herself into the vaults of the Old Ones. She pored over ancient books and scrolls day and night. She dug into the deepest caverns of the Tyrenian libraries to find others. She stalked the warrens of their museums for forgotten relics. She crept into dark alcoves and abandoned rooms of the palace, ferreting out any secrets they might hold.

Each time I saw her, I looked for signs of Janos' affliction when Raveline tempted him with knowledge in exchange for his soul. Janela seemed weary, eyes red-rimmed with reading, but each day she buzzed with fresh excitement, and if anything, her spirits seemed to rise while mine grew stale.

Thinking to impress me, Prince Solaros ordered a grand military display and asked me to review his forces. I must admit they made a handsome parade. The chariot regiments with their mighty steeds and dazzling vehicles filled the air with thundering menace.

Battle wizards showed off wondrous machines that could turn a single attacking spell into a veritable swarm of magical missiles. Archers bent bows that would test a giant. Slingmen hurled shot amazing distances. Spears and javelins were thrown with similar results, and brawny warriors shouted war cries guaranteed to strike terror in the heart of an enemy and admiring lust in that of a Tyrenian maid.

But in the exercises that followed the parade, the chariot heroes outflanked their mock opponents in the first few moments of maneuvering, the magical war engines had no sorcerous opponents at all, and the brawny warriors turned back every attack with suspicious ease.

The prince and I watched the martial amusements from his royal box in the company of his friends, Lord Emerle and Lord Thrade—both Tyrenian generals—as well as Lord Vakram, who behaved more like a barracks chum than a wizard.

Whenever a particular feat caught Vakram's attention—which was more often than not—he'd display those huge horsey teeth and neigh, "Good show!" or "Mark that swordsman!" or "The demons will be chewing our dust for breakfast!" He'd slap either Emerle or Thrade on the back, depending on whose forces had most recently roused his generous admiration.

Later, when asked my opinion, I was most diplomatic, throwing up clouds of comments that might be taken for praise—if one did not blow too hard on those clouds and reveal the implied criticism.

"You have made a lovely art of war," I said. "It seemed almost theatrical."

The prince and the generals beamed with pleasure, and Vakram brayed, "Well said, sir! Well said!"

Then, after stringing together more creative dodges than it takes to make a fishing fleet's net, I couldn't help but ask: "Since this was merely for show, I assume the strategies and attacks were well-choreographed in advance?"

"With certainty," Lord Emerle said. "We practice those moves constantly, as well as whole volumes more."

"Your comparison to the arts was most apt," Lord Thrade added. "I like to think of my men as musicians who must dare tedium to pipe the most perfect refrain."

My sister Rali would have burst her buckler laughing. I merely cleared my throat. "What an interesting notion," I said. "Warriors as musicians."

Then I said: "Some armies like to occasionally test their forces with—how shall I say this without revealing how much a foolish amateur I am?—ah, yes . . . Test them with more active and unplanned opposition. What is your opinion, my lords, of such schools of thinking?"

The generals frowned. "What use is that?" Lord Emerle asked. "We have detailed records of every strategy used in history. For every action there is a known counter."

"With study and practice," Lord Thrade said, "there is no need to risk injuring our men."

"And it's a well-known fact," Lord Emerle concluded, "that injury is bad for morale."

"I suppose it would be," I said. "Yes . . . I can see that now."

My teachers smiled in pleasure for being the architects of my new understanding. But when I glanced at Lord Vakram, he appeared more amused than pleased.

And for just a moment I thought I saw a glimmer of intelligence in those strange, wide-set eyes.

DESPITE MY DISAPPOINTMENT, I did not think ill of the Tyrenians. I was guest of honor at many a banquet—Janela was always too engrossed in her studies and experiments to attend—and the number of newborns named for us would sorely test the king's prediction that we would soon be forgotten by his fickle subjects.

They were the pleasantest people one could meet at a banquet—where much is discussed and little said. When I had enough wine to fog my cares and warm my good nature, I had to admit I'd never seen such a handsome race. Even the graceful citizens of Irayas would look plain beside these folk, who were tall and slender with broad foreheads, wide clear eyes, and skin so healthy it was almost translucent like a child's. They wore clothing of the most artistic designs with splashes of tasteful color, and the whole time I have been in Tyrenia I have never seen one costume that was like another. Since the days are always warm here, the nights balmy, such costumes might consist of only a swatch of fine cloth for modesty's sake and a few baubles of simple jewelry to subtly light the wearer's most prized feature.

My band of companions were also well-entertained. Kele and Quatervals said the whole company was constantly showered by romantic proposals and gifts of more money and goods than they could ever hope to carry away; they were so pampered by the servants in their commodious quarters that they feared their limbs would wither from lack of use.

Kele shook her head in weary amazement. "Keep havin' t' pinch meself, Lord Antero," she said. "Folks actin' like we was the Old Ones 'stead of them. Gonner get one'a me mates t' bedevil me ever' mornin' so's I don't ferget I'm just Kele."

Quatervals had similar comments. "Now I see what it's been like for you all these years, my lord," he said. "Not sure I like it. When my duties're done I favor a bit of time to myself. Thinkin' on whatever needs thinkin' on. And I like to walk when I think. Put the head down and charge along until I run out of walkin' room or brains. But you can't do that when you're famous, my lord. People come up and want to talk to you. Shake your hand and invite you to dinner—or bed. And that's all very nice, and all very kind, and I like a tumble more than most, thank you very much, lass, but can't you see I'm presently occupied?"

As any merchant knows, the best source of information about the habits, customs, and secrets of potential customers are the men and women who meet them daily: his employees. Although I as yet did not know what goods I had to offer, I knew the day would come when I might have to sell or die.

So I asked them both: "What do you make of these people?"

"First I thought they was lubbers through and through, my lord," Kele said. "Nice, kinder stupid, but not *that* nice and not *that* stupid, if yer can catch that bit'a driftwood when it floats by."

I shook my head. I'd missed it by a league.

"Okay, let's try a new set'a signal flags, my lord," she said. "The Tyrenians I meet fall over the deck t' make certain I'm happy. But if I was a bad'un, they'd toss me over the side quicker'n fish oil squints through a gull."

"Good," I said. "They have spirit—unlike their king. Go on. What about the, ahem, stupid part?"

"They're kinder stupid, my lord," Kele said, " 'cause they won't face facts. They're inna starin' match wi' the demons and ever'one knows demons don't blink. All scaly balls, 'n' no eyelids. 'Stead'a lookin' fer what's on the horizon, the Tyrenians study the deck fer ever' speck 'n' put it in a log book wit' lots'a other specks. And they reorganize that log over and over till she's pretty near perfect 'n' they know ever' speck in ever corner of the ship. 'N' any day now, when she's perfect . . . maybe they'll scour 'n' varnish."

"It's sort of like they're frozen, my lord," Quatervals said. "Like they've nearly lost confidence in which way to go. And so they walk the same path till it's worn out in fear they'll lose the direction. 'Course, who can blame 'em with the king they've got? Never know what's going to happen from one day to the next. Also, when you've been at war off and on so long, you tend to live your days as they come—'cause you know there's not likely any comfort in tomorrow."

Kele nodded. "Which brings me course back t' the not *that* stupid part, my lord. They don't like King Ignati much. Trust him not at all. So whyn't they hoist him off the throne? These're fierce folk 'n' they don't swim in schools like fish, hopin' the sharks notice their sister afore they spots them. Got a mind of their own, they do, my lord. Thick-skulled as they be. But still they let the king be king."

I shrugged. "Why do you think that is?"

"Who would replace him, my lord?" Quatervals said. "They love Prince Solaros, but they think of him more as a favorite nephew than a leader. They know he's too young, too green, and too bold."

"A dangerous medley," I said.

"We all sang that cracked-voice tune at one time, my lord," Quatervals said. "Anyways, the Tyrenians think the prince is gonna make a first-rate king. Someday. But he'll be needin' a lot of seasonin'. 'N' then, I'll tell you, Lord Antero, they'll follow him into the Hall of the Doomed itself."

"If they live long enough to see the day," I said.

Kele grunted and Quatervals said, "There is that, my lord."

The two of them eyed me for an uncomfortable moment. Then Quatervals, who knows me best, baited the question and made the cast.

"We've been sort of wonderin', my lord," he said. "Now that we're here and all. Now that we found what we was lookin' for and it isn't anythin' like we expected. And considerin' further that we maybe've got a whole bunch of demons breathin' on our necks . . ."

"You want to know what we're going to do next," I said.

Quatervals sighed. "Yes, my lord. We've been wonderin' about little things like that."

"Not so small," I said, "and not so simple that we ought to act in haste." I felt a little like Tyrenia's indecisive king. "Lady Greycloak, as you know, is engaged in vital investigations. And I have been charting the political map quite carefully. Te-Date willing, a plan should make itself clear quite soon."

"That's good to know, me lord," Kele said.

"Yes, my lord," Quatervals said. "We'll pass the word to the others. They'll take comfort in that."

But as we parted, none of us felt at ease.

JANOS' GREATEST CRITICISM of me was that he thought I was too softhearted.

"Mercy is a much overrated virtue," he once admonished me. "It blurs the eye when you stand over your defeated enemy. It slows you, spoils your aim, and bleeds the anger you require for the final thrust. All these things are needed most when your enemy is at your feet. For if he is worthy of your hate, he will save just enough of himself to strike out as his life flows away. Mercy may make your dreams less bleak, my friend. But I'd rather dream bleak than not dream at all."

As usual, Janos was correct. But I did not change my ways. I am not the same cold, hard metal Janos was. Still, I *have* reached a much greater age than he. Although it's true I'm softhearted, I am no fool. When I stayed my hand and let Cligus and Modin live, I did not make the mistake of clutching my son's viperous soul to my bosom. I let them live, yes. But I made certain they were caged and defanged.

Janela and I were given spacious and luxurious quarters near the prince's rooms. At my request, he made certain those quarters included chambers suitable for imprisoning Cligus and Modin. They shared three large rooms with no windows and only one door leading out. I had the door exchanged for one made of heavier material—which could be barred from either side.

Quatervals, my most trusted and able man, was in charge of guarding them. He kept one man posted inside and one without, changing them frequently so they would always remain alert. He also made spot checks both day and night and berated any guard who so much as yawned while on duty. To make doubly certain, I stepped in to check on them myself from time to time—usually using their comfort as an excuse.

The only flaw in this arrangement was that by keeping them close, my son preyed more on my mind. At odd moments—and always without warning—I would recall him as a child. I'd remember him at innocent play in the garden or sprawled at the feet of Omerye as she piped a joyful tune. We had such hopes for him, such dreams, such long discussions in the privacy of our bed, spinning fanciful scenes of his later life when he would grow from our golden boy to a golden man.

Similar things must have been on his mind, for one day when I entered, he seemed glad to see me. Modin, as usual, turned his scarred, blind face away. When I tarried, he hissed a curse and demanded his servant lead him from my presence.

"Is all well?" I asked Cligus. "Do you lack anything I can have fetched?"

He glanced after the wizard's retreating form and made a wan smile. "Only better company," he said. "He made such a great wind when we had the upper hand. I never knew a wizard who talked so much—except maybe Palmeras. But now that he's met defeat, if he talks at all it's only to curse or complain about his injuries."

A rush of anger nearly overtook me. I wanted to snarl: "That is the company you chose! Be damned to you!" Then I felt sad and said nothing.

"I had a lovely dream last night," Cligus said. "Do you remember the time when I was a boy and was taken very ill?"

I nodded. I recalled it well. It was before we had mastered the sorcery we'd gained from Irayas, and had few defenses against seasonal disease. Cligus caught a summer chill that lingered many weeks despite all our efforts to cure it. I had already lost one wife and a child to a plague, so I was possibly even more frantic than Omerye. Gradually he recovered, but while doing so he spent many weeks confined to his nursery—fretting to go out and play but too weak for us to allow it. So we plied him with treats and amused him with games and toys to make his confinement more pleasant.

"Mother used to make my meals with her own hands," Cligus said, smiling in gentle reflection on Omerye's many kindnesses. "She'd concoct the most amazing delicacies, which never disturbed my poor stomach. But my favorite dish was the simplest."

"Toasted cheese," I said, caught up in his reverie and smiling back. "And soup made from the tomatoes we grew in our garden."

"With butter and pepper floating on the top," Cligus added.

"Yes," I said. "I left it off when I fetched it to you once. And you curled your lip and wrinkled your nose and said, 'Where is the butter and pepper?' Your manner was that of a learned gourmand whose taste buds had been offended by a peasant kitchen."

We both laughed.

"When I woke from the dream," Cligus continued, "for a minute I thought I was that sick boy again, kept in his nursery by kind and caring parents. At any moment there'd be a tap at the door and Mother would enter with toast and melted cheese and rich soup to dip it in." He sighed. "Then I realized where I was, and . . . Ah, well. Life certainly takes its twists, doesn't it?"

And I replied, quite softly: "If you're asking my forgiveness, you can have it. I've forgiven villainy before. Besides, your mother would have demanded it. But if you are asking me to relent as well . . ." My voice turned harsh. "I will not!"

Cligus flushed, angry. "You think I'm asking you to forgive me? I piss on your forgiveness! You are to blame, sir. If you had dealt with me fairly, none of this would have happened. I was merely reminiscing with someone who *knew* me. With someone whose many faults do not include poor conversation. And as for asking you to relent . . . why would I waste my breath? The only thing I ask of you, sir, is to join me for supper. And turn your back long enough for me to insert my dinner knife!"

I shrugged and left, allowing him the last word.

As I passed the sentries guarding my son, I thought of Janos. And wished to the gods I could pluck mercy from my breast.

SOME WEEKS AFTER the parade, the prince summoned me to his quarters. I had been there many times since our arrival, but it was always to discuss my adventures or to listen to his views—so passionately held that they had small merit.

This time, however, Solaros surprised me.

As I was ushered in, he was pacing the room, hands clasped behind his back and head bowed in thought. Vakram sat by the table that bore the globe.

When he saw me, the prince broke off his pacing. "Lord Antero! How glad I am to see you! I badly need your advice."

I asked him what had happened, and he said: "My father has been visited by emissaries from King Ba'land."

"I was expecting as much," I said. "I assume they are here concerning Lady Greycloak and myself."

Solaros shook his head. "Your names weren't mentioned," he said.

Vakram's long face was split by a cynical grin, exposing his long, thick teeth. "Your presence," he said, "is certainly known, Lord Antero. It has been the unspoken current beneath all the discussions."

The prince looked at him a moment, then nodded. "I suppose it was," he said slowly. "My father has been papering together a truce with the demons for some time. The negotiations came after King Ba'land agreed to cease hostilities, which is a jest for so many reasons and more violations than I care to number just now.

"Regardless, my father has made one concession after another, which as you know is the source of my disagreement with him.

From his viewpoint, however, much progress has been made and the demons' final demands met. And the truce required only the formality of signatures."

"Allow me a guess," I said. "King Ba'land has sent his regrets, claiming new matters have come to light that require renegotiating the entire document."

Lord Vakram neighed. "What a wise fellow you are! Those are nearly that devil's exact words. Weren't they, Your Highness?"

The prince ignored him. "Ba'land's emissaries have informed us he is presently drawing up a new treaty with the additions, which they will shortly present to us."

"I assume these additions," I said, "are not negotiable."

"Nothing is negotiable," the prince said.

"What nerve!" Vakram said.

"Furthermore," Solaros went on, "they expect us not only to agree, but to sign the treaty formally at our annual Creator's Day, when we honor the ancient founders of our kingdom and the gods who blessed us."

"Very canny," I said. "The demons intend to smother your most symbolic day with symbolism of their own design. If your father agrees, it's as good as a surrender."

Lord Vakram slapped his forehead. "I hadn't thought of that!" he said. "The bastards!"

"Well *I* certainly had," the prince huffed.

"Do you think your father will agree?" I asked.

"He hasn't said no," Solaros said. "I would have thrown them out. Immediately!"

Lord Vakram's wide eyes swiveled forward. "But that would also mean *immediate* war, Your Highness," he said.

The prince's features grew very hard for one so young. "That is why I asked to see you, Lord Antero. My most pressing goal is to convince my father to refuse. And when—not if—that happens, there will be war. I want us prepared to wage it."

Vakram seemed surprised, his lips drawing back over his teeth. "What you are suggesting, Your Highness?" he asked.

The prince replied, "That I want Lord Antero to help us in that task."

"I am no soldier," I said.

"I know that," Solaros said. "But you have wide experience and knowledgeable soldiers in your company."

While I chewed this over, he said, "I caught your comments to my generals at the parade. At first I didn't see what was beneath them. Frankly, when I did, I was irritated. My pride was hurt. I may command all my father's forces—in his name. But at heart I am a charioteer, and a charioteer is kin to the stallions who carry us into battle, all courage and speed and quick reactions to a continuously changing terrain. We fight where you aim us and do not think of the consequences, much less the plans that lead to those consequences.

"So I was slow in understanding your implied criticism. Which is that we fight by rote. And that we are defenders, not attackers. I can see that now. And I mean to set it right."

"What you are suggesting, Your Highness," Vakram broke in, shedding the last of his jolly nature, "would be considered madness if it came from another source."

"If insanity is called for," the prince said, "so be it! From now on we will train as if it is an enemy who opposes us, not tavern friends."

"But your generals will never agree, my liege," Vakram said. "There will be injuries. And think of the morale of the men!"

"Be damned to morale!" the prince replied. "If what the demons conspire to achieve comes to pass, we'll be considering the morale of slaves instead of soldiers."

Vakram champed off a retort and bowed his head.

Then the prince said to me, "Will you do it, Lord Antero? There's time, although barely, to get ready. If a confrontation comes, it will be at the Creator's celebration. Which is some months away."

I said yes, we'd teach them how Orissans make war.

MY AGREEMENT may have endangered the morale of the Tyrenians, but it certainly had the opposite effect on my company. When I called them together to explain what was to be done my remarks were greeted with much enthusiasm.

As if they had been given a magical command, Quatervals and his ex-Scouts snapped to as one.

"First thing we do, lads," Quatervals said, "is get 'em off the parade ground and show 'em the Scouts' way, which no man has ever seen in a book."

"Me bottom's gettin' lardy with all the sittin' and the sippin' we been doin'," Kele said. "I may be a seafarin' woman, but me and me captains got a trick or three that's confounded more lubbers'n not."

Towra and Berar made loud noises of agreement.

"If'n they wants t' know how t' sneak," Pip said, "cain't find a better sneak master'n me."

The Cyralian brothers got into a heated discussion on flaws they'd seen in the use of the archers, and before I knew it, the whole lot of them had forgotten I was there and were arguing the fine points such instruction might include.

When training commenced I thought the hardest part would come not from the troops, but from foot-dragging generals. No general enjoys instruction, even when the order comes from their commander and crown prince. But such was the stature of myself and my fellow voyagers among their own men that their objections were drowned out by the loud cheers of the soldiers when the prince assembled them for the announcement.

And they trained with a will, their spirits fired by the thought that such training was in itself an act of defiance against the demons. Soon all Tyrenia was caught up in the fever, making it very difficult for King Ignati to do more than grumble about the expense and the difficulty it would cause him in his dealings with Ba'land.

Even my mood brightened. I found myself thinking that the Tyrenians weren't such a disappointing lot after all.

Still, I harbored no delusions about Ignati. He *was* king. And monarchs are rarely moved to risk their crown.

SOMETIME LATER Janela came blinking out of the archives like a mole into the sudden sun. She was wan and weary when she stumbled into our rooms. But victory glowed in her hollowed eyes.

"I'm almost there, Amalric," she said. "I'm at the same point my great-grandfather was when he told you he was a wisp away from discovery."

"What have you found?" I asked.

Janela shook her head, the weariness catching up to her. "I can't say, yet," she said. "But I'll *show* you what I can tomorrow."

Then she dragged herself off to bed.

JANELA SLEPT LATE the next day and we didn't set out from our quarters until early afternoon. Although there were crinkles of tiredness at the edges of her eyes, she seemed filled with energy.

She led me outside the main building for a stroll through the palace gardens that sprawled beside the outermost walls.

"Actually, it's well I was such a slugabed," she said. "We need to approach what I have found with some care. I don't intend to keep it secret long, but it might be better as a whole piece rather than fragmented—which is how my mind feels just now."

I looked about, then gave her a puzzled smile. It was a bright cheery day, and courtiers were strolling by us on the same garden path, inspecting the wares at the market stalls that lined the walls. Others were picnicking in a lovely park, while scores of highborn children were at play in a broad field.

"If it's secrecy that's required," I said, "this hardly seems the proper time. A good skulking session requires wet breeches as part of your reward. And if you want to truly test the mettle of your bladder, I've found the night much better. It comes with so many more alarming shadows and sounds than day."

Janela laughed. "And if someone sees you," she said, "suspicion is automatic."

"There is *that*," I admitted.

Janela took my hand. It was warm and smooth as silk off a caravan. "If we make this look like a romantic stroll," she murmured, "no one will approach."

She was right. Although our fame drew stares, those looks quickly turned away when they saw us walking like lovers on a summer day. After a time her closeness and the smell of her perfume began to make me feel less like an actor in a play.

We came to a small tavern near one of the museums she'd been working in. It was set under an enormous tree, and with a start I saw it appeared to be the same breed as the silver-leafed giant we had seen on the island after we took leave of Queen Badryia.

"Don't stare at it, Amalric," she whispered. "And yes, it's exactly what you think."

I tore my eyes away and we went into the tavern, which was lightly attended since it was past the midday meal. The owner beamed when he saw Janela and hurried over to tell her everything she'd requested was nearly ready and would we care to sample his best chilled wine while we waited?

Janela said we'd be delighted and led me to a table resting at the edge of what I took to be a dance floor. Once again I was surprised. Instead of a floor, it was a large, thick glass window, and looking down, I could see a lighted chamber. In that chamber was an ancient bath with room for twenty or more. It was made of milky stone, and graceful statues of unclad serving women rose up on all sides, each tilting a pitcher into the bath. At one time water would have flowed from those pitchers to fill the pool. The walls were frescoed, but so damaged by age I couldn't make out the scenes they portrayed, although they gave the impression of soothing femininity.

"When the prince told us he was restoring part of the original palace," Janela said, "I mistook him to mean that all the Tyrenian monarchs had lived there since the beginning. Actually, this kingdom is much older than that. The palace we see and the grounds around it were erected over the redoubts of even more ancient monarchs. When they constructed the museum, they came upon the ruins you are looking at. No one saw any use in such a thing so they were going to cover it up."

I smiled. "And a clever man or woman of business came along and saw profit where they saw a hole in the ground, no doubt." I looked around the tavern. The few patrons were very wealthy, very cultured Tyrenians. "What better place to sup and dine than on the mysteries of your ancestors?"

Janela chuckled. "Money makes you clear-headed, Amalric," she said, "where it confounds others. Yes, that is what happened. When I supped here the first day I came to the museum, my realization was somewhat different. I saw the tree outside and the view through that floor and doubted there was a coincidence. I cast a spell and found the tree to be near the age of that chamber. My interest was minor at first, but the more I've delved into what I hope will be our deliverance, the more I thought these ruins deserved greater study."

She pointed at the chamber. "That was the bathing room of King Farsun's queen," Janela said after the tavern owner had delivered the wine and retreated. "You know . . . the king in the dancer's scene."

"Yes, yes," I said impatiently. "I know who you mean. The fellow Solaros said was Tyrenia's first cowardly monarch."

"Her name was Monavia," Janela continued. "Legend has it she was sorely wounded by her husband's cowardice. When they wed, the whole empire celebrated the joining of such a handsome couple. When Monavia took her oath as queen, she swore she'd buckle on armor herself if that became necessary to defeat the demons. But everything changed after her first child was born. On the feast day of her son's first year of life, the demon king sent his diplomats to sue King Farsun for peace. By odd coincidence, that day was also the day when Tyrenia holds its most important event."

"It wouldn't be Creator's Day, would it?" I asked.

It was Janela's turn to be startled. "Yes. How did you know?"

I quickly filled her in on my meeting with the prince and the deadline set by King Ba'land.

Janela grew troubled, then brightened. "Yes. That makes things much clearer now." She resumed the tale.

"When the emissaries presented themselves, they behaved so familiarly many suspected this was not the first meeting. The suspicion grew when one of the demons boldly asked for a private audience and the king obediently cleared the chambers and had the doors barred and guarded. No one knows what was said in that room, but the secret meeting lasted all that day and into the next.

"As you can imagine, it cast a pall on both celebrations, with the whole kingdom worrying what might be occurring. Was the king dead? Was he a hostage? Just when the queen was at the point of ordering soldiers to burst into the chamber, the doors came open and the king called everyone in to announce this had been the most historic day since the founding of Tyrenia. The war with the demons had ended, he said.

"From this moment forward they would be welcome whenever they chose to visit his court. Furthermore, the demon king, Ba'land himself, would be arriving soon and a month of feasting would be decreed to honor his arrival."

I sipped my wine, reflecting. "I wonder what was said?"

"No one knows," Janela answered. "I've scoured all the old parchments for a hint. There was all kinds of speculation, of course. The life of the crown prince threatened. Or the queen's. The king was possessed, or he'd made a bargain to keep his throne. I've finally concluded it doesn't matter and any further effort to find out would be a waste of valuable time. After all, a demon's greatest talent is delving into one's most secret, most weak self, and using one's greatest fear—or most shameful desire—against you.

"More important is Queen Monavia's reaction as Ba'land and his demon courtiers swarmed her palace and took increasing liberties. She did her best to resist, even threatened to break the royal marriage. But King Farsun locked her child in a tower and said he'd keep him prisoner there until he could make a child on another queen, and when that child was born, the crown prince would be assassinated."

"How bold cowards can sometimes be," I said.

"I thought the same thing," Janela said. "Fortunately, the queen was no fool. And she was patient, as well. She put on a royal face and braved it out for some years. Meanwhile she conspired with a woman she had in her service who was a very powerful witch. Her name is lost to history. Her birthplace, however, is not. One old historian, who was a devil when it came to thickly laid prose, spent several glowing pages describing it. He said she came from a wondrous lake district where the River of the Heavens is born."

"Our river?" I asked.

"The very same," she answered.

I just had to laugh. "So it's likely this witch was kin to Queen Badryia?"

Janela grinned. "Remember how she lectured us like an old schoolmistress on the nonexistence of Tyrenia?"

"*Very* well," I said. "Badryia reminds me of a teacher I once had who insisted on the truth of facts that were nonsense. Such as— and he swore this to the gods—that women had fewer teeth than men."

This drew a belly laugh from Janela. "Didn't he ever count them?" she asked.

"No," I replied. "But I did. My father dismissed him soon after. Thank Te-Date I was blessed with a wise father."

"And he a wise son," Janela murmured.

I flushed, feeling like a small boy hearing welcome praise.

"To continue," Janela said. "The witch coaxed roots to grow from a stem of a magical leaf, a leaf from a rare tree that grew in her homeland. When it became a sapling, she planted it by a spring whose waters were reputed to be an elixir of renewal and protection. It grew swiftly, and before long it was one of the larger trees in the kingdom. Its roots were becoming a nuisance, boring through the foundation in some places. But the queen would let no one touch it, declaring its leaves a beauty aid of much importance to her.

"The spring that fed the tree, by the by, was also used for the queen's bath, which the old historian said kept her from being harmed by the demons, who knew she opposed them."

I started to ask her a question, but the tavern owner bustled over with a large wicker basket. He assured my Lady Greycloak that only the most excellent food had been prepared, with samples of their very best spirits to complement each dish. Would she wish a servant to assist us while we picnicked? Janela said thank you, no, but this was to be a very private affair. She winked. The tavern owner floated away on a wave of good humor.

Janela finished her wine and rose. "Shall we, my lord?" she asked in mock formality.

"Yes, yes, of course," I said, too distracted by her tale to take note of all the trouble she'd gone to. "But tell me one thing before we leave."

"If I can."

"What was the tree's purpose?" I asked.

"That's one of the reasons for the picnic," Janela said. "I intend us to find out. But I do have a guess."

"And that is?"

Janela tossed a silver coin on the table, saying, "She used it to murder the king."

MURDER IN
THE PALACE

An arbored path wound around the tavern and tree. It emptied into a secluded garden the tavern owner rented for romantic trysts, such as he imagined ours to be. A colorful
pavilion had been set up for our picnic, but Janela only dumped the
basket next to it and motioned for me to follow her to a wide spot
between two mighty roots. The ground there was moist and covered
with a carpet of thick moss.

She pointed to a depression about four feet square. "That's
where we dig." She dropped to her knees and started cutting a fur-
row into the moss with her knife.

"Why, pray tell, do we need to?" I asked.

"To get into the old palace," Janela said. "I've cast spells to find
an entrance, but they're all either too deep or lack seclusion—such
as through the tavern floor. Except for here. Now if you'll only help
me all we should have to do is peel away this moss."

I did as she said although I was still mystified.

"I've been experimenting with measurements of sorcerous energy," Janela explained. "And from what I can determine, there is more of a disturbance in the ethers in this area than just the presence of the witch's tree can account for. I don't know what it is, although I have my suspicions. I thought it important enough to investigate. I found old builders' sketches of Farsun's palace and managed to trace the source of the disturbance. If fortune smiles, we should soon learn if I'm right."

With that she made a final cut, and we gingerly rolled back the mossy carpet. The damp earth beneath it crumbled under our fingers and I could hear the sound of rushing water. Janela brushed at the dirt, revealing an old stone grate. Cool, sweet air wafted up between the openings.

"That's odd," I said. "I'd expect the air to be dank and foul-smelling."

Janela didn't answer. She scratched a faint impression around the edges of the grate. Her knife glowed, and the damp stone hissed where the knife touched. The grate fell away and splashed into the watery recess below.

Her action amazed me. I hadn't seen her lips move in a chant, much less heard her mumble. But before I could ask how she'd accomplished it, she fumbled firebeads from her purse and they'd barely winked to life before she'd swung over the side of the hole and was clambering down—using impressions cut into the stone sides as foot and handholds.

The hole was only ten or so feet deep, and she quickly reached the bottom. I saw the firebeads shift this way and that as she investigated.

"It's a culvert," she called up to me, her voice light with victory. "Just as I hoped. Come on, Amalric. It's not very wet."

I dropped in after her and found myself standing on a stone path that rose above a stream of water. The culvert was quite wide, and high enough for us to stand comfortably straight. I raised my own firebeads and saw the water came from a small pool that on closer inspection proved to be an overflowing well. The water ran along the culvert into a tunnel that appeared to head off under the tavern.

Janela bent to scoop up some of the water, drank, then nodded in satisfaction. I did the same. It tasted exactly the same as the elixir spring we'd encountered on the island. She motioned and we set off into the tunnel.

As we walked along the path, I heard a roaring sound that grew louder, until we couldn't have made one another out if we'd talked. But we didn't have to go far to find the source of the noise, for abruptly the tunnel widened and we came into a small chamber. The water was channeled through the center of the chamber, then plummeted over a rough, natural ridge. I looked down, but the bottom was so distant light couldn't reach it. Janela nudged me and I saw an alcove cut into the opposite side. We leaped over the stream and went to it. I saw a heavy door made of some metal that didn't seem to be affected by the elements, since it was as smooth as the long-ago day when it was first cast in one solid piece.

There was a depression for a handhold, and Janela got a good grip and heaved. But the door came open so easily I had to catch her when she lost her balance and nearly fell. As I righted her she shook with mute laughter at her clumsiness. Her eyes were dancing with excitement and she gave me a quick hug and said something I couldn't hear over the deafening sound of the waterfall. She shrugged, giving up, and signaled for me to follow her.

We entered into a large room filled with shadowy objects. Janela shut the door, which was so well-designed that the water's sound vanished. She whirled the firebeads about her head and the whole room lit up as ancient, magical torches flared into cold life.

The objects were now clearly visible as well-made vases and jars of various sizes and shapes. We examined a few. They were wondrously decorated. The larger vases showed various scenes of women bathing in natural settings. The smaller ones had glazed pictures of different flowers. Janela broke the seal on one and a delicious, sensual odor wafted from it.

"How lovely," she murmured, dabbing a little behind each ear. "Still fresh after all these centuries."

To one side was a pot large enough to hold a person. Beneath it was a small furnace with the coals and ashes heaped into it from a long-dead fire.

"This is where the queen's maids came to fetch her bathwater,"

Janela said. "They went through that door to dip it out of the spring. They heated it in that pot. Perfumed it with the fragrances in those jars. Then carried it in the vases to wherever the reservoir is that fed the bath."

I had no doubt she was correct, but as further proof she showed me a small door with a peephole about two fingers wide. I peered into it and could make out the bath chamber we had seen in the tavern. By stooping and craning my neck I could even catch a glimpse of someone walking past the glass floor in the tavern above.

There was one other door in the chamber, and on the other side of that was a long corridor with three more doors set into its length, which carried on around a dark bend. One door was warped by the heavy weight of rubble on the other side, so it was impossible to investigate. Janela guessed it was Queen Monavia's bedchamber. A second door opened easily, revealing a warren of corridors leading into the ruined palace. The third was a little stiff on its hinges, but when we looked inside we found a small empty room with what I at first took to be a raised stone pallet for a mattress. When we looked closer, however, we saw the familiar decorations carved into it. In the center was an even more familiar boxlike recess. Except this one was empty.

Janela got out the stone box we'd found on the island and held it over the recess. It was the same size and shape. For a moment I thought she was going to place the box into it and I became alarmed, my heart quickening, palms perspiring, as I recalled the mysterious and intoxicating incident on the island—an intoxication that both attracted and frightened me.

"Don't," I said.

Janela looked at me. "What's wrong?" she asked.

"Something will happen if you do," I said. "I'm not sure what. But I don't think we'll be pleased."

Janela didn't question me, and to my relief she put the box away. Then she closed her eyes and stood very still for a long time.

Finally she opened them, saying, "You were right to warn me, Amalric. The queen's witch used this room for her magic. Perhaps even to charge the box with whatever sorcery she intended."

"Is our box the same one?" I asked. "Or its twin?"

"The same, I think," Janela said. "If so, the witch must have returned to her homeland and made a holy place on the island to keep it safe in case it needed to be used again."

I licked dry lips, not wanting to ponder long on what that use might be. Janela must have known something of my feelings for she gave me a quick kiss, then beckoned me out of the witch's room and down the long corridor.

We walked along it for nearly an hour, Janela whirling the firebeads over her head every now and again to cause the ancient lights to bloom and the shadows to retreat like an army that had lost heart. We came to other doors and other corridors, but Janela barely glanced at them, staying close to the sorcerous trail she'd sniffed out. Then the corridor sallied out into a vaulted chamber with mighty double doors on the far side. The metal of those doors was inscribed with the crown of a king. As we approached them I felt suddenly cold, as if a draft were blowing beneath—although I felt no disturbance in the air.

Janela paused at the doors. She felt the metal, then put her ear against it as if listening.

"This is it," she said in a low voice.

She stepped back and flung her arms wide. The doors swung swiftly open, booming loudly as they jarred against the walls. She took a few paces forward, whirling the beads, and the great room beyond those doors burst into light.

We entered and found ourselves in the court chamber of King Farsun.

I could see the twin thrones where he and Queen Monavia had reclined in the dancer's scene. I could see the white stone platform where she'd danced, the pit where the musicians had played—and on one side the boxed seats where the demon king had watched and lusted.

Cobwebs and clots of dust made a ghostly curtain over every object in the room. They cloaked the thrones and chairs and small round refreshment tables where goblets and plates still sat. Two enormous banquet tables rested in one corner, and they were still covered with mummified and dust-covered food. There were whole roasted animals set on tarnished trenchers of rare metals, tiered cakes decorated with confectionery figurines, platters of what had once been delicacies but were now lumps of gray and black stone. In many places tree roots had burst through the vaulted ceiling and walls, then continued on through the stone floors. The roots were thick and latticed together in some areas, forming veined canopies of cobwebs and feathery shoots.

We walked toward the thrones in silence, intimidated by the spectral scene.

There was a bejeweled goblet lying at the foot of King Farsun's throne. Janela went to it and picked it up. She stood quite still for a moment, then said, "This is where the king died."

She sniffed at the goblet as if there would be an odor still remaining after all this time.

"Was he poisoned?" I asked.

Janela nodded, then indicated the goblet. "But not by anything in this."

She set it on the seat of the throne. She went to the dancer's platform, circling it a few times. Then she stepped out a few paces, paused, glanced down at the floor, then grimaced as if the ghost of what she saw there had touched her greatly. Janela continued on until she came to the demon king's viewing box. She opened the gate set into the low wall, revealing several gilded chairs. She sat in the chair I knew to be King Ba'land's, shut the gate, then leaned an elbow on it, staring out at the dancer's platform. After a while she exited and came back to me, but her brow was furrowed and her eyes glazed in thought.

Her brow cleared. "I think I know what happened here," she said. Then the frown returned. "But I don't know how it *could* have happened."

She looked around the room, staring here and there, twitching with sorcerous energy as she probed with all her power. She became pale as the blood drained from her face, and suddenly she started to sag as she called on more reserves. I thought she was going to collapse and rushed to her. I embrace her and I could almost feel her energy draining away. I became alarmed.

"Janela!" I shouted.

She shuddered at my shout. A moment later I could sense

her strength returning. She straightened, pushing gently away from me.

"Now I know the *how*, Amalric," she said, voice quite weak. "And as quickly as we can, we'd better tell the prince."

With that she collapsed into a faint.

THE NEXT DAY, while Janela rested, I sought an audience with the prince. I did not tell him all that had occurred, for Janela insisted that knowledge of things such as our possession of the magical box should remain a secret.

"It's a wizard's natural caution," she said. "We always like to hold at least a few things back—if not all. More to the point, however, is we don't want to alert the demons. Oh, they'll know something is up—if they don't already—and they'll learn soon enough some of what I plan. But the more I can keep secret, the better our chances of surprising them."

She sipped the frothy elixir she'd prepared to restore her vitality. "Besides, there is still much to know about that box. I want to study it at my leisure, with many safeguards in place. Not only for the reasons you think.

"If you recall, my dear Amalric, we still have King Azbaas' demon inside. When we let him out, I assure you he won't be a happy fellow."

With those cautions I approached the prince and told him enough to convince him that Janela had made an important discovery. And that if the discovery were put to a proper use it might turn the demon tide.

It took Janela two days to recover from her ordeal and a little over a week to prepare for her demonstration. A fat purse convinced the tavern owner to close his doors to the public and take a holiday while Janela had the floor removed and the bath chamber door opened for easier access to the underground palace.

When all was ready, the prince summoned the wisest wizards, as well as the city's most important men and women, and bade them to attend Janela's demonstration. He urged his father to come as well, but the old king said he would have nothing to do with such foolishness.

"The very idea," he was reported to have said, "that a barbarian magus—and a woman to boot—should instruct our learned wizards is ludicrous to the extreme."

But the prince was so impassioned that Ignati at least didn't forbid it. He called his son a goosecap and said the lesson in humiliation he would learn might serve to temper his judgment when he assumed the throne.

When the day came for Janela's demonstration, however, I saw that the king's attitude had crept into the gathering that assembled outside the tavern. There were cynical mutterings and much rolling of eyes as Janela and I led them through the bath chamber door and retraced our steps to King Farsun's ancient court chamber.

During the journey Lord Tobray and Lord Vakram were the most vocal in their complaints and made the greatest faces whenever Janela spoke. Tobray, who after all was Chief Wizard and King Ignati's closest adviser, didn't surprise me. Vakram, however, did. Although he'd at first raised objections to our training the Tyrenian forces, he'd reverted to his old hail-fellow self once that training got under way. Moreover, he'd made no objection when I'd put Janela's request before Prince Solaros. But now that I thought on it, I recalled he hadn't said anything in favor of it, either.

The comments and childish grimaces ceased the moment we entered the court chamber. The men and women stared in awe at the ghostly tableau. Amazed glances took in the remains of the banquet, which looked as if it had been interrupted in the middle of the feast.

They gawked at the thrones and the upturned goblet, which Janela had replaced precisely as she'd found it.

But their ill-humor sparked when Janela asked them to be seated at the edge of the court chamber in chairs she'd had provided; and grew into full flame when they saw the assembled objects and magical implements she'd laid out on a long table nearby.

Janela ignored their sour looks and began as if they were all wise and kind and true.

"My lords and ladies," she said, her voice confident and strong, "thank you for coming today. I doubly thank you for being so amiable as to listen to a wizard such as I without judging me an ignorant upstart. I know you all have reputations for open and inquisitive minds. It is in that spirit of inquiry and discovery that I approach you with my findings.

"Ours is a demanding and sometimes dangerous art. So dangerous, in fact, it is the reason given for keeping the curious but unblessed by Talent at wand's length. Although it is not an area I will dwell on today, I should warn you that in the near future secrecy may not only be impossible, but harmful. For if I am correct, every man, woman, or child—even improperly trained—can perform and *will* perform feats which in the past could only be done by men and women such as ourselves."

There was grumbling and much rude laughter at this last comment.

"I suppose the street sweeper will dispose of pig dung with a finger snap," Vakram said to his neighbor, loudly enough for all to hear and to spur further laughter. "He'll turn it to gold and then he'll no longer sweep our streets but retire to a villa which he'll conjure up with another snap."

Tobray, as scoffing as the others, was at least manful enough to direct his remarks at Janela.

"We've all heard such nonsense before," he said, to a rumble of agreement from the others. "The fact of the matter is the gods, for reasons we cannot fathom, bless only a few with sorcerous Talent. Even then it is in varying degrees. A market witch can cure the warts on a cow's udder. I, on the other hand, can stop—or create—a plague of those blemishes."

"Without delving too deeply into your belief in the source of such ability," Janela replied, "I will accept the remainder of your statement as law, not theory. Some are better than others. There is a wide gulf between a mere practitioner and a genius such as yourself."

Tobray coughed at the flattery, but I noticed he did not deny it.

"In any human endeavor, there is a difference in ability," Janela said. "Anyone can pipe a flute. Even make a pleasant sound—with practice and training, of course. But few can claim the ability to beguile us like a master musician. When I said all could perform sorcery, I did not mean they would be able to do so with equal ability.

"And talent or genius aside, who would want to? Not everyone would give up a normal life with normal loves and simple pleasures that we have denied ourselves."

When she said that, I thought of Gamelan, the Evocator who had befriended Rali, and how he'd confessed that he'd been forced to give up the love of his life for magic, and how bitterly he'd resented it the rest of his days.

"But as I said," Janela continued, "that is not the subject of my remarks today. It is only one of many logical outcomes. I think if you will only give me a fair hearing you will eventually agree."

"Very well, my Lady Greycloak," Tobray said. "You shall have it. Carry on, if you please."

Despite his diplomatic words, I noted his features were hard with doubt.

"As you all know," Janela said, "it was my ancestor's theory that all things obey the same laws, and that in a manner of speaking all things are created through similar means and even with some similarities in content. It is the arrangement and structure of these things that make the difference."

She smiled at Vakram. "There very well could be gold in pig shit," she said. "It depends on what that pig ate. But there can't be pig shit in gold unless you frequent a very bad jeweler, for gold is pure in itself."

Vakram's neighbor laughed, drawing a scowl.

"But even gold, pure as it is, can be broken down further. Using magic, its particles can be released—although I don't think you'd want to do so casually. Besides the financial loss, my calculations show that such a division would unleash a terrible force."

"Come now, my lady," Tobray broke in. "Gold has no force other than what I impart." He drew off a gold bracelet and tossed it to her. "Such as when I exercise my arm to throw it to you."

Janela caught the bracelet. She held it up high for all to see, turning this way and that as if it should be of the most absorbing importance.

"You saw him throw it?" she asked them all.

And everyone agreed they did.

"Lord Tobray has just demonstrated quite ably several natural forces at play," she said. "One was the force he imparted to the object. The second was the disturbance the object made as it moved through the air. The third was its fall as it approached me. The fourth, the force I absorbed when I retrieved it."

Tobray made an impatient noise. "Yes, yes. We've all heard of your illustrious ancestor's theories on such matters. Some of us have even read them, and some of our younger members have wasted valuable time in experimentation."

A few youthful faces in the audience ducked in embarrassment or looked stubbornly defiant.

"Janos Greycloak, for instance," Tobray continued, "said light may have substance. This may be so. But what can one *do* with such knowledge—if it is indeed true? I cannot eat it. I cannot form it into a tool. So what earthly use can it have besides lighting our way or disturbing our sleep?"

"Earthly use?" Janela said. "Why, there are many. But I won't take your time with such an accounting. For it is the *unearthly* use of it that I want you to consider . . . as I shall demonstrate."

She held up the bracelet again. Then she picked up a goblet and dropped the bracelet inside. We heard a satisfying rattle. Janela waved a hand and the goblet glowed.

"Now it is light."

She shook the goblet and we heard nothing. She picked up another tumbler, held it a foot or more beneath the first, then poured.

The wizards gasped as light flowed like water from one goblet to the next. Some of the liquid even spilled to the floor and made glowing droplets. Janela took an experimental sip from the light-filled tumbler. Her brows arced as if in pleasant surprise.

She wiped a faint phosphorescent trace from her upper lip. "Why, it tastes like . . . light!"

She gave the goblet to Tobray, who examined it critically. He, too, took a sip, and amazement crossed his features. Then he passed it on for the others to examine and sample.

"It was good you gave me gold, my lord," Janela said. "For that is the metal light most resembles. It would have not been so easy to concentrate using something else. A feather, for instance."

Vakram snorted. "A parlor trick, nothing more," he said. "Any of us could do it with a little practice."

"I said you could from the start, my lord," Janela said.

There was laughter, and Vakram flushed.

"Still," he said, "it's sorcery. Nothing more."

"Yes," Janela agreed. "Nothing more, except a demonstration of magical force behaving like an ordinary liquid and obeying ordinary laws. I tilted the goblet and it had no choice but to pour.

"As for the trick being simple sorcery, that is only partly true. The trick required energy, although I did not draw on the power required from the usual sources. As an aside, you might have noted I made no chant, nor did I use any magical ingredients."

She looked about the crowd. "Would you all agree that magic requires energy and produces energy—sometimes seeming like more is produced than is drawn?"

There were mutters and nods of agreement.

"Would you also agree that you draw that energy from . . . elsewhere . . . which is why more force may be displayed than is easily observable to the casual viewer?"

Some frowned, but many repeated the nods and murmurs of acceptance, especially the younger wizards Tobray had scorned.

"And that energy you use is finite, and sometimes when you cast your mind to that . . . other place . . . too soon after your first action, there is not enough left to repeat the spell. So you must cast . . . farther, so to speak, to find more?"

Fewer still agreed. But those who did beamed as if in sudden understanding.

"I won't ask you to take my word for these things," Janela said. "That is against the very nature of my great-grandfather's beliefs. All assumptions must be tested and tested again. Afterward, if you are interested, I will show you how I conducted my experiments, and where I found my insights—many of which are from your own archives."

When she said that, many who seemed in doubt relaxed. Tobray was in this group. It heartened me to see that he, at least, had a practical mind and sound instincts.

"What did you mean, my lady," he asked, "when you said you used a different energy source for the bracelet trick?"

"Why, I got it from the power produced when you threw and I retrieved," Janela said.

"That's not possible!" Vakram snapped.

He seemed worried, although I couldn't make out why. He hadn't a reputation as a wizard who proposed ideas that were worthy of threat.

"As I said, my lord," Janela replied, "you may test all I've claimed afterward. But I tell you, my fellow magi, that *any* power can be used for sorcerous purposes. Just as your breath has force enough to turn a child's wheel toy, it can also power a small bit of magic, such as sweetening your breath if you fouled it at lunch with a garlic dish." Janela grinned. "But I doubt it's enough to sweeten a foul temper."

There was much laughter at Vakram's expense. He glowered about him, which only made everyone laugh louder. But when his eyes caught the prince's wide grin, he quickly turned away.

Janela moved on. "Now, we can all speculate quite easily on what forces are at work in this, the common world. The natural world. There is heat and light, the force that makes things fall, the force that draws a compass needle, the various forces imparted by motion and that displayed when lightning strikes. And so on and so forth.

"Then there are uncommon forces. The forces of the spiritual, of magic and sorcery. Which again take may forms. All of which I think may someday prove to be mere counterparts of common forces. The opposite side of the coin, if you will."

"What of the gods, my lady?" Tobray asked.

"What of them?" Janela said. "They must obey the same laws as you and I. If they exist at all."

There were gasps at this heresy. But I noted the gasps were few. There were more doubters than I would have imagined in Farsun's ghostly court chamber.

"Are you saying magic is no more important than these other forces?" Tobray asked quite calmly, showing by his mild tones that he was among those doubters.

"It isn't a question of importance, my lord," Janela answered. "Use determines such things. If I need to cook that garlic dish Lord Vakram favors, then heat must rule or he will go hungry or eat a poor meal."

Vakram flushed deeply but said nothing. The laughter was subdued. Janela saw her mistake in pressing her advantage over an already defeated opponent and shifted ground.

"The real importance," she said, "is that all the forces we've discussed—and those we skimmed over—are actually one force. We separate it only because that is what we observe. Heat cooks. Light lights. And so on."

"It's as if there were one god," Tobray said, "but with many faces. And we see the face we wish to see or are forced to."

"And that god—" Janela began.

"—would be a force himself," Tobray completed for her. "And therefore merely a part of the whole."

"Assuming," Janela said, "that He—or She—exists."

"Yes, yes," Tobray muttered. "Assuming that."

Vakram roused himself. "Might I be so bold, my lady," he said, "to ask a question and be spared your sharp wit?"

"I'm sorry for that," Janela answered. "I was nervous from being in such august company and spoke without thinking."

Vakram nodded but I knew he hadn't accepted her apology. "My question is this: What does it matter if there is one force or many? As Lord Tobray so aptly put it, I cannot eat this knowledge. Even with garlic. And I cannot form it into anything useful."

"You can by using the tools you are most adept at, my lord," Janela replied. "Which are your magical tools. It is the practice of sorcery, not religion, that leads not only to understanding, but the ability to manipulate at will."

She waved to the table of objects. "I had many things I was going to use to demonstrate," she said. "But I don't think it's necessary now. I'll teach any and all of you my methods. And in my notes you'll find my proofs. I'm certain I erred in many things. I was in a rush. Even if I did, I'd stake my life on the results.

"As for practical use, why, that is the only reason I pleaded for this assemblage. If it were merely academic, I would have spoken to you separately."

"You mean the demons?" the prince broke in. "You've found a way to turn your knowledge into a spear against the demons?" His eyes sparkled with youthful hope.

"Yes, Your Highness," Janela said. "I believe I have."

She swiveled, pointing to a pair of the tree's great roots.

"You have all seen the tree that towers over these ruins," she said. "Just as you all know it is magical."

"We do indeed, my lady," Tobray said. "But its magic isn't of any importance. The tree is just a pretty that makes a day more pleasant for lovers."

"I beg your forgiveness for contradicting you, my lord," Janela said, "but it is more than a romantic pretty. If you examine it you will see it gives off more power than it could possibly require for its needs. The very demonstration I made with the gold bracelet was much easier to perform because we are in its presence.

"I believe it and its kinds were bred to produce such energy, like flowers are improved by gardeners for their fragrance. It was grown here for a purpose of vast importance in your history. Its presence, sirs and ladies, is not the result of idle fancy, but the design of a witch who discovered a magical spring that is twin to or even the same spring that flowed in her homeland."

"Where does the tree get this power, my lady?" Tobray asked.

"From the world the demons rule," Janela answered. "From the realm of King Ba'land himself."

The wizards were rocked by this. Loud argument raged between them until Tobray brought them to order with an imperious wave of his hand.

"Please explain further, my lady," he said.

"Gladly," Janela said. "The tree draws on the power of the demons' natural world—if you can imagine such a thing—just as they draw on ours. Except they are leeches, consuming all they can. Especially human misery, a force we haven't spoken of. But it's there, my lords and ladies. It's there. And it is that hunger for our misery and greed for our resources that drives them, that has led them to ravage us all these thousands of years.

"You should know this as well. All that is common in our world is magical in theirs. And all that is common there is magical here. Which is what the tree feeds on—the tree that can give us an entirely different kind of power. That is: power over our enemies."

Another uproar. But this time I heard no debate. These were long-suffering people, anxious to grasp at the smallest hope.

"You all know the story," Janela said, "of King Farsun and his queen, Monavia."

There was a buzz of agreement.

"We know it well," Tobray said, smiling. "It's one of Tyrenia's most popular children's fables. The good queen and the cowardly king. The demon who lusted after and used his evil to win the dancer."

Solaros broke in, adding, "And the prince who was kept in the tower by his father's cowardice." He looked around at the others. "You didn't know that, did you?" he said. "That's part of the tale that's never told. Lord Antero recited it to me just the other day. Just another example of the things Lady Greycloak has dug up that have been under our noses all along."

Janela laughed. "Thank you, Your Highness," she said. "I couldn't have begged a greater testimonial than that."

She took a deep breath, as if resigning herself about what was to come. She withdrew the figurine of the dancer from her sleeve.

"Do you all recognize this, lords and ladies?" she asked.

"Indeed we do," Tobray said. "It was once a popular toy in Tyrenia. Any number of them were produced."

Bitter humor filled me when I heard that. So much had been gambled, twice, counting Janos, for what turned out to be a child's amusement.

"I am going to attempt to show you the true story of Farsun and Monavia," Janela said. "And in that story you will readily see how we can confound the demons."

Janela turned to me. She smiled, but I could see she wasn't looking forward to her final demonstration.

"Amalric," she said, "I'm likely to be affected as before. I've put some things by my bedside, and written directions as well. Will you administer them to me . . . if I cannot do it myself?"

"I think we should give the entire thing a miss," I said. "It's too dangerous."

"But necessary nevertheless," Janela said.

With that, she walked out to the stone platform, placed the doll in the center, and retreated.

She bowed her head in concentration. The light dimmed and the room was hushed as the familiar scene of the tiny dancing maid shimmered into view. Then the dancer vanished, leaving only the doll-like figures of the courtiers.

Janela made a great motion and we all gasped as the scene blossomed larger and larger until it filled the chamber we sat in. We became a shadowy audience peering into a past that lived again. We heard the low chatter of the courtiers as if we were among them. We listened to the music swelling from the instruments the musicians played in the pit. The air was warm from all the bodies present, and as I gaped about the court chamber I could see it was all new again. Gone were the cobweb mantles, gone were the invasive tree roots, gone was the feeling of long-dead ghosts.

The banquet table groaned under the weight of fresh and tempting food. The smell of delicious sauces and spices mingled with the pleasing aroma of delicate incense. Jolly servants passed among the crowd, refilling their plates and goblets.

But there was an evil edge to the festive spirit. There was an aftertaste in the air we breathed of sour demon flesh. Now I saw the demon courtiers moving through the crowd, and in the private viewing box King Ba'land glared out with his single yellow eye. I looked over at the thrones and saw that Tyrenia's monarch, King Farsun, was sullen and drunk. Queen Monavia sat beside him, attempting a gay smile at something a jester said. But she seemed pensive, as if waiting for something to happen.

Then Ba'land roared, "Your court is wearisome tonight, sir." The music stopped and the court chamber grew silent. Farsun shrunk and grabbed up another wine cup to hide his shame at being so rudely addressed.

"Where is the dancer?" the demon demanded. "Where is Thalila? Bring her on, if you please!"

Farsun gulped down the last of the wine and motioned for a

servant to fill it again. "Yes, yes," he said. "You are right, my friend. I was growing bored myself." He clapped his hands, signaling for the dancer.

The musicians piped the overture and all eyes—both past and present—swiveled to the dancing platform.

It was as if an invisible curtain had parted as the maid twirled into view. She was as beautiful and seductive as ever. But before, her sensuality had sprung from innocence, as if the lovely maid was unaware of the musical musk that emanated from her dance and infused the air.

This time, this dance, the innocence was gone. Thalila danced like a courtesan. Each thrust of hip and bounce of breast begged a caress. Her eyes burned with sinful wisdom and her fingers traced slow, graceful paths along her fine white limbs. Her lips were swollen, entreating a kiss. Her slender thighs trembled to be parted and pierced.

I was as aroused as I have ever been in my life. My member rose up and became like the engorged snake that had once hunted Melina, the woman who stole my innocence and left only a faint trace of her hot perfume, which still disturbs my sleep. For a moment I was even carnal twin to King Ba'land, who gnashed his teeth and roared obscenities at the dancer.

I tore my eyes away to shed her spell. I glanced at the thrones and saw that Queen Monavia had gone, while King Farsun was slumped over, snoring in a drunken stupor.

When I had somewhat recovered I looked back and noticed for the first time that Thalila held a rose in one hand. She ran the blossoms along her body and waved it teasingly at the demon king, smiling coyly and casting her eyes down. The demon squirmed in lustful pleasure, his talons needling out and withdrawing, over and over again.

Then horror chilled what passion remained as I saw Thalila dance off the platform and twirl toward Ba'land. She teased him for a time, coming forward, then retreating. But each sequence took her closer to him, until she stood before his box. She laughed and held out the rose. Ba'land's paw stretched—slowly, as if in wonder at her offer. Then he grinned hugely and snatched the rose from her hand.

He kissed the flower and held it up for all to see. His demon courtiers bellowed their approval. Thalila twirled gaily about, her gossamer veil swirling around her naked hips. Once again she stepped
forward, and a pretty hand darted out and plucked a single petal
from the rose. The demon reached for her but she danced away,
shaking a teasing finger.

Ba'land rose from his seat and threw open the gate to his box.
He lumbered toward Thalila but she retreated, moving back until
she once more stood on the platform.

There she waited. Still. Trembling. Ba'land mounted the platform and went to her. He stopped, his yellow eye glaring at the
court chamber crowd.

"Leave us!" he shouted. And the courtiers, human and demon
alike, made a hasty retreat.

He turned back to Thalila. I thought I saw her shudder, but if
she did, she quickly recovered, lifting up her lovely face to smile at
the demon. Ba'land clawed her into his embrace, his black cloak
covering them both.

The court chamber was empty now, save for King Farsun, snoring on his throne.

There was a stirring among our group. We thought it was over
and were frankly puzzled at the purpose of the display. Then
Janela's shadowy form moved and the scene of the unlikely lovers
dissolved before our eyes—to be replaced by another.

We found ourselves looking into the room of the queen's witch.
It had been empty when Janela and I first saw it. Now it contained
a small, lacquered table covered with sorcerous symbols. Against
one wall was a case filled with odd-shaped containers. The others
were covered with tapestries with mysterious scenes woven into
them. And standing at the table, grinding ingredients in a crucible,
was a woman in a witch's cloak. She was tall, with striking features,
and when I looked close I could see her resemblance to the Lake
People. There were several silver leaves next to the crucible, which
I realized were from the magical tree. She put them in and ground
them up, one by one.

The door opened and Queen Monavia entered. "The king
sleeps," she said. "We must hurry, Komana."

The witch said nothing but continued grinding with her pestle. There was a tap at the door and both women turned, startled. Then came a series of taps and they relaxed. The queen opened the door.

To my surprise, I saw the dancer enter. She looked frighteningly young and vulnerable in the white robe she'd donned since we saw her last. There was a faint trail of blood on her cheek.

"Ba'land waits for me in his chamber," she said. " I have to go soon or he will become suspicious."

The queen embraced her. "I'm so sorry, Thalila," she said. "If only there were another way—"

"Well, there isn't!" the witch broke in. "And do not pity her. There's a price we all must pay for this night's work."

Komana gestured to the dancer. "The rose petal. Where is it?"

The dancer fumbled it from her sleeve. The witch snatched it and turned back to her work.

Monavia and the dancer looked at one another for what seemed an eternity.

"I will love no other but you," Thalila said.

"And I, you," the queen replied.

"Ba'land may possess me," the dancer said. "But he will receive only coldness, only hate from my embrace."

The queen wiped a tear. Then they both kissed, a long, lingering meeting of lips.

"I'm ready now," the witch said.

The two lovers parted. After one last look, the dancer fled the room, her feet a ghostly patter on an ungentle stone floor.

The witch moved to the stone altar and drew out the box set in its center. She lifted the lid, set the petal inside, then closed it again. Long witch fingers pinched powder from the mortar on the table and sprinkled it over the box. The powder sparkled as it floated down to coat the engraving of the dancer.

Komana chanted:

"Life from darkness,
Grace from evil;
Part the demon curtain
And let us walk free.

Dancer to rose
And rose to dancer
And power
From a demon's kiss.
There is no barrier
From one world
To the next."

And I saw an eerie light glowing through the box.

But the witch wasn't done. Komana set the box aside, then lifted a jug, poured clear water into the crucible, and quickly mixed the dregs. I needed no one to tell me that the water was from the underground spring. Then the silvery liquid the witch created was poured into a small goblet.

She gave it to the queen, saying, "Fill your mouth with it, Your Highness, and hold it until the proper time. Don't let one drop trickle down your throat, for it will kill you, and then where will your son be?"

The queen nodded. "I understand," she said.

We all watched as if in a trance as she did the witch's bidding.

Next came the box. Without instruction Queen Monavia opened it and removed the petal.

She shuddered as she took it, and the witch moved quickly to grab the box as it fell from her hand.

The queen stood still, as if frozen. And then we saw a most marvelous form float from her body. It was the queen's other self, a self that I had once been, if only for a moment. The queen's ghostly self shimmered with life and power. She didn't hesitate but walked away, the witch staring after her.

Monavia's spirit didn't bother with the door. She walked through it, leaving her temporal body behind. We were amazed witnesses to her progress, watching her move down long corridors through the walls of other rooms, past men and women who did not see her ghostly form.

Finally we were back in the darkened court chamber with the remains of the abandoned feast—and King Farsun, who snored on his throne, his wine goblet still clutched in his hand.

The queenly ghost floated to him. She leaned over, gently turned his head, and spit the liquid into his ear.

She floated back, smiling at her husband. And she said: "Wake up, my lord and master."

King Farsun groaned up, silvery drops spilling onto his cheek. He brushed at them absently.

"Who's there?" he demanded.

And she said, "Hurry, my lord. Your son awaits your throne."

"Monavia?" he said, peering this way and that but not seeing his wife's spirit. "Where are you?"

He shook himself. "Too much drink," he muttered. "The bitch gives me nightmares. But wait till she sees her son's head. I'll cut if off tomorrow. Then we'll learn whose dreams are sweeter!"

The queen's other self laughed, and it was like garden chimes in a soft wind.

King Farsun swiveled, nearly falling from his seat as he looked to see where the sound came from.

Then the poison struck and he shrieked in agony, flinging his wine goblet to the floor and clutching his ear. The pain must have been awful from his cry.

Our blood turned cold, but the queen only laughed and floated away.

When the doors slammed open and the alarmed courtiers poured in, their queen was safely gone and their king lay dead on the floor.

Confusion reigned in that room for long minutes as the court-iers ran about, saying, "What's to be done?" and "What could have happened?" and "I blame the doctors for this! They should have known he was unwell."

A hush fell as Queen Monavia came through the doors. This was the *real* Monavia, not the murderous ghost we had seen. She had a robe cast carelessly over her sleeping clothes as if she had dressed in a hurry. She saw the king on the floor and walked over—quite calm—ignoring the whispered condolences of her subjects. She brushed aside the doctors and knelt down by the corpse.

Monavia stared long at her husband's florid face.

Then she hissed, "Coward!" And spat in it.

The courtiers were plainly shocked, although we saw nods of satisfaction from some. But they said nothing as their queen rose and turned to them.

She said: "My husband is dead, no doubt from over-indulgence."

There were murmurs of agreement.

Monavia continued. "I want my son released tonight. He'll assume the throne tomorrow, and despite the ill treatment he received at his father's hands, I expect he'll declare an appropriate period of mourning."

The courtiers murmured approval. There were many smiles breaking out now that it was plain which way the winds would blow. Farsun had not been a popular king.

The queen looked at the remains of the feast and wrinkled her lips in disgust. "This has been a most shameful time in our history," she said. "And this room and this palace have seen us all humiliated by Ba'land and his fiends. But that has ended, lords and ladies. My son, I expect, will order them from Tyrenia the instant he dons the crown.

"As for this chamber, none of us are ever again to set foot in this hall of shame. I want it closed up, you hear? Leave everything as it is. And shut the doors.

"The first thing I shall urge my son to do is to empty this entire palace and seal it off. We can build another, more worthy home for our monarchs. And I, for one, shall not sleep another night in these halls."

The queen stalked out amidst the applause of her citizens.

Then I heard Janela sigh; the scene dissolved, and we were all back in the cobwebbed court chamber again.

My heart leaped when I saw Janela sprawled over the dancer's platform. I ran to her and lifted her up. She gave me a weak smile.

"Did they see how it was done, Amalric?" she asked.

"Yes," I said. "Now rest, my dear."

Tobray leaned over us. "Do as he says, my lady. We can discuss this later."

"Still," she said. "You understand now, don't you? There's a gateway here. A gateway to the demon world."

"Yes, yes," Tobray said. "I understand. Now rest. When you are well you can teach us how to open it."

Janela nodded, then closed her eyes and slept. I didn't think I have ever seen her look so peaceful.

I TOOK HER BACK to her room and put her to bed. I followed the instructions she left, dribbling elixirs between her lips. Then I disrobed her and bathed her slender body with sweet-smelling potions, working them in as tenderly as I once cared for my own daughter, gone to the Seeker so many years now.

I covered her up and was about to depart when she murmured for me to stay. So I curled up beside her and held her until I, too, slept.

Late that night I was startled awake. Janela was up, hastily pulling on a robe.

"What's happening?" I said, speech slurred by sleep. "Get back in bed. You're ill."

Janela ignored this, saying, "Come with me, Amalric! Quickly!"

I bounded up and followed her out of the room. We ran to my son's quarters and I cursed when I saw the open door and the sentry asleep at his post.

"Sorcery!" Janela hissed and ran inside.

The other sentry was slumped on the floor, also victim of a spell.

Another body made a heap in the center of the room. But this was a corpse—and blood was spattered about him in a wide circle.

It was Lord Modin.

Fear added strength to my limbs and I burst ahead of Janela and flung open Cligus' door.

The room was a welter of blood. My son was stretched out on the gory sheets of his bed, his eyes fixed on the ceiling in a dead man's stare.

I stood over him, the room spinning as if I were at the center of a devil's top.

Janela's voice slipped through the mad whirl: "They aren't just dead, Amalric. They've been drained. Soul and all."

"Who?" I said, limbs numb. "Who did this?"

"Only a demon could have done it," she said. "And even then . . . it was very powerful."

"King Ba'land?" I asked.

"Yes," she said. "King Ba'land."

CHAPTER NINETEEN

JOURNEY'S END

The grief I experienced over Cligus' murder nearly overwhelmed me. If someone had said only a day before that I would feel so wounded I'd have called him a liar. But when I saw the soulless husk that was his corpse, all the pent-up emotion, all the anger and the guilt, joined with a whole confusion of other human frailties to paralyze me. I didn't weep. I didn't faint. I stood there unable to move, gazing at the man the gods had decreed would be my son.

Weak as she was, Janela summoned strength enough to send for Quatervals to do what was necessary, and then, assisted by Pip, helped me back into our quarters. She gave me a draught to make me sleep, then held me in her arms until weariness overtook her.

But we didn't rest long. In the morning there came a hammering on our suite's outer door. I heard voices, and as I struggled into awareness, Quatervals was tapping at our chamber entrance and saying we had been summoned by the king.

Still numb from the potion, I grumbled up to splash water on my face and don my clothes. Janela stirred and asked what was wrong.

"The king calls," I said. "You go back to sleep. I can deal with him myself."

"Beggin' your pardon, my lord," Quatervals broke in, his voice tight with worry. "But the messenger says you *both* must attend his majesty. I tried to argue, but there's king's soldiers in the hall to make certain his orders are carried out."

Janela bolted up. "What's wrong?" she asked. Her face was gray from fatigue and her eyes were feverish. I didn't have to look twice to see she would take much longer to recover her strength than the last time she'd been stricken.

But I could only repeat what Quatervals had said, for when a king sends his messenger—and that messenger comes with soldiers attached to his message—you'd best follow his commands to the letter.

FOR SUPPOSED HEROES we made a less than glorious entrance when we entered King Ignati's court.

It was as gloomy as before, with only the throne area lit, and the soldiers seemed nervous as they ushered us across the floor, which was engraved with the names of so many of their own heroes. It seemed to me that they performed their task with reluctance and no little shame.

And they seemed as startled as I was when we saw the demon standing next to Ignati's throne.

He was large, as most demons are, and shaped like a lizard. But this lizard stood on two feet like the reptiles who run with the jackals in the hills outside Jeypur. His snout was broad, his eyes were small red coals, and he had venomous sacs on either side of his neck that were engorged and scarlet with anger.

As we approached, a feathery snakelike tongue darted out from his snout, tasting the air for our fear. "So these be the mortals," he hissed, "that have given so much trouble to my king."

Ignati glared down at us from his throne. "It's my kind heart that's to blame," he said. "Shouldn't have tried to please the rabble. Isn't that so, Tobray?"

I wrenched my gaze from the demon to see who else was with us. Besides the soldiers and a few other guards, I saw only Tobray at first. Then I spotted Vakram's long form leaning lazily against a far wall, and I wondered what he was doing here. I did not see his master, Prince Solaros.

Then I realized Tobray hadn't answered and turned back to see the king glowering at his chief wizard.

"I *said*," the king repeated, "isn't that so, Tobray?"

The wizard seemed disturbed as he forced an answer. But it was not the answer I expected.

"In this case, Your Majesty," he said, "I believe you have been wise in listening to your people."

The demon emissary hissed displeasure. "How dare you address your king in that manner? Are you a fool or a traitor?"

Ignati squirmed. He plainly didn't like the demon taking such liberties with his own man. Even if he plans to have you beheaded, no king appreciates such open interference from an outsider. The way a monarch sees it, he might as well be introducing a termite queen to his throne.

"Yes, yes," the king said to the demon. "I quite understand your pique, Yasura. But pay no mind to Tobray. He's a good fellow. Means well. Only saying what he thinks. Which I like to encourage in my court." And then he added, reflexively, "Isn't that so, Tobray?"

Tobray gulped. "Yes, you do, Your Majesty. That is what makes you a great sovereign. And if I am to continue to serve Your Majesty honestly and faithfully, I must again risk your wrath and beg you to spurn this demon—and any of his king's demands."

My estimation for the wizard grew immensely. It's nothing for a brave man to say a brave thing. But for one such as Tobray, it was an act of extreme courage.

"Do you want war?" Yasura screeched.

Ignati shook his head. "Of course we don't. And I wish you wouldn't use that word. Can't two reasonable kings differ on a teensy thing or two without shouting war this and war that?"

His hand came out as if to give the demon a placating pat, then he snatched it away scant inches before he touched the demon's scales.

I sallied into the gap. "What is it we have done, Your Majesty?" I asked. "Have we violated any of Tyrenia's laws? I can't see how we could. All our actions have been in the open, and we sought and received your permission every step of the way."

Prince Solaros' voice rang out. "That's absolutely true, Father."

The prince, boiling out of a small private entrance, rushed to the throne breathless, clothes in disarray from hurried dressing.

"Before we get into that, Father," he said, "I must beg you to tell me why I wasn't notified of this meeting. You know my friendship for these two. And you know my deep interest in our future relations with King Ba'land."

Ignati snorted. "I also knew you'd try to interfere," he said. "The time for that sort of thing has passed. Much at stake here. Much at stake. Take my word for it."

The prince eyed Vakram. "And what are you doing here, my lord?"

Vakram remained at ease. He did not seem troubled by his prince's displeasure. "Observing, Your Highness," he said. "Nothing more."

"I find it odd," Solaros said, "that my personal wizard should attend such an affair without notifying me."

Before a confrontation could erupt, Ignati swatted the air as if the whole matter was all a buzzing of pesky flies. "Lord Yasura requested his presence, my son," he said. "He wanted details of that little incident in the old palace."

The king shook his head. "I must say it seemed a nasty business. All my wizards taken in by a charlatan. And a gods-denying charlatan, at that?"

"If you had attended yourself, Majesty," Janela said, "you might have acquired a different view."

"View of what?" Ignati snarled. "Parlor tricks and war mongering, from what I've heard."

"It is King Ba'land who seeks this crisis, Father," the prince said. "He makes demands on us that will leave us helpless if we agree. And all his demands are unconditional. That's war talk if I ever heard it."

"And what is the intent of your recent military training, Your Highness," the demon said, "if not to make war?"

"There's that word again," the king said. "War, war. I wish we'd all start using more positive language. Peace is so much nicer on the tongue. It has a sound like a tempting dish. Pear, for instance. In a sauce of cherry wine. Whereas war, why that sounds like . . ." The king racked his brain, then shrugged. "Well, I don't know what it sounds like in particular. But if I *did* think of something, I'm certain it would be nasty."

Despite his silly talk, I could see that Ignati's temper was beginning to fray.

"King Ba'land insists this training must stop," Yasura said.

Ignati nodded. He turned to the prince. "There you go," he said. "That's not so difficult a demand. And if you think on it, my son, you can see how one's, ah, former, ah, competitors—that's it . . . competitors—might take offense at our actions." He looked at Yasura. "Which were merely to keep our forces from growing bored. Yes, that's it. The training was merely for the purposes of improving morale . . . Isn't that so, Tobray?"

The wizard started to answer, but the king quickly waved for silence. "Never mind," he said. "Can't tell what may come from your mouth these days, Tobray. I say, are you feeling quite well?"

The demon hissed, impatient. "More will be required than that, Your Majesty," he said.

The king looked at him sharply. "I must speak to your master," he said, "about his choice in representatives. I don't appreciate fellows who run around *requiring* me to do things. I wear the crown here, and if there's any requiring to be done, I'll do it. On the other hand if there's a *request* you want, why request away, sir. A good king considers all requests."

The demon bowed. "As you wish, Your Highness," he said. "Request it shall be. However, it should be noted these are very *firm* requests."

The king frowned at this dicing of terms. Then he nodded. "What is it exactly that your master requests, then?"

Yasura looked at us. "Punishment," he said.

Ignati looked relieved. "That's quite reasonable," he said. "Tell him that I shall severely punish these two." Then to Solaros: "You see how simple it is, son?"

"I fear that won't be satisfactory," the demon said. "King Ba'land requires more than your reassurance."

Ignati looked concerned. "How's that?" he said.

The demon emissary didn't answer, but only stared hard at the king. The king broke first.

"You can see how it is?" he said to Janela and myself. "My subjects' lives against your own. But rest assured I shall person-ally"—and he glared at Yasura—"*request* that King Ba'land dispose of you quickly, with as little torment as possible."

He smiled at Yasura. "There you go," he said. "Problem solved. Misunderstandings set straight."

Solaros boiled forward. "I won't permit it, Father!" he cried. "Lady Greycloak and Lord Antero are under *my* protection. Ba'land might as well ask for *my* life as theirs!"

"That, too, can be arranged, Your Highness," the demon said.

Ignati was shocked. Then the shock turned to fury and he tore at his beard. "How *dare* you?" he shouted. "How dare you threaten the life of my son? And don't tell me it was a slip of that filthy thing you call a tongue! You are impertinent to the extreme and you shall languish in my dungeons, sir, for that impertinence until your master sends me his immediate apologies. And that is a firm *requirement*, sir, not a request!"

He turned to his wizard. "Isn't that so, Tobray?"

Tobray smiled hugely. "As usual, Your Majesty," he said, "your choice of words is perfection itself."

The king nodded, pleased. Order had once more been restored to his court.

Then he said, "Guards, remove Lord Yasura from my presence. You know where to put him. I needn't spell it out."

The soldiers grinned, snapped salutes, and started forward.

"You see?" the king said to his son. "That's how it's done. Mark well my actions for your future reference when I am gone. Speak kindly but never let the other fellow mistake kindness for weakness. Isn't that so—"

"Enough of this foolishness!" Vakram shouted. He shot up from his perch and stalked toward the throne.

"Beware!" Janela cried, running forward. "It's Ba'land!"

She drew her dagger as she ran. I didn't ask, I didn't ponder, but drew my own dirk and leaped after her.

Vakram turned to face us. He roared, and as he did, flesh peeled from his face and a snout exploded through, showering us with flesh and blood, and his body twisted up and up, scaly bone and muscle rending his courtly wizard robe; and he was Ba'land, the demon king, and his single eye was a horrible torch of fury, his breath a hot sulfurous reek, and his hands were gory talons that stretched out for us.

Smoke and fire burst from those talons with such force that we were hurled back many feet. As we lay there another burst struck us and I was screaming agony and then had no breath and was fighting to draw it in but all that came seared my lungs.

Then stillness. A shudder of cool air. I could breathe. But I couldn't move. I heard Janela groan beside me.

Ba'land stood over us. His fangs parted in a yellow sneer. Then he turned away as if we needed no further attention.

I could see two guards slumped against the throne, blood leaking from their wounds. King Ignati sat frozen on his throne, his son beside him with a drawn sword.

Ba'land laughed. It was a thick and liquid sound, like the effluent in a sewer.

I heard the rasp of many taloned feet, and demon soldiers came out of the gloom to join their master.

Ba'land gestured, and the sword was ripped from Solaros' grasp and clattered to the floor.

"Now, shall we discuss my *requests*," he said to the king, "in a more reasonable manner?"

Ignati was silent. He looked very old and weak. He clutched at his son's hand.

"My first request is this," the demon king said. "On Creator's Day you will kindly sign whatever I put before you. And in honor of the improved relations between our realms, you will bring these two to the ceremonies. Where I request that they be sacrificed. Furthermore, until that day—which I believe is only a few months off— you will hold them and their comrades under a guard of my choosing. And if they should escape, I promise you the penalty will be severe.

"You see, my interest in peace is such that I want to end any possibility of future conflict between us. The sacrifice I plan will assure not only that Lady Greycloak and Lord Antero can no longer trouble us, but it will also seal the way against any other mortal upstarts who might attempt to follow."

He glared at the two royal figures, who still did not speak. I saw the prince glance down at his sword, weighing his chances.

Ba'land gestured, and the sword flew across the room and was caught in his talons.

"Also, I mustn't forget," he said mildly, "your recent military preparations. I want one thousand of your finest troops to be present that day. They are to appear disarmed, disrobed, and in chains. At the proper moment I will use them for the final blessing. A thousand heads should do quite nicely, I think."

Ba'land turned, mocking. "Isn't that so, Tobray?"

The chief wizard's mouth gaped open, but before a word could be said, Ba'land flung the sword at him. The blade tumbled in its flight, glowing with magical life, then pierced the wizard's arm, going through it and the stone wall behind him—pinning the wizard to it.

Tobray groaned but he did not cry out. I saw blood flow from lips from his effort to prevent it.

"Well, Majesty," Ba'land said. "What do you think of my requests? Will you *require* them to be carried out like the wise monarch you are?"

Ignati, too weak from shock to answer, shook his head—no.

His son spoke for him. "You saw his reply. If our deaths are the result of it, so be it. But I tell you this, Ba'land: Once we are dead, you had best flee as quickly as you can, for our subjects are certain to revenge us. And if you escape, their resolve for war will only be greater."

"I see you still think there are choices," Ba'land said. "I'd best put that notion to rest."

He gestured, and Ignati suddenly jerked forward. Another gesture and the king screamed. His chest bulged out, his kingly robes swelling.

The prince jumped forward, but Ba'land struck him down. The king's awful shrieks echoed through the chamber, then his heart burst through the cloth and flew into Ba'land's claws. The demon king squeezed it, and the king's cries grew more terrible still.

Ba'land held out the heart for the prince to see. Solaros gaped at it from the floor.

"Here is your father's life," Ba'land said. "Think quickly now. You can accede, and I'll restore it. Or you can continue to refuse, in which case I shall—"

Again he squeezed and again Ignati cried out.

"We agree," the prince gasped. "Now please, don't torment him anymore."

"Are you certain?" the demon king asked.

Another squeeze, another scream.

"I'm certain," the prince wept.

Ba'land bowed. "If that is Your Highness' wish."

He walked slowly to the throne, smiled down at the suffering Ignati, then placed the heart back in his chest. He blew on the bloody hole, and in an instant all signs of the wound and even the tear in the garment were gone.

Ba'land patted the king. "I'm glad you finally see things my way," he said.

He turned to Yasura. "See that my wishes are carried out," he said. He pointed at us. "Especially concerning those two. Until I return, I do not want to have to think of them again."

His servant bowed, and as he did so, darkness swirled about Ba'land. He drew it on him like a cloak . . . and was gone.

*   *   *

SO FOR THE LAST TIME I became the prisoner of a king. But this was no savage king like Azbaas or despotic wizard like the Archons who once ruled Lycanth.

Ignati is a civilized man who shrinks from pain and bloodshed. Despite his many faults, he loves his son. And his son loves him.

Because of this love, we and a thousand others will die.

I do not suffer physical torment in these last days. They've locked us up in our chambers, and I'm assured by Quatervals and Kele—who were allowed to stay with us as servants—that our company is well-cared for under similar confinement.

Demons guard us day and night. Demon hounds sniff us for signs of sorcerous work several times a day.

There is no hope of escape.

It took a long time for Janela to recover from her ordeal. But she's well now and tells me daily not to despair. And I say yes, my love, I know the old wives' adage about life and hope. And I pretend to take comfort so as not to cause her more worry.

You noticed perhaps my expression of endearment. It was not a slip of the quill. She *is* my love. And I suppose we both knew it was inevitable from the start.

I do not long to recast those wasted days and nights when we stayed apart. For it would not have been seemly if we had come together before. It would have spoiled our partnership in this grand adventure. It would have soiled our embrace with guilty thoughts about Janos and betrayed friendships and a whole score of other confusions, such as—was this love or was it a man's most petty means of revenge?

I don't recall the very moment we came together, for my recollections mix up all the other moments when it nearly came to pass.

I don't even know if it was day or night. But I believe I was writing in this journal. Janela's hand fell on my shoulder and I turned to see what she wanted. She had a cup of wine for me in her hand and a smile on her face, but when our eyes met, the smile vanished and I found myself plunging into those dark depths.

Then we were at the jungle pool where Janela and the other women had bathed. Instead of turning away, I swept her up and carried her to a soft bank where we made love until the fireflies came out to taste the perfumed night.

And then we were in that chaste bed in Irayas, pretending we were lovers to foil Modin's unseemly plans. Except this time I was young and Janela's hand crept down and found my strength. She laughed and threw off the covers and mounted me—riding me like a wild plains woman, her dark hair lashing about like a mane.

She has been Omerye and Deoce to me all in one. Our love-making has been full of fire and spirit, but it's also been tender and dreamy, with magical pipes playing songs that speak just to me. And yes, she's even been Melina once or twice. With smoldering eyes and teasing caresses and thighs that part at a touch.

Mostly she's been Janela. All mystery and smoke, with a laughing woman behind that witch's veil. A woman who transports us in our lovemaking to places that are free of all care. We've made love in mountain vales. Run through the snow to warm geyser springs. Crept under forest bowers and shed our clothes. Lay spooned in a hammock on a gently swaying ship where the waves and the winds made the motions for us.

Once she even conjured a pitcher of warm wine and honey that we dribbled on each other's bodies then sipped off until only lovers' musk remained.

But I treasure most of all the lazy times after we've made love, when we talk of far-flung lands and people and their dreams. For to speak with Janela is to converse with a woman who has sought and found the riddle to the stars. Why the moon shows only one face, and what the sun will be when its fires die out.

Once she reminded me of Solaros' comment about the Old Ones who said they'd found a door to a more perfect world and fled there, never to return.

"I think I know how to open that door, Amalric," she said.

"Then open it at once," I said. "And we shall flee after them."

Janela shook her head. "There's more involved," she said.

"Such as?"

"To begin with," she said, "there's a small thing required. Like death."

"So?" I said. "Ba'land is going to kill us anyway. Why give him the pleasure?"

"That's the other small thing," Janela said. "We'd have to rid ourselves of Ba'land before it would work."

"So much for a grand escape into an afterlife," I said, only half in jest. "But what of it? I'd probably be disappointed. I've seen two Far Kingdoms, after all, and neither one measured up to its mythical reputation.

"To tell you the truth, Janela, if it weren't for our manner of going and the mess the world will be in when we depart, I wouldn't mind ending my life right now. Even without something so enticing as a perfect *other* world attached. I'm old. Even in a young man's body, I'm old. I've had enough of this life. My only regret would be leaving you. Ending this most enchanted of affairs. I've climbed the mountains. I've seen the desert stars. I've sailed ships to nowhere and come back.

"It's time for a rest, I think."

Janela didn't answer.

"Have I offended you?" I asked. "I'm sorry if I did. I was only speaking my mind. Sometimes that's not such a wise thing to do."

Janela wiped away a tear. "You didn't offend me, my love," she said. "I'm only sad that I can't give you the ending you wish."

I hugged her. "Nothing to be sad about. Besides, I've got the journal to finish. It's taking longer than I thought, but I must make certain nothing is left out."

I looked over at the desk, where the pages I'm adding to now were heaped in the corner—waiting for this addition. "Creator's Day," I said, "is nearly here. And now that I think of it, it's best if I continue writing until the last possible moment. What if the one event I missed was the key to Orissa's rescue? It's not likely. But if it were so, it would make me a most unhappy ghost."

"Oh, you'll be a wonderful ghost, Amalric," Janela said. "Quite sexy, too. I'll have to watch out for all the women ghosts who'll want to get you in their clutches. And you'll be walking about all confident, commanding with a look, praising with a smile. And you'll never know it's your body they want when they say, 'Yes, my lord.' And, 'No, my lord.' And, 'Thank you so much, my lord, for your kind words.' "

"I think I'm being mocked," I said.

Janela pointed a finger at her breast, eyes widening into great round innocence. "Me?" she said. "Mock the great Lord Antero? Oh, no, not I, sir. Not your sweet Janela. Not your—"

And I kissed her to make her shut up.

I BEGAN THIS JOURNAL shortly after Janela's recovery.

The two of us, plus Quatervals and Kele, talked for many hours about the situation and realized we must warn Orissa at any cost.

I pray to all the gods who seem to have forsaken us that in this journal a means will be found to stop King Ba'land from unleashing the demon hordes on our world.

It has taken many generations to rise from the ashes the demons left behind the last time they fell upon us. I fear if it occurs again, they will make certain that recovery is not repeated.

Most of our world is still in darkness. Only in Orissa and a few places like it has savagery been shed. Left to our own devices, we could create a world that would humble even the Old Ones in its enlightenment. For as we have learned in Tyrenia, the Old Ones were sadly lacking in many areas. They slew and looted and enslaved to make their kingdom. They jealously guarded their magical secrets so they would have power over all.

In the end it was the Old Ones who were to blame for humanity's defeat. When the demons came, the Old Ones had only their own resources to fall back upon. The rest of the world had no means to aid them. And the Old Ones abandoned their fellow mortals with little concern about what would happen to them, until finally they'd given up all except one last redoubt they could claim as a realm.

The place so aptly named the Kingdoms of the Night.

When I am done with this journal, Quatervals and Kele will carry it away. We have found a means for them to escape, but I will not detail it or name the Tyrenians who will assist us, to guard against retribution if our two companions are captured.

The reprisals their escape may cause should not be too severe.

Ba'land will think them too unimportant to waste his energies upon. Which is not what would happen—as the demon king warned—if Janela and I joined them.

We plan for our friends to stay behind when we are all called to the sacrifice. Janela will use magic to cover their absence. Quatervals and Kele will depart after the slaughter, when the demons are certain to be intoxicated with all the gore and misery they caused.

And may Te-Date grant our friends wings to speed home with the news.

THE DAY WE ALL dreaded has finally arrived. These will be the last words I write to you, my dear Hermias.

I promise we shall go bravely to our fates. Know that King Ba'land's only satisfaction will come from our deaths. He will not hear one man or woman in our company weep or beg for mercy.

This we have resolved. This we have sworn.

I hear the demons in the hall.

I hear the creak of their harness, the rattle of their weapons, and the scraping of talons on the floor.

They are coming for us.

Farewell, my dear nephew.

Farewell.

BOOK THREE

BEYOND TYRENIA

CHAPTER TWENTY

THE RETURN

My dear Hermias. As you can see from these pen scratchings, I still live.

Before I enlighten you on how this came to be, I beg you to reward Pip and Otavi handsomely. They have gone through much with us and will have endured much more to deliver this addendum to my journal.

I presume you have already made Captain Kele and my faithful Quatervals as rich as any two such brave hearts could ever possibly dream. I urge you to do the same for the pair who carry my final message to you. Otavi's family has given us long and honorable service. And Pip, genial rogue though he may be, has made the difference many a time when all the odds seemed weighed against us.

Others of our company should be trickling home soon, although I cannot say as yet who and how many they may be. But I've told everyone to seek you out when they return to Orissa and you would see that their lives are made comfortable and that they get credit for the grand part they played in history.

You may have drawn the conclusion in reading thus far that I don't expect to return myself. If so, you are correct.

These words—added to the journal you have already received—are my parting gift to the world.

A world I shall soon leave.

When last I wrote, the demons were at our door. And I was scribbling hastily lest some crucial detail be left out.

As far as I can tell, I was successful. But much followed that will open even the most skeptical eyes to the greatness of Janela's achievements.

And how much more can still be achieved.

I THOUGHT I had seen every twist in every road Fate could possibly scratch out. I thought I had been flung as high as any giant could manage and borne to depths as low as the Dark Seeker can carry us and still hold life.

So much for an old man's arrogance.

We were bathed and dressed in our best when the demons came. I chose a military look to show my defiance, although there might also have been a phantom motive involved—such as literally girding my loins for the coming ordeal. Janela wore a scarlet tunic over black leggings, and her favorite boots. And in her hat was a graceful feather to match her tunic.

When she put on her jewelry, she held back two bracelets. These went to Quatervals and Kele.

"There's a spell on them that will hide you when the demons arrive," she said. "When I signal, think only of darkness. Concentrate on the night and all the shadowy things that night holds, and the demons won't see you when they enter. Not only that, but their thoughts will be turned away whenever they attempt to think of you. So your absence from our ranks will not be missed."

They put them on as she directed, but the whole time she talked they hung their heads and mumbled their replies—as if they were ashamed.

"If these are our final moments together," I said, "can't you manage cheerier faces? Do you want my last thoughts of you to be those sour and wrinkly gourds I see clinging to the end of your necks?"

Quatervals grumbled and Kele muttered as my first attempt missed its mark by many lengths.

So I uncorked the last bottle of Orissan brandy we had brought with us and poured all around.

"Try a little of this magic," I said. "If you drink enough, you'll be as blind as the demons."

A good administrator must lead by example, so I drained my cup and filled it again to the brim. Janela laughed and followed suit.

Very grudgingly, first Quatervals and then Kele drank.

"Drink, drink," I urged, gently pushing at the bottom of Quatervals' cup until the last drop had flowed between his lips.

"Here, now," Kele warned. "I'll be me own rudder." And she too drank to the dregs.

I sloshed more brandy around. "I know you're both thinking we've come all this way together, so we should continue until the end, and somehow you are abandoning us even though you know your mission is more important than all our lives combined."

I chuckled. "But the fact of the matter is you're not likely to make it either, so what's the point in feeling so guilty?"

Quatervals brightened. He took a healthy drink. "That's quite true, my lord," he said. "Chances are we'll be picked up faster'n a green legate can piss his britches in his maiden fight."

He looked at Kele. "They'll probably torture us first," he said. "For makin' 'em go to so much bother."

Kele smiled, encouraged by this bleak picture. " 'N' even if they don't catch us," she said, "what do yer thinks our chances are of ever makin' it all the way back to Orissa?"

Quatervals nodded. "By the gods, you're right!" he said. "Don't know what we're so worried about. The journey'll kill us, if the demons don't."

He finished his drink and held out his cup for a refill. Which I did. Quatervals was positively beaming.

"Thank'ee, my lord," he said, "for pointin' out how hopeless our situation is. I'm feelin' much better now."

"Not so quick wi' tha' bottle, me lord," Kele said, knocking aside Quatervals' cup with her own. "I'm a delicate lass, as yer know, 'n' I must get me proper share so's I don't shriek or faint."

Quatervals snorted. "You mean pass out." Another snort. "Delicate lass, my arse!"

"Yer arse is what I'll be puttin' me boot up," Kele said, "if yer continue t' question me sensitive nature."

"Children, children!" I admonished. "Is this how you're going to behave on the way back?"

Quatervals and Kele looked at each other, then laughed.

"Too right, my lord," Quatervals said. "How else're we supposed to stave off boredom?"

Kele nodded in agreement. "Fer a lubber," she said, "he ain't bad in a quarrel. Given a century or three, might even make a sailor outter him."

Quatervals bristled. "Never," he said. "I hate water. And I hate fish even more."

"There yer go, then," Kele said with relish. "Yer halfway there already."

EARLIER, while Janela was dressing, I'd seen the pouch containing the stone talisman dangling from her neck. After she'd pulled on her tunic, covering it, she'd studied herself in the mirror, patting and tugging until the outline of the talisman couldn't be seen.

"A last minute plan developing, perchance?" I'd asked.

"I wish I could say yes, my love. But I have nothing in mind that might save us."

"Then why are you bringing the box along?"

"I thought of all the weapons we could have smuggled in and hide about our persons," she'd said. "On the far-off hope that we might be able to inflict a wound or two before they killed us."

"I've considered the same," I'd replied. "But I couldn't see what use it would be—even if we could manage it. Considering the stakes, what's a scratch or two on a demon's hide? I think I'd rather keep my dignity and not go out flailing like an hysterical old fool."

Then I'd eyed her. "You still haven't told me why you're bringing along the box."

"An off-chance, really," she'd said. "The more I've studied it, the more certain I am that the box the queen's witch created increases the power of spells. How greatly, I'm not so certain.

"Still, it occurred to me that when Ba'land is performing whatever sorcery he has in mind, if we are very, very fortunate—so fortunate all the gods would have to be favoring us in unison—he might choose a spell I can use against him. We'll still die. But there's a slim chance we might do him damage, as well."

"From your lips," I'd said, "directly to the ears of Te-Date."

"That, my dearest Amalric, is exactly what I'd had in mind."

WHEN THE DEMON SOLDIERS led us away, we had no idea where they were taking us. I couldn't imagine they'd slaughter us at the amphitheater in front of the whole population. No matter that Ba'land held the king's life ransom, the anger such an action would cause would certainly spark a great riot.

As we were marched along I prayed King Ba'land would do something so foolish. There was no way he and his soldiers could halt the furious mob.

The possibility of such a revenge diminished the instant they prodded us out of the palace. Instead of heading toward the amphitheater, they turned us toward the path Janela and I had taken the day we found the ghostly court chamber.

The rest of our party was waiting, heavily guarded, in a park, and as we came up they hailed us, calling our names—and Quatervals' and Kele's as well, evidence enough that Janela's spell was working.

Our comrades defied the demon guards and crowded around us, some laughing, some crying angry tears, some cursing the fates for marooning us on such foul shores of circumstance.

"T' think of alla coin I pissed away on sacrifices, my lord," Pip complained, " 'n' this is me payment fer it! Wish't yer'd writ somethin' in yer journal warnin' me family 'bout it. Tell 'em how much a waste it be. Why, they been tithin' ten percent of all they steal fer long as I c'n 'member. And what good's it do, I ask yer?"

"Watch your blasphemin', Pip," Otavi warned. "There's others about might not feel the same. 'N' the gods might mistake your black soul for one'a ours."

"No chance'a that," Pip said, gloomy. "They've marked me in their sights right square, they have." He gave me a shaggy-toothed grin. "Mayhaps I could cling t' your lordship's sleeve when we finally go," he said. "Sure t' be more riches where yer head'n than what's laid on for poor Pip."

"Cling away," I said. "But be warned. There's some who say that in the afterlife the quarters for the rich are hovels while the poor are treated as unto kings and queens."

Pip snorted. "Beggin' your pardon, my lord, but I never smelt such a foul wind since the last time my dear granny tucked away a plate'a bad beans. The rich stay rich, I warrant, no matter where the gods takes 'em."

I laughed, clapped him on the back, and said he was speaking nonsense. Although I knew what he said must be true. If there was an afterlife, I thought, why would justice be any different there? Power loves the powerful. It only follows that the gods must love the rich.

Why else would more villains succeed than fail?

The guards were impatient and prodded us into line with their spears, then herded us off with Janela and myself in the lead.

I was shocked when we came to the place where our picnic had been prepared. An immense raw hole had been gouged into the earth where the tavern had once stood, and a wide tunnel led down into the ruins of the Old Palace. Surly Tyrenian workmen were clearing away the last of the debris as we approached, snarling under the lash of demon soldiers urging them to make haste.

The magical tree gave me a greater shock. It was axe-scarred and lines had been thrown around it and men were working winches trying to rip it out of the ground. The earth groaned, and water from the underground spring showered up along its roots to run down a swiftly deepening path in the center of the tunnel.

"They been at it near two weeks," Pip whispered to me. "First wit' axes 'n' saws. But that darlin' tree turned the blades away— ev'n when the demons themselves went at it. Now they're tryin' a new one, they is. Pull 'er down if they can't cut 'er down."

He cackled. A little louder perhaps than he ought. "Don't look like that's workin' either."

A guard growled at him and jabbed him with his spear. Pip slapped at it.

"Get away from me, ya shit-breath lizard," he said. "Or ol' Pip'll put his fist up yer wobblies."

Two more guards joined the first and Pip gave up with a smile, falling behind us again. "Allus pickin' on the little guy, they is," he said.

We trooped into the tunnel.

It was eerie. Sorcerous light sputtered and flickered as if power were being drained away. Water dripped from the ceiling and sides, and it was difficult to dodge the stream in the center, much less keep our footing in the heavily trodden mud.

Janela hissed for my attention.

"Drink some water," she whispered. "Tell the others to do the same."

Without breaking stride, she bent down, scooped up a palmful, and quickly swallowed the muddy brew. I followed suit, signaling Pip and the others to do the same.

Despite the mud, the water was as delicious as ever. I felt a surge of energy. I seemed to walk taller now, with firmer stride and clearer eye. I heard mutterings of similar reactions from the men and women in our company.

I nudged Janela. "A plan?" I whispered.

She shook her head, whispering back, "Just do what you can to delay the inevitable."

With those mysterious words still ghosting about my brain, we were brought into the ancient court chamber of King Farsun.

Enormous though the chamber was, the crowd inside was densely packed and the air was hot from all their bodies and thick with the moisture of their breath. On one side, hemmed tight to the walls by demons, were Tyrenian officials and representatives of the highborn families. On the other were the soldiers Ba'land had condemned to be sacrificed. They were shackled, with chains running from their hands and feet to broad metal belts welded about their waists.

Standing in front of them were their generals, Emerle and Thrade. They were not chained, and stood as stiff and proud as they could in front of their men. When I looked close I could see them twist their lips to the side to mutter words of encouragement.

Above us we heard the groaning and creaking of the machines struggling with the stubborn tree. Below I could hear the rush of the underground spring. Its flow had increased to a torrent from being disturbed.

There was a clear area running from the dancer's platform to the twin thrones. As we moved toward it, demons hissed orders, shoving Janela and me forward while forcing our company away from us. Some of our people called good-bye, but we couldn't turn to make our own farewells.

We were brought up short at the platform. Steps climbed to the thrones. A bright light flared and I had to shield my eyes to look. I could see King Ignati seated in one throne, Prince Solaros in the other. The light lessened somewhat and I could see that Ignati's features had been squeezed by despair. Flesh drooped from his jowls, and his eyes were tunneled from pain and fatigue.

Solaros looked little better, although he tried mightily to smile with encouragement when he saw us.

The light shifted to a cold blue and I could see much better now. It emanated from a third throne half-again the size of the others. A wide area around it sputtered and crackled with a sorcerous shield. King Ba'land took his ease on that throne. Crouched in front of him like a dog was a naked man. Every bone stood out from starvation and his long hair was tangled. There was a metal band about his neck with a chain leading from a welded ring to Ba'land's hand. I saw with dismay it was Tobray.

The demon king yanked on the chain when he saw us. The chain glowed white-hot and Tobray moaned in pain.

"Look who's come to see us, Tobray," Ba'land said. "Sit up and bark your greetings like the good dog you are."

Tobray didn't move. The demon king gave the chain another yank, hissing, "Sit up, I said!"

But Tobray refused, curling up instead, as if by making a tighter knot he could escape the agony. I winced as smoke curled from the flesh on his neck, and I saw a puddle suddenly form on the floor beneath him as he lost control of his bladder.

Ba'land wrinkled his nose. "What a dirty animal you are, Tobray," he said. He gave him a kick. "I'd make you lap it up, but then I'd be forced to smell your breath until I was done with you."

The demon king looked up at us. He gestured at Tobray. "You see. It was all for nothing. You sought a golden land where the streets are paved with myths. Instead you came to a place where you can't even find a decent dog."

I struck a casual pose as if not bothered by Tobray's misery. "I know where you can find one, my friend," I said. "There's a place my sister visited. A realm of seaweed and rotted ships. The fellow who rules it would make an admirable dog for you. If you're ever out that way, stop by and see him. He'll leap in your lap and lick your face if you tell him an Antero sent you."

I was babbling nonsense, trying for delay, as Janela had urged. For some reason, the demon that Rali had bested sprung to mind.

Nonsense or not, Ba'land liked it. He slapped his thigh and roared humor.

"Elam?" he said. "You want me to make me a dog of Lord Elam? Why, he'd bite my throat out. And yours afterward for suggesting it."

"I'm fairly certain my neck won't be around for the honor," I said. "But come now, are you saying a mighty king like yourself fears a lowly creature like Elam?"

"Not fear him, exactly," Ba'land answered. "I choose to keep my distance." He waved, taking in his ferocious soldiers. "It may surprise you to know," he went on, "all demons aren't civilized like us. Sometimes they cause us almost as much trouble as you and the Greycloaks have. But there's too few of them to bother with so we let them alone.

"Besides, they add to the misery of mortals. And you make a much more delicious dish that way." He smacked his lips in illustration.

"Too few?" I asked. "Or too powerful?"

Ba'land didn't like the way the conversation was turning. "Don't speak on something you know nothing about," he said. "It is you who stands before me. And that, little man, is the only power you need consider."

I chanced a quick look aside and saw Janela slowly drawing something from her tunic. What she was up to I didn't know. But I did my best to keep Ba'land's attention.

"You make a weighty argument," I said. "Here *we* are. And there *you* are. My only possible retort can be: Why did it take you so long to accomplish this deed if you truly are such a majestic majesty?"

Ba'land's yellow eye glowed in amusement. "I haven't the faintest idea," he said. "I've commanded whole legions of demon wizards to answer that very question. What is it about the Anteros and Greycloaks—especially when combined—that creates such danger for us? My best wizards have spent years on it. But to no avail. I've chained them, flogged them, ripped their limbs from their trunks, but the riddle remains steadfastly unsolved."

"You didn't get to be king by not doing some thinking of your own," I said. "Surely you must have your own theories."

"As a matter of fact, I do," Ba'land replied. "It's in your blood. I know that's a market witch's explanation. But there's a ring of truth in its haggish simplicity. The blood of the Anteros and the blood of the Greycloaks bears a seed of much power and greatness. Few mortals are blessed with it, which is fortunate for us.

"When we first came to your world and found a moving bounty to feed upon, we encountered a few such as you. They fought the hardest and wounded us most severely. But we killed them in the end and killed their brothers and their sisters and all the children we could find. We have legends of a few who escaped to live and breed to haunt us in a future time. Perhaps those legends are true and you and Lady Greycloak are a result of that breeding."

"It makes more sense than any theory I've had," I said. Then I grinned. "I hope greatly that someday you're proven correct. Living proof would be the best. Yet another Antero and Greycloak pairing, say?"

"Alas for scholarly inquiry," Ba'land replied. "For that is also quite unlikely. The odds an Antero and Greycloak would combine more than once are greater than most could imagine. That it should happen more than twice is beyond the fortunes of even the most persistent dice shaker. Still, I won't chance it. The spell I shall make from your blood today will see to it no others appear. To make doubly certain, I will seek out all your kin and even the ghosts of your kin and sup on their souls and make them mine."

"Beware of your digestion, my friend," I said. "I intend to make my soul as bitter as I can."

"Oh, that's very good." Ba'land laughed. "You know, I'm almost sorry this day has come," he said. "It's given me genuine peace of mind to have you locked up where I could get to you whenever I wanted, instead of you traipsing about causing me no end of worry."

I bowed, mocking him. "We did our best," I said.

"I'm sure you did," the demon king said. "And for that your deaths will be as painful as I can manage. I have a few regrets. It's comforting to know your enemy. More comforting still to have him at your mercy. But once you kill him, where are you? Back to the days of faceless enemies and troubled sleep. Then you wake up wondering if you really did kill the fellow or did the crafty devil manage to escape once again."

"May your dreams be as unquiet as my ghost can make them," I said.

"No chance of that," Ba'land replied. "Didn't I already say I wouldn't even leave a ghost?"

Janela laughed harshly. "You certainly did, Ba'land," she said. "Ghosts trouble you, do they? Such a mighty fellow you are, fearing weak spirits who can do little more than tap on your walls and moan at night."

"I've been waiting to hear from you, my dear Lady Greycloak," the demon answered. "You've convinced many that you are a great wizard, as great perhaps as even your great-grandfather, Janos Greycloak. Tell me, O Wise One: What words of wisdom do you have for us this day?"

Janela shrugged. "Wisdom never interested me," she said.

"Wisdom is someone else's reflections on what they observed. I prefer to do my own observing. When I reach a conclusion, I do not reflect—I relate what I have seen."

"Tell me what you see, then," Ba'land said.

Janela studied him a moment, then said, "I see an uneasy king. So uneasy it makes one wonder at the stability of his crown. You seem to fear many things, which makes one wonder even more.

"I'll list them. You feared *us*, which you can't honestly deny. You fear ghosts. You fear wild demons like Elam." She pointed to the roots shaking above us as the workmen made another try. "You even fear that tree."

Ba'land hissed. He didn't like her words. But he said nothing.

"I also think in your own world you and your kind have consumed more power than is wise. It's like a city that cuts down all the forests to build their homes and heat them as well. Eventually they have to travel very far and pay a dear price for something that was once so close. That is what you have done. In more places, perhaps, than just our world. There must be other demon kings with similar problems, kings who would love to see their brother monarch fall. If so, it follows that you are stretched quite thin, Ba'land, merely defending what you hold."

Ba'land recovered his foul humor. "Pity I didn't catch you sooner," he said. "I could have made you into such an amusing little pet." He kicked Tobray. "Much better than this."

Janela put a hand to her breast. "Oh la, sir!" she said coyly. "Such words stir a maid's poor heart anticipating your demonly attentions. We all saw what an effect you have on mortal women. How you charmed the fair Thalila, who so willingly danced her way into your arms."

"Willingly or not," Ba'land growled, "I had her."

"Did you, now?" Janela said. "Or did she have *you*? You saw how she played you the fool. How she conspired—and quite successfully—against you. And you never knew, did you? Not until I revealed it in this very chamber."

"I saw nothing you didn't intend, witch!" Ba'land snarled. "The vision was nothing but a trick. And a low one at that."

"Was it?" Janela asked.

She held her hand out. In it I saw the stone box with the carving of the dancing maid etched clear by the blue light.

"Shall I call her back for you?" Janela asked. "Would you like to see her dance once again?"

As she spoke, Janela's free hand traced a curving figure in the air. Ba'land turned his head, perhaps to command a guard to have the box taken away. But as he turned, a familiar seductive figure wavered into view and his head snapped back. The dancer's music swelled from the empty pit and the faint figure of the maid firmed into flesh.

The demon king gaped as Thalila's slender limbs moved in graceful time to the music.

She was ice in the pale light, but ice that begged to be melted. Hips twitching to be grasped, breasts heaving for a lover's kiss, lips blowing promises of future delights. Her perfume charged the air with the spice of seduction, and I saw Ba'land shudder when her hands rose in a long slow caress from thighs to breasts.

Janela motioned and the dancer vanished. It was so abrupt that it left Ba'land gaping like a wide-jawed sea snake.

She stepped forward, holding out the box. "Here," she whispered. "Thalila. For you?"

Ba'land gnashed his teeth and held out a hand. Janela mounted the steps. When she reached his magical shield she said, "She's waiting, Ba'land. Waiting only for you."

Ba'land gestured impatiently and the shield dissolved.

Janela took one more step, then suddenly snatched the lid off the box.

The demon Mitel exploded, howling in fury for being trapped inside so long. King Azbaas' Favorite saw Ba'land first and bounded toward him bellowing blood-lust.

Ba'land was so frozen in surprise that Mitel nearly got him, but the demon king kicked his throne over backward. It shattered into splintered ruins, and Tobray scrambled out of the way as Mitel plunged after Ba'land.

The demon soldiers rushed to help their master, who had rolled to his feet to match Mitel talon for talon. King Ignati shouted, bolted from his throne and tried to block the first demon who came up the stairs. But he was pushed aside contemptuously and a blade run in and out of his chest.

His son shouted an oath and leaped on his father's killer, curling a brawny arm around his neck and snapping it.

Solaros jumped free and called to his men. The shackled soldiers struggled in their chains as other Tyrenians boiled over to help free them. The prince raced across the room to join his men.

Beyond the thrones Ba'land was locked with Mitel. The two demons grappled, Mitel trying to sink his teeth into Ba'land's throat while Ba'land clawed at Mitel's abdomen with his feet. The demon king broke away, lashing out with all his might.

The blow sent Mitel staggering back into the first wave of Ba'land's soldiers. Demons went down in a wild tumble and a sword came skittering almost to my feet. I snatched it up and instinctively started forward.

Janela grabbed my hand and shouted, "Wait, Amalric!"

On the throne platform Ba'land caught Mitel behind the neck. Mitel lashed back with his taloned feet, but then Ba'land's soldiers were on him and he went slack as they plunged their swords into his body.

Ba'land reared up, roaring for his soldiers to surround him, then swiveled about to hunt us with his big yellow eye.

I heard Pip and the others cry our names and knew they were charging to our sides.

Ba'land saw us and Janela clutched my hand harder, hissing for me not to let go. The demon king flung his arms high, summoning a mighty spell to strike us down.

Janela held up the box and shouted, "Open!"

The floor fell away, and just as Ba'land sent a rolling ball of lightning crackling toward us, the underground spring exploded out of the earth. It wasn't cooling, life-giving water, but a deadly sheet of silver fire.

The two forces met. There was a great blast, sweeping Ba'land and the demons away and up.

The blast caught us, and my ears were filled with a great howling and a wind of pure white light flung us high.

Then we were falling and Janela was gripping my hand tighter and tighter as we fell.

We fell so far I thought we'd never stop.

BATTLE WITHOUT END

I stood on a great plain ringed by mountains that belched fire into a sky spattered with dark clouds against a red sunset. Behind me gaped cave mouths, and somehow I knew I'd come from them, not fallen from the sky as my mind had foolishly told me.

I wore a rough fur tunic that fell below my knees, and there was a crude rope of dried vines around my waist, a dagger laboriously chipped from flint stuck in it. I carried a club that had a jagged shard of obsidian buried in it.

Around me were men and women, more than one thousand of them, dressed much like I was and armed with clubs or thrusting spears topped with flint or jagged rock. They stood in ranks, expecting battle. I recognized them: There were Pip, Otavi, Towra, Berar, all *four* Cyralian brothers, and the others who'd sailed from Orissa with me. The others were the Tyrenian soldiers we'd trained, among them their generals, Emerle and Thrade—the sacrifice Ba'land had demanded. I looked about and didn't see Prince

Solaros—for some reason he hadn't been carried into this world with us.

Quatervals stood in front of me, and not far behind him in the crowd was Kele.

"They caught you," I sorrowed. "Now Hermias will know nothing."

"No," Quatervals said. "We are far down the road now, not far from that haunted village."

"Then—"

"We are, we shall be, where we are needed . . . when we are needed."

Before I could ask another question, the drums began. To one side of my small army danced half a dozen chanting shamans, Tobray the loudest of the chanters. To their fore was Janela, naked, her hair swirling as she danced, her arms moving in wild supplication. I felt lust and my member stiffened, then anger gripped me as the drums grew louder and across the plain the demon army moved against us . . . against our homes.

At their fore was the demon king I'd known as Ba'land. I screamed rage and we charged forward, running down the slopes to meet them, our bare feet not feeling the sharp rocks.

As we charged, the demons also broke into a run and our armies crashed together. Then there was nothing but a melee of cutting and slashing, the demons' talons and fangs ripping at us. I saw Otavi smash one monster's head away, and the monster keened pain through the ruins of his throat and fell, ichor pouring. Another horror, this with four arms and armed with scythelike claws, slashed, cutting Otavi's arm off. Bellowing laughter, my former stableman sprayed blood from the stump of his arm into the demon's face, blinding him, then stove in the creature's chest before he died.

Pip dueled with an equally small monster, bow-legged, squat like a toad; then they staggered together and went down, daggers buried in each others' bodies.

There was a creature in front of me with the face of a tiger, but surrounded by tentacles. A long-clawed forearm whipped at me, and I smashed my club into his throat, pulling it free as it went down.

It was a mass of killers and killed, a heaving, groaning throng that swayed back and forth, the rocks under our feet slippery with gore and what strange and many-colored fluids the demons had running through their bodies.

As I fought on, trying to stay alive, trying not to notice when I was cut here, torn there, my eyes scanned the battle, looking for Ba'land. I saw him surrounded by his demon nobles and fought my way through the mass toward him.

There were shouts from behind me to follow, to help, to bring down the demon king, and I was at the point of a spearhead.

But as we forced our way forward, all changed about us. I don't know quite how to put it, but it was as if direction changed at will, so suddenly I would be alone on this plain, then surrounded by my foes, then by my own forces. Now I'd be striding forward toward Ba'land, then my steps were taking me back, back toward our caves.

I shouted in rage, helpless against the spell the demon king was sending against us, and then I heard Janela's steady chant, a long rhythm in a language I did not know, but it sent new blood and energy rushing through me and I knew how to travel in this strange world, stepping now forward, now back, and then Ba'land was not ten feet in front of me, waiting, his talons scraping the rock. I started for him, then heard screams and had a moment to glance around.

The demons had swept around my comrades, almost encircling them, and there were shouts to me to fall back, we must run.

But their deaths, my death, meant nothing if I could slay Ba'land. Then he was no longer in front of me, but far, far away, standing atop a boulder, shrieking in joy.

The blood-roar and -lust left me and sense returned and I was shouting orders, as was Towra. I knew Berar lay dead on the field, although I'd not seen her fall, and at my side was Quatervals, parrying a lunge from a horned monster and driving a spear through a gap in its carapace. It hissed in agony, twisted, and was dead.

"Back! Back! Flee!" came the cries, and so we did, not falling back as an army did, but running, broken, defeated.

Janela stood in front of me, her eyes flaming.

"We'll turn here," I gasped, my lungs searing.

"No," she shouted. "We cannot fight on! Not now! Not here!"

I turned and looked back, and the demoniac army was coming up the slopes toward our caves, screaming in triumph at their victory, Ba'land at their head. He was taller, stronger than before, full-fed on the deaths of my friends.

I turned—to the hells with sense, they'd not desecrate our homes!—bringing my club up for a last stand, Quatervals, blood pulsing from an ignored wound, beside me, my ears deaf to Janela's pleas and . . .

. . . We were falling, falling, endlessly . . .

It was a green and beautiful pasture, gentle rain seeping down from the skies. My horse nickered impatiently, scenting the battle to come.

I wore the uniform of an ancient horse soldier: leather helm with a strip of steel from crown to nose with steel cheekplates, steel cuirass, breeches tucked into high boots that had steel sideplates against slashes. My horse was also armored, with an eerie helm over its head and eyes and leather skirts that hung below the saddle. I was armed with a saber hung on my saddle, a dagger, and a long lance that a pennon floated from, a pennon matching the small one that trailed from my helmet's crest.

But our dress, while familiar in period, was unlike anything I've ever seen, the cuirass worked with strange designs in unusual colors, and the pennon above of no city I knew.

Beside me rode Janela, dressed much as I was but armed with a more slender sword. Flanking her were my captains, Towra, Berar, Kele, and Quatervals.

Waiting impatiently, their horses sometimes dancing in eagerness, were the rest of my soldiers, Orissan and Tyrenian.

We were half hidden by trees, looking down from this pasture at rolling meadows. Far across them the demon army was marching forward stolidly, moving in two great wings. Their cavalry was a ghastly array of demons mounted on strange beasts and other demons.

Closer to my right was the rest of our forces, infantry in two divisions, reinforced by war elephants and hunting cats.

Trumpets blared and drums thundered as the two armies closed on each other.

"This time we'll have 'em," Quatervals murmured.

Janela reached out her hand and I held it, without taking my eyes from the battlefield below, waiting for our moment.

Then she began a chant:

"You see nothing
You see naught
Naught but trees
Naught but grass
Nothing here is of hurt
Nothing here is of harm
Your foe waits
There
You need not look
You need not see."

The two armies met below us, arrows reaching out to begin the battle, and then the spear- and swordsmen clashed and the killing began once more.

I heard a mutter from Kele about now being the time but paid no attention, watching closely as first one side then the other held the advantage. I grinned as I saw—just as I ordered—our left wing retreat as if they were being beaten back. Back and back and I heard the demon shrieks of mastery, they'd broken us.

Now was the moment, and I drew my sword, rose high in my stirrups and shouted the charge. My cavalry stormed down from the heights full on the demons' right flank.

I have never been a soldier, but somehow the commands were known to me and fell easily from my lips:

"At the walk . . . forward!

"At the trot . . .

"Couch . . . lances!"

More than one hundred fifty steel fingers dropped down, each one promising death.

"At the gallop . . . *Charge!*"

They did not see us, did not sense us until we smashed into their flank, our long spears smashing into their ranks, and screams and howls of pain and surprise shattered the heavens. I left my lance buried in the body of a two-headed fanged beast with scales and oozing slime, pulled my saber, and we hewed on.

My mount shrilled agony and reared, pouring blood where a demon had slipped through and slashed its throat, and I kicked free from the stirrups and slid back and away as my horse fell, kicking, crushing the monster that had slain it. I heard shouts, "The lord's down . . . Lord Antero's down . . ." and then Janela was beside me and I pulled myself up on the back of her steed and we plunged deeper into the throng, cutting, slashing, forcing our way to the center of the demon army to where Ba'land's banners rose.

We were surrounded by the demons, some frantic to kill us, others equally eager to escape our bloody blades. But the press kept us alive—there wasn't room enough for our enemies to close and destroy us, and we kept moving, always moving, always closer to Ba'land.

He rose above me, now wearing the silks of a dandy under his half-armor. He was armed with a shortspear and dagger. He was no more than a dozen feet away, his standard bearer beside him—an awful creature I could not bear to look at for longer than an instant.

Ba'land lunged at Janela and she ducked aside as I flung myself off her horse at him. Spearthrust . . . brushed away by my slashing saber, his dagger plunging at me, and I knocked it aside, dancing away and cutting at him, blade whipping across his side, below his armor, and he howled and his blood—an awful black and green slime—gushed.

Ba'land bellowed and stumbled back and I slashed at his color bearer, missed him, but slashed the halberd that carried the demon's standard in half. Before the monster could recover it, I had it in my free hand, held high, and the demons screamed rage and fear.

Janela shouted and I turned and saw a demon had pulled himself up on her horse and had her throat in his claws, strangling, and her hand blurred back and forward, steel-toothed dagger burying itself in the monster and he fell away.

Ba'land was a few feet from me, waiting my attack, but as I advanced, a swirl of battlers came between us and I lost him.

Janela was beside me, and then others. Blood ran down from a wound across my forehead; I wiped it from my eyes and had a single instant to look about.

Around me were the surviving members of my band, no more than thirty men and women, all of them wounded. The demons boiled about us, shouting in glee that they had me trapped.

The rest of my army was far, far away, fighting desperately forward to rescue me.

Quatervals somehow had picked up my lance and buried its butt deep in the earth. The blood-soaked pennon atop it with the house flag of the Anteros snapped in the wind. He grinned at me.

"Now they'll have somethin' to aim for," he said.

There was a phalanx of my war-elephants ripping through the mass not fifty yards distant from us, but far, too far, as the demons charged forward once more, their blades singing our deathsongs.

But this time, I thought, *this time I'd hurt Ba'land sore, perhaps a deathwound, and we'd hurt his army sore. If I died now, it mattered little if he went down with me.*

I cut down a four-armed demon with a sword in each hand but little skill to use them, pivoted aside from a thrust and . . .

. . . We were falling, falling . . .

Our ships rolled mightily as the swells bore in from the east, so none of us, not the most experienced seaman, could stand alone. But none of us had mind for that, for we'd pinned the demon fleet against a long bank that crossed from horizon to horizon and we held the weather gauge, thanks to Janela's magic.

Their ships were huge and consisted of three types. The first and most impressive were great hulks that were almost round; low, single-deckers towed by smaller galleys. On these ships the demons had their war engines mounted and their soldiers waited in the ranks, ready to board any vessel that came within reach. The other type was also large, tall three-masters that towered far over our craft. They also had catapults, trebuchets, and other engines on their decks. They wallowed mightily but showed little signs of being otherwise troubled by the building storm we had sent down on them, nor were they aware they were being blown to certain doom on the banks unless they broke through us.

Our ships were much smaller and of a strange design I'd never seen before. They were galleys and single-masted, but the foredeck was covered with a curved shield, as was the poop. The oarsmen were shielded by high-curving bulwarks. The only open areas of our ships were amidships. Forward of me were two catapults, behind me two more on a deck raised above the rowers, and I stood with Janela, Kele, Quatervals, and Otavi on a round open tower that was the quarterdeck. Otavi, I guessed, was our helmsman, since he stood at what was the ship's wheel—two vertical poles that came up through slots in the deck that he moved forward and back at Kele's commands.

I was reminded of the turtleships that Rali had faced in a great sea battle far to the west.

This was strange, but still stranger were my sailors. Some of them I could make out and recognize as the Orissans and Tyrenians who'd battled with me. But those were hardly enough to make up a fleet's complement. There were others, but I could not hold my eyes on them. Somehow looking at them hurt, and I was glad to let my gaze slide past them, not letting my mind register any of their details.

Janela knelt on the deck, which was chalked with a pentagram inside a circle, with a second circle outside of that and symbols drawn around that arc. Empty leather bags—bags that would have held wind—were scattered around her. A candle burnt beside her with a flame that never flickered in the near-gale blowing behind us.

Suddenly the wind died and we began to lose way, almost caught in irons as it suddenly picked up again, blowing directly into our faces. Ba'land's spell had broken our control of the winds.

"No you don't," Janela muttered, and held the candle to a nearby brazier. A multicolored flame blazed up, twice the height of a man, a flame that was barely a handspan across, and her magic was stronger as the wind whipped through half a compass arc and was as before.

"That's held him," she said, and then geysers rose in the sea around us as the demon catapults found our range.

I had my ships in an arrow formation, striking straight for the heart of the enemy's fleet, our oarsmen pulling with all their strength, our windspell filling our sails. This would be unexpected, for a sea battle should be fought with ships in two lines face-to-face, the greater seeking to enclose and destroy the lesser.

But I intended to fight differently—my signals were already on the halyards and my captains had their orders.

How I knew this, when and how I told them, I cannot say, although now I wonder if some things my sister had told me years ago when she returned from Konya might have been remembered.

"We're in range, lord," Quatervals said.

I nodded to him, and now our own catapults sent heavy stones lofting through the air toward the enemy, long bolts from the catapults behind them.

But this was not our main weapon—*that* lay hidden just under the water that foamed around our bows.

Each of us had a demon ship as target. My own ship was holding true for the greatest of the enemy, Ba'land's flagship.

We closed on it and the demons aboard howled in pleasure at our stupidity, our willingness to come alongside a much larger ship and be taken by storm.

But we were not. At the last minute Kele ordered the course shifted slightly and then corrected, until we would strike Ba'land's craft just off the port bow. Now the demons realized we intended to ram, and their helm was put over, the wallowing ship turning slowly.

"Brace for it," Kele shouted, and the oarsmen below went flat and we found handholds.

We struck hard and many of us were knocked down in spite of our being ready for the shock. The demons recovered and raced to their rails high above us, ready to leap down and attack.

Kele shouted orders and the oarsmen pulled hard, one side forward, one back, and just as she planned, our ship spun, and with a great rending sound our ram broke away and we were free, backing off from the stricken flagship.

Quatervals' catapults were sending their messengers thudding onto the decks of the enemy or smashing through the sides of the crippled ship.

"All hands aft," Kele shouted, and men rushed to the stern, bringing our bow slightly up.

This again was as planned, and the seamen forward opened hatches, swiftly unbolted the remains of the broken ram and slid a new one into place, tightened the bolts and slammed the hatch shut, taking but little water in the process.

"Hands to their stations!" And our ship sat as before, level in the rolling seas, but now with a fresh and deadly beak.

Still at full sail and with the oarsmen pulling hard we struck on, straight through the enemy, almost onto the killer banks. I saw rollers breaking, although the bank was hidden, just under the surface, before I ordered Kele to turn and attack their fleet once more, like direwolves cutting apart a flock of sheep.

The rest of my ships were behind me and pivoted like so many trained ponies at a show. I'd lost but a handful in my first attack, as I'd hoped.

This time we struck from the rear, finding another ship and smashing into its stern and then pulling away, leaving it sinking, some of the crew trying to swim for the wreckage that littered the water, some for the boats that had been lowered.

This was not a day for mercy or kindness. We ran down three boats, archers skewering drowning monsters as they clawed at our sides, and then we were through the demons' line of battle once more.

The storm was about to break, wind shrieking, and the demon fleet was being blown down on land to its destruction. Ba'land's fleet was shattered, each ship now fighting for survival.

I looked around for the flagship, intending to finish it on this approach and . . .

. . . We fell, but it seemed to be more slowly . . .

The ground, a pleasant land of lakes, was far below us. Behind us was the rising sun as our twenty ships floated toward the mountains that was the demon king's stronghold.

I did not know what world or what time we were in, for I had never heard or thought of a craft such as the ones we flew.

They were huge tubes, eight or nine hundred feet long, pointed at the edges, with a long deck slung below each cylinder. On the decks were my soldiers, armed and waiting for the battle.

But to describe the cylinder and deck as if it appeared simple is a mistake, for on either side of it jutted long masts, fitted with sails and swarming with sailors furling and unfurling the canvas to hold our course in the wind that blew from astern.

I didn't know how we stayed in the air but suddenly recollected being a boy folding small pyramids of paper, holding them over the fire and letting the hot air lift them up the chimney. Perhaps these cylinders held such air, kept heated through sorcery.

Kele shouted a warning and pointed, and from the caves and canyons of the brooding mountain range the demons rose to meet us. Some rode on the backs of winged beasts, some, as before, *were* those beasts. They were armed with lances and long swords.

I heard a humming in the air and then one of my ships of the air gouted flame, twisting, burning, and falling, again like one of my paper toys that came too close to the fire.

Janela was working the counterspell, lighting a candle, then as she chanted, closing her hands about it, snuffing the flame:

"You cannot burn
You will not burn

I deny you life
I deny you fuel
I command you die
I command your death!"

The humming was gone and the monsters swarmed in on us. I was no longer commander but a common soldier, and I worked the crank of a crossbow until the string clicked over the fingers. There were clips on the rails with bolts, and I dropped one into the bow's channel.

A four-winged beast that looked like a heavy-bodied dragonfly soared close, its claws reaching to rip one of our sail workers from his perch. He screamed, seeing death on him, and I quickly aimed and fired. My shot missed but snapped between the creature and its intended prey, startling it so its claws closed on emptiness. It shrilled anger, banked away, and I lost it.

Some of the demons had jumped from their mounts and were on our decks, fighting with claws or weapons. Men closed, wrestled with each other, and then someone, monster or man, would fall screaming into the abyss. Not infrequently two bodies went twisting down to doom, still battling, hands clenched around each other's throats.

It was the time for our flames.

Janela held her palm out with a smear of oil in it, whispered, and fire blazed up—a magical fire that did not sear her flesh.

She picked up a paper tube from the deck that was inscribed with symbols, held it next to her palm and blew gently.

A great flame, a finger of fire, shot out and burnt a winged demon to a blackened crisp, sought on across the sky, found others and sent them searing to their deaths.

There was an immense roar, and a long snake with three sets of wings along its body whipped toward me and I knew it to be Ba'land. My hands were turning, winding, but far too slow—the creature was almost on me—then I fumbled the bolt, lifted and pulled and the string twanged and the bolt went home, burying itself in snake-Ba'land's body, and the monster rolled and convulsed, whipping back and forth as it fell . . .

We were tumbling, drifting, like autumn leaves falling toward the distant ground . . .

There was no land, no sky, no sea.

All around was blackness, but there was light. I existed but was in no body.

Beside me was Janela, invisible yet visible.

Something smashed past me, sending me skittering to the side, something that if it had been visible might have been flame but here was naught but pure force.

I was terrified, naked, unarmed, but then felt Janela's strength touch me and her knowledge teach me and I *reached*, found and gathered a force, a power that was my own, and sent it lancing out to where Ba'land floated. It struck him hard and this world/ notworld shook to his agony.

Then there were others, the other demons, but they also were without body, raw will, evil itself, coiling for a snake strike . . . but then the thought, for there was nothing to see, was gone and the world rolled and tore as demon turned against demon.

I sensed the wild demons tearing at their brothers, trying to end this agony, trying to break free from this world, and I sensed demons meeting the real death in this strange civil war in the void.

Another shaft came at me, searing my thigh above my knee, and then twin bolts were returned, one from each of us, and the universe was a shatter of Ba'land's pain.

WE STOOD on the bare rocky plain where the silver fire had first sent us.

There were but three of us. Janela and I were naked and held what might have been swords but were flaring torches of that pure light, pure energy.

Before us crouched Ba'land, holding up his clawed hands in supplication.

"Mercy, Antero. I beg mercy, Greycloak. Your soul was indeed too bitter for me."

"Mercy?" Janela's laugh was hard.

"Yes. Leave me—leave us with what remains of our power, our lives, and I swear we shall come to your worlds no longer."

"You expect me to believe you would honor such a pact?" I asked.

"I do," he said. "Look, here, graven on my chest, here is the sign, and you will see why you must believe me, why you must let us live."

Reflexively I leaned close . . . and Ba'land's talons shot out, straight for my heart. But silver flashed and his blow was stricken aside and my own weapon seared across, striking of its own volition, and Ba'land's head rolled on the rocks.

His great eye burnt yellow, then went dark, and I felt his going and something was missing from the world, something dark, something deadly, something that had hung around all of our kind like a leaden weight for ages and generations.

Janela was beside me, and for just an instant she was all silver, like the dancer Thalila, and then the force she'd used to save me was gone.

I reached out for her and then we were in the ancient throne room of King Farsun.

Around me clustered the soldiers that had fought the demons for our world and won. Quatervals . . . Kele . . . Otavi . . . Pip . . . the other Orissans . . . Tobray, and the men of Tyrenia.

There was no one else in the chamber, not Prince Solaros, not any of the other Tyrenians. But there were three bodies: King Ignati, the demon Mitel, and, sprawled headless on his throne, now black and corroded, the corpse of King Ba'land.

My body was unscathed, but I felt the agony of each of the wounds I'd suffered in those long battles in many worlds.

Quatervals grinned and began to say something, then he and Kele shimmered and were gone, now far-distant on their trek toward Orissa.

I was suddenly unsure of where I was or if I even existed, but I felt Janela's hand firm in my own, and I held her, and the world was real and mine.

Then we turned and limped up the long tunnel toward the light of day.

THE SEER GHOST

When the joyous Tyrenians poured out to hail us I felt like a ghost—so distant but so close. Like a ghost, I longed more for peace than the glad spirit of life displayed all around me.

Ghosts, I have been told, see more clearly than those with living eyes. They're chained to the past with links they cannot break and are therefore intent observers of the present and cunning predictors of the future.

So it is in my Seer's robes, my dear Hermias, that I will address you next.

Solaros will make a good king. I've watched him closely in the glorious chaos that followed our triumph over Ba'land and his demon hordes. He dealt well with the praise his subjects showered on us all. He showed no jealousy of Janela and me for getting the greater share. As soon as the long celebration was over, while the others slept off drunken cheer, he set to work planning a future for those boozy celebrants.

That Tyrenia will be different there is no doubt. With no demon enemy to defend against, the kingdom must melt down its weapons and forge a new will. It shall be difficult. These are people who have lived behind walls for more years than it took bricks to build them. They were humiliated long ago by their great retreat, giving up region after region until the only possession remaining was that barricade. The memory of that shame is bound to linger.

As for those who dwell outside Tyrenia—particularly those I love in Orissa—the challenge will be greater. The Tyrenians live in an invulnerable fortress. But even with Ba'land gone, your homes are set in a dark and angry wilderness. There will be many dangers to face, including from within as you quarrel over which direction to take. Be warned, nephew. That kind can be more fearsome than even a demon king.

I have made a pact with King Solaros. All the knowledge Janela gained will be shared with Orissa. A company of wizards will depart soon, and I beg you to make them welcome in Orissa. They bring truth that two Greycloaks stole from the gods. If that truth is freely and generously bestowed to all, then we will at last be free of our masters who so jealously guarded it. There will be nothing you will fear to dare. But if it is kept locked away in a miser's treasure house, there will come the fated day when all will curse the ones who slew Ba'land, and call his lashes a father's stern kindness.

Now I come to the part I'd most dreaded. I know as you read this you are asking, "But what of you, my dear uncle? What of you?"

Ah, well.

Ah, well.

I plan to end my life.

There.

I've said it.

I hope you don't hate me for it and call me a foolish old man who is too cowardly to face his natural end.

If so, what I have to say next will make you think I've gone mad, as well.

It is Janela who will kill me.

Why, you ask, would a woman who loves me agree to such a thing? Does she secretly harbor designs for revenge because I killed Janos? Is her love a pretense?

The answer is that it will be her love for me that makes her grant this gift.

She came to me while I was assembling my thoughts for the final segment of this journal. She'd seen my mood since our return but said nothing out of respect for my privacy.

"I thought, Amalric will tell me soon enough," Janela said. "But then you didn't speak, and the longer the silence grew, the more I was hurt you hadn't confided in me."

"I'm sorry, my love," I said. "It's nothing so deep or complicated. It's only the old malaise that's crept into my bones again."

"You are weary of life," she said.

"Yes," I said. "I was weary when I first met you, when you came knocking at my door saying, 'Come with me to the Far Kingdoms, old man.' "

"Was it worth it?" she asked.

I sighed. "Of course it was. But I only got the spirit up because I owed it to Janos to finish what we started."

"And now that it's done," she said, "you see nothing that beckons you onward?"

"What else could there be?" I said. "I'm an old vagabond and it's getting late and I'm anxious to come to a place where I might rest."

Janela studied me in silence for a time. Then she reached a decision. "Do you recall when we last had this conversation, Amalric?"

I said I did. It was when we were waiting for the demon guards to take us to Ba'land.

"Do you also recall that I proposed a second choice?"

"I do. You said you knew how to open the door the Old Ones fled through."

"But I couldn't do it," she added, "as long as Ba'land lived."

"He's dead now," I said, mumbling because my mouth was suddenly dry.

"Yes," Janela said.

I struggled to answer, for my reply wasn't the one she wanted to hear.

"You said then it would be a gift," I finally managed. "But I can't accept it. I'm nearly done with this life, and glad of it. Why should I want to be condemned to toil long in another?"

"Before you refuse," she said, "do you want to see what you'll be spurning?"

I shrugged, believing my mind had been solidly cast. "What's the point in it?" I asked.

"How do we know," she said, "if we don't look?"

I hesitated, which made her laugh. "I have you now, Amalric Antero," she said. "You never could resist a new place, if only for a look at the wares in the market."

Her response made me smile, and with that smile I accepted and was rewarded with her embrace.

That night she dimmed the lights and sat me at a small table. She lit incense, then sat across from me so close that our knees touched. She set the stone box in the center of the table. She directed me to place my hands on it, then put hers on top of mine.

And she said, "Close your eyes."

I did. I waited, but she said nothing more.

"What do I do next?" I asked, impatient.

"Nothing," she said.

"Should I think?"

"If you like."

"What should I think of?"

"Anything you wish."

"Good," I said. "Then I'll think of you."

I relaxed, building her image in my mind. I found myself peering through the grated window in my garden walls. I saw her mounted on a fine steed, fair of skin and form but with a presence that commanded you to look beyond her beauty. She beckoned, and I opened the gate and ran to her. I grabbed her hand and vaulted up behind the saddle. No sooner had I clutched my arms about her waist then she kicked the horse into a gallop. We thundered along the road to Orissa until it made a fork where no crossroads had been before. We took the unfamiliar path and soon we came to a steep hill. The horse seemed charged by the obstacle, and bounded up the rocky trail like a goat in high pasture.

We came to the top and dismounted, Janela taking my hand and leading me to the hill's edge.

"Look, Amalric," she said.

And I did.

I saw a land of silvery forests, sisters to the tree that humbled Ba'land. I saw a river flowing through those forests, making a golden, shimmering run to a distant sea. I saw ships with marvelous forms and glowing sails the color of the last sky before night falls. And on those ships I saw elegant creatures, neither man nor beast nor spirit, but all those things in one. Creatures of sublime light and curiosity. A wind out of a mariner's sweetest dreams filled the sails, promising swift passage to ports of wonder.

I longed to go, wept to go.

Janela whispered, but the whisper was from a great distance.

And I was back in the room sitting across from her once more.

I was so overcome by the vision that I couldn't speak for a long time. Janela fetched me brandy, curling up beside me until I had sipped enough to find a voice again.

"Did you know it would be like that?" I asked.

"How could I?" she said.

Her voice was rough, and I looked up to see she had been weeping as well.

"Can I truly go there?" I asked.

"Yes, Amalric," she said. "*We* can."

I was alarmed when I realized she'd included herself in the answer. "But Janela," I said, "you told me that death was a requirement for that journey."

"It is," she said.

"But why should you want to die?" I protested. "You are a young woman. Already you have achieved greatness no one else has ever managed. You have many years to accomplish still more."

"But I could never match it," she said, "no matter how long I lived. I tell you, Amalric, when I found the answer my great-grandfather sought, I cried from the joy. But then I wept out of despair because there could never be such a great riddle as that. I've been your sister in misery since we returned to Tyrenia. I am a seeker by nature and breeding. But I *must* have a goal worthy of the seeking. And what could that be, Amalric? What could that be?"

How was I to answer her, my nephew? Knowing my heart, what could I say?

So we made our pact.

I nearly reneged when I learned how it must be carried out. We would drink wine, drugged just enough to soothe us. We would cushion ourselves on soft pillows. The stone box would be opened, revealing the magical rose petal inside. Then Janela would prick my arm to draw a bit of blood and administer the killing potion through the small wound. As I died she'd sprinkle blood on the petal to bless it. And then she'd do the same for herself.

"But I'm not such a coward," I protested, "that I can't find nerve enough to take my own life."

"It's the only way," Janela said. "You must be a spirit first so you are ready for me to carry away."

Still, I resisted the notion that she should end her span so young. But she begged, saying if I loved her I wouldn't make her stay in this place alone. And so it was we finally made the plan that would free us from our mortal burden.

Do you see how it is, Hermias? If you do, I love you. If you don't, I love you still.

I must go now. Janela is waiting and I've wrung myself dry of farewells.

The tides are beckoning and the captain's called the last warning.

Where Janela and I go, no sea has known a ship's rough hull. The wind blows only east there. All shores are legend. And every voyager's soul flies for the horizon.

Where all dreams await our embrace . . .

In Far Kingdoms.

ABOUT THE AUTHORS

ALLAN COLE and CHRIS BUNCH bring their lifelong addiction to distant lands and cultures to the Far Kingdoms. Bunch is still haunted by youthful memories of Asian temple bells and snow leopards, and the thousand-year-old tomb of a Korean princess, while Cole recalls hearing *The Tempest* for the first time as a child sitting on an ancient wall in Cyprus—the island Shakespeare had in mind when he penned the play. As adults, their wide travels have taken them from misty gull-haunted islands of Ireland to the frozen wastelands of Antarctica. When not traveling, they live in Chinook and Ocean Park, Washington, with their strongest supporters, Karen and Kathryn.

DEL REY® ONLINE!

THE DEL REY INTERNET NEWSLETTER (DRIN)

The DRIN is a monthly electronic publication posted on the Internet, GEnie, CompuServe, BIX, various BBSs, and the Panix gopher. It features:

- hype-free descriptions of new books
- a list of our upcoming books
- special announcements
- a signing/reading/convention-attendance schedule for Del Rey authors
- in-depth essays by sf professionals (authors, artists, designers, salespeople, and others)
- a question-and-answer section
- behind-the-scenes looks at sf publishing
- and much more!

INTERNET INFORMATION SOURCE

Del Rey information is now available on a gopher server—gopher.panix.com—including:

- the current and all back issues of the Del Rey Internet Newsletter
- a description of the DRIN and content summaries of all issues
- sample chapters of current and upcoming books—readable and downloadable for free
- submission requirements
- mail-order information
- new DRINs, sample chapters, and other items are added regularly.

ONLINE EDITORIAL PRESENCE

Many of the Del Rey editors are online—on the Internet, GEnie, CompuServe, America Online, and Delphi. There is a Del Rey topic on GEnie and a Del Rey Folder on America Online.

WHY?

We at Del Rey realize that the networks are the medium of the future. That's where you'll find us promoting our books, socializing with others in the sf field, and—most important—making contact and sharing information with sf readers.

FOR MORE INFORMATION

The official e-mail address for Del Rey Books is

delrey@randomhouse.com